Praise for *New Y*

B

"Brenda Novak do…
stories, she writes keepers."

—Susan Mallery, #1 *New York Times* bestselling author

"Heartwarming, life-affirming, page-turning… I can always count on Novak to make me weep, laugh and fall in love!"

—Jill Shalvis, *New York Times* bestselling author

"Any Brenda Novak book is a must-read for me."

—Sherryl Woods, #1 *New York Times* bestselling author

Praise for *New York Times* bestselling author Brenda Jackson

"Brenda Jackson writes romance that sizzles and characters you fall in love with."

—*New York Times* and *USA TODAY* bestselling author Lori Foster

"Jackson's trademark ability to weave multiple characters and side stories together makes shocking truths all the more exciting."

—*Publishers Weekly*

New York Times bestselling author **Brenda Novak** has written more than sixty novels. An eight-time RITA® Award nominee, she's won the National Readers' Choice, the Booksellers' Best and other awards. She runs Brenda Novak for the Cure, a charity that has raised more than $2.5 million for diabetes research (her youngest son has this disease). She considers herself lucky to be a mother of five and married to the love of her life.

Brenda Jackson is a *New York Times* bestselling author of more than one hundred romance titles. Brenda lives in Jacksonville, Florida, and divides her time between family, writing and traveling. Email Brenda at authorbrendajackson@gmail.com or visit her on her website at brendajackson.net.

New York Times Bestselling Author

BRENDA NOVAK

FIRST LOVE, SECOND CHANCE

Previously Published as *A Family of Her Own*

HARLEQUIN
BESTSELLING
AUTHOR
COLLECTION

HARLEQUIN®
BESTSELLING
AUTHOR
COLLECTION

Recycling programs for this product may not exist in your area.

ISBN-13: 978-1-335-97992-6

First Love, Second Chance

First published as A Family of Her Own in 2004. This edition published in 2020.

Temperatures Rising
First published in 2009. This edition published in 2020.

This edition published by arrangement with Harlequin Books S.A.

For questions and comments about the quality of this book, please contact us at CustomerService@Harlequin.com.

Harlequin Enterprises ULC
22 Adelaide St. West, 40th Floor
Toronto, Ontario M5H 4E3, Canada
www.Harlequin.com

Printed in U.S.A.

CONTENTS

Also by Brenda Novak

Christmas in Silver Springs
Unforgettable You
Before We Were Strangers
Right Where We Belong
Until You Loved Me
No One but You
Finding Our Forever
The Secrets She Kept
A Winter Wedding
The Secret Sister
This Heart of Mine
The Heart of Christmas
Come Home to Me

For a full list of Brenda's books,
visit www.brendanovak.com.

FIRST LOVE, SECOND CHANCE

Brenda Novak

To Sugar Novak, my mother-in-law,
who will leave the world a much better place
for having been part of it. Sug, I'm grateful to
have you in my life. You're one of the few people
I know who truly understand the meaning of
family. Here's to all for one and one for all…

PROLOGUE

BOOKER ROBINSON SAT in his truck at ten o'clock on a warm Thursday night, staring at the small rental house where Katie Rogers lived and telling himself he was crazy to even be here. He wasn't the type to ask for anything. He'd made it a habit never to need anyone. He'd learned as a child that showing vulnerability was never rewarded.

But he'd heard that Katie and Andy Bray were almost engaged, that she was going to leave town with Andy soon. And he knew if she did, she'd be making a big mistake. Andy wouldn't take care of her the way he would. Andy wouldn't love her as he did. Andy loved only himself.

Taking a deep breath, Booker cut the engine, got out and walked up the driveway. He'd hoped Katie would come back to him on her own. For a few short weeks, they'd shared something that was heady, powerful and very mutual. He was sure she felt everything he did. But her family and most of her friends had convinced her she'd be ruining her life by taking a risk on someone like him, a man with a criminal past and not much of a future. And now she was running scared and on the verge of marrying someone else.

She might end up marrying Andy, Booker told himself, but she wasn't going to do it without at least knowing how he felt about her. He lived with enough regrets already....

It took several minutes for someone to answer his knock. When the door finally opened, Katie's best friend, Wanda, peered out at him.

"Oh...uh...hi, Booker."

He could tell she was nervous about seeing him, so he didn't bother with small talk. Wanda was one of the people telling Katie that he'd never amount to anything. "Is she home?" he asked, not bothering to specify Katie by name because they both knew who "she" was.

"Um... I don't think—"

He broke in before she could finish. "I saw her pull into the garage from the end of the street."

"Right." She chuckled self-consciously. "I wasn't sure if she actually came in or not, but she must have if you saw her. Just a minute."

While he waited, Booker's pulse raced. He'd never laid his heart open to a woman before, and he wasn't sure where to start now. He hadn't let himself love many people.

You're a fool for even trying, you know that, don't you? Who are you to say you're any better than Andy? At least Andy comes from a good family and has a college degree. What do you have to offer?

He almost turned to leave, but then Katie appeared at the door.

"Booker?" She sounded surprised to see him. He'd known she would be. He hadn't contacted her since they'd had that big argument several weeks ago—when she'd told him it was over between them, that she wanted to start seeing Andy, and he'd thought he could let her go.

He took a deep breath. "Can we talk?"

"I don't think so," she replied. "There's really nothing to say."

"You're making a mistake, Katie."

"You don't know that."

Maybe he didn't *know* it. But he felt it. Letting her marry *anyone* else was a mistake. It had taken him nearly thirty years to fall in love, but the hell of living without Katie for the past few weeks had left little doubt in his mind that he was there now. "What we had was good."

"I—I can't argue with that, but..." She tucked her long blond hair behind her ears in a nervous gesture and glanced over her shoulder. "I'm sorry. I've already made up my mind."

The expression in her large blue eyes was tortured. He could tell that she was torn between what she thought and felt and what others were telling her. He knew she was afraid of what he'd once been. He wouldn't want a daughter of his to marry an ex-con, either. But he couldn't change his past. He could only change his future....

"Katie..." Reaching out, he ran a finger along her jaw. The contact made him yearn to hold her, and she seemed to feel something similar. She closed her eyes and pressed her cheek into the palm of his hand as though she was dying for his touch. "You still care about me," he murmured. "I can tell. Come back to me."

Tears glittered in her eyelashes, reflecting the porch light. "No," she said, suddenly pushing his hand away. "Don't confuse me. Andy tells me I'll feel differently after a few months away from here. We're going to get married, have a family—"

"But you don't love Andy," Booker said. "I can't even imagine you with that self-serving yuppie."

"He's a nice guy, Booker."

"Why? Because he helped you raise the money to replace that old floor at the Elks Club?"

"That was no small thing. Without him, I probably wouldn't have been able to start my singles club for seniors."

"He only did it to impress you. Can't you see that?"

"Booker, I don't want to argue about Andy. I'm trying to make a good decision for my future, and yours, too. I've got to go—"

"Marry me, Katie," he said suddenly, passionately. "I know I can make you happy."

Her eyes widened, and two tears slipped down her cheeks. "Booker, I can't. You're not ready to be tied down by a wife and family. You love your freedom too much. I knew that when we first started seeing each other."

"Katie, maybe it wouldn't have come to this quite so soon if—"

"I'm sorry, Booker. I've got to go." The door closed in his face. When she drove the bolt home, he knew he'd lost her.

CHAPTER ONE

Two years later...

KATIE ROGERS SMELLED SMOKE coming from the engine of her car.

"Come on, you can make it," she muttered, her fingers tightening on the steering wheel of the old Cadillac, which was pretty much the most valuable possession she had left. She'd purchased the vehicle three days ago after posting a Garage Sale sign near her apartment and selling off the last of her and Andy's furniture. Then she'd packed up what remained of her belongings and headed out of San Francisco before he could come home and plead with her to give him one more chance. She couldn't bear to deal with Andy Bray anymore. Not with a child on the way. Not when it seemed as though she was the only one who was finally growing up.

The smell of smoke became more pronounced. Katie wrinkled her nose and remembered, with longing, the nice new truck she'd owned when she lived in Dundee. She and Andy had used that truck to move to San Francisco. But once they'd arrived, Andy had talked her into selling it for the security deposit on a better apartment. "We don't want to stay in a dump," he'd said. "And we don't need a car.... We're in the city now, babe. There're plenty of ways to get around. As soon as I start making the big bucks we can get another set of wheels...."

As soon as he started making the big bucks... Ha! Katie would've been satisfied had he earned just a *few* bucks. Or at least used some caution in the way he threw *her* money around.

Because they couldn't afford parking, she'd finally agreed to sell the truck. But it was a decision she'd long regretted. If she'd had a reliable vehicle, maybe she would've left sooner.

The Welcome to Dundee, Home of the Annual Bad-to-the-Bone Rodeo, Population 1,438 sign she'd seen thousands of times in her youth appeared in her headlights. Breathing a huge sigh of relief, Katie began to relax. She'd make it home safely. After traveling 640 miles, she was only another ten or so from her parents' house—

Suddenly the Cadillac gave a loud *chung,* and the lights on the dashboard blinked out. Katie frantically pumped the gas pedal, hoping to get a little farther, but it didn't do any good. The car slowed, trailing smoke.

"No!" Katie shifted the transmission into neutral so she could crank the starter. Returning to Dundee in her current situation was pathetic enough. She didn't want anyone she knew to see her stranded on the side of the road.

But the car wouldn't start. She was pretty sure it was dead.

Her tires crunched on the snow-covered shoulder as she managed to pull over without the aid of the power steering that had gone out when everything else did. Then she sat, listening to the hiss coming from the engine and watching smoke billow out from under her hood. What now? She couldn't walk the rest of the way to her folks' house. The doctor didn't want her to be on her feet. Just two weeks ago, she'd experienced premature labor pains and he'd told her she had to take it easy.

Sitting inside a dead car wouldn't get her anywhere, though. For all she knew, the engine was on fire and the car would momentarily explode, like so many seemed to do on television.

Wrestling her luggage out of the back seat, she dragged it a safe distance. Then she perched on the bigger suitcase and shivered in the cold night air as she watched several cars pass. She didn't have the heart to stand or make herself noticed. She'd hit rock bottom. Life had finally gotten as bad as it could be.

And then it started to rain.

BOOKER T. ROBINSON switched on his windshield wipers as he descended into Dundee. It was a chilly Monday night, cool enough that he thought the rain would turn to snow before morning. Dundee typically saw a lot of snow in February. But Booker didn't mind. He was comfortable living in the farmhouse he'd inherited from Grandma Hatfield. And any kind of extreme weather was good for business.

Sticking one of the toothpicks from his ashtray into his mouth, a habit he'd developed when he quit smoking over a year ago, he calculated how much longer it would be before he had Lionel Richman paid off.

Another six months, he decided. Then he'd own Lionel & Sons Auto Repair free and clear. He could buy the lot next door and expand. Maybe he'd even give the business his name. He'd kept "Lionel & Sons" because it had been that way for fifty years, and the people of Dundee didn't like change any more than they'd liked him when he first moved to town. But since he'd taken over, he'd developed a solid reputation for knowing cars and—

The sight of an old banged-up sedan parked off the highway up ahead piqued Booker's curiosity enough that he braked. He owned the only tow truck in the area, which was currently at his shop. But he hadn't received a distress call on his radio. Yet.

Where was the driver? He couldn't see anyone inside or around the vehicle. Whoever owned the Cadillac had probably already walked or hitched into town, looking for help. But if the smoke pouring from beneath the hood was any indication, the car hadn't been sitting too long.

Chewing thoughtfully on his toothpick, he pulled up behind the stranded vehicle, left his lights on so he could see and climbed out. If the car was unlocked and he could get under the hood, it would probably be smart to take a look while he was here. Chances were the car had a busted hose—a problem he could solve without going to the trouble of towing the Cadillac to his shop in town.

The moment he stepped out of his truck, however, he realized he wasn't as alone as he'd thought. Someone—a woman, judging by her size—peered at him from around the front of the car. She was wearing a man-size sweatshirt with a hood that shielded her face from the rain, a pair of faded jeans with bottoms a little wider than he typically saw in these parts and—his eyes darted back to her feet—*sandals?* In *February?*

The car had California plates. Leave it to someone

from sunny California to run around in sandals all winter.

He shrugged on his leather jacket as he walked over, stopping well short of her. He didn't want to frighten her. He only wanted to get her car going so he'd be able to meet Rebecca and Josh for a drink at the Honky Tonk and not be interrupted later. "Having trouble?" he asked above the sound of the wind.

"No." She pulled the hood of her sweatshirt farther forward. "Everything's fine."

The wind made it difficult for him to hear. He took the toothpick out of his mouth and moved closer. "Did you say everything's fine?"

She moved back a distance equal to his advance. "Yes. You can go on your way."

Booker glanced at the smoke rising from her car. He might've thought it was just steam coming off a warm engine on a cold night. Except steam didn't explain the luggage or why this woman was standing on the side of the road in a sweatshirt so wet it dripped along the hem. And it sure as hell didn't explain the distinctive scent of a burned-up engine.

"Everything doesn't *smell* fine," he said.

"I'm just letting the engine cool."

The engine was going to need a lot more than a good cooling. He could tell that without even looking at it. But Booker didn't say so because this time when she'd spoken, something about her voice had sparked a flicker of recognition.

The California license plate flashed through his mind. He didn't know anyone from California, except… God, it couldn't be…

"Katie?" he said, trying to make out her face despite the shadow of her hood.

He saw her shoulders droop. "It's me," she said. "Go ahead and gloat."

Booker didn't respond right away. He didn't know what to say. Or how to feel. But gloating was pretty far down on his list. Mostly he wanted to leave so he wouldn't have to see her again. Only he couldn't abandon her, or any woman, on the side of the road in the cold rain. "You need a lift?"

She hesitated briefly. Then her chin came up. "No, that's okay. My dad's good with cars. He'll help me."

"Does he know you're out here?"

A slight hesitation, then, "Yeah, he's expecting me. He'll know when I don't show up."

Booker put the toothpick back in his mouth. Part of him suspected she was lying. The other part, the stronger part, felt immediate relief that she was somebody else's problem. "I'll take off, then. Your dad can call me if he has any questions."

He strode briskly to his truck, but she followed him before he could make his escape.

With a sigh, he rolled down his window. "Is there something else?"

"Actually I'm here a little earlier than planned and—" she hugged herself, shivering "—well, it's possible that my parents won't miss me for a while. I think I'd be better off taking that ride you offered, if you don't mind."

Everything's fine.... She'd said so when he first pulled up. Why couldn't he have taken her at her word and let her remain anonymous?

The pain and resentment he'd felt two years ago, when she'd closed the door in his face, threatened to consume him again. But considering the circumstances, he had to help her. What choice did he have?

"What's with the sandals?" he asked.

She gazed down at her soaked feet. "I bought them in San Francisco. They're one of a kind, designed especially for me."

They were still only sandals, and it was raining, for Pete's sake. She must have realized that he didn't understand the full significance of what she'd just said because she added, "The day Andy and I bought these was the best day of the past two years. And the only day that turned out anything like I'd planned."

So they were a symbol of her lost illusions. Well, thanks to her, Booker had a few lost illusions of his own. Not that he'd possessed many to begin with. His parents had taken care of that early on. "Hop in," he said. "I'll get your luggage."

KATIE SAT WITHOUT TALKING, listening to the hum of the heater and the beat of the wipers as Booker drove into town. Of all the people in Dundee, he was the last person she'd wanted to see. So, of course, he'd been the first one to come along. It was that kind of day—no, *year.*

Clasping her hands in her lap, Katie stared glumly out at the familiar buildings they passed. The Honky Tonk, where she used to hang out on weekends. The library, where her friend Delaney, who was now married to Conner Armstrong, used to work. Finley's Grocery. Katie had once knocked over a whole display of Campbell's soup there, trying to get a better look at Mike Hill, a boy she'd had a crush on all the time she was growing up.

"You warm enough?" Booker asked.

He'd already removed his jacket so she nodded, even though she was still chilled, and he turned down the heat.

"So," she said, hoping to ease the tension between them, "how've things been since I went away?"

She could see the scar on his face that ran from his eye to his chin—souvenir of a knife fight, he'd once told her—and the tattoo on his right biceps. It moved beneath the sleeve of his T-shirt as his hands clenched the steering wheel more tightly. But he didn't respond.

"Booker?"

"Don't pretend we're friends, Katie," he said shortly.

"Why?"

"Because we're not."

"Oh." Booker's friends had always been few. He regarded everyone, except maybe Rebecca Wells—Rebecca *Hill* since she'd married Josh—with a certain amount of distrust. So considering their history, Katie knew she shouldn't be surprised. She'd lost his good opinion along with everything else. If she'd ever really had it. Even when they were seeing each other before she left, she'd never felt completely certain that he cared about her. He'd driven her around on his Harley and shown her one heck of a good time. But he was somewhat remote, and she'd always approached their relationship with a sense of inevitability, believing that it wouldn't—couldn't—last. Then he'd shown up at her door and *proposed!* She didn't know how to explain it, except that his widowed grandmother, Hatty, had just died. He and Hatty had been so close throughout her final years that Katie could only suppose his sudden marriage proposal was triggered by his loss.

Now he was obviously holding a grudge that she'd

turned him down at a difficult time, or been the one to cut things off between them. "I make a left at 500 South?" he asked after several minutes.

She pulled her attention from the rain beading on the windshield. "What?"

"Your parents still live in the same place, don't they?"

Last she'd heard they did. But she didn't *know.* She hadn't talked to them since a year ago last Christmas, when they'd told her not to call again. "They've been on Lassiter nearly thirty years," she said, infusing her voice with as much confidence as she could muster. "Knowing them, they'll be there another thirty."

"Seems I heard your father say something not too long ago about building a cabin a few miles outside of town." He shifted his eyes from the road to study her. "They give up on that?"

Apprehension clawed at Katie's insides. Her folks still had the same telephone number. She'd definitely heard her mother answer when she used the pay phone yesterday. She'd wanted to tell her family she was on her way home. Only she'd lost her nerve at the last moment and hung up.

"Yeah." Having the same number didn't necessarily mean they hadn't moved within a certain geographic area, but Katie was sticking with the gamble. Doing anything else would reveal a rift she preferred to keep private. "They like living so close to their bakery. That bakery is their life," she added.

The Arctic Flyer appeared on the right, evoking bittersweet memories. Katie had worked there the summer of her junior year because she'd wanted to try something besides her parents' bakery, and she'd broken the ice-cream machine her first week. Harvey, the owner, had complained every day about the money she was costing him, until the part to repair the darn thing finally came in.

Booker turned up the radio, and she glanced surreptitiously in his direction. Her memories of him didn't go back nearly as far as her Arctic Flyer days. She'd heard tales of him visiting for several months when he was about fifteen; he'd raised enough hell that the entire town still regarded him as trouble. He'd mentioned a few things about that visit himself, like stealing Eugene Humphries's truck and wrecking it only a few hours later. But Katie was nine years old at the time. She hadn't met Booker until years later when he moved in with Hatty.

"Aren't you curious to know what I'm doing back?" she asked, turning to conversation to stanch the flow of memories.

He looked pointedly at her two suitcases, which he'd wedged into the back seat of his extended cab. "That's pretty obvious."

"Actually, it's probably not what you think. San Francisco was fabulous, for the most part," she said. Which was true—if she confined her comments to the city itself.

When he made no reply, she plunged ahead. "It's just that I'm a country girl at heart, you know? I decided that San Francisco is a great place to visit, but nowhere I'd want to stay."

He slung one arm over the steering wheel, and she supposed it was his rebel attitude that made him look both bored and on-edge at the same time.

"Don't you have *anything* to say?" she asked.

His toothpick moved as he chewed on it. "Where's *Andy?*"

"He—" she scrambled for something to crack Booker's reserve "—he's laid up and couldn't come along."

Booker arched an eyebrow. "Laid up?"

"He was…um…hit by a cable car," she said with a grin to let him know she was joking.

She'd hoped to elicit a smile, but the line of Booker's lips remained as grim as ever. Slowly he slid the toothpick to the other side of his mouth. "You mean life in San Francisco wasn't the nirvana you expected."

She resisted the urge to squirm in her seat. "We all make mistakes," she muttered as he parked in front of her parents' white-brick rambler.

He easily yanked the suitcases that she could barely lift out of his truck, carried them to the door and punched the doorbell. Then he pivoted and headed back, leaving her on the doorstep without so much as a "goodbye" or a "good luck."

"Haven't you ever done anything you regret?" she called after him. She knew he'd done plenty; she just didn't know if he regretted any of it. He certainly had never acted as though he felt any remorse.

But she didn't listen for a reply. The door to her parents' home opened almost immediately, and her stomach knotted as she saw her mother's face for the first time in two years.

"Hi, Mom," she said, praying that Tami Rogers would be more forgiving than Booker.

Her mother's expression didn't look promising. And when Tami glanced at Booker and his truck, her features became even more pinched. "What are you doing here?"

Katie peered over her shoulder at Booker, too, wishing him gone, well out of earshot. “I…” The pain inside her suddenly swelled. She couldn’t even remember, let alone recite, the eloquent apology she’d prepared on the way from San Francisco. All she wanted was for her mother to reach out and hug her. *Please...*

Her mouth like cotton, she searched for the right words. “I… I need to come home, Mom…just for a little bit,” she added because she thought it might make a difference if her mother understood she didn’t expect any long-term help. Just a place to stay and some kind of welcome until she could find a job that wouldn’t require her to be on her feet.

“Oh, *now* you want to come home,” her mother replied.

“I know you’re angry—”

“Andy called here looking for you,” she interrupted.

“He did?”

“He told us you never got married.” She folded her arms and leaned against the lintel. “Is that true?”

“Yes, but only because—”

“He also said you’re five months pregnant.”

Instinctively Katie’s hand went to her abdomen. She hadn’t gained any weight yet, so the pregnancy wasn’t apparent, especially in Andy’s baggy sweatshirt. “It—it wasn’t something I planned. But once it happened, I thought maybe Andy would—”

Her mother put up a hand to stop her. “I don’t want to hear it. I raised you better than this, Katie Lynne Rogers. You used to be a good girl, the sweetest there was.”

Katie tried not to blanch as her mother’s rejection lashed a part of her that was already terribly raw. “I’m still the same person, Mom.”

“No, you’re not the girl I knew.”

Katie didn't know how to combat such a statement, so she switched topics. "Andy had no right to tell you anything. He's the one who—"

"He's a bum, just like we said. Right?"

Andy was handsome and debonair. He certainly looked like a stand-up guy. But he was full of empty promises and false apologies. She couldn't refute that, either, so she nodded.

"We tried to tell you," Tami went on. "But you wouldn't listen. Now you've made your bed, I guess you can sleep in it."

The door closed with a decisive *click.*

Katie blinked at the solid wood panel, feeling numb, incredulous. Home was the place that *had* to take you in, right? She'd hung on to that thought for miles and miles. She didn't have anywhere else to go. She'd spent nearly every dime she possessed reaching Dundee.

She considered the last twenty bucks in her wallet and knew it wouldn't be enough to get a room. She couldn't even walk back to town, where there was a motel, without risking the baby.

Slowly it dawned on her that Booker hadn't pulled away from the curb. Which meant he'd probably heard the whole thing.

Embarrassment so powerful it hurt swept through her as she turned. Sure enough, he was standing at the end of the walk, leaning against his truck with the rain dripping off him, staring at her with those shiny black eyes of his.

His learning about the baby this way, seeing what Andy had reduced her to—it was more humiliating than Katie could've imagined. She'd broken off her relationship with Booker because she'd wanted more than he could give her. And here she was….

A lump formed in her throat and her eyes began to burn. But she had a few shreds of pride left.

Bending, she picked up her small suitcase. She couldn't lift the large one. It was too heavy to carry with any dignity, and she wouldn't get far trying to drag it. So she sucked in a quick, ragged breath in an effort to hold herself together a little longer, threw back her shoulders and started down the street.

She didn't know where she was going. But at the moment, anywhere was better than here.

CHAPTER TWO

BOOKER COULDN'T BELIEVE what he'd just heard. Katie wasn't only down on her luck, she was pregnant. Andy Bray, that sorry son of a bitch who'd come through town bragging about everything he was and everything he was going to be, when he wasn't anything at all, had gotten her pregnant and left her to cope on her own.

Booker longed to make Andy pay for what he'd done. Then he reminded himself that he had no stake in Katie's life. He might have loved her once, but she'd chosen someone else. Someone with all the trappings of respectability—the preppy clothes, the supportive family, the college degree. That removed Booker from the picture completely. He should head over to the Honky Tonk, he told himself, and forget he'd ever seen her.

Climbing into his truck, he decided to do exactly that. But that damn suitcase sitting alone on the front porch nagged at him. Surely Tami Rogers would change her mind and take her daughter in. Any moment now, the door would open and some member of the family, Katie's little brother perhaps, would go after her.

Booker waited, but the door didn't open. Lightning darted across the sky, thunder boomed in the distance and the wind rose before Tami so much as peeked out a window. Booker felt a moment of hope when he saw her glance furtively into the street. But when she realized he was still there, she jerked the curtains shut.

"She's not my problem," he finally muttered, punching the gas pedal. But he didn't get farther than half a block before Katie's parting words came back to him: *Haven't you ever done anything you regret?*

He'd done plenty of things. He'd been so angry as a kid that he'd been kicked out of more schools than he could remember. He'd put a guy in the hospital simply for looking at him the wrong way. He'd spent two years in a jail cell for stealing a car he didn't want in the first place. When he reflected on everything he'd felt and done before the age of twenty-five, he knew it was a miracle he'd ever reached thirty. If not for his grandmother, he might never have turned his life around.

In his rearview mirror, he watched Katie round the corner at the end of the street. With her wet clothing and sandals, she had to be freezing. And she was pregnant.

Slamming on his brakes, he spun around and pulled into the driveway of the Rogers house. He retrieved Katie's suitcase, then rocketed down the street.

KATIE HEARD BOOKER'S TRUCK coming up from behind and instantly improved her posture. She hadn't managed to hold back her tears for long, but with the rain she doubted he'd notice.

He slowed as he drew parallel, and shoved open the passenger door. "Get in!"

She refused to look at him. She had to live with what she'd made of her life, but she didn't have to show Booker her pain. "Go away."

"I'll put you up for a few nights until you can work things out with your folks," he hollered. "Just get in before you catch pneumonia."

"I'll be fine," she replied. But she didn't feel fine. She felt sick at heart and angry and ashamed….

"Where are you planning to go?" he asked. "It's after eleven o'clock."

She didn't answer because she didn't know. She had friends in town, people she'd grown up with, gone to school with, worked with at Hair and Now. She was sure *someone* would take her in for a night or two. But asking wouldn't be easy when she hadn't been in touch with anyone since she'd left—except her best friend Wanda, who'd married and moved to Wyoming.

"It's going to start snowing soon," Booker added.

"I realize that."

"You'll ruin your sandals."

"They're already ruined." *Everything* was ruined and had been for a long time. The sandals were just the last to go.

Booker gunned the engine. The truck lurched forward but came to a squealing stop right in front of her. Leaving his door open despite the rain, he got out and walked over to confront her. "Give me your suitcase."

She held her suitcase away from him, but he caught her hand and relieved her of it. Then they stood facing each other in the pouring rain and, as Katie gazed up at him, she was suddenly so hungry for one of his rare smiles she could have cried for that alone.

"I'm sorry," she said softly.

The harshness in his face eased. "We've all done things we regret," he said, and loaded her suitcase into the truck.

THE OLD HATFIELD PLACE hadn't changed much. Booker went for a towel as Katie stood dripping in the mudroom off the back, remembering the woman who'd lived here, alone for the most part, for so many years. Hatty had been a fixture in Dundee for Katie's entire life. She might have had blue-gray hair and looked as fragile as a bird, but she was more headstrong than anyone Katie had ever met. Hatty generally wore bright-red lipstick and a red suit to match, drove a giant Buick—if one could call what she did behind the wheel *driving*—and had a no-nonsense approach to everyone and everything.

But Hatty was gone now. She'd died just before Katie left. Katie had been so intent on getting away that she hadn't given Hatty's passing much thought. But she knew Hatty's death must have hit Booker hard.

"Here," Booker said, returning with a plush burgundy towel and a pair of sweats. He'd peeled off his own wet shirt and was wearing another simple T-shirt that stretched taut across his wide chest and showed the bottoms of the tattoos on his arms. He hadn't bothered changing his jeans.

"I've got some sweats of my own," Katie said when she realized the pair he'd handed her were probably his.

"I didn't want to dig through your suitcase. You can give them back to me in the morning."

He left her to dry off and went into the kitchen. Katie could hear him moving around, opening cupboards and drawers while she changed. She was still freezing and knew it would take some time to warm up, but she was glad to be out of the storm.

She entered the kitchen with her hair up in the towel and Booker's sweats hanging loose on her body, trying to ignore his scent, which lingered on his clothes, and all the pleasant associations attached to it.

"You hungry?" Booker asked.

"Not really," she said because she felt she had no right to impose on him any more than she already was.

He considered his sweats on her. "Looks as though you could stand to gain a few pounds."

"I'm sure I'll be gaining plenty over the next few months."

When he frowned, she knew he'd made the connection to her pregnancy. "Eggs and toast okay?" he asked.

Secretly grateful for the promise of a meal, Katie nodded. She'd been so afraid she wouldn't have money for gas that she'd skimped on food. "It's really nice, you helping me out like this. I appreciate it."

She took a seat at the kitchen table, recalling the day Hatty had made Booker varnish it. "The varnish seems to be holding up."

Booker looked at her. "The what?"

"The varnish. We tried to tell Hatty that this set was mostly plastic. But she wouldn't listen, remember? She wanted you to varnish it, anyway."

A ghost of a smile curved Booker's lips. "I remember. She had me wash the walls before I could paint them, too, and she made me restarch her doilies. I must be the only guy my age who's ever starched a doily."

Katie couldn't help chuckling. Toward the end of Hatty's life, Booker did almost anything she asked of him. Some people thought she'd bullied him like everyone else. Others claimed he was afraid of losing his inheritance. Katie had seen Booker and Hatty together often enough to know Booker indulged Hatty for only one reason—he loved her. "The place looks great," she said.

"Gran had it in top shape before she died."

But she'd been gone more than two years, and while

the house hardly seemed different, Booker did. He'd always been a survivor, a man who could take care of himself. But he suddenly seemed so much more… domestic. Maybe it came with owning his own home. "I'll bet you miss her."

He dug through a drawer until he found a spatula. "What's Andy doing these days?" he asked, changing the subject.

Andy was partying. But she wasn't about to tell Booker that. "I'm not sure."

He studied her in that way he had of looking right through people. "How long ago did you leave him?"

"It's been three days."

"And you've lost track of him already?"

Most of the time she hadn't known what he was doing even when he was in the next room. Because she hadn't *wanted* to know. It was rarely something of which she could approve. "I don't want to talk about Andy."

He went to the fridge. "One egg or two?"

"Two."

"When did you eat last?" he asked, setting the egg carton on the counter next to the stove.

"Today."

He paused. *"Today?"*

"Yeah, you know, earlier." She tried to avoid a more specific answer by drawing his attention back to the food. "Anyway, it smells good."

He broke the eggs into a frying pan, and Katie listened to them sizzle. As awkward as it was between her and Booker, she was beginning to get warm—and to appreciate the fact that she hadn't been forced to knock on someone else's door in the middle of the night.

When the silence grew to the point of discomfort,

however, she asked, "What have you been doing since I left?"

"Working," he said simply.

"Doing what?"

"He owns Lionel & Sons Auto Repair," a third voice proudly announced.

Katie looked up to see Delbert Dibbs standing in the doorway between the living room and the kitchen, rubbing the sleep from his eyes. A rottweiler the size of a small horse sat at his heels.

"You're back," he said, recognizing her immediately. Delbert was wearing a pair of Buzz Lightyear pajamas that weren't buttoned quite right. Where he'd found such a large size, Katie couldn't even guess. He was her age. At least five foot eleven, he had to weigh a good hundred and seventy pounds—only about thirty pounds shy of what Booker probably weighed. "I'm so glad," he added. "I missed you, Katie. I missed you cutting my hair."

Katie didn't have a chance to stand up before Delbert hurried across the kitchen and gathered her tightly in his arms. They'd never been close, but she'd cut his hair every once in a while. They'd also gone to the same elementary school for kindergarten and first grade. By second grade, it had become apparent that he wasn't developing normally, and he was put in a special school. But she'd still seen him around town. Especially after he dropped out of school altogether and took to rambling up and down Main Street, hanging out at the Arctic Flyer or loitering near the auto repair shop.

Katie frowned at Booker while Delbert squeezed her with all the exuberance of a child and the dog sniffed her curiously. But Booker neither came to her rescue nor offered any explanation.

"What—what are you doing here?" Katie asked Delbert when he finally released her and she could draw enough breath.

"I live here now," he said, showing crooked teeth in a wide smile. "I live with Bruiser and Booker."

Bruiser was obviously the dog, but Katie didn't get the connection between Booker and Delbert. How did such an unlikely pair wind up as roommates?

"Since when?" she asked.

His face clouded as he slumped into the chair next to her. Bruiser went over to Booker and wagged his tail in greeting. "My dad died. Did you know that, Katie? I came home one day, and he was just staring at me. Wouldn't say a thing."

"How awful," she said. "I'm sorry to hear that. I didn't know."

His sadness lifted as quickly as it had descended. "Want me to show you what I made?"

"Uh...okay."

He got up and raced from the kitchen, and Katie slanted a questioning glance at Booker. "*Delbert* lives with you? How did that come about?"

"I met him at the shop once I took over."

"And?"

"You heard him. His dad died."

"So you took him in?"

"He works for me," he said. "I've actually been able to teach him quite a bit about cars."

Teaching Delbert anything had to be a slow, frustrating process. That Booker would have the patience and go to the trouble when almost everyone else in town—including the local minister—barely acknowledged Delbert impressed Katie. "There must be more to the story than that."

"Not really," he said. "Delbert's dad was all he had. Once he died, there wasn't anyone left to care for him."

Katie shook her head as she toyed with the salt and pepper shakers in the center of the table. Somehow Booker never failed to surprise her. "That's really nice," she said. "What would've happened to him if you hadn't stepped in?"

"He would've gone to a special home in Boise."

"Most people would've let him go," she said.

He set her eggs on the table and went to the counter to butter the toast that had just popped up. "Maybe, but it didn't make any sense to me. He grew up around here. Dundee is comfortable and familiar to him. And they wouldn't let him have a dog or work on cars. Delbert lives for those two things."

As if to confirm his words, Delbert returned with a model of an antique Ford. "See?" he said. "This is a Model-T, one of the first cars ever made. It came in pieces. Booker helped me put it together."

"He did, huh?" Katie watched Booker clean up the mess he'd just made.

"Yeah." Delbert gazed lovingly at his model. "Booker can do anything."

Katie lifted her eyes to meet Booker's and found him wearing a wry grin. "Some people are easier to please than others," he said.

"WHERE ARE YOU?" Rebecca demanded as soon as the bartender at the Honky Tonk brought her to the phone. "Josh and I have been waiting here for over an hour."

Booker returned the frying pan he'd dried to its place beneath the stove. "I ran into a slight complication."

"What kind of complication?"

He looked toward the kitchen door to make sure he was still alone. "Katie."

"What?" Rebecca nearly screamed the word. The fact that she could scarcely hear above the music pounding in the background probably had something to do with it. But he knew hearing Katie's name on his lips had more impact than anything.

"Katie Rogers is back in town," he explained.

"No way!"

"It's true."

She fell silent for a moment. "I thought you were over Katie. Just last week, you told me to quit bugging you about her. You said she was never going to contact you, and it didn't matter anyway because you didn't—"

"I remember what I said," he interrupted.

"And now she's back? *Out of the blue?* How do you know?"

"I found her stranded on the side of the road a few miles outside town." He didn't add that she'd been driving a hunk of junk, had dark circles under her eyes, looked as thin as a rail and was five months pregnant.

"Was Andy with her?"

"What do *you* think?"

"I think they lasted longer than I ever dreamed they would."

They'd lasted longer than Booker had thought possible, too. For a while, he'd held out hope that Katie would reconsider his proposal and come back to tell him she'd made a mistake. But as month marched on to month, he'd finally realized he was stupid for continuing to hope and had forced himself to get on with his life.

Only now she *was* back. She just hadn't come back to *him.*

"She should never have let you get away," Rebecca said.

"Let me get away? Hell, she practically ran in the other direction."

"Maybe it's because you don't give many people a chance."

"She had more than a chance."

Rebecca wasn't listening. "You're not unsociable, exactly. Just a little rough around the edges, stubborn—definitely stubborn—and a bit of a cynic."

"That's pretty funny, coming from you," he pointed out, but Rebecca's mind had already shifted gears.

"Hey, do you think she'll want to work at the salon again?"

"Aren't you ready to give up managing that place? It's not as though you need the money."

"I'm not managing the salon anymore, I'm buying it. I like having something that's all my own. It helps me hold on to Rebecca so she doesn't get lost in being Mrs. Joshua Hill."

"You expect me to understand that psychobabble bullshit?"

She laughed. "You understand, and you know it."

He only understood that Rebecca was one of the few people he could trust, and he valued her friendship. "So you want me to have Katie call you in a day or two if she's interested in coming back to work?"

"Wait a second." Suspicion entered Rebecca's voice. "She's staying at her folks' house, right?"

Booker blew out a sigh. "Wrong."

"Don't tell me she's staying with you!"

"I *had* to bring her home," he said. "Her parents refused to take her in."

"Why?"

If he'd been talking to anyone else, he might have said, "Because she's pregnant and not married." But he wasn't talking to just anyone. He was talking to Rebecca, and she was very sensitive these days about who was having a baby and who wasn't. Mostly because *she* wasn't. She and Josh had been married a couple of years and they'd been trying to have a baby the whole of that time, but nothing they did seemed to work. Booker knew Josh had gone in for testing because Rebecca had shown up on his doorstep, when the doctors determined that she was the one facing fertility problems, and ranted about the unfairness of life. Of course it would be *her,* she'd said; Josh was never to blame for anything. Then she'd done something he'd never seen her do before—she broke down in tears.

"I guess they're still upset about her leaving on such bad terms," he said, glossing over the facts.

Rebecca snorted. "Give me a break. I didn't like Andy any more than you did, but Katie's got a right to make her own choices."

"Tell her parents that." He thought she just might, which was a happy possibility. Maybe Rebecca would get through to Tami Rogers. Maybe then Katie could move home....

"So you're not going to make it out to see us tonight, is that it?" Rebecca asked.

"It's pretty late."

"That's okay. Delaney and Conner decided to join us."

Delaney had been Rebecca's best friend while they

were growing up. She'd married Conner Armstrong nearly three years ago. They had a kid right away and built a huge resort out of the Running Y Ranch. Booker knew Delaney and Rebecca would always be close. They weren't much alike—but then, Rebecca wasn't much like anybody.

"I beat Josh at pool," she told him.

"Freak luck, that's all," Josh said in the background.

"Don't listen to him. He's a sore loser."

"Play me again, and I'll show you a sore loser."

"I have to go," she said. "Josh needs me to humble him."

Booker figured she wouldn't have any trouble bringing poor Josh to his knees. Josh loved his wife more than Booker had ever seen a man love a woman. But there were days when Booker thought this baby thing would tear them apart. He was glad they seemed to be getting along so well tonight. "Good luck," he said.

"Booker?" Rebecca caught him just before he hung up.

"Yeah?"

"How did it feel to see her again?"

"It wasn't any big deal," he said.

But as he went off to bed, he hesitated outside Katie's door, remembering the nights they'd spent together. There hadn't been a lot of them. He'd known even then that he was fighting an uphill battle for her affections. She'd had a crush on Josh's older brother, Mike, when they first met, but she'd had that same crush for over a decade and nothing had ever come of it. Booker hadn't been intimidated. He'd assumed he'd have all the time in the world to convince her that loving a man who loved her back beat the hell out of idealizing some family friend who'd never shown any interest.

But then Andy Bray had shown up and changed everything....

Booker winced as he recalled the night he'd tried to talk Katie into staying with him. *Marry me, Katie. I know I can make you happy.* She'd almost made an honest man out of him.

Close call, he thought, and moved on to his own bedroom. If she'd made a different decision, she'd probably be carrying *his* baby right now.

Unfortunately that didn't sound nearly as bad as he wished it did....

CHAPTER THREE

KATIE BLINKED AT the ceiling, wondering where she was. Letting her gaze sweep the room, she took in the white eyelet drapes, the faded roses on the wallpaper and the white finish on the dated furniture. Then it came to her. She was at Granny Hatfield's, staying with Booker Robinson, the Harley-riding ex-con who'd made the whole town groan when he moved in, the guy who'd ruined her reputation before she'd ruined her life. Her parents hadn't been pleased when she became engaged to Andy; their only consolation was—in her father's muttered words—"At least she didn't end up with Booker Robinson."

Covering her eyes, she chuckled mirthlessly. In an ironic twist of fate, she *was* with Booker. Because he'd been kinder to her than her own parents....

But she wouldn't stay with him long. She'd find herself a job and move out. She might be single and pregnant, easy pickings for the gossip-hungry, but she was going to get back on her feet.

Grabbing hold of that fresh resolve, she climbed out of bed. Then she caught herself in the dresser mirror, saw the way her short blond shag was standing up and noticed the dark circles around her eyes and the paleness of her skin, and sank back onto the bed. Who was she trying to kid? No one was going to hire a woman who looked ill and wasn't allowed to stand for any length of time. She couldn't work at the library, or the convenience store, or even the Arctic Flyer. She couldn't wait tables at Hokey Pokey's Ribs and Barbecue. She couldn't even do day care because of the lifting, not to mention the possibility of picking up some virus or other infection that could harm the baby.

How was she going to survive until the pregnancy was over?

Andy should be helping her, she thought with no small amount of resentment. He was just as responsible for her situation as she was. But "responsible" was about the last word anyone would use in connection with Andy. She knew better than to even contact him. The best she could hope for was that he'd stay out of her life. If she went back to him, she'd only sit in their small San Francisco apartment day in and day out—an apartment that had no furniture now—wondering if she was going to be evicted while he was out snorting cocaine and chasing other women.

She'd sunk pretty low. But she hadn't sunk low enough to go back to that….

A knock on the door startled her, made her heart thump loudly, because she assumed it was Booker and felt reluctant to face him in the light of day. "Yes?"

"Booker told me to bring you this," Delbert said, entering with a tray of oatmeal, toast and jelly, Bruiser at his heels. "We've gotta go to work. I work for Booker," he added as though he'd never mentioned it before. "I fix cars."

"That's wonderful," she said. She was truly happy for Delbert, that he'd found someone who was so good to him. But Booker liked her considerably less and made no secret of it. "Do you think he could use any more help down at Lionel & Sons?"

Delbert nearly tripped on the rug, so she helped him steady the tray. "You want to fix cars?" he asked.

Katie put the tray on the nightstand. "I'd do anything at this point."

"I change oil and air filters and spark plugs. I could show you how."

"I was only joking," she said. "I don't think I'll fit beneath a car very much longer."

"Oh." He gave her a puzzled look, but didn't ask why. He just stood there, blinking at her.

"What's wrong?" she asked.

"Booker said to tell you—" his brow furrowed in concentration "—he said the keys to Hatty's old Buick are on the counter, if you wanna go anywhere today."

"How nice of him."

"Booker's never hit me. Not once."

That announcement made Katie wonder how Delbert's father had treated him. But she wasn't about to ask. She wasn't sure she could take the answer right now.

"Delbert, let's get going," Booker called from downstairs.

"Tell Booker thank you," she said.

"Sure, Katie. I'll tell him." Delbert gave her a sloppy grin as he and Bruiser hurried from the room, obviously anxious to reach Lionel & Sons.

Outside, the engine of Booker's truck roared to life. Katie stood at her window and watched the dog jump in the back before they drove off. Then she ate, grateful for the meal in a way she'd never been grateful for such simple things before, and showered. Without Booker, she wouldn't have had any clean clothes this morning, she realized. He'd been the one to retrieve her suitcase from her parents' porch.

Carefully folding his sweats, she set them aside, wondering if her mother had gone out looking for her last night. If so, why hadn't Tami contacted Booker? Surely she'd seen him at the end of the walkway. If her parents cared about her, if they were worried about her at all, they would've called to see whether—

A job. She needed a job, she reminded herself, steering her thoughts away from her parents' hurtful behavior. If she didn't remain focused on practical considerations, the sting of their rejection would quickly immobilize her.

Opening the larger of her two suitcases, on the floor because it was too heavy to lift onto the bed, she tried to decide what to wear. When she lived in San Francisco, she'd combed through the factory outlet stores at least once a week and found garments worthy of New York, Paris or Milan, all for pennies on the dollar.

But she'd had to sell most of her clothes, along with her shoes. Gone was the Jones of New York sweater with the faux fur. Gone was the low-riding, tight-fitting pair of Bebe jeans with the trendy dirty-denim look. Gone were the cool jackets, Ann Taylor blouses, Kenneth Cole boots and fine Italian leather heels.

Good thing she didn't need much in Dundee. Wranglers were considered high fashion in this part of the country.

That brought her back to the issue of earning a living. The sooner she found work, the sooner she'd have options. The sooner she had options, the sooner she could stop taking help from Booker.

Unfortunately news of her illegitimate pregnancy was going to travel fast, which would definitely have a negative impact on her chances. Especially in a town so conservative and so small.

Hoping to beat the gossips, she pulled on a simple black dress so she wouldn't look quite so silly wearing the sandals that were her only shoes. Then she put on some makeup and fixed her hair in a much more conservative style than she generally wore in the city, and located the key for Hatty's Buick.

"Welcome back to Dundee," she whispered.

KATIE SPENT THE MORNING searching for a job. She approached the real estate office on the edge of town, hoping to get a receptionist position or a secretarial job, but Herb Bertleson, the broker, wasn't hiring and his only agent, Fred Winston, couldn't afford any help. She tried Lester Greenwalt, an insurance agent located not far from the real estate office, but he was content to have his daughter answer the phones and his wife do the filing.

After Greenwalt's office, she visited the local elementary school to see if she could take lunch tickets or something. But the school year was more than half over and all they needed was a temporary crossing guard because Rosie Strickland had come down with mononucleosis a few days earlier. Standing out in the rain and cold was something Katie couldn't do while she was pregnant, so she moved on, but the answer was the same everywhere she checked.

Jerry's Diner was at the very end of her list. When she'd stopped by Finley's Grocery a few minutes earlier to see if anyone there had heard of any openings,

Louise, the cashier, told her to talk to Judy at the diner. Louise said she heard Judy's daughter was quitting her job at the video store to go back to school. Katie wondered if working there would require her to be on her feet much and if the position would pay her enough to get by.

Managing to squeeze the boatlike Buick into the only parking space available at the diner, Katie got out.

"Isn't that *Hatty's* car?"

Katie shaded her eyes to see Mary Thornton standing beneath the small overhang of the restaurant. "Hi, Mary," she said. Six years older than Katie, Mary walked and talked as though she considered herself some kind of perennial prom queen. But she was really just the divorced mother of an eleven-year-old boy—a woman with the single-minded ambition to capture one of Dundee's eligible bachelors.

"Don't tell me you're back with Booker," Mary said, eyeing the Buick.

Everyone who saw the Buick was going to jump to the same conclusion. Katie hated that. She had enough disadvantages already. But she needed some way to get around. She couldn't seclude herself at the old Hatfield place for long. Not if she planned to survive. "Booker and I are just friends. He—he's helping me out."

"Booker's not the type to do favors for free." A taunting smile curved Mary's freshly glossed lips.

"How do *you* know?" Katie asked, but before Mary could retort, Mike Hill strode out of the restaurant. He was in the process of returning his credit card to his billfold, but when he glanced up, his face lit with recognition.

"Katie! I didn't know you were back."

While she was growing up, the sight of Mike Hill had always made Katie's knees go weak. Even when she was only five or six, she'd stand on her front lawn and wait for him to come by on his bicycle while he was delivering papers.

He was still the handsomest man she'd ever met, in a predictably pleasant, hometown sort of way. With the long thin body of a basketball player, he was always clean-shaven and kept his fine brown hair neatly trimmed. Better yet, his green eyes crinkled at the corners when he smiled, which he did quite often—far more often than Booker, for instance. But as attractive as he was, he was thirteen years her senior. He'd always treated her like a baby sister. And she was through with men. At least for a few years.

"Hi, Mike," she said. "How've you been?"

"Good. What brings you to town?"

The fact that she was broke and pregnant came to mind, but Katie knew he'd find that out soon enough. "I moved back yesterday."

His eyebrows shot up. "Really? So you're home for good?"

She nodded.

"That's great."

In the past, his words would've left Katie stewing over the sentiment behind them. "Great" as in he missed her? Or "great" as merely a generic "that's nice"? Today she took them at face value. Cynicism had its advantages.

"It's good to be back," she lied. Then she realized that Mary hadn't moved and was looking up at Mike as though—as though they were *together.* When Katie left town, Mike had been dating someone from McCall.

They'd been seeing each other for months, so everyone had expected them to get married. That must not have worked out. But Mike was thirty-eight and had never even been engaged, so maybe she shouldn't have been surprised. "You two just have lunch?" she asked.

Mary smoothed her hands over a suit that was, to Katie's trained eye, a designer knockoff and not nearly as impressive as Mary seemed to think. "We did."

Had Mike picked up where his brother, Josh, had left off when Josh married Rebecca instead of Mary? The thought made Katie feel ill even though she no longer had designs on Mike. Mary had her better moments—when she'd helped Katie start the Senior Singles Club two years ago, for instance—but on the whole, Katie had never liked her much.

Mike glanced at his watch. "We should go. I promised Slinkerhoff I wouldn't keep Mary over an hour."

"You're still working at the law office, Mary?" Katie asked.

"We're taking a deposition this afternoon," she explained, as though that made her someone important.

"Who's getting divorced?" Katie asked. Everyone knew Slinkerhoff's practice survived on marital unrest. When she'd passed his office a few minutes ago, she'd half expected to see a sign posted near the door saying, "Leave him now. Ask me how."

"This isn't a divorce case," Mary said. "It's a *criminal* trial."

Katie shifted her purse to the other arm. "Slinkerhoff is moving into criminal law?"

"His nephew is accused of robbing two houses in your old neighborhood," Mike explained.

"His nephew?" Katie responded. "I didn't realize he had a nephew."

"You've probably seen him around," Mike said. "He's got to be twenty-two."

"Oh." Katie thought the mother of Slinkerhoff's young nephew would be much better off hiring an attorney from Boise to defend him, preferably someone who knew what he was doing. But who was she to offer advice? She only knew that Warren Slinkerhoff and his sidekick, Mary, were the last two people she'd trust with the freedom of anyone she loved.

"You planning to go back to work at Hair and Now?" Mike asked.

"No, I'm looking for something else." She kept her answer vague because she didn't want to face Mary's reaction to the truth.

"That's too bad." He pulled his cowboy hat a little lower. "No one cuts hair as well as you do."

"I could come out to your place and give you a trim once in a while," she said. Staying on her feet for only one or two cuts certainly couldn't hurt the baby, and Lord knew she needed the money.

He grinned. "That'd be great. Give me a call once you get settled."

Their exchange was simple enough, but Mary's eyes narrowed and her gaze suddenly dropped to Katie's feet. "Are you wearing sandals for a reason?" she asked.

"I bought them in San Francisco." Katie smiled as though her shoes weren't completely out of season.

Mike shrugged indifferently. "They're nice."

Mary chuckled and shook her head. "There's snow on the ground, silly," she said, then she tugged on

Mike's arm, scarcely giving him a moment to wave, and they were gone.

Katie watched them drive away in a new champagne-colored Escalade before trudging into the restaurant. "What do guys see in her?" she muttered, but when the bell jingled over the door, she promptly forgot about Mary. She needed some sort of break. And she hoped to find it here.

The place was packed, as usual. Several waitresses wearing maroon uniforms bustled around, carrying plates back and forth, getting drinks, taking orders. Judy was busy wiping the coffee area, so Katie sidled up to the bar between an older man and a woman with a young girl. Nothing at Jerry's had changed since she'd left. Katie felt momentarily relieved about that. She wanted to go back in time....

"I'll be with you in a second, hon," Judy said in her deep smoker's voice and rushed off, carrying a stack of menus.

Katie toyed with the sweetener packets next to the napkin-holder, trying to distract herself from the food coming out of the kitchen. The smell of onion rings, French fries and burgers was making her stomach growl. But she wasn't about to spend her last twenty bucks on lunch when she'd already had breakfast.

Judy returned a moment later, her weathered face breaking into a smile. "So our girl's come home, huh?" she said. "When did you get back?"

"Last night."

"How long you planning to stay?"

"For a few months, at least."

"Great." She wiped up a spill on the back counter, near the hot chocolate machine, then tossed her cleaning rag into the sink and pulled a pad and pencil from the pocket of her apron. "What can I get you?"

Jerry's Giant Baconburger sounded good. Katie nearly broke down and ordered it, but 5.85 was 5.85. "Nothing, thanks. I stopped by to talk to you, if you've got a minute."

Judy's shoes made a sticking sound as she moved closer. The floor obviously needed to be mopped, and the lampshades needed dusting. But folks ate at Jerry's because the prices were right and the portions were large. They weren't excessively concerned with cleanliness. "What's up, kiddo?"

The man on Katie's right had his face close to his plate, devouring an open-face turkey sandwich. The child on her left picked at a club sandwich. Both meals looked so *good.* Forcing her attention away from the food, Katie said, "Louise told me she heard your daughter might be quitting her job over at the video store. I was wondering if that's true."

"It better not be," she said. "She's got to buy diapers and formula for Nathan."

"So she's not going back to school?"

Judy shielded a quick cough. "No. She talks about it constantly, but she blew her chance at school when she got pregnant. If she's going to live with me, she has to contribute."

"I see. Of course." Katie tried not to let her disappointment show, although she had no idea where she could turn next.

"You looking for a job, kid?"

"Yeah."

"What about doing hair?"

"I—I can't do hair right now."

"Why not?"

"I can't be on my feet."

"That pretty much narrows things down." She shoved her pad and pencil back into her apron.

Katie blinked several times, once again fighting tears. She wanted to say, "Everything will be fine." Only the words wouldn't come.

Judy moved closer. "You want to tell me what's going on?"

Katie knew she could lie and keep people guessing for a few weeks, or at least until she began to show. But there wasn't much point, not anymore. She'd already applied for every job available and been repeatedly turned down. And everyone was going to find out eventually. Especially if her mother and Booker were sharing what they knew of her situation. "I'm pregnant," she said. "My doctor told me I could lose the baby if I don't take things easy."

Leaning on the bar, Judy lowered her voice. "Where's that fella you married?"

"We never actually tied the knot."

"Oh."

"He's still in San Francisco."

"And I take it he's not coming back."

"No."

Her face registered compassion. "Well, I'll put the word out that you're looking for a job." She straightened. "But I'm afraid there's not a lot around here."

Katie forced herself to get up and step away from the counter, even though it felt strange to leave the diner hungry. "I know."

"Can't your folks use you at the bakery?"

"No…er…not right now."

"If I hear of somethin', where can I reach you? Their place?"

Katie shook her head. "No, I'm staying out at Hatty's."

One eyebrow lifted toward the black roots of Judy's bleached hair. "You mean Booker's? You're staying with *Booker?*"

Katie sighed. "Yeah."

An appreciative smile stole over her face. "If that's the case, I'd give just about anything to be in your shoes."

"It's not like that." Katie felt her cheeks heat. "He… he's just helping me out for a little while."

Judy fanned herself as if the mere thought of living with Booker was enough to give her heart palpitations. "Well, I know I'm not the only one who'd love to trade places with you."

"I'm not interested in a man."

"Are you crazy? Even Booker? I've never seen a better pair of bedroom eyes."

Booker's hands weren't bad, either. Katie knew from experience the havoc they could wreak on a woman's body. She'd been a bona fide Goody Two-shoes before she met him, yet he'd broken through her reserve. He seemed to know moves the average man, like Andy, didn't. But at twenty-five she'd already made more than her share of mistakes. If she'd learned anything, she'd learned that life wasn't about personal gratification. It was about deeper things, lasting things, and it was time for her to grow up and start building the right foundation. "I don't care about bedroom eyes. I'm going solo for a while."

"Then I suggest you move out of Booker's house immediately," Judy said. "Because the bedroom's where you're going if you stay."

CHAPTER FOUR

KATIE RETURNED TO Booker's around four o'clock. She'd spent the afternoon at Hair and Now, catching up on all the gossip and getting reacquainted with the people she used to work with—Mona, the middle-aged manicurist, Erma, who was selling the shop to Rebecca but still worked part-time, Ashleigh, who'd been there about two years, and Rebecca.

Rebecca had been a little reserved at first. Considering how close Booker and Rebecca were, Katie could understand why Rebecca might not be thrilled to see her. But then Delaney had walked in to have her little girl's bangs trimmed, and Rebecca had warmed up considerably while playing "aunt." They'd all sat around talking and laughing—until LeAnn, Andy's cousin, arrived for an appointment. At that point, Katie decided it was time to leave. Mona wanted to trade a manicure and pedicure for a haircut and color, which sounded pretty appealing, but Katie felt she should have dinner ready when Booker and Delbert came home. She had to do *something* to repay Booker's generosity in letting her stay with him, *something* to compensate him for the fact that he didn't really want her around. Her self-respect demanded it.

Besides, she was so hungry she could almost eat cardboard, and she wasn't about to help herself to Booker's food without working to earn it.

Unfortunately Booker's cupboards weren't well-stocked. Salt, cold cereal, a few cans of tuna, the heel of a loaf of bread… Probably he and Delbert ate out a lot.

What was she going to do?

She opened the refrigerator. Beer, a cube of butter and some eggs. Not much better.

Sitting down, because her empty stomach was making her a little light-headed, she considered her options. She could make tuna salad. Or she could go to the store, spend her last twenty dollars on groceries and make a meal of which she could be proud.

Somehow, after her mother's poor reception, the rejection she'd experienced while attempting to find a job and facing one of Andy's cousins, she needed to be able to contribute—even more than she needed money. Getting up, she grabbed her purse and headed back into town.

GLANCING AT HIS WATCH, Booker realized it was nearly eleven o'clock. Much too late to tear apart the wheels and repack the bearings on Helen Dobbs's Chevy Suburban, which was next on his list.

Shoving himself out from beneath the red Mustang he'd just fixed, he dodged the space heater that hummed nearby and crossed to the sink at the corner of the shop. He'd let his full-time mechanic, Chase Gardner, leave hours ago. Delbert had taken Bruiser and wandered over to the Honky Tonk at nine o'clock to play some pool. But Booker had kept working. For once, he wasn't interested in hanging out at the Honky Tonk. And he sure as hell didn't feel like going home. Not with Katie there. Word was spreading that she was staying with him. He'd been hearing about it all day.

"Hey, I hear Katie's in town… You two back together…? Is she finished with Andy…? Why is she staying with you instead of her parents?"

In retrospect, Booker wasn't sure exactly how he'd wound up with Katie under his roof. There was her smoking car, then the rain, then her mother standing at the door looking down her nose at both of them. And suddenly he had a roommate.

It was just plain bad luck that he'd come across her before anyone else had.

Peeling off the heavy coveralls he typically wore over his clothes in winter, he pushed up the sleeves of his long-sleeved T-shirt, lathered his hands and arms with laundry detergent and used a brush to scrub off the grease. In the extra hours he'd spent at the shop, he'd worked on Katie's car, which he'd towed into town first thing this morning, and finished repairing a Mustang and a Nissan truck. He was tempted to keep working through the night. Heaven knew he had enough backlog. But he had to go home sometime, or he knew he wouldn't be worth anything tomorrow.

The telephone rang. It had rung at about ten, while he was working under the Mustang, but he hadn't wanted to talk to anyone badly enough to interrupt what he was doing. Now he thought maybe Delbert hadn't been able to catch a ride home, as he normally did if Booker wasn't around, so he headed into the small front office.

"Hello?" He propped the handset against his shoulder while he finished drying his hands on the paper towel he'd brought with him.

"Is everything okay?"

Not Delbert—Katie. Mildly surprised, Booker threw the paper towel in the garbage. “Of course. Why?”

“I thought maybe there’d been an emergency.”

“No.”

“So what’ve you been doing?”

“Working.”

“Just working?”

“Were you expecting something else?”

“You didn’t think to let me know you wouldn’t be coming home tonight?”

“Was I *supposed* to let you know?”

“Well, I assumed—I mean, I made…” She sighed. “Never mind.”

“What?”

“Nothing. Forget it,” she said and hung up.

Booker blinked at the phone, then called her back, but she didn’t answer.

Rubbing his temples, he gave a long sigh. One day. She’d been there one day. And it was already one day too many—for a variety of reasons.

BOOKER SHOOK HIS HEAD as he read Katie’s note taped to the refrigerator. *There are plenty of leftovers if you’re hungry. K.*

“Smells good in here,” Delbert said, coming in from the mudroom, where he’d just taken off his boots.

Booker opened the fridge and gazed inside to see a large pan of lasagna, a green salad, a foil-wrapped loaf of garlic bread and a pitcher of lemonade. Judging by the number of pans drying in the drainer next to the sink, Katie had gone to a lot of effort.

He felt a *little* guilty for not bothering to let her know he wouldn’t be home. He’d considered calling but refused to feel as though he needed to check in. It wasn't as though he owed her anything. Two years ago, he'd asked her to marry him. She'd turned him down flat, then she'd left town with another man. That hardly obligated him.

"There's food in the fridge if you want to eat," he told Delbert.

Delbert was feeding Bruiser, who'd actually started out as Booker's dog. Earl Wallace, owner of the local feed store, had found him roaming around his back lot. When no one claimed him, Booker stepped in to keep him from going to the pound. But Delbert moved in about the same time, and Booker simply couldn't compete with the kind of love and devotion Delbert lavished on the dog. Bruiser became Delbert's dog and began shadowing his every move. Now the pair were almost inseparable.

Delbert got Bruiser some fresh water before pulling the lasagna out of the fridge. Booker headed into the living room, where he could hear the television. He wanted to talk to Katie, to find out whether she'd spoken to her parents today or made any decisions about her future. He recognized the difficulty of her situation. He blamed Andy for much of it. But he was determined not to get personally involved with Katie again—on any level. Which meant they had to make other arrangements as soon as possible.

The television flickered in the corner, providing the room's only light. Booker could see Katie lying on the couch in front of it, but when he drew closer, he realized she was asleep.

He was just deciding whether to wake her, so they could get their little talk out of the way, when the telephone rang. Who'd be calling at midnight? he wondered and grabbed the cordless phone off its base.

"Hello?"

Whoever was on the other end slammed down the receiver.

"Was that my parents?" Katie asked, obviously struggling to wake up.

"Maybe." He replaced the phone. "Why? Are you expecting them to call?"

She blinked up at him. Her mascara was smudged, her face bore the imprint of the fabric covering the couch, and her hair stuck up on one side. She looked her worst. But he didn't care. His mind immediately conjured up the feel of that soft pouty mouth beneath his and the expression in her blue eyes when he'd first cupped her breast....

Resenting how the past two years seemed to fall away so easily, he reminded himself that what they'd had was over. For good.

"Not really." She tried to smooth down her hair. "I... I thought they might try to contact me. You know, just to check up."

Her brittle smile and casual tone didn't ring true, but Booker refused to feel any sympathy. He needed to get rid of her, and he needed to do it fast, before his memories undid all the progress he'd made over the past two years. "Maybe we should call them in the morning," he said.

She grimaced and stared at the phone. "If they wanted to talk to me, they would've done so by now, don't you think?"

He settled in the recliner. "What about your father?

Have you tried contacting him? Maybe he doesn't feel quite as strongly as your mother does."

"Maybe," she said, but her voice held no hope. And Booker knew her father usually took a harder line than her mother did. "I—I'll stop by the bakery tomorrow."

"Good." Booker thought perhaps he should visit the bakery beforehand and try to rouse Don to his familial duty.

"What did you do today?" he asked, even though he already knew a little about her movements. Lester Greenwalt had stopped by to pick up the flat he'd brought over for repair, and mentioned that Katie had visited him looking for work. Why she'd applied at an insurance office, Booker couldn't say. He'd assumed the beauty shop would be her first stop.

"I put in a few job applications," she said.

"Did you go by Hair and Now?"

"I popped in this afternoon. Why?"

"Was Rebecca around?"

"For a while. Until she went into the back room to take her temperature. Then she rushed off to meet Josh."

The baby thing again. Rebecca wasn't giving up, yet every time it didn't work out she got that much more upset. "Didn't she tell you she'd hire you back?"

"We talked about it briefly."

"And?"

"I'm going to try something different for a while."

From all indications, she was on her last dollar. Now wasn't the time to be selective. "Why?" He scowled to let her know he didn't agree.

She scowled right back at him. "Maybe I need a change of pace."

"Katie, I towed the Cadillac to my shop and got it running again, but—"

"How much do I owe you for that?" she interrupted, worry clouding her face.

"Six hundred dollars."

She winced.

"That's giving you a good deal," he said because it was true. Six hundred dollars represented his costs in labor and parts, nothing for profit. "You cracked the block, and I had to have the engine rebuilt. It took my top mechanic nearly all day. I worked on it some more tonight, and we're still not quite finished. I'm waiting for another part to come in."

"I appreciate the effort," she said, "but you didn't even ask me if…if I wanted it fixed."

"What were you planning to do? Leave it on the side of the road?"

"No, I…" She closed her eyes and rubbed her temples. "I hadn't decided, I guess."

Silence fell, during which Booker could hear Delbert talking to Bruiser in the kitchen.

"How much is the car worth out here, if I wanted to sell it?" Katie asked after a few seconds.

Booker couldn't supply an exact figure, but he knew it wouldn't be much. "I don't know."

"Well, it's probably not worth the 4,000 I paid for it, but as soon as I sell it, I'll give you the money."

God, she was *that* desperate? What had happened in the two years she'd been gone? "I'm not going to let you sell your car," he said flatly.

Her troubled eyes finally met his. "But I can't pay you, Booker. Not now, anyway. I don't even know when."

Booker had dreamed of running into Katie again, thousands of times. She'd hurt him so deeply when she left that he'd thought he'd like nothing better than to find her penniless and repentant. But he felt no triumph. Only anger, plenty of anger, directed at her *and* Andy. Maybe he didn't have a family who'd supported him all the way through college, like Andy's. Maybe he wasn't a slick talker with wrinkle-free clothes and a pretty face. But he would've starved before letting Katie go without. "What happened in San Francisco?" he finally asked. "Why hasn't Andy been taking care of you?"

She drew up her legs and hugged them against her. "You can be so old-fashioned," she said with a slight grimace. "I wouldn't need anyone to take care of me if it wasn't for this baby. I was working in a nice salon, making good money. I was the one paying all the bills. But then—"

He waited when her words drifted off, watching the emotions play across her face.

"—then I got pregnant and the pregnancy hasn't been going well."

A trickle of unease heightened Booker's senses, telling him the story was about to get a hell of a lot worse. "What does that mean?"

She shrugged, but it was hardly a careless movement. "I can't work on my feet."

"Or…"

"Or I could lose the baby, okay? That's why I can't cut hair. That's why I can't go back to Hair and Now."

Releasing a long sigh, Booker wiped his face with one hand. "And you have no savings."

"No. Andy made sure of that. He barely waited until I could make the money before he spent it."

"Wasn't he bringing home a paycheck of his own?"

She shook her head. "I tried to get him to work, but—" She fell silent. "Never mind. I'm sure you don't want to hear about that."

Booker's heart was pounding against his chest. He wasn't even sure why. Maybe it was because, painful though it might be, he *did* want to hear the details. "What about Andy's parents?"

"What about them?" she asked. "Have you ever met them?"

"No, but from what his cousins say, they're pretty damn supportive of their only boy. According to LeAnn and her brother, Todd, he never had to work a day to put himself through school."

"His parents cut him off a few months after we reached San Francisco."

"Why would they do that after paying his way until then?"

She turned her attention to the remote and muted the television, but he got the impression it was just to give herself something to do so she wouldn't have to look at him. "They had…reason."

"Are you going to tell me what that reason is?"

She dropped the remote into her lap. "I'd rather not talk about it."

"I'd like to know."

"Fine." A touch of belligerence entered her voice. "They came to visit us in San Francisco and were pretty disappointed by what they saw, okay? At that stage, Andy was hardly someone to be proud of."

He raised his eyebrows in place of demanding an explanation, but she got the point. Groaning, she rested her forehead on her knees. “Andy rarely bothered to come home. When he did, he was usually wasted.”

“You mean drunk?”

“High, although he drank, too. He got involved in the party scene almost the first week we lived there.”

Booker didn’t feel he could say much about Andy’s partying. There’d been a rough patch in his own life when he’d deadened the pain with whatever he could beg, borrow, buy or find. And he’d acted out in other ways, too, and paid a heavy price. Only now, years later, was he glad his actions had caught up with him. Prison had changed him. Forced him to realize that his behavior was more self-destructive than anything else. Taught him to appreciate the simple things in life. He wasn’t proud of his past, but he’d finally come to terms with who and what he was.

“By the time his parents left, his mother was crying,” Katie went on. “And Andy’s father told him not to bother calling with any more sob stories about being laid off or losing his last paycheck. He said they weren’t going to send him any more money and, as far as I know, Andy hasn’t heard from them since. I’m guessing he’ll contact them now, though. I’m not sure he can survive without me there to pay the rent.”

“So his folks don’t know about the baby?”

“Not yet.”

“Are you going to tell them?”

“I don’t know. Andy wanted me to have an abortion. Right now, I feel the baby’s pretty much exclusively mine.”

Wonderful. Katie’s life was the complete mess he’d been hoping for since she’d rejected him, yet Booker couldn’t feel good about it.

He got slowly out of the recliner. “Don’t worry about paying for the car. You need some way to get around.”

“Booker, I can’t accept—”

“We can settle up whenever you have the money,” he said brusquely and started to leave before he could ask the one question that burned in his mind. But he only got as far as the door. Then he stopped, turned and asked it anyway. “You love this guy?”

Katie twisted a lock of hair around one finger as she stared at him. He could see a shine in her eyes and thought maybe they were filling with tears, but the room was too dark to tell for sure. “I don’t think I even know what love is,” she said softly.

The smell of freshly baked doughnuts enveloped Booker the moment he entered Don and Tami’s Bakery the following morning at six o’clock. The bell went off over the door, but Don barely glanced up before going right back to what he was doing—transferring fresh apple fritters, glazed doughnuts and maple bars from rolling metal trays to the display case.

“I need to talk to you,” Booker said.

“We don’t have anything to say to each other,” Katie’s father responded.

Booker knew Don didn’t like him. Don was one of the locals who still took his car to a neighboring town or to Boise for service and repair. But Booker wasn’t asking for his business. He just wanted Don to take Katie off his hands and to see that she was safe and well cared for. “I think we do,” he said. “Katie’s staying out at my place.”

Don shifted to the bottom shelf and start lining up custard and jelly-filled doughnuts. “That’s what I hear.”

"She's pregnant."

Don craned his head around, as if he expected Tami to come out of the back room where they did their baking, but no one appeared. "I'm afraid that's her problem. We tried to tell her what she was in for with Andy, but she wouldn't listen. He lived here in Dundee, off those cousins of his, for months and never got a job. What does that say about him?"

Booker didn't want to get into an argument over Andy. "You're her parents," he said. He knew from experience that parents didn't always care. But from what he'd seen in the past, Don and Tami Rogers were certainly more supportive than his own parents had been.

"She's of age." Don finally stopped long enough to catch and hold Booker's gaze. Eyes narrowing, mouth tightening, he added, "So don't come in here thinking you can criticize us. She probably wouldn't have made the mistakes she made if she hadn't gotten involved with you first."

Booker felt the old anger—the dark kind of anger he hadn't felt for years—coil inside him. He'd loved Katie. That should have redeemed him somehow. But because of his reputation, it didn't seem to matter. Even though his reputation didn't have a damn thing to do with any of this. "Don't you care what happens to her?" he demanded.

"We love her enough to let her feel the natural consequences of her actions." Don wiped powdered sugar from his hands onto a towel. "How will she ever learn if we're always there to rescue her?"

"There's a *baby* involved," Booker said. "The baby hasn't done anything wrong."

Tami poked her head out from the back. "I've been

reading some of those parenting books that are so popular these days," she said, "and they all say you've got to have tough love."

"What's tough love? Telling someone you care about, 'tough luck'?" he asked.

"I'm sure Rebecca will hire her back at Hair and Now," Don said. "Katie will pull herself up by her bootstraps eventually."

"And when she does, she'll thank us." Tami nodded self-righteously. "She'll gain perspective and confidence from working through her own problems."

The only catch was that Katie *couldn't* work. Obviously they didn't know that. Booker considered breaking the news to them. He wanted to see their faces when they realized they were expecting the impossible. But something inside him rebelled. The only reason they didn't know about the difficulty with Katie's pregnancy was that they'd treated her so poorly. They hadn't even bothered to ask how she was doing. In his view, they didn't deserve contact with her or the baby.

"Forget it. She'll be better off without the two of you," he said and walked out.

CHAPTER FIVE

THE PHONE RANG, finally waking Katie at eleven o'clock. She'd actually opened her eyes earlier, when she heard Booker and Delbert leave for work, but she hadn't been able to drag herself out of bed. She didn't have anything to get out of bed for. No job opportunities. No one to see. She didn't even know if Booker and Delbert would be home for dinner, or if she'd spend the entire day alone.

She remembered that Mona had offered to give her a manicure....

A manicure was a hopeful thought. But when she considered the logistics of getting to the salon... She'd have to get up. Then she'd have to shower, which meant washing her hair and shaving her legs. Then she'd have to brush her teeth and put on makeup....

It was simply too overwhelming. Besides, by now, word of her pregnancy would've spread, and she had no way of knowing who she might encounter at Hair and Now. She could run into her own mother, for crying out loud. Or Mike and Josh's mother, who wouldn't think any better of her than Tami did. Or worse, the smug Mary Thornton.

It no longer felt safe to go anywhere. When had the world become such a dangerous place?

With a groan, she pulled the covers over her head.

She wasn't going to answer the phone. Whoever was calling could leave a message on Booker's answering machine. It was probably for him, anyway.

After another few moments, blessed silence fell, and Katie began drifting off to sleep—only to have the phone start ringing again.

"Go away!" she yelled at it. But whoever was calling wouldn't give up. If she wanted any peace at all, she had to answer.

Stumbling out of bed, she moved slowly into the hall. Hatty's house was too old to be wired for a phone in the bedroom, and Hatty had been too set in her ways to change that.

"Hello?" Katie snapped.

"Katie?" It was Booker.

Katie softened her voice. "Yeah?"

"Where've you been?"

"Uh…in the shower," she said, because she didn't want to tell him the pathetic truth.

"Are you going over to the bakery to talk to your father?"

"I was thinking about it." *Not.* She'd pretty much decided it was useless. Her parents hadn't even called to check on her. She could be living on the streets for all they cared. Which was a distinct possibility for the future. But she wouldn't think about that. That made her feel even more tired, and she was barely moving as it was.

"Well, don't bother," he said.

She could hear the wind outside, the trees brushing against the house. If she hadn't been staring at the sun streaming in through the window of the closest bedroom, she would've thought it was storming. "Why not?"

"I'm working on a different plan. We'll talk about it when I get home."

"Fine." She covered a yawn, too indifferent to wonder what he meant, let alone ask. Nothing Booker did would make any difference. Straightening out the mess she'd made of her life was something she'd have to do on her own. Only she couldn't manage it today. She'd deal with it tomorrow, when she felt better.

"I'll be home at six o'clock," he told her.

"Okay. I'll have dinner waiting," she said. But then she went back to bed and slept the entire day.

WHEN BOOKER AND Delbert got home, there was no dinner on the table. The place was dark and seemed empty.

"Where's Katie?" Delbert asked as he and Bruiser followed Booker inside.

Booker couldn't hear anything. No TV or radio. No one speaking on the phone. "Katie?" he called.

"She's gone," Delbert said, and Booker felt a trace of hope. He'd been planning to offer her a bookkeeping job at his garage. Even though he knew it wouldn't be easy to spend so much time around her, he hadn't been able to think of anything better. But maybe someone had come to pick her up. Maybe she'd found another place to stay and a job that wouldn't require her to be on her feet. If so, her problems, which had become his problems, might already be solved....

If only he could be so lucky.

Heading upstairs, he knocked on the walls as he neared Katie's bedroom to announce that he was coming. "Anyone home?"

No answer. Darkness had fallen outside, but her door

was shut, and there wasn't any light glowing beneath it. "Katie?"

"Did you find her?" Delbert asked, standing at the bottom of the stairs.

"Not yet." Booker turned on the hall light and knocked softly on her door. No answer. He looked inside to see a round lump in the middle of the bed—a round lump that was beginning to stir.

"What? Who is it?" Katie sounded groggy. Shoving herself into a sitting position, she blinked against the light spilling into her room.

Booker let the door swing wide, and leaned against the lintel. "This shouldn't come as any kind of a shock, since I own the house, but it's me."

"Booker?"

"You got it."

She groaned and fell back. "God, I thought I was only dreaming that I was pregnant and broke and having to rely on the pity of someone who hates me."

Booker felt a wry smile claim his lips, and stuck his toothpick in his mouth to stave it off. He wasn't about to let his heart soften where Katie Rogers was concerned. Not after the way she'd thrown his proposal back in his face two years ago. "What did you do today?"

"Nothing."

"Is she there?" Delbert called up to him.

"She's here," Booker said. "Go ahead and make yourself a sandwich."

"Oh, good, she's here," Delbert told Bruiser, as though the dog was especially worried, and galloped to the kitchen.

"What time is it?" Katie asked.

"Six-thirty."

"Six-thirty!"

He pulled the toothpick from his mouth. "Time flies when you're having fun, hmm?"

"Ugh." Her voice sounded muffled because she'd ducked completely under the covers.

"What's the matter?" he asked.

"I just slept the whole day away and I still feel too tired to move."

"Tell me that has something to do with the pregnancy."

"I don't know. I've never been pregnant before. But then, I've never been shunned and penniless, either. This is all new to me."

Booker couldn't help chuckling. "You'll get through it."

"That's easy for you to say," she told him, now sullen. "*You've* never been pregnant."

"No, but I've been shunned and penniless most of my life."

No response.

"Are you getting up?" he asked.

"No."

"Do you think you might get up later?"

"No."

"You're not making me feel particularly comfortable here."

Nothing.

Booker searched his mind for something he could say or do. "Can you feel the baby move yet?" he asked at last.

The question obviously took her off guard. Rising onto one elbow, she stared at him. "I felt the baby move for the first time while I was driving here."

"What did it feel like?"

Her expression mellowed. "Like…like a butterfly's wing inside my belly. Why?"

"Because you need to remember that moment. Tomorrow you'll get up for the baby," he said and left.

LETHARGY WAS SPREADING through her like a slow-moving drug, incapacitating one muscle after another until she felt almost paralyzed. She'd been in bed for two nights and a day, but it didn't seem to matter how long she slept. She was more tired now than when she'd first hit the sack. Worse, she knew she looked terrible, but she didn't care. Brushing her teeth was suddenly too much effort.

There was a brisk knock at her door.

Katie didn't respond. She was afraid it was Booker coming to make her get up, and she wasn't ready. She needed more time.

He didn't seem to receive her telepathic "Stay away," because he came in anyway. But he didn't say anything. He paused briefly at the foot of her bed. Then he opened the blinds and left.

Grateful for the reprieve, Katie rolled over on her side and stared at the square patch of sky he'd revealed. The sun was just beginning to rise, painting the horizon a delicate pinkish-orange. Booker had said she'd get up today—for her baby—but he didn't understand. She couldn't get up for *anything.*

Booker's truck started outside.

Tomorrow, she promised herself as he drove away. She'd get up for her baby tomorrow. Surely she'd feel better by then.

"THAT OLD CADILLAC'S RUNNING, but I can't promise how long it's going to last," Chase said, standing in the doorway of Booker's office.

Booker glanced up from his cluttered desk to acknowledge his mechanic's words. Chase was only nineteen, but he had a real talent with engines. "It's old. There's nothing we can do about that."

"You wanted the keys?"

"Yeah."

Chase tossed them over. Booker caught them and slid them in his pocket. The Cadillac might be running, but Katie wouldn't be driving it anywhere if he couldn't get her out of bed.

"Go ahead and start the tune-up of Lila Bronwyn's Jeep," he told Chase. Then he turned down the radio they had blasting and tried to reach Katie. He let the phone ring nearly twenty times, hung up and called again. But she wouldn't pick up.

"Answer, damn it," he muttered, losing patience.

"What's wrong?" Delbert wiped his grease-covered hands on a rag as he and Bruiser came into the office. "Are you mad? Are you mad at me, Booker?"

"I'm not mad," Booker said, but he *was* getting worried. What was he going to do with Katie? She'd completely withdrawn from life. She wasn't getting up. She wasn't eating. She wasn't doing *anything.*

He thought of her parents. Should he have told them that she couldn't work? Would it have made a difference?

He certainly wasn't the best person to handle this, but remembering how Tami had treated Katie at the door, how both her parents had reacted to him at the donut shop, quickly convinced him that they were part of the problem, not the solution. And it wasn't as if he saw anyone else stepping up to help her.... She'd been gone too long and apparently hadn't kept up with relationships. Which meant, crazy as it seemed, he was the closest thing she had to a friend.

Mike Hill's new Escalade cruised by out front, catching Booker's eye. Watching Mike turn on First Avenue, he thought of all the times he'd heard, from almost everyone in town, that Katie had had a crush on Mike nearly her whole life. She'd once told him herself, flat out, that she wanted to marry Mike Hill someday. But Booker hadn't taken her too seriously. He'd never seen Mike show any interest in her, couldn't imagine them together. They were both...*good.* In his opinion, they each needed a counterbalance.

But Mike *was* rich and dependable. Maybe the best thing Booker could do for Katie and her baby was to throw them into Mike's lap. A friend would do something like that, right?

Picking up the phone, he called Rebecca at the salon.

"Hello?"

"Is Rebecca there?"

"Hi, Booker."

From the voice, it was Ashleigh Evans. "How's it going?"

"Good. Where've you been? I've missed you."

They'd danced last Friday at the Honky Tonk, but Booker knew if he pointed that out, she'd just say Friday seemed too long ago. "I've been busy."

"You promised me a ride on your bike, remember?"

How could he forget? She reminded him whenever he talked to her. "I'll stop by the salon sometime."

"I'm looking forward to it."

The phone changed hands and he heard Rebecca's voice. "I think she has a thing for you."

"Ashleigh?"

"Yeah."

Booker already knew that. She'd been coming on to him ever since she'd broken up with that bull rider from Boise. She'd even invited him to her place last Friday night, but his response had been decidedly lukewarm. "I need a favor," he said.

"Really? Wow! You've never asked me for anything before," Rebecca said. "You must be desperate."

He ignored her teasing because it hit a little too close to home. He didn't like asking for favors. He didn't like needing anything. But this wasn't for him—exactly. "Katie's looking for a job."

"I heard she's pregnant."

Booker braced himself for her reaction. "That's true."

"Why didn't you tell me?" she asked, her voice filled with accusation.

"I figured you'd find out soon enough."

She released a long sigh. "Some people have all the luck."

Booker pictured how rumpled and dispirited Katie had been sitting up in her bed last night and doubted she was feeling very lucky. "I'm sure Katie would be surprised to hear you say that."

"I'd do anything to have a baby, Booker. Especially Josh's baby. Sometimes I love him so much I can't even breathe, and yet I can't give him the one thing we both want most in the world."

Bill Peterson arrived to pick up his Camaro. Booker could hear Chase talking to him in the garage, and started searching his desk for the work order. "You're too tense about it, Rebecca."

"But I'm nearly thirty-three."

"A lot of women have babies at thirty-three."

"And everyone else is having one."

"Everyone?"

"Delaney's pregnant again."

"She is?"

"She's been holding off telling me, hoping I'd get some good news, too. But she's gaining weight, and I guessed."

"You'll just have to keep trying," Booker said. "I'm sure Josh doesn't mind that."

"No, he likes all the trying. He just doesn't like how upset I get when it doesn't work out."

"It's that watched-pot thing. You need to forget about it, and then it'll probably happen." Finding the paperwork he was looking for, Booker waved to let Mr. Peterson know he'd be right out.

"I don't think it's the watched-pot thing. I'm going to start taking fertility drugs," Rebecca said.

"Do whatever works, Beck."

"A lot of people have fertility problems."

Fortunately Chase came in and took the paperwork out to get Bill on his way.

"I know." Booker cleared his throat. "About that job…"

"I already offered Katie a job," she said. "She came by here a couple of days ago. But she told me she can't be on her feet."

"I wasn't thinking of having her work at Hair and Now."

"Where, then?"

"What about the resort?"

"It's wintertime, Booker. The resort's overstaffed as it is because Conner and Delaney won't lay anyone off. They're trying to limp by until summer, but I have the impression that finances are getting tight. They need to be careful."

"Do you think Josh and Mike might have an opening out at the ranch, then? She could do bookkeeping or answer phones behind a desk, couldn't she? Katie's a good friend of their family's. Surely they can help her out until she has the baby."

"They could probably come up with something for her to do but… I never would've suggested it because of you. Are you sure you want her working with Mike, Booker?"

Booker shoved away from his desk and stood. "I think it's time Katie got what she wants."

Silence. "What about what *you* want?"

"I already have what I want."

"O-kay." She didn't sound convinced, but after a moment she said, "I'll call Josh and get back to you."

BOOKER REFUSED TO GO AWAY. He stood over Katie's bed, scowling at her. When that didn't work, he started pulling off blankets.

"Leave me alone," she grumbled. "I'm tired."

"How can you be tired?" he asked. "It's nearly three o'clock in the afternoon, and you've been sleeping for two days."

"I think there's something wrong with me."

"It's called depression."

"I've never had trouble with depression."

"Then get up."

She curled into a ball to compensate for the warmth she'd lost when he stole the covers. "I'll get up tomorrow."

"You'll get up today," he said, and from the determination in his voice, she could tell he meant it. "I've set up a job interview for you."

"Where?" she asked, but she didn't really care. Who'd want her? She couldn't even function anymore.

"Mike Hill is looking for a secretary."

She raised her head to blink at him. *"Mike Hill?"*

"That's what I said."

"You've got to be kidding!"

"No."

She covered her eyes with her arm. "I don't know anything about ranching."

"You'll be doing some type of bookkeeping."

"I don't know anything about bookkeeping, either."

"He'll teach you."

"I'm not going out there." She didn't want to see anyone in her current state, but she *especially* didn't want to see the man she'd always hoped to marry.

"Oh, yes you are."

"Does he know about the baby?" she asked.

"I have no idea."

"I'll go anywhere *but* there."

"Come on," he said. "This is the man of your dreams, remember?"

She definitely detected sarcasm in his voice. Men weren't part of her dreams at all anymore, but she didn't feel quick-witted enough to explain that right now. "He's seeing Mary Thornton, so don't talk to me about my dreams."

"There's no accounting for taste." Booker jabbed

a finger at the small brown sack he'd brought in with him. "There's a deli sandwich in there. Eat it, then go shower."

"Okay," she said, but only so he'd leave her in peace. As soon as she heard him move away, she grabbed the covers he'd thrown off the bed and burrowed beneath them again. *Mike Hill... No way!*

"Katie?" Booker spoke from the doorway, his tone a warning.

"I thought you'd left," she grumbled.

"Don't make me drag you out."

"Aren't you supposed to be at work?"

"That's it." He stomped back to the side of her bed and yanked off her covers. Then he put his hands under her arms and lifted her to her feet as though she were a child.

Katie's legs didn't feel strong enough to support her. She swayed and nearly crumpled, but Booker caught her against him. For a moment, before she came to her senses, she wanted to grab him and hold on for dear life. He had more street smarts than anyone she'd ever met. He was tough. And he was *always* his own man.

After living with a chameleon like Andy, Katie admired that. Booker was probably the only person she knew who did what he wanted and offered no lies, excuses or apologies. To anyone.

And he could be gentle. She remembered the way he'd lightly rub his whiskers on her neck while they were watching TV, then chuckle deep in his throat when she tried to fend him off. They'd end up laughing and wrestling until—

She didn't want to remember what happened next. She'd been right to break things off with Booker. If only her intuition hadn't abandoned her when it came to Andy…

She needed to go back to bed.

"Don't even think about it," Booker said when she tried to slip out of his arms. "You're going to get cleaned up, and you're going to do it now."

"Yes, sir." She tried to salute in response to his commanding tone, but she made no effort to stand by herself, let alone walk toward the bathroom.

"We can do this the hard way. Or we can do it the easy way," he said. "Which will it be?"

Katie wasn't sure what he was talking about. There wasn't an easy way for anything anymore. "I told you, I'll get up tomorrow," she said. "I just need a little more time."

"You need a shower, that's what you need." He was impatient now, and who could blame him? He was the last person she had any right to impose on. At twenty-five, she had no right to impose on anyone. But she couldn't stay with Andy, she couldn't work, and she couldn't rely on any of the people who were supposed to love her. She didn't seem to have a whole lot of options. Who would've thought one tiny baby could make such a difference? She should never have let her birth control lapse. She wouldn't have, if she and Andy had been making love. But before they created this baby, they hadn't touched in weeks. Then one day Andy broke down crying, acknowledged his need for help, agreed to go into rehab, and begged and pleaded with her to make love with him one more time to prove that she was willing to forgive him. Katie had been stupid enough to feel sorry for him, to want to console him. And they'd used a condom, but it hadn't been enough.

Booker sat her on the bed and stalked into the bathroom. The pipes clanged as the water went on a few seconds later. She could hear him moving around, walking in and out of the room, but she wrapped herself in the covers and paid no attention.

When he returned, he didn't drag her off the bed again. He merely pushed the bedding away and started pulling off the sweatshirt she'd been wearing, with nothing but a pair of panties, for two days.

She used her arms to block him before he could discover that she wasn't wearing a bra. "What are you doing?"

"What do you think?" he asked. "Since you won't get up and take a shower, I'm going to give you a bath."

"Don't you think I'm a bit too old for that?"

"You're not leaving me any alternative."

"Fine. Good luck." Strangely indifferent, she dropped her arms. He'd seen her naked before. He didn't seem particularly interested in seeing her again. And she had no energy with which to fight him. A woman had to *care* to be humiliated, and Katie simply didn't.

Cursing, he left her sweatshirt on and lifted her in his arms.

When they reached the bathroom, she caught a glimpse of herself in the mirror and cringed. No wonder Booker wasn't impressed enough to continue undressing her. She didn't know any man who would be. She hadn't showered for three days, and she'd brushed her teeth only once or twice.

Turning her face resolutely from the sight of her dirty hair and sunken cheeks, she let him place her on the closed lid of the toilet while he tested the water.

After he'd adjusted the temperature, he propped his

hands on his hips, looking like some kind of bouncer. "Take your clothes off and get in."

She didn't move.

"Now," he said.

She was too numb to feel anything, so it came as quite a shock when tears began to slide down her cheeks. Especially because she couldn't do anything to stop them.

A pained expression appeared on Booker's face, telling her he'd definitely noticed, but he didn't back off. "Are you going to get undressed, or am I going to have to do it for you?"

A tear dripped off her chin as she stared at the water in the tub.

"Katie, I think you'd rather do this next part on your own," he said. "But if you want my hands all over your body, then…"

She dashed a hand across her cheeks, sniffed and peeled off her sweatshirt.

Booker's eyes dipped briefly to what she revealed, but his expression remained implacable. "Hurry up," he said.

With a deep breath, she stood and started pulling down her panties, and he finally stepped out. It was easier to obey than fight—especially because he banged on the door every few minutes to keep her moving.

When she finally finished the laborious process of washing herself, she pulled the plug on the drain. It took several more minutes, and another pounding on the door by Booker, before she could summon the energy to stand.

As soon as she'd wrapped herself in a towel and

opened the door, Booker half-dragged her into the bedroom. "What do you want to wear?"

She thought of her only shoes, and Mary Thornton's snide comment, *There's snow on the ground, silly....* "Sweats."

"To a job interview? Glad to see your sense of humor is returning." He let her lie back while he rummaged through her suitcase. "You couldn't have unpacked this stuff?"

"I didn't think I'd be staying long enough."

"From what I can tell, it doesn't look as though you're leaving anytime soon."

"That's the problem," she muttered, but she had to admit she felt slightly better now that she was clean.

He brought her fresh bikini underwear, a lacy bra, some jeans and a long-sleeved sweater. "This stuff okay?"

"Does it go with sandals?"

"How the hell should I know? *Popular Mechanics* doesn't exactly cover that."

She laughed, actually *laughed,* at the thought of Booker becoming any kind of fashion guru, and that gave her the strength to move again. Sitting up, she continued to clasp the towel around her. "I guess that outfit's as good as any," she said. "We're only talking about a stud ranch."

"Exactly." He handed them to her. "If I leave, can I trust you to get dressed?"

"Yes."

"If you don't, I'll take you to see Mike Hill just as you are now."

She rolled her eyes. "I doubt he'll care about seeing me naked any more than you did."

Something flickered across Booker's face, some expression Katie couldn't have named if she tried. "Just hurry," he said. "Your appointment's in less than an hour, you still have to eat, and we're going to stop off and buy you some boots."

CHAPTER SIX

BOOKER FELT A great deal of relief when Katie emerged from the kitchen. She'd taken her time getting dressed and eating, but at least she'd managed to get ready. Now, with the blue of her eyes more vivid than ever because of the paleness of her skin, she looked downright pretty in a fragile sort of way. Not that he wanted to notice.

"Did you have enough lunch?" he asked.

She nodded.

"Good."

"This seems rather sudden," she said as he guided her out of the house and across the driveway to where he'd parked his truck. "Is it—is it a *formal* interview?"

It was more like a favor from Rebecca and the Hill brothers, but Booker was afraid Katie would go right back to bed if he admitted that. Mike had said he'd be happy to help, and Rebecca had called later to say it was all arranged.

"I don't think they'll be too hard on you, if that's what you're worried about," he said. "They know you, know what you can do."

"I cut hair," she said pointedly.

He let her get in the truck without assistance but closed her door. "Don't you know how to use a computer?" he asked as he slid behind the wheel.

She seemed to consider the question. “I’m pretty good on one,” she said a moment later.

“Then you can do computer work.”

“I’m savvy on the Internet. I can find what I want, pay my bills online and reconcile my checkbook, but I’m not very familiar with business-related programs.”

“You can learn.” He started the engine and pulled out of the driveway. “At least it’s a job.”

“Right. A job.”

They drove in silence for several minutes.

“But a job won’t solve everything,” she blurted when they turned onto the main highway. “At least not right away.”

Booker propped an arm over the steering wheel and refused to let himself glance at Katie. Whenever he looked at her, he remembered the way he’d wanted things to be and couldn’t believe how different they actually were. “What do you mean?”

“In order to get an apartment, I’m going to need first and last month’s rent and a security deposit,” she said, her voice full of worry. “And the baby comes in only four months.”

Rebecca had mentioned something about a place where Katie could live. But nothing had been resolved in that area, so he said, “First things first,” and simply hoped Rebecca would come through.

As Booker drove, he let his mind wander to another troubling subject. Rebecca had asked him earlier what doctor Katie was planning to see. He’d told her it was none of his concern, but she knew as well as he did that wasn’t entirely true. Katie didn’t have any money and she hadn’t been working recently, which meant she probably didn't have medical insurance. So how was she going to pay for the care she needed?

"Rebecca told me you should find a doctor right away," he said as they came into town. "Do you have any idea who you're going to see?"

Katie shrugged and kept her face averted.

"You don't know?" he pressed.

"Maybe Dr. Hatcher." Her voice sounded noncommittal.

Booker couldn't help the frown that tugged at his lips. Hatcher? He definitely didn't want her seeing Hatcher. Just after Katie left town, the Pruitts filed a malpractice suit against Hatcher for misdiagnosing a serious disease and prescribing the wrong medicine for their six-year-old. Granted, that illness might have had little to do with delivering babies, and the charges were eventually dropped, but Booker knew Hatcher had problems. "From what I hear, he's a drunk," he said.

"Well, unless another doctor's moved to town, there isn't anyone else close by. And I can't drive all the way to Boise. My car's too old to keep making that trip."

Booker had to agree with her there. He'd had Chase put a lot of time into that car, and he still didn't trust it. The parts he hadn't replaced were old, and he didn't think the car had ever been properly maintained.

"Maybe someone from Hair and Now can give you a ride when you have an appointment, or let you borrow a car," he suggested. Hell, he'd be willing to let her take Hatty's car. He had his truck and his Harley. Except he was working on getting *out* of Katie's life….

"Hatcher can't be that bad," she said. "He delivered me. And I think he might let me make payments."

She was already having trouble with the pregnancy.

Booker couldn't see her taking the risk. But what Katie did or didn't do wasn't any of his business.

Even though it was difficult, Booker purposely clamped his mouth shut and pulled into Saba's Western Wear, the only clothing and boot outlet in town.

SITTING ACROSS MIKE'S wide and rather cluttered desk, surrounded by expensive wood paneling and framed pictures of horses with ribbons on almost every wall, Katie sat rigidly in her stiff, new boots while she waited for him to end the phone call that had interrupted them shortly after she sat down.

"… We have two of the best stallions in the country right here.… Yes, I've heard that.… Well, sir, you get what you pay for.… We have quite a few mares coming in that week already, so you might want to let us know as soon as possible.… Sure, no problem."

Hanging up, he smiled at her. "Where were we?"

"We were, um…talking about my hours," she said, scrambling to recall where they'd left off. She'd become a little distracted watching Mike and remembering all the times she'd followed him around when she was just a girl, spying on him with her friends. She could see that he'd aged a bit while she was gone. The lines bracketing his eyes and mouth were more pronounced, but they did nothing to detract from the chiseled planes and angles of his face.

"Right, hours," he said. "You could do a normal workday from, say, eight to four. Or you could come in a little later, if you'd like."

Katie didn't dare tell him she had trouble getting out of bed regardless of the time. She hoped that wouldn't last. And he was being so flexible! She'd already told him she didn't know anything about any of the computer programs he'd named, and he'd said it didn't matter. He was happy just to have her back up the girl who was already answering the phones and doing the filing. At fifteen dollars an hour, she wouldn't be making nearly as much as when she did hair, especially when she'd worked in San Francisco. But in Dundee, she could definitely get by on a salary like that.

She could even raise a child.

Feeling the fear that had spread through her recede just a bit, she smiled more freely. A job would make such a difference. It might not fix everything all at once, but it would enable her to rebuild her life, halt her downward spiral.

Katie knew she'd work any hours Mike required, but as long as he was giving her a choice, she wanted to pick the schedule that would help her be the most dependable. "I think nine to five might be best. That way I'd have some extra time in the mornings, in case there's snow on the road. I'm not sure exactly where I'll be living yet, but the ranch is a bit of a drive from town. Not that I mind driving—"

"Rebecca didn't tell you?" he interrupted.

"Rebecca?" Katie echoed.

"She's reserved one of the cabins for you to live in. You won't have to drive anywhere."

"What cabins?"

"The cabins we built out back a year ago. They're primarily for the cowboys we hire during breeding season, but—"

"Isn't breeding season coming up?"

"It is." He shuffled a few papers around on his desk. "But I'm sure we can make do."

Make do? Not many employers tried so hard to accommodate a new hire, at least not one coming in at entry level. "How much is the rent?" she asked.

"Don't worry about the rent. It's part of your salary."

"You're going to pay me fifteen dollars an hour *and* provide a place for me to live? And all I have to do is back up the person you've got filing and answering phones, and do it according to whatever schedule is best for me?"

He hesitated as though unsure of the edge in her voice. "That's the plan, I guess. For the next few months, anyway."

"Until I have the baby."

He showed no surprise when she mentioned the baby, confirming the fact that he already knew. "You'll probably want to go back to doing hair after that, right?"

She could tell he was hoping her answer would be yes, providing further proof that she wouldn't be fulfilling any real need on his end.

Suddenly her stomach hurt, reminding her of the early labor pains she'd suffered, and she feared her anxiety might bring them back. In any case, it was difficult to breathe. "So this isn't a job interview at all."

"Pardon me?"

"This is a handout."

He looked uncomfortable. "It's not a handout, exactly, Kate. I mean, there's no reason to look at it like that. We can always use some extra help around here. And…with a baby on the way, you…well, it's no trouble to let you live in one of the cabins until you get back on your feet."

"Who asked you to hire me?" she asked.

"No one."

She gave him a "we both know better than that" look.

"Well, Booker mentioned it to Rebecca," he said, backing off. "Then Rebecca called me. But I don't mind, really. Neither does Josh. Hell, I'm sure Conner and Delaney would let you stay out at the Running Y, if you'd rather."

Briefly, Katie closed her eyes and rubbed her temples. Did she have to be humiliated in front of everyone who'd ever meant anything to her? How had it come to this? She was tempted to blame Andy and the general unfairness of life. But *she* was the one who'd made the decision to leave with him. *She* was the one who'd softened and let him back in her bed that day he was crying. And, if she didn't want to be a charity case, *she* was the one who'd have to figure out a way to solve her problems.

"Thanks for the offer." She stood with as much dignity as she could muster. "But I'm afraid I won't be able to accept."

Mike's eyes widened. "Rebecca said you don't have any other options. What are you going to do?"

"I'm going to salvage what I can of my self-respect." The weariness that had pressed her back into bed whenever she'd tried to get up during the past couple of days stole over her like a lengthening shadow. But she managed to lift her head high and walk out.

She found Booker leaning against his truck, chewing on a toothpick. He watched her cross the driveway, wearing the lazy, somewhat insolent expression that was so characteristic of him—and so deceiving. He never appeared to be paying close attention to anything or anyone, but Katie knew nothing ever slipped past him.

"How'd it go?" he asked.

The way Booker took the toothpick out of his mouth and straightened told Katie he already knew something was wrong. He'd probably noticed the stiffness of her walk the moment she stepped out of the ranch office.

She wished she could hide in a dark corner, away from the rest of the world. But time out wasn't an option. "It might be a while before I can pay you back for these new boots," she said, brushing past him.

He turned and, from the corner of her eye, she saw him raise his eyebrows. "What does that mean?"

"It's not going to work out."

"But you had the job before you ever came here."

"That's just it." She climbed into his truck and shut the door, forcing him to get in if he wanted to continue the conversation. But when he got behind the wheel, he didn't say anything. He started the truck and, except for the radio station playing Van Halen, they drove to the farmhouse in silence.

"So what's the plan?" he asked as they turned into the driveway.

She'd been working that out, ever since they'd left High Hill Ranch. Now she took a deep breath and shifted toward him. "I want to make a deal with you."

BOOKER CUT THE ENGINE. "What deal is that?" He resisted the urge to check his watch. Delbert and Chase had been expecting him at work for quite a while now, but it didn't look as though he was going to get there anytime soon.

"I don't have any money, and I don't have a place to stay."

This was not late-breaking news. "You just walked away from both," he pointed out.

She grimaced and stared out the window for a few seconds before turning soulful eyes on him. "Letting you buy me these boots was hard enough. I just couldn't… Tell me, would you ever accept that kind of charity?"

"I've never been pregnant and unable to do what I normally do," he hedged.

"Yes or no?" Her voice demanded absolute honesty.

He sighed. "What's your offer?"

"If you'll let me stay here, I'll do all the cooking, cleaning and laundry for you and Delbert, to cover my rent."

Booker didn't see how this solution got her out of his life. Having her wash his boxers and change his sheets seemed pretty much the opposite. "How can you do that without risking the baby?"

"I'll do it a bit at a time, rest in between, be careful not to overdo."

"*That's* your plan?"

"Not all of it, but—" she fidgeted with the bottom of her sweater "—I'm afraid you won't go for the next part."

Booker wasn't sure he wanted to go for the *first* part. What had Mike Hill said or done to blow what Rebecca had arranged? He hesitated, but his curiosity finally got the best of him. "Try me."

"I need a computer. I want you to help me sell the Cadillac so I can buy one and pay you back for the repairs."

"You want a computer instead of a car?"

"Yes."

"What for?"

"So I can start a home-based business."

"In *my* home?"

Her gaze never wavered, but her knuckles turned white as she clasped her hands in her lap. "Just until I make enough money to get out on my own."

"What type of home business did you have in mind?"

"I'm going to design Web sites. When I was in San Francisco, I worked with a designer to construct a site for the salon. I don't have a background in graphics or computers, but the designer said I have a natural eye. She also told me it's much easier than it looks. And everyone liked what I came up with."

Katie was supposed to be packing up to move over to High Hill Ranch....

"How long do you think it would take to get this business going?" he asked.

"Maybe six months."

"And the baby's coming in four."

She caught her lip between her teeth. "Right."

He had to give her credit for being straightforward. But he didn't want to face Katie with Andy's baby every time he came home. "That's it?" he said. "That's your plan?"

"That's all I've got at the moment," she said softly.

Booker knew he'd be crazy to risk having Katie so close. But this went beyond romantic hurts and confusion. This was one heart, stripped absolutely bare, appealing to another for a simple hand up. And six months wasn't so long....

The situation reminded Booker of ten years ago, when he'd just gotten out of prison and didn't have a penny to his name. If it hadn't been for Hatty... His grandmother had been the one to tip the scales in his favor, because she'd absolutely refused to give up on him, no matter how bad he tried to convince her he was. She'd made a profound impact on his life. Surely, in her honor, he could put aside his own preferences… for a few months.

This one's for you, Hatty. "I like fried chicken," he said, forcing back a sigh. "And Delbert likes meat loaf."

TAMI ROGERS STARED at the phone. She longed to pick it up and call her daughter. Sometimes she dialed Booker's house just to hear Katie answer.

"Don't even think about it," Don said, glancing over from where he sat in his recliner, holding the television remote in one hand. He knew exactly what Tami wanted to do because she was tempted every night. Especially when it grew late and she felt her loneliest.

"But I went by Hair and Now today, and she wasn't there," Tami said. "As far as I can tell, she hasn't been there all week. When will she start working?"

"I don't know, but we've drawn a line, and we can't cross it," he told her. "You heard what Pastor Richards said. Are you going to ignore him the way Katie ignored us?"

"No," she said. But was it truly necessary to shun their only daughter? Granted, when she'd first heard of Katie's illegitimate pregnancy, Tami had been shocked and angry. She'd been angry ever since Katie left with that no good bum two years ago. But now that Katie was back, worry was quickly eating away her resolve. "The only thing is—"

"We've been through this before, Tami. We have to let Katie suffer the consequences of her actions, so she'll feel some remorse and change her life. 'The ultimate goal,' Pastor Richards said, 'is to reclaim her soul for

God.' And we agreed. Don't you want her to get back on the straight and narrow?"

"Of course I do, but..."

"But what?"

"I just keep seeing her standing on the porch in the rain. And wondering why she isn't working."

"She's fine. Fine enough to be staying with Booker Robinson," he muttered.

Tami didn't bother to mention that Katie wouldn't be at Booker's if they'd taken her in. Or that she didn't see how associating with Booker was doing Katie's soul any good.

"All people in church can talk about is what a disappointment our sweet Katie has turned out to be," Don said. "They're holding her up as an example to their own kids. And now we're facing the same thing with Travis. If we don't stick to our guns on this, he'll keep acting up the way he has for the past few months."

Don had a point. He always managed to convince Tami by bringing up the trouble they were having with their fourteen-year-old son. Travis was hanging out with the wrong crowd, ditching school, flunking classes and getting into fights. She was desperate to get him straightened out.

"I suppose you're right," she said. Then, because she knew she'd break down if she didn't, she went to bed although it was only eight o'clock.

KATIE COULD HEAR the television in the living room and, for once, she couldn't sleep. She supposed it was because of all the thoughts whirling through her head about what she was going to do and how she was going to do it. Regardless of the cause, her wakefulness was a refreshing change from the depression that had buried her in such a dark hole. If her Internet business succeeded, she could take care of herself and her baby on her own terms. She'd be able to work with the baby around, which meant she wouldn't have to hire a baby-sitter and, depending on her ability to build her business, she could make a lot of money. She could do even better than she could cutting hair.

Her idea had so many advantages to recommend it, she couldn't believe it hadn't occurred to her before. She'd lived in the big city, witnessed how many people made their living via computers.

But she was still frightened. There were so many variables. Would she be able to get enough money for her car to pay Booker *and* buy the computer and software she needed? Would she be able to manage without a car once she let the Cadillac go? Would she be able to learn everything she needed to know from reading books on Web-building and design? Most people in Dundee didn't even have Internet service, so she couldn't build her business by relying on local contacts. If she sold her car and her business failed…

Her baby moved, a subtle reminder that focusing on her fears wouldn't help. Putting a hand to her stomach, Katie smiled for probably the first time since the pregnancy test had come back positive. "Everything's going to be okay, baby. I'll take care of you," she whispered.

The television went off and she heard Booker climbing the stairs. It felt strange to be living under the same roof with him, strange that he was so indifferent to her after everything that had once passed between them.

She remembered the day, not long after she'd met him, when he took her down by the river. It was autumn and cold already, but after lunch they'd dared each other to go into the water. Booker had eventually taken off his shirt and gone in. She'd realized then just how beautiful his body was. When she refused to join him, he'd carried her in with him and kissed her for the first time. He'd bent his head to hers, right there in the icy water, her whole body freezing cold except where his hot mouth connected with hers.

He was an expert kisser. Katie had to give him that. She should've known that he was bound, at some point, to claim her virginity.

Did Booker ever think about that day? He probably thought more about the night she'd told him she wanted to stop seeing him and start seeing Andy, which made her curious as to why he was letting her move in with him. Stranger than his generosity in letting her stay was the fact that he hadn't belittled her ideas, hadn't complained about her turning Mike down. He'd simply listened in silence at dinner, nodding occasionally as she'd gone on and on about the possibilities of making it big in Web design. When she'd asked him for his opinion on the value of the Cadillac, he told her he thought it was worth about three thousand dollars. He'd even offered to park it out front at his garage in hopes of generating buyer interest. And she didn't get the impression it was because he was worried about the repair money.

Getting up to use the bathroom, she tried to put Booker out of her mind. She didn't need anything to confuse her right now. She had enough to deal with. But when she walked across the hall, she bumped into someone going to the same place and knew instinctively it wasn't Delbert.

"Go ahead," Booker muttered, pulling away.

"Booker?" she said before he could retreat to his room.

"What?"

"Do you really think I can get three thousand dollars for that old car?"

"You should be able to get that much."

"Good. I called the Web designer I was working with in San Francisco today—"

"Was that what the two-fifty you left on the counter was all about?"

She'd given him the last of the change she had in the bottom of her purse. "I wanted to reimburse you for the call. Anyway, she said I should be able to get a quality computer, monitor and printer for around fifteen hundred. And the software I'll need should run me about nine hundred."

"What software are you going to need?" he asked.

"She said I could get StudioMX from Macromedia, which will include Dreamweaver for creating pages and sites, Fireworks for building graphics and Flash for building complex animations. It also includes a few other things, but I'm not sure yet what it all means."

"Have you ordered Internet service?"

"Not yet. I'm waiting until I sell the Cadillac. How long do you think that'll take?"

"The market's soft right now. Around here, there's no telling."

She hoped it would be soon. With a baby on the way, she felt as if time was like sand running through an hourglass, forever dwindling. For her child's sake, she had to be much better prepared to make a living—and soon.

He started moving back to his bedroom, but she stopped him again. "Did you…did you like dinner,

Booker?" she asked. "Do you think it's going to be okay to have me here?"

"Dinner was good," he said.

"I was hoping maybe we could be friends. You know, like you and Rebecca."

"I've never slept with Rebecca. I've never even wanted to."

"Well, you don't want to sleep with me anymore. That should count for something, right?"

"Just let me know when you're out of the bathroom," he said.

CHAPTER SEVEN

BOOKER COULD TELL THAT Katie was feeling better. She was getting up in the mornings, showering and riding with him and Delbert into town, where she studied at the library all day. Then she caught a ride home with him or someone else going the same way and started dinner before doing laundry and cleaning house. A couple of times, Booker had to tell her to go easy. He was afraid she was working too hard and might hurt the baby. But she insisted she felt no pain. And he found that having her around wasn't nearly the torture he'd expected. Life could certainly be worse than having someone wash his clothes and cook him a hot meal every day. He and Katie had even started playing chess at night while Delbert took Bruiser out for a walk.

"So, did you get any calls on the Cadillac this afternoon?" Katie asked as they sat across the chess board, a week after their new arrangement had begun.

Booker hadn't received one call on that car since the day he posted the For Sale sign. But he couldn't keep telling Katie "no." After her depression those first few days, he was afraid that if good news didn't come soon, she'd lose her newfound energy and optimism.

He pretended to study the board so he wouldn't have to answer, but the second he moved his bishop, she asked him again.

"Booker?"

"Hmm?" He finally looked up and was pleasantly surprised to notice that one week of eating regular meals and having a sense of purpose had made a big difference in Katie. Already the dark circles beneath her eyes were gone, and her normal color was returning.

"Has anyone called about the Cadillac?" she asked.

"One guy," he lied.

Her face lit up. "Really? Who was it?"

"Just someone passing through town."

"What did he say?"

Her pressing questions and the eagerness in her voice made Booker wish he'd stuck with being honest. "He just stopped by and looked at it, that's all."

"Did he make an offer?"

"Not yet."

"Do you think he might?"

Booker rubbed his chin and pretended to concentrate, hoping she'd let the conversation go. He saw a move he could make with his knight that would seriously damage her ability to defend her king.

Predictably she kept badgering him about the car. "Well?"

"He could. I don't know."

"I'll go as low as twenty-five hundred," she said. "If anyone mentions anything close to that, take it, okay?"

She'd said so dozens of times, but he didn't point that out. He knew she was just nervous. "I'll keep it in mind."

"Thanks." She moved her queen across the board to take his rook.

"That's what I get for letting you distract me," he

grumbled, realizing she'd just ruined the fancy move he'd planned for his knight.

"What did I do to distract you?" she asked.

She couldn't fit into her jeans anymore and had to wear them unbuttoned at the top because she didn't have any maternity clothes. And her breasts seemed bigger every day. Booker found *that* pretty distracting. But the desperation in her voice was why he'd lied to her in the first place. "Nothing."

After a few more moves, he managed to take her queen, which went a long way toward making him feel better about having lost his rook.

"Do you think maybe we should advertise the Cadillac in one of those car magazines in Boise?" she mused as he closed in on her king.

Now he knew *she* was distracted because she was usually much tougher to beat. Sometimes he couldn't beat her at all. "No one's going to drive all the way out here to look at such an old car when there're so many in the city," he said. "Especially during the winter."

She propped her chin on her fist and gazed at him. "It's *got* to sell, Booker. My whole plan hinges on that money."

"It'll sell," he promised.

But two more weeks passed without a single nibble, and she began to ask about it less and less. He knew it was because she couldn't bear the answer.

After four weeks of watching Katie wring her hands, Booker had had enough. When she called him at the shop under the pretext of asking if he wanted chicken and broccoli casserole for dinner—when she knew he'd eat anything she made—he told her the Cadillac had sold. Then he had Chase follow him out to his place, where he hid the old car beneath some scrub brush in a gully about a half mile from the house, and went to the bank.

"YOU MEAN THEY paid full price?" Katie's expression was one of stunned disbelief as she fanned out the stack of one-hundred-dollar bills Booker had just handed her.

The door slammed, and Delbert and Bruiser came in from playing in the soft swirls of snow that had started to fall earlier in the afternoon.

"Isn't that how much you need?" Booker asked.

"It is," she said. "I just can't believe we got the whole three thousand. I was getting so scared."

Delbert frowned as he glanced over Booker's shoulder. "You sold the Cadillac?"

Booker cleared his throat. "Yeah."

"When?"

"Today."

Delbert scratched his head in confusion. "Was I there?"

Booker stretched his neck. "You were busy."

"Oh." His frown lingered as he tried to puzzle it out, but he didn't question Booker. After a moment, he shrugged, led Bruiser over to his bowl and sat on the floor next to him while he ate. "Gee, you're hungry, Bruiser, aren't you, boy?"

Katie twirled around, oblivious to everything except the money. "And they paid you in cash," she said. "After all this waiting, it happened just like that." She snapped her fingers. "Thank you, God!"

Not exactly God, Booker thought wryly. Most people pictured Booker T. Robinson with a pitchfork and tail. But he couldn't help feeling pleased by her excitement.

She'd studied so hard. Every night she rambled on about all sorts of Web-related things—whether she should actually get Dreamweaver software from MacroMedia or GoLive from Adobe, the beauty of flash graphics, which allowed such complex animations, writing HTML code. He didn't understand half of what she said, but he liked seeing how animated she became when she talked about her business.

"Are you going to get your computer tomorrow?" he asked, crossing to the fridge.

"I'm not sure." She counted out six hundred dollars and handed it to him. "This is yours for the repairs."

Booker hesitated. He didn't care about the money, knew she needed it more than he did. But she seemed so proud that she could pay him.

Taking the money, he shoved it in his pocket while she gathered the rest of the bills into a neat stack and put them safely in her purse.

"Boise is probably where I can get the best deal on a computer, at least around here," she said. "But I don't have a car anymore. I need someone to give me a ride."

Someone? He heard the hint and glanced over his shoulder to find her smiling coyly at him. "Oh no," he said. "Not me. I have to work. You can take the truck or Hatty's car, if you want."

She wrinkled her nose. "It isn't any fun to go alone. I mean, this is sort of a celebration. And I might want another opinion."

"I don't know anything about computers." He got out a glass and poured himself some milk.

"You can still help me."

He scowled. "I have a business to run."

"Can't Chase take over for one day?"

Booker didn't answer right away because letting Chase take over for such a short time was entirely feasible. She must have sensed this, since she immediately began to press him even harder.

"If I have any money left, I'll buy you dinner."

Shopping bored Booker to tears. He'd sooner stab a knife in his foot. But a night out could be fun. For some reason, the Honky Tonk and forward little Ashleigh didn't hold the same appeal as they used to, which wasn't a whole lot to begin with.

"It's my turn to make a deal with you," he said.

"What kind of deal?" She sounded justifiably leery.

"You forget about going to Hatcher. Start seeing a doctor who really knows what he's doing when it comes to all the things that can go wrong in a pregnancy, and tomorrow I'll drive you to as many stores as you want."

"But Hatcher's the only doctor close by. Boise's too far for regular trips, don't you think? And Boise doctors will probably be more expensive."

"We'll work it out."

She sank her teeth into the soft flesh of her bottom lip. "I don't know, Booker. I'll feel too dependent…."

He leaned against the counter. "If you want me to go tomorrow, you're going to have to trust me on this."

"Why should I?"

"Because we're friends, remember?"

"Friends?"

"That's what you wanted, isn't it? Like me and Rebecca?"

She hesitated for a moment. She wasn't sure their "friendship" was like his and Rebecca's at all, but she supposed he was right about Hatcher. "Okay, we've got ourselves another deal."

STEAM ROLLED OUT OF the bathroom as Booker opened the door the following morning, his dark hair so wet it gleamed.

"What are you doing up so early?" Katie asked, surprised to bump into him at five-thirty.

"I've got to go in to work and get things ready for Chase," he said. "I'll take my bike. You can pick me up in the truck when you're ready to go."

She tried not to let her eyes drift lower than his freshly shaved chin. With only a towel wrapped around his lean hips and that scar on his face, not to mention the tattoos on his muscular arms, he looked like some kind of storybook pirate. A pirate with nice teeth. And one who smelled pretty good, too.

But Katie knew better than to let herself gawk. They seemed to have reached neutral ground. She wasn't going to let her thoughts, or her eyes, drift in any direction that might jeopardize their tentative peace.

Think of him as no different from one of your girlfriends, she told herself. But he was simply too male to be anything like a girlfriend.

"I think it snowed all night," she said. "Are you sure it's safe to take the motorcycle? Why don't you drive the truck, and I'll bring Hatty's car?"

"I'll be fine."

Stubborn *and* reckless. Just as she'd thought—too male. "Do you want me to bring Delbert into town with me?" she asked.

"Yeah, there's no need to wake him this early."

"He'll probably be heartbroken that you left him. You're his idol."

"It doesn't take much to be his idol," he said, but he was smiling affectionately when he said it, which surprised Katie. Booker wasn't really the type to care about someone like Delbert Dibbs, was he? He wasn't the type to care about anybody.

Or maybe he just wasn't the type to show it….

Now that she'd been away for a while, and grown up some, Katie felt she could read Booker a little better, although it was entirely possible that *he* was the one who'd changed.

"I gather his father wasn't very good to him," she said.

He grimaced. "Bernie Dibbs was a bastard, just like my old man."

Booker had never talked much about his parents, but from the bits and pieces he'd said and town gossip, Katie knew they'd drunk to excess and fought something terrible while he was growing up. They'd separated and reunited so many times, he'd never known from one day to the next whether their marriage was going to last or whether he'd have a home with either one of them. Only Hatty had stood by him.

"Is your father still alive?" she asked.

"Last I heard." Turning back, he gathered the boxers he'd left on the bathroom floor, and Katie realized that if she'd been fifteen minutes earlier, she would've run into him in his underwear.

"Is he still with your mother?"

"No. They finally split last year."

"Where do they each live?"

"I don't care, so long as it's not here."

She wanted to ask more about his parents, but it seemed odd to be carrying on this conversation while he was standing in front of her almost naked. He didn't seem to notice his state of undress, or feel concerned about it if he did, but Katie was having difficulty ignoring it.

"I'll see you in a while, then," she said and turned sideways to squeeze past him without touching, which wasn't easy now that her stomach had grown. She wasn't this careful to avoid inadvertent physical contact with her other friends. But none of her other friends looked quite so good in a towel.

"WHAT ARE WE DOING HERE?" Katie asked as Booker pulled into the parking lot of a large shopping mall.

"We're getting you some maternity clothes." He glanced pointedly at her booted feet. "And maybe another pair of shoes."

Katie was already exhausted. They'd spent the whole day visiting electronics stores, where she'd bought the software she'd decided on. When she'd educated herself on what kind of computer she might be able to buy new, she'd had Booker stop and purchase a local newspaper. Then they'd scoured the used market, trying to get more for her money. Driving house to house had taken time, but they'd come away with a fairly good computer, monitor, printer and scanner for only eleven hundred dollars.

Overall, Katie was incredibly pleased with her purchases, but satellite Internet service didn't come cheap and, after purchasing the software as well as the computer and everything else, she had only three hundred dollars left, which she thought she should probably save for baby items.

"It's almost April, so it's going to warm up soon," she told him. "I'll buy some clothes when I get paid for my first Web site."

"You can't be comfortable in those tight jeans," he said.

She wasn't. Which was why she unbuttoned them every time she got into the truck. Evidently, he'd noticed. "I don't *have* to button them. This sweater you lent me hangs low enough to cover the top of my pants, see?"

She regretted drawing his attention when his gaze ranged over her as though he was seeing her for the first time in a long while. She'd gone to Hair and Now and traded haircuts and manicures not four days earlier. But her hair and nails were definitely her only high points. She was bursting out of her clothes, including her bra, and her boots didn't match what she was wearing. She'd been so attuned to fashion, it hurt to realize how far she'd fallen.

"You can only get by without new clothes for what, maybe another couple weeks?" he said. "You think you'll be making money by then?"

"I'm not sure," she replied. "It all depends on how much business I can drum up."

"Well, I don't see the point in waiting. I'll lend you some money, if you need it." He got out and waited for her to open her door before hitting the "lock" button on his key ring.

She stuck her head out so he'd be sure to hear her. "Do we really have to do this today?"

His expression conveyed his feelings on the matter.

"All right," she grumbled, "but if I don't have the money to buy you that dinner I promised, don't blame me."

The mall was crowded. Long lines of people waited to get in to the cinemas at one end, reminding Katie that it was Friday night—and that she hadn't done anything fun in a really long time.

Booker stopped to check the store directory near the entrance. "See anything?" he asked as she peered at it with him.

"Anna James Designer Maternity looks like the only specialty store they have. But it sounds pricey. Maybe we should check the larger department stores."

"Let's see what Anna James has."

They took the escalator to the second floor and walked the length of one wing until they found a narrow boutique filled with expensive but stylish maternity clothes. Katie riffled through the racks, looking for something she could afford, and found an attractive black wrap shirt with stretch bengaline pants. She held them up for Booker to consider. "What about this outfit?"

"Try it on," he said.

While she was changing, she could hear Booker and the saleswoman talking as they found more clothes, which Booker kept delivering to her. Surprisingly enough, for a guy who wore mostly jeans and leather, he had better taste in women's fashions than she ever would've guessed.

When she finished tying the wrap shirt over the bengaline pants, she examined her reflection in the mirror and decided they were quite flattering. Stepping out of the dressing room, she waved Booker over. "What do you think?"

The face she thought she was beginning to read quite easily suddenly became shuttered as he looked at her.

"You don't like it," she said.

He shoved his hands in the pockets of his leather

jacket and leaned against the wall, chewing on his damn toothpick. "It's nice," he said indifferently.

Her ego could've used something better than *nice.* Or maybe "nice" with a little more enthusiasm would've worked. As it was, he made her feel like a woman who'd lost whatever looks she'd once possessed.

Tucking her hair behind her ears, she swallowed a sigh. "I'll manage with what I have."

She started back into the dressing room, but he caught her by the arm. "Buy it," he said, and this time his voice, if not his words, held some kind of meaning. Their eyes met, and warmth spread through Katie, starting at the point where he held her arm.

"Your wife might like this." The saleswoman came around the corner, holding an A-line skirt with a matching gray jacket, and Booker immediately let Katie go. Katie expected him to set the woman straight on the nature of their relationship, but he didn't. Silently taking the clothes, he handed them to her, then went out to wait, sitting on one of the benches in front of the store.

KATIE GAZED AT THE BAGS of clothes and shoes piled in the chairs on either side of her at the food court. She'd tried to hold back, to save some of her money for later, but Booker had insisted she needed this and had better get that. Now she was the proud owner of two pairs of maternity pants, two blouses, a dress, a sweater, a pair of loafers, some maternity underwear, two giant-size bras—and only enough money to buy pizza.

A purple lingerie sack sat closest to her. She chuckled as she fingered the delicate ribbon handle, remembering Booker's reaction to what was inside. He hadn't been very impressed with her new underwear, which were plain white panties and looked as though a regular woman could pull them over her head. But he'd grinned in appreciation at the bras. Holding one up, he'd lazily slid the toothpick in his mouth over to one side, gazed directly at her chest, and said, "Are you sure this can handle the job?"

She'd slugged him in the arm so he wouldn't know that his sultry look had made her heart race, and pretended to buy bras that were as utilitarian as her underwear. But when he wasn't watching, she'd purchased the lacy ones he preferred, and thanked whatever kind soul had found it in her heart to design something in a large size that was actually a *little* flattering. Katie was finding it increasingly important to feel pretty once in a while.

Like now, she thought dully, frowning as a curvy blonde hopped into line behind Booker. Shapely and attractive, she had ankles that wouldn't be swelling with water retention in the near future, and she was looking Booker over as though she might have *him* for dinner.

Of course she'd like what she saw. There wasn't much about Booker *not* to like, at least physically.

Folding her arms on her stomach, Katie took a deep breath and willed away the sudden tension knotting her muscles. What was wrong with her? Booker was only a…a *friend,* for lack of a better title. He had every right to flirt with or date whomever he pleased. But the thought of Booker making love to this Daisy Duke lookalike in the room next to hers stole Katie's appetite. She hoped she wouldn't be around if and when it came to that—

"Are you okay?"

Katie glanced up to see an old woman sitting at a nearby table, wearing an expression of concern.

"I'm fine," she said.

"For a moment there, you looked so unhappy."

Katie consciously replaced the glower on her face with her best stab at a smile. "It—it was just something I was thinking. I'm actually doing great. Better than great." Then, from the corner of her eye, she saw Daisy Duke open her purse and write down something that was apparently being dictated to her by Booker, and Katie felt her smile wilt. Getting up, she asked the kind lady sitting next to her to watch her packages, and marched over to them.

Booker raised his eyebrows when he saw her bearing down on them, and motioned to the left. "The rest rooms are that way, remember?"

She knew exactly where the rest rooms were. Much to his irritation, she'd been there several times already. "I don't need to go right now," she said. "I just… I came over to tell you that…" Her eyes slid to the blonde and she tried to ascertain whether Daisy was as pretty up close as she seemed from far away.

Katie was minimally relieved to discover that the woman had a rather big nose and slightly crooked teeth, but her hair was a beautiful honey color and her figure was quite stunning. Even up close.

"What?" Booker prompted, drawing Katie's attention back to him.

"I'd like a salad with my pizza."

"You just told me you *didn't* want a salad."

"That's why I came over. I changed my mind."

He shrugged. "Okay."

"Is—is this your wife?" Daisy asked, glancing from one to the other.

Booker removed his toothpick. “I don’t have a wife. This is my…roommate.”

“And his good friend,” Katie added.

“I see. So you two aren’t… I mean you don’t—”

“No,” Booker said.

“Oh.” She giggled in obvious relief and stuck out her hand to shake with Katie. “I’m Chevy.”

“Chevy?” Katie repeated. “You mean like the car?”

“Yeah. It’s just a nickname. My real name is Chevelle.”

“Chevelle’s pretty,” Booker said, then looked pointedly at Katie. *“Anything else?”*

She blinked. “Hmm?”

“Did you need anything else?”

“Oh…no. Just a salad, that’s all.”

“Fine. You might want to go sit down and *get off your feet.*”

“Right, in a second.” Katie glanced back at Chevy. “So where are you from?”

“Cedar Ridge. It’s only about fifteen miles from Dundee. I was just telling Booker that I drive out that way all the time to visit my stepfather.”

“What a small world,” Katie said.

“I was thinking I might stop by some time. Booker gave me your address and telephone number.”

“We’d love to have you, wouldn’t we, Kate?” Booker said.

Katie straightened her spine and pasted on another false smile. “You bet.”

CHAPTER EIGHT

KATIE NEVER FELT closer to heaven than when sitting in a cool, dark theatre, eating buttery popcorn and drinking a large, ice-cold Coke. But somehow her movie experience just wasn't the same tonight. She was wearing her brand-new clothes, which meant she could breathe easily for the first time in a long while. Yet she couldn't concentrate on the picture.

"You're not *really* going to start seeing that woman, are you?" she whispered to Booker.

"What woman?" he responded, his eyes on the screen.

"Chevy."

He glanced at her. "I don't let my friends get involved in my love life," he said. "Even *good* friends."

She grimaced at his words. "I'm not getting involved in your love life. I just can't believe you're attracted to that…to that—"

"What?"

"You don't think she's *that* pretty, do you?"

Katie was already regretting the fact that she'd let Booker help her shop for industrial-size panties, but her remorse grew by leaps and bounds when he said, "What's not pretty about her?"

"Well, I know she's slender and…"

"Friendly," he supplied.

"Right, and—"

"She has sexy eyes."

Katie knew how much Booker liked eyes. Eyes, lips and legs, in that order. "She's all collagen and silicone," she said.

"And you know this how?"

"I have X-ray vision. What do you think? I'm a beautician. I notice these things."

"Maybe I don't have a problem with a little medical enhancement. At least she's *emotionally accessible.*"

Emotionally accessible? That phrase hadn't come from Booker. Dropping her voice because the people behind them were starting to murmur about the noise, Katie said, "How did that come up?"

"She just said so."

"In the ten minutes you were standing together in line, she told you she was emotionally accessible?"

The man directly behind snapped at them to be quiet, but he improved his attitude considerably the instant Booker turned in his seat and glared. With that scar on his face and his mysterious eyes, Booker didn't look like anyone to mess with.

"I don't think she was talking about her *emotions* when she mentioned she was accessible," Katie said as he faced front again. "Did she ask you if you carry condoms, too?"

She thought she heard Booker chuckle, but when she opened her mouth to speak again, he nudged her.

"Be quiet. You're going to get me in a fight."

"You like fights."

"I've already been in more than my share."

"That probably goes for beds, too," she muttered. She was suddenly spoiling for a good argument and hoped Booker would oblige. He didn't. He gave her one of his crooked grins, which could be sexy or infuriating, depending on the situation. Today it was both, and that bothered Katie more than ever. Since taking up residence with him, she couldn't seem to regain her center....

She was just out of sorts. Probably because the movie did little to capture her interest. It had a lot of karate stuff going on, and people blowing up cars and bridges and pretty much destroying everything in sight. Booker had chosen it, of course. But she couldn't complain too loudly. He'd also bought the tickets.

Closing her eyes, she decided to let herself rest, just until her eyes stopped burning.

When she woke up, the movie was over and she had her cheek pressed into the soft cotton covering Booker's shoulder.

"I CAN'T BELIEVE you fell asleep during that movie," Booker said when they were nearly home.

Katie covered a yawn. "That good, hmm?"

"It had some of the most awesome fight scenes I've ever seen."

"I'm sorry I missed it."

She knew he'd picked up on her sarcasm when he looked over. "Okay, next time we'll see something guaranteed to make us cry. Will that make you happy?"

She didn't answer. She'd been trying to start an argument earlier, but that impulse seemed to have passed.

"Why so quiet?" he asked after another few miles. "Don't tell me you're still tired. You slept through the movie and almost the whole ride home."

"I'm not tired." She stretched her legs out to admire

her new loafers. “I was just trying to imagine you crying in a movie. Or crying at all, for that matter.”

“Sorry I asked.”

“Has it ever happened?”

“Hell, no. I’m too much of a badass,” he said, but his accompanying scowl was more of a half smile, and she could hear the laughter in his voice.

“Okay, so you have broken down. Tell me about the last time. What did it take?”

He cocked an eyebrow at her. “Hey, I’ve got an idea. Why don’t I poke my finger in my eye instead?”

Katie couldn’t help laughing. “What a baby.”

“You want to probe my deepest pain? Tell me something I want to hear first.”

“Like what?”

He turned down the radio. “Like why it took you two years to leave Andy if he started using right after you arrived in San Francisco. Were you using, too?”

“No.”

“So you put up with Andy as an addict for two years?”

She adjusted her seat belt so it wasn’t pressing against the baby. “I knew I’d made a mistake almost the moment I hit the city,” she said.

“Yet you stayed.”

“I’d made a commitment. I felt responsible for my own bad decision and was determined to make the best of it. And…part of it was pride. I didn’t want to give up and come home with my tail between my legs—like I had to do once I got pregnant.”

Booker opened the ashtray. Katie knew he was looking for a toothpick. When he found it empty, he snapped it closed. “What then?”

"Then I caught him in bed with the stylist from the station next to mine."

"Not *your* bed."

She turned toward the window and watched the snowdrifts, piled high on the side of the road, blur as they drove past. "No, her bed. I stopped by to drop off a tip one of her clients had brought to the salon. It was a big tip, and I knew she'd be excited about it because she needed the money. When I arrived, Andy was there." She took a deep breath and faced Booker, realizing that this incident seemed to have lost most of its sting. "Needless to say, they were both surprised to see me."

Booker's jaw tightened. "You were already pregnant at the time?"

She nodded. "That was a horrible day, but—" she hesitated, examining her feelings "—now I'm kind of glad it happened."

"You want to explain that?"

She found herself smiling again. "Because it forced me to make a decision. Was I doing my baby any favors by staying with this man? No. He didn't even want the baby. He kept trying to talk me into getting an abortion so the baby wouldn't 'cramp our style.' So I finally quit trying to make the relationship work and got out."

Katie listened to the tires on the wet, shiny pavement, astonished at how rarely she thought about Andy anymore. She wondered if that would change once she had the baby as a constant reminder.

"Okay, it's your turn," she said.

"My turn for what?"

"You owe me a deep dark secret."

"What kind of secret?"

"I don't know…something juicy. How old were you when you lost your virginity?"

"Fifteen."

"Who was she?"

"My best friend's mother."

"What?" Katie supposed this was information she should have already known, but the relationship she'd had with Booker two years ago was so different from what they had now. They'd never really talked before, at least not so honestly.

"She was divorced and bored and wanted to feel desired again, I guess."

"How did she approach you?" She frowned. "She *did* approach you, didn't she? I mean, you didn't seduce her at fifteen!"

He rolled his eyes. "I didn't have *that* much confidence at fifteen," he said. "*She* did the seducing."

"How?" she repeated.

"She'd have Gator invite me over to stay the night, flirt with me, brush up against me whenever possible. I could feel her interest from clear across the room. It didn't take a rocket scientist to figure out what she wanted."

"Your parents must have been furious when they found out."

He gave her a funny look. "Are you kidding? They never knew what was going on in my life. They were too busy trying to kill each other."

"Is your friend's mother still alive?"

"She was only thirty-something at the time."

"Then she could've gotten pregnant!"

"She was on the pill."

Katie adjusted her seatbelt again. "Have you had any contact with her recently?"

"Hell no, not for years. And I don't plan to."

Katie could easily imagine Booker catching the eye of an older, lonely divorcée. He was a tough kid with parents who didn't look after him. He'd probably matured early, judging by the five-o'clock shadow that covered his jaw only a few hours after a shave. And, although Katie knew it wasn't a conscious thing, Booker's chocolate-colored eyes carried the promise of knowing how to please a woman. Judy at the diner had said it best—he had bedroom eyes.

"Did Gator ever find out?" Katie asked.

Booker slowed as he turned off the highway toward the farmhouse. "God, I hope not."

"Where is he now?"

"I don't know. I lost track of him when I went to prison."

Katie studied his profile. "What was prison like?" She'd never asked him that before, either. She'd purposely avoided any mention of it.

He knitted his fingers over the top of the steering wheel and hunched forward, showing the first sign that he might finally be getting tired after their long day. "Lonely," he said simply.

"Is that when you cried?"

His eyes briefly met hers before moving back to the road as he continued to dodge the potholes that made this part of the trip so slow after a storm. "No."

She wanted to press him for details, but as they turned into the farm, their headlights swung across the snow-covered lawn and she saw someone sitting on the porch swing, hunched against the cold.

LEANING FORWARD, KATIE squinted as a boy no older than thirteen or fourteen stood up. Tall and gangly, he had shaggy blond hair and—

"Oh my gosh! It's Travis," she said.

She nearly hopped out of the truck before Booker could come to a complete stop, but his hand shot out to grab her. "Hold on," he said.

As soon as Booker parked, she got out. "Travis, what are you doing here?" she cried, hurrying toward the house.

Her younger brother shoved his hands in the pockets of his jeans. The way he held himself, tense and sullen, told her this was not the social visit she'd craved since her return.

"What's wrong?" she asked when she was close enough to see his troubled face.

His breath misted on the cold night air. "It's Mom and Dad. I just—" The muscles in his jaw worked, and he pulled his hands out of his pockets and made fists, as though he longed to hit something or someone.

"What?" she said.

"They threw me out of the house."

"But you're only fourteen!"

"They don't care. They don't care about anyone."

Booker came up behind her and stood silent, listening.

"What happened?" she asked Travis.

"I got kicked out of school. Again."

Again? As far as Katie knew, Travis had never been a stellar student. But he'd never been a behavioral problem, either. "For what?"

"For bringing nunchakus to school."

She felt a moment's confusion. "Nunchakus?"

“Martial arts weapons,” Booker explained.

“But where did you get them in the first place? There’re no karate instructors in Dundee.”

“I bought them off a kid who moved here from Utah.”

“Oh.” She considered what to say next. “Didn’t you realize they wouldn’t be allowed at school, Travis?”

Her brother shrugged. “I didn’t think it was any big deal. It’s not like I hit somebody with them.”

“That’s good at least.” Katie gave him as much of a hug as he’d allow in his agitated state. “How did you get all the way out here?”

“I thumbed a ride down to the turn-off and walked.”

“Don’t ever thumb a ride. It’s dangerous.”

“Billy Joe and Bobby Westin picked me up,” he said, his tone suggesting that she was overreacting by a wide margin.

Billy Joe and Bobby Westin *were* pretty harmless most of the time. A couple of good ol’ boys in their thirties, they hung out at the Honky Tonk and had the beer bellies to prove it. “Maybe that wouldn’t be a problem during the day. But Billy Joe and Bobby are usually drunk this late at night,” she said.

“Why didn’t you go into the house?” Booker asked. “Isn’t Delbert home?”

“I guess not,” Travis told him. “I rang the bell, but no one answered.”

“Delbert likes to play pool. He’ll be along.” Booker nodded toward the front door. “Let’s go inside where it’s warm.”

Katie followed her brother and Booker into the house. She was thinking she should probably call her parents, have them come and get Travis, but she didn’t particularly want to talk to them after the way they’d treated her. She knew her brother wasn't going to be happy with that course of action, either. Only she didn't have a lot of alternatives. She didn't have a car to drive him home herself, and she was already a guest in Booker's house. She couldn't invite him to stay with her.

"Wow, you really are pregnant," Travis said, focusing on her stomach the second Booker flipped on the light.

"I'm not *that* big," Katie said. From the corner of her eye, she saw Booker grin and thought he mumbled something like "yet," but Travis drew her attention back to him before she could respond.

"It's just… I couldn't picture you…like this," he said. "Mom and Dad have been bitching about you having a baby for weeks now, but I haven't seen you once."

"*Bitching,* Travis? Don't talk like that."

"I didn't think you were a Goody Two-shoes anymore."

"I'm the same person I was."

"Why haven't you called me?"

"I didn't want to upset Mom and Dad."

"Well, you did the right thing. Mom and Dad wouldn't have let us talk, anyway. They told me I'd be grounded for three weeks if I had any contact with you."

"They obviously don't mind any more," she said. "They've practically chased you into my arms."

"They don't understand anything." He peered at Booker as though expecting him to agree with this defiant statement, but Booker said nothing.

"So." Travis shoved his hands in his pockets and shifted nervously on his feet. "You don't mind if I stay here tonight, do you?"

Katie refused to look at Booker. "Um… I don't know… Let me…well, you see…" She took a deep breath. "Why don't you go watch TV in the living room while I talk to Booker?"

"Okay."

Travis left the kitchen, and Katie waited for the television to go on before braving a glance at Booker. When she finally turned, she found him leaning against the cupboards, his thumbs hooked in the pockets of his jeans.

"I know this doesn't look good," she said. "But I think, if we let Travis stay the night, I could probably work things out with my parents in the morning."

"Because the three of you are so close?" he said, wearing a pained expression.

"No, of course not. But this situation is a little different from mine. I mean, I'm an adult. My parents had every right to turn me away. Travis is only fourteen, and—"

"He can stay," he said.

"Surely they'll see that—" Katie had been so busy thinking of what to say next that it took her a moment to realize she didn't need to say anything at all. She'd already gotten what she wanted.

Booker scooped his keys off the counter. "I'm going into town to see if I can find Delbert. He and Bruiser should've come home by now. I'm thinking he might not have been able to get a ride."

He let Travis stay that easily? And he was going into town after Delbert?

Katie covered her mouth to hide the fact that she was tempted to laugh. She'd always considered Booker so dark and mysterious, so dangerous and unreliable. He was an ex-con. Who would've guessed he had a heart too soft to turn anyone away? First Delbert and Bruiser, then her, now her little brother…

He squinted at her suspiciously. "What?"

"Nothing," she said, but her lips were twitching so badly, she couldn't hold back any longer. Booker didn't just let people move in—he took care of them. She thought of the way he'd helped her sell the Cadillac, bargained to get her to go to an obstetrician Rebecca regarded as especially good and had taken her to buy a computer. He was tired, but he was going back out because Delbert and Bruiser weren't home.

"You mind telling me what's so damn funny?" he asked.

"I don't think you're such a badass after all," she said.

"Oh, yeah? Well, go ahead and laugh. When I run out of beds you'll be the first to go," he grumbled and stomped out the door.

BOOKER SLOWED AS HE reached the edge of town. The Dundee police force—which consisted of a whopping three members—liked to catch people speeding just as they were coming past the feed store. It helped swell the public coffers. But Booker knew better than to get pulled over. Ever since he'd broken the police chief's sprinkler system by peeling out on his lawn when he was visiting Dundee at fifteen and driving Hatty's car, Chief Clanahan hadn't liked him. And that sentiment had definitely filtered down to Officers Bennett and Orton.

Besides, going slow suited him just fine—tonight. He hadn't found Delbert along the highway as he'd expected, and was hoping to spot him walking around town. Or at the Honky Tonk. The Honky Tonk stayed open until two o'clock on weekends. Delbert was never out that late, but it was still the best place to start looking.

When Booker drove into the parking lot, he saw Officer Orton sitting in his patrol car and rolled down his window as he pulled alongside him.

"What you doin' out so late, Booker?" Orton said.

Booker ignored the question. "Have you seen Delbert?"

"He was here for a while. That dog of his was tied out front, just like always."

"When did he leave?"

Orton rubbed his chin with his thumb. "I guess it's been an hour or so."

"Was he on foot?"

"Isn't he always?" Orton said, chuckling.

Booker began to roll up his window but paused when Orton spoke again.

"What's between you and that retard, anyway?" he said. "Prison turn you a little funny, boy?"

Booker's muscles bunched as the desire to break Orton's jaw washed over him. Like so many of the prison guards Booker had met while serving time, Officer Orton was drunk on his own power. But Booker wasn't going to be stupid enough to let Orton draw him into a fight. "If that's an invitation, I'm not interested," he said and drove away.

A glimpse of Orton's normally pallid face turning bright red siphoned off some of Booker's anger. Orton was simply too small-minded to bother with.

Heading deeper into town, Booker stopped at the new Gas N Go. Delbert liked to buy candy and play the video game near the entrance. But when Booker didn't see Bruiser sitting dutifully outside, he knew Delbert wasn't here, either.

The bell sounded over the door as he went inside. Shirley Erman, the night clerk, glanced up from cleaning out the ice-cream dispenser. "Hi, Booker. What are you up to these days?" she asked.

"Right now I'm looking for Delbert. Have you seen him?"

"Not since I started my shift. He bought a pack of gum—I swear that guy's gonna rot his teeth. Then I think he went over to the Honky Tonk."

"Thanks."

Booker drove up and down Main Street two more times without any luck, then started winding through the darker side streets. Delbert had lived in the trailer park behind the baseball diamond when his father was alive. Maybe he'd gone back for some reason. Or maybe he'd gone to the cemetery. He didn't seem to miss his father much. Bernie Dibbs didn't deserve to be missed. But some relationships were more complicated than others. No one understood that better than Booker.

He decided to go to the trailer park by way of the cemetery, but a dog, barking wildly, caught his attention before he reached either place. He was just passing Center Park and could see movement on the far side, several shadows among the trees.

Slowing, he bent his head, trying to figure out what was going on—and that was when he realized he'd found Delbert.

CHAPTER NINE

WHERE WERE BOOKER AND DELBERT?

Katie was tempted to pace, but she knew better than to be on her feet. Her back ached already, just from the walking they'd done in the mall earlier. And her stomach felt tight and hard. She wasn't sure how much of her discomfort stemmed from her pregnancy and how much from her frayed nerves, but she hadn't been so miserable since she'd first returned to Dundee.

She forced herself to remain seated in front of the television but glanced nervously at the clock every few minutes. Travis had gone to bed and was asleep, as far as she knew. He *should* be asleep. It was nearly 4:00 a.m. But she hadn't so much as dozed off. Booker had been gone for three hours, and she felt as though she'd been counting every second. He could've driven to Boise and halfway back in that length of time!

Setting the telephone in her lap, she called to see if anyone was still at the Honky Tonk. She needed to find out what was going on. It was cold out, and the roads were slick. She kept picturing Booker crashed in a ditch, slumped over the steering wheel, slowly freezing to death....

Surely there hadn't been an accident. Booker was an exceptional driver. He loved cars, motorcycles, anything with an engine, and he handled almost any kind of vehicle expertly.

But he was tired, and accidents did happen.

God, please don't let him be hurt....

No one answered at the Honky Tonk. Evidently Bear, the bartender who generally closed up on weekends, had finished cleaning and gone home for the night. Katie didn't have many other options. Who else could she call?

She tried Rebecca. When the answering machine came on, she didn't leave a message. Rebecca was probably asleep, which meant Booker wasn't there, either.

The wind rose, howling under the eaves, promising more snow. Another fifteen minutes dragged by, then Katie decided she couldn't wait any longer. She was calling the police.

"Dundee Police Department. Officer Orton speaking."

Katie gripped the phone tighter. She knew Officer Orton. He and his family attended the same church as her own family. But she was too worried to bother with any kind of greeting. "Could you…could you please tell me if there've been any accidents involving a black 4X4 this evening?"

"None that I know of."

"Could there be one you don't know of?"

"I suppose that's possible, if it happened out on one of the back roads, but—"

"Officer Orton, this is Katie Rogers."

"Oh, yes. My wife mentioned you were back in town."

His voice wasn't particularly friendly, so Katie released herself from any obligation she might have felt from their past acquaintance. "Then I'm sure you've also heard I'm staying out at Booker's."

"That's exactly what I've heard."

She hadn't imagined his chilly tone. "Well, the reason I'm calling is that Booker went out a few hours ago to find Delbert, and neither one of them has returned—"

"They'll be home in a few minutes."

Katie would've been relieved, except she still didn't like the sound of Orton's voice. "You've seen them, then?"

"Yes, ma'am."

"What happened?"

"I'll let Booker tell you when he gets home. But you should have an ice pack handy. And you might want to call him a good lawyer."

He laughed, there was a click in her ear, and he was gone.

KATIE'S HEART POUNDED when she heard Booker's truck pull up outside. She was grateful to have him and Delbert home, but apprehensive at the same time. Orton had mentioned an ice pack.... What could possibly have happened?

Anxious to find out, she opened the front door, and Bruiser shot over to her as soon as Booker cut the engine. He wagged his tail, but when she stepped aside to let him in, he circled back to Delbert and licked his fingers as he approached.

When the porch light fell on Delbert's face, Katie saw why Bruiser was so hesitant to leave his master. Delbert had a black eye and was holding a bloody napkin to his nose. He moved gingerly, protecting his right side with his free hand.

"Delbert, you're hurt!"

"Hi, Katie," he said sadly.

She held out a hand to stop him so she could get a closer look. "What *happened?*"

"I don't know."

"You have to know! Tell me where you've been."

"We were at the police station. The police—Officer Orton—he put Booker in jail." Tears gathered in Delbert's eyes, and Katie realized that, despite whatever had caused his injuries, seeing Booker in jail was the most traumatic part. "They wouldn't believe me. I tried to tell them, Katie. I tried to tell them it wasn't Booker's fault. But they wouldn't listen."

"I'm sure everything will be fine," she said, giving him a quick hug for comfort.

Booker reached the porch, allowing Katie her first look at his face, which wasn't in much better shape than Delbert's. He had a cut above his eye, a busted lip and a red spot high on his cheek. Delbert's hands were uninjured, but Booker's were more battered than his face.

"You okay?" she asked.

"I'm fine." He walked with an economy of movement that told Katie he was in pain, but the tautness of his body and the gravity in his voice told her he was also angry, almost explosively so.

She stepped out of the way so he could move past her. He got himself a drink of water and headed upstairs.

Katie let him go, knowing instinctively that he wanted to be alone. Then she had Delbert sit at the kitchen table so she could clean his cuts. "Tell me about the fight," she said as she dabbed antiseptic ointment on his injuries. "How'd it get started?"

"I was just walking to the cemetery, Katie. I wasn't bothering anybody."

"And?"

"Some men were in the park. They were drinking. Drinking and laughing. When they saw me, they asked if my dog could do tricks. They wanted to see some tricks. I told them Bruiser doesn't know any. Then they said he was a worthless piece of—" His face reddened. "They said some mean stuff about Bruiser."

He winced as she held a bag of ice against his swollen eye. "I tried to tell them he was a good dog, but they said, 'I'll bet you fifty bucks we can get him to turn on you.' I said Bruiser would never turn on me." He frowned and the eye that wasn't covered looked at Katie beseechingly. "He wouldn't, would he, Katie? Bruiser would never turn on me."

"Of course not. He loves you."

"Yeah, he loves me."

"What happened then?" she asked.

"They wouldn't let me go. Two guys stood in front of me and two were behind me. They said they'd share their vodka with me if I'd kick Bruiser. I said I wasn't thirsty. I wouldn't kick Bruiser."

"Good for you, Delbert," she said.

"Only that made them mad. They shoved me. Bruiser started to growl. They said I'd better tie him to a tree, or…or the police would take him away."

Katie knew Delbert would do anything to protect Bruiser and wasn't smart enough to realize the dog was his only defense. "And you did it."

"I had to, Katie. I didn't want Bruiser to bite anyone. Then someone hit me, and I fell down. They were hitting me and kicking me and…and hitting me. Until Booker came."

Katie could only imagine the scene and understood, from her own feelings at the moment, how furious Booker must have been to see grown men attacking someone like Delbert. "Booker tried to stop them?"

"He pulled them off me. Then everyone was fighting. I ran to the Honky Tonk. Officer Orton was there. But when he came, he took Booker to jail." He blinked several times in an attempt to stanch emotions that were obviously still very near the surface. "I shouldn't have gone there."

"You didn't know, Delbert. Don't feel bad. What about the other guys?"

"They went home, I guess."

Fresh anger surged through Katie's blood. "They weren't taken to the station with you?"

"No. Officer Orton told them, 'You're free to go. Tell your dad I said hello, Jon.'"

"Jon Small? *Councilman* Small's son?"

"Yeah."

Katie gritted her teeth. "Who else was there?"

"I don't know."

No wonder Booker looked the way he did. She got a couple of Tylenol out of the cupboard and handed the pills to Delbert, along with a glass of water. "Take these and go to bed," she said. "Everything will be better in the morning."

"I hope so, Katie." Delbert started shuffling across the kitchen but turned back before he reached the stairs. "Is Booker going to be okay?"

She couldn't help smiling at the worry in his voice. "I'll make sure of it."

"Good. That's good, Katie. You take care of Booker. You make sure he's going to be okay."

KATIE HEARD THE SHOWER turn off while she waited in Booker's room for him to cross the hall. He'd been in the bathroom a long time. Were his injuries worse than she'd originally thought? Or was he simply letting the water pound down on his sore muscles while he grappled with the emotions raging through him? She could certainly identify with what he had to be feeling. Councilman Small's son wasn't some stupid teenager caught up in peer pressure. He was at least thirty-five and had no business tormenting a man who was more like a child, no business ganging up on *anyone* four to one.

And what did Orton think he was doing, taking Booker to jail instead of Jon and his friends? *Tell your father hello for me....*

Katie was sitting on the foot of Booker's bed, holding the first-aid kit in her lap, when the bathroom door opened. She knew Booker saw her as soon as he entered, but he didn't acknowledge her presence. He flipped off the light and dropped his towel as if to say it was her problem if she saw more than she wanted to, since he hadn't asked her to come into his bedroom.

Without the light on, she couldn't see much, just a quick shadowy view of his backside as he pulled on a pair of boxers. Then he got into bed, yanked the covers up and turned away from her.

Katie wanted to talk about what had happened. But she knew Booker was in pain—from more than his injuries. She also knew he didn't deal with emotional issues the same way she did and wouldn't want to discuss it. At least not yet.

Taking a deep breath, because it was difficult to stay when he'd made it abundantly clear that he didn't want her there, she walked around to the other side of the bed.

"Move over," she said.

"Katie—"

"Move over." She spoke more firmly the second time and it came as a shock when he did as she asked.

She turned the light back on, opened the first-aid kit, and sat beside him.

He flung an arm across his eyes. "Do you have to do this? I've been in plenty of fights. I'm sure I'll live without your assistance."

But she had to see how badly he was hurt so she could put her own mind at rest. "This won't take long." She glanced up at the light, which did seem rather bright. "I guess I don't have to blind you, though."

Adjusting the door to let in enough light from the hall, she darkened the room again and returned to his bed. Then she pulled the covers down to his waist so she could see the extent of his injuries.

She'd seen Booker before—all of him. She knew he had a body women admired and men envied. She especially liked his sinewy chest and the dark hair that swirled so perfectly across it. But she hadn't been aroused in at least a year and certainly didn't expect the desire that overtook her now.

Licking dry lips, she lifted her eyes to find Booker watching her. Time seemed to stand still as they stared at each other. She wanted him to touch her, to make love to her the way he used to, when she'd been foolish enough to take him for granted and then cast him aside. But he made no move, except to close his eyes and turn his face away.

He wasn't interested. Of course he wouldn't be. That realization cost her some self-esteem, but she couldn't really blame him. She was six months pregnant with someone else's child. Why would he want her when he could have a woman with a body like Chevy's? A woman with no immediate promise of future responsibility?

Katie's chest constricted, making it difficult to breathe. She'd been crazy to let the thought of making love, to anyone, cross her mind. What was the matter with her? She was finished with men, remember? Probably she was just hormonal. Pregnant women got that way.

Squeezing some antiseptic ointment onto her fingers, she dabbed it on the cut over Booker's brow and a couple of the gouges on his hands. He wouldn't allow any Band-Aids, said they'd only fall off, but he let her raise his chin so she could reach the cut on his lip. While she worked, she could feel the roughness of his whiskers, the softness of his lip and his steady regard beneath his lashes.

"Your hand is swelling pretty badly," she said, releasing his chin as soon as possible. "You don't think it's broken, do you?"

"No."

"Is there any way to be sure?"

"Short of having it X-rayed? No."

"Maybe we should take you to the doctor."

"No."

"Why not?"

"Because I'm going to sleep now."

"We could go in the morning, when you wake up."

"Or I could go to the garage instead."

"Booker, you work with your hands."

No response.

"Fine. If you won't have the injury X-rayed, I won't go to Rebecca's OB in Boise. I'll head straight over to Dr. Hatcher," she said, infusing her voice with a threatening note.

"You can't," he said simply.

"Why not?"

"Because you already traded me for that, and I'm not going to let you out of it."

"Fine. I'll trade you something else."

A muscle flexed in his cheek. "Like what?"

"What do you want?"

His gaze lowered to her belly.

"What?" she said when he didn't speak right away.

"Let me feel the baby move."

"Are you serious?"

"Of course."

"But that could take a while, Booker. This baby doesn't exactly move on command."

"Are you in some sort of hurry?"

"Not really," she said. It wasn't as if she had to get up early for anything specific. But she wasn't far enough along that it was easy to feel the baby move from the outside. Booker would have to put his hands up her shirt, right against her belly....

"Then what's the problem?" he asked, challenge glinting in his eyes.

"There's no problem," she said. "I—I guess we could give it a try."

He slid over to make more room for her, and she got into bed with him. For propriety's sake, she sat against the headboard.

"You'll be more comfortable if you lie down," he said, using the hand that wasn't swollen so badly to cover her legs with his blankets.

The appealing scent of Booker's warm body engulfed her. "That's okay," she said, swallowing hard. "I'm fine."

He shifted closer, and she took a deep breath before guiding his hands under her shirt. She had to rearrange them more than once searching for the perfect place to feel the baby. But the baby seemed to have settled for the night and wasn't moving. By the time Booker shook off her hands and began to explore on his own, she was shaky and weak and wishing she hadn't put herself in such a vulnerable position.

Closing her eyes, she tilted her head against the wall as Booker felt her stomach. He didn't touch her anywhere else, but she couldn't help remembering other times when he'd instinctively responded to her every desire…and thought she might melt on the spot.

"The—" She cleared her throat so she could speak, hoping to gain some perspective—and some emotional distance. "The baby is in a sac of fluid, so it's kind of hard to feel. It'll get easier as I get bigger. Do you—would you rather take a rain check?"

"Don't talk," he said.

"Why not?"

"Silence is part of the deal."

"You didn't mention that before."

"Do you want to change your mind?"

No! She was on fire, scarcely breathing, burning both where he touched her and where she wanted him to touch her. The heady sensations coursing through her were all bittersweet, but sweet enough that she didn't want him to stop. "I'm okay if you are," she lied, trying to sound unaffected.

"Then relax."

Relax? She couldn't relax. She could see his bare shoulders gleaming in the light filtering into the room, the strong profile of his rugged face, and wanted to comb her fingers through his thick, tousled hair.

But she didn't dare. He was just curious about the baby. And the baby seemed to like his touch. After a few minutes, as Booker held his palms against her belly, the baby moved.

Katie glanced down to see if he'd noticed. But his dark lashes rested against his cheeks, and his breathing had become deep and regular.

Too late. He was asleep.

CHAPTER TEN

BOOKER FELT AS IF he'd been hit by a freight train. "I'm getting too old for this shit," he muttered, staring at his cut and bruised face in the mirror.

He could smell bacon frying downstairs and knew that Katie was already up, fixing breakfast. He wondered how Delbert was doing. Delbert had cried the whole time Booker was being taken into custody.

He washed his hands and brushed his teeth, thinking about the fight and wishing he'd had the chance to inflict a little more damage before Orton arrived with his gun. If anyone deserved a beating, it was Jon Small. He had a mean streak a mile wide, drunk or sober, and always managed to hide behind daddy's name. He was a coward, and Booker hated nothing more than a coward....

The phone rang. Booker grabbed the sweatshirt he'd taken into the bathroom with him and pulled it over his head as he made his way downstairs. He hadn't bothered to shave. He wasn't planning to open the garage today.

As he neared the kitchen, Booker could hear Katie on the phone. "I think he's going to be okay. Just a minute." She came around the corner and nearly collided with him.

"Oh, there you are. Rebecca's on the phone."

Booker remembered the feel of Katie's bulging tummy beneath his hands and purposefully turned his mind to other things. *She* wasn't the one who'd finally brought him peace last night. He was just fascinated by the baby. She was the first pregnant woman he'd ever associated with on an up-close basis, and the changes he witnessed in her from day to day were pretty damned amazing.

"Hello?" he said, wondering why, if he was only interested in the baby, he had such a tough time taking his eyes off her nicely rounded behind when she moved away.

"What happened last night?" Rebecca asked.

"Haven't you heard?" Booker covered a yawn. "It's got to be all over town."

"The rumor that you were arrested for attacking Councilman Small's son is all over town. Josh heard it at the feed store and just called me. Not exactly the kind of news I like to hear about my good friend first thing in the morning. Especially when I don't believe it."

Booker glanced into the kitchen to see Travis seated at the table with Delbert and wondered how he now had three people and a dog living with him when, not too long ago, his Harley had been the closest thing he had to company.

"Jon needed to learn a lesson," he told Rebecca.

"So you taught him one."

"I did my best." He stared down at his swollen knuckles and decided his efforts had been well spent in spite of everything. "Unfortunately he had his brothers with him, and a cousin."

"You took them all on? Are you crazy?"

"It was what you might call a time-sensitive issue."

"I like the story so far. What's the rest?"

Booker heard Katie putting plates on the table and

felt his stomach growl. She made the best biscuits and gravy. From the smell, he was willing to bet…

"Booker?" Rebecca said.

"I'm here," he replied. "That's pretty much it. Orton came, broke up the fight and hauled me off to jail."

"Just *you?*"

"Yeah."

"Not such a great ending. Why? Did you start the fight?"

"No. But this isn't Mayberry, Beck. Orton hates me."

She snorted in disgust. "Orton's an idiot. What's the charge?"

"Misdemeanor Assault."

"Can you get jail time?"

"I guess it's possible, but I'm betting on a fine."

"How much of a fine?"

"Maybe five hundred bucks. There were four of 'em, so it's tough to fine a guy too much for taking the worst of it."

"I can't believe the fight was four to one, and *you're* the one who went to jail."

"I know. Delbert was so upset, they almost arrested him because he wouldn't let go of me."

"*Delbert* was there?"

"He was there before I was. The Smalls were having a little fun at his expense. That's what started the whole thing."

"You're kidding! They were picking on Delbert? Is he okay?"

"He'll live. But I'd hate to see him if I'd gotten there any later."

"Where was Bruiser?"

"Being the nice guy that he is, Delbert tied Bruiser up so he wouldn't bite anybody."

There was a long pause. "What happened is sickening, pathetic," she said at last. "I'm going to tell my father."

Rebecca's father was the mayor of Dundee, but Booker knew better than to count on any help from him. He was the one who'd told the police chief to keep an eye on Booker when he'd moved to town two-and-a-half years ago. "I think you're missing something here," he said.

"What's that?"

"Your father hates me, too, remember?"

"Actually, now that I'm married, I think he's starting to mellow," she said. "A couple of days ago, he told me to see if you can check out his Lincoln. It's making a knocking noise."

Booker carried the phone into the kitchen and sat down next to Travis. "Have him bring it to the shop."

Katie put a big plate of biscuits and gravy, bacon and eggs in front of him.

"I will." Rebecca sighed. "So are you going to be okay?"

He studied his food eagerly. "I'm fine."

"Katie said you look like hell."

"She's the one who's putting on weight," he said, and knew Katie had heard him when she narrowed her eyes and tried to snatch his plate away before he could take a bite.

"Just tell me one more thing," Rebecca said.

He curved an arm around his plate to protect it. "What's that?"

"Tell me you're not going to do anything to get even with Jon."

"I can't promise you anything there."

"Booker, you don't need this kind of trouble. Don't let him—"

"He has to understand something, Beck."

"Like what?"

"Like if he ever touches Delbert again, he'll need more than his daddy's name to protect him."

ON SUNDAY, KATIE sat in a booth at Jerry's, with Travis across from her. She shifted, straightening her new maternity top. Thanks to Booker, she had clothes that fit and was wearing a nice pair of loafers. And she had twenty dollars in her pocket, which he'd insisted on paying her for work around the house. That was all good. Except the new clothes and shoes, and even the money, did little to soothe her anxiety when her parents walked in.

Taking a bolstering sip of hot cocoa, she resisted the urge to glance across the street at Booker's shop, where he was handling a few details, and looked pointedly at Travis. "They're here," she said, patting the seat next to her so her brother would move there.

He stuffed another French fry in his mouth, shoved his plate across the table, and came around. "I don't see why we have to meet Mom and Dad. I like living with you and Booker."

Katie had let him stay two nights. Since he was expelled and didn't have school anyway, Travis had wanted to stay longer. But Katie felt it was time for Travis to make amends with their parents and go home.

"Booker has enough people to look after right now,"

she said, thinking of that whole mess with Delbert and the fight. Fortunately, after a little badgering, Booker had made good on their trade and visited Hatcher's office yesterday, so they knew his hand wasn't broken.

"Booker doesn't care if I stay," Travis argued. "Booker's cool. He gave me a ride on his Harley this morning."

Katie tried not to feel a twinge of jealousy. She'd wanted a ride on the bike, too, but Booker had refused to take her until after she'd had the baby. "You're fourteen, Travis. You need to be at home, and somehow, you need to get back into school."

"You sound like Mom," he grumbled under his breath.

Katie didn't have time to respond. Her parents had reached the booth and were sliding in on the other side.

"You wanted to see us?" her father said, his voice clipped.

"Yes, I—"

Judy showed up almost immediately to offer them coffee, and winked at Katie as she walked away. Obviously she thought Katie and her parents were finally resolving their differences. But this meeting wasn't about Katie. Her parents had taken their stand where she was concerned, and Katie had no intention of trying to change that. This was about her brother.

"Travis should be at home," she said.

"He knows what he has to do if he wants to live with us," her father said.

Her mother didn't speak. She just kept looking at Katie. Katie got the impression that Tami was curious about the baby, but the table hid most of her belly and she folded her arms to conceal the rest. Her mother hadn't wanted any part of her pregnancy before, and Katie didn't feel inclined to share it with her now.

"I was hoping you could go over the rules with him, one more time," she said.

"We've been over and over them," her father said.

"He has to attend school, pass all his classes and do his chores every Saturday," her mother recited. "No more rap music, no more coming in late, no more getting into trouble."

"That doesn't sound like too much to ask, does it, Travis?" Katie said hopefully. Booker had had a long talk with him on their way into town. He'd told Travis how important it was to get an education and not make the same mistakes he had. And Katie felt Booker's words had made an impact. Travis respected Booker. She'd sensed a maturing in her brother, a recognition that he'd have to do better.

But despite those inroads, Travis grimaced now, obviously put out by their parents' attitudes. "How can they tell me what kind of music to listen to?" he asked her.

"Have you heard the lyrics to some of those songs?" their father jumped in, obviously ready to do battle. "I've never heard such trash in my life."

Katie searched for a quick compromise. "They have advisory labels on the worst ones. How about if Travis agrees not to buy or listen to anything with an advisory warning?"

"That's not good enough," he said. "Rap is nothing but a bunch of people screaming obscenities into a microphone."

"Maybe his taste is different," Katie pointed out, and to her surprise, her mother agreed.

"I think we could bend there, Don."

Don glanced at Tami, clearly not pleased with her defection, but without her support, he gave in, too. "Fine. But I'd better not find one CD with an advisory warning. Not one."

"Okay, Travis?" Katie said.

"They've given me an eleven-o'clock curfew on the *weekend,*" he complained. "All my friends can stay out until midnight."

"I'm not going to change that until you show me you can be responsible about staying out later, young man," their father said.

"How long would he have to keep out of trouble and come in at eleven o'clock before you'd trust him to stay out an hour later?" Katie asked.

Their parents exchanged a look. "I don't think he's capable of—" Don started, but Tami interrupted with, "Three months."

"Can you handle three months in order to get your curfew extended?" Katie asked her brother.

Travis shrugged. "I guess so."

"Great."

Judy came with Don and Tami's coffee, and Katie pushed her empty plate aside. "If you both keep your bargains, things should be easier around the house. Booker tried to tell Travis how—"

"Booker has no right to tell Travis anything," her father snapped.

Katie felt her spine stiffen. "Booker has been good to Travis. He's been good to me, too."

"Booker's no better than Andy. He was tossed into jail for fighting the other night."

Katie's fingernails curled into her palms. "Don't pass judgment on something you know nothing about."

"I know enough to—"

Tami touched Don's arm. When he fell silent, she looked at Katie. "What about you, Kate?"

"What about me?" Katie said.

"Have you learned your lesson?"

Katie thought of the depression and desperation that had nearly destroyed her after her parents had closed their door in her face. How badly she'd needed a kind word from her mother. How hard it was to accept the fact that her parents didn't love her enough to forgive her.

She was still struggling with that one. "I've learned a lot of lessons lately," she said softly.

"So you're ready to come home?"

Katie heard the hopeful note in her mother's voice, but Tami's offer was far too late and far too conditional. "I'm not coming home, Mom. Ever. You asked me about lessons. Well, I've learned that people aren't always what they seem. And that I can't count on you to be there for me if I ever make a mistake." She felt a faint smile curve her lips. "Maybe when I'm perfect, I'll give you a call."

Tami's cup hit its saucer with a *clank,* spilling coffee, but Katie ignored it. She'd done what she'd come to do for her brother.

Nudging Travis so he'd let her out, she gave him a hug. "Be good," she said and threw her twenty-dollar bill on the table.

BOOKER LOOKED UP the moment Katie came through the door of his office. He'd been paying his vendors—a slow, laborious project because of his injured hand—but he was finished now. Returning the checkbook to his desk drawer, he said, "So how'd it go with Don and Tami?"

"Great." She smiled, but Booker thought she looked a little pale. Her parents seemed to have that effect on her.

"They're going to take Travis back?"

"As long as he lives by their rules."

Booker considered her answer. "Fortunately he can't get pregnant."

She chuckled. "Actually they said I could move back, too."

Sudden panic raised Booker's pulse, but he told himself it had everything to do with losing the comfortable existence he'd come to know with Katie's cooking and cleaning. Surely it had nothing to do with her on a personal level. Surely he wasn't beginning to count on having her around. He'd known from the outset not to count on her for anything.

"Are you going home to your folks, then?" he asked, turning his attention back to the papers on his desk as though her answer didn't matter.

"I will if you want me to."

From the corner of his eye, he could see her toying with the strap of her purse. "It's your decision."

She didn't answer for a while, and eventually he looked up at her.

"Do you want to know what I'd rather do?"

He nodded, but felt his stomach muscles tighten.

"I'd rather stay with you."

Relief swept through him, but Booker wasn't about to let Katie know that. "If you stay with me, you're seeing the doctor this week," he said.

"Booker, you know I have to find someone who'll let me make payments—"

"We're going to Rebecca's doctor," he said. "Delaney's been to see him, too. They both recommend him. If he won't let you make payments, I will."

THREE DAYS LATER, on Wednesday, Katie visited the doctor. According to the nurse, her blood pressure was fine. Her weight gain was on target. There wasn't any protein in her urine, and the baby seemed to be growing at a healthy rate. She felt she was in good hands and was glad Booker had brought her. Until just before she left. Then the doctor suggested she start childbirth classes right away and asked if she had a friend, parent or significant other who could be her coach.

Katie thought of Mona, Erma, Rebecca, Delaney and Ashleigh. She supposed she could ask one of them. She thought briefly of her mother, too. But no matter how many faces passed through her mind, she kept coming back to one—Booker's.

Only she couldn't imagine him in a childbirth class with her, let alone joining her for the actual delivery. And she had no idea how she'd even ask him.

"Is something wrong?" he asked as they drove home.

She hesitated. "No, why?"

"You haven't said much about the doctor. Did you like him?"

"He was nice." She kept her eyes on the road.

Booker opened the ashtray, and she knew he was getting one of the toothpicks she'd put in there after grocery-shopping yesterday. "What did they do?" he asked.

"They weighed me, measured the baby, that sort of stuff."

"That's it?"

"That's it."

After another few moments, she could feel his attention on her again and finally turned to face him. "What?"

He opened and closed his right hand, stretching his injured fingers, and she wondered how badly they still hurt. "Are you going to tell me what's wrong?"

"There's nothing wrong," she said. Except that she was terrified. Terrified of having a child she wasn't prepared for. Terrified to experience so many "firsts" on her own. She had three months before the baby was due. Then she'd be facing the actual delivery, getting up at night to nurse, worrying about Sudden Infant Death Syndrome and jaundice and all the other things that could go wrong with an infant. And she was living with her ex-boyfriend....

Suddenly her existence seemed very precarious indeed. She'd been so excited about learning how to build Web sites, so optimistic, that she'd grown complacent and hadn't really considered what her life would be like in the very near future. How was she going to care for a newborn *and* launch a business?

She didn't have a bassinet or a crib. She didn't even have a diaper bag.

"Have you ever been around a new baby?" she asked.

He studied her, frowning, obviously trying to guess at her thoughts. "No."

Just as she'd figured. What if he didn't like all the fussing? What if he asked her and the baby to leave?

When I run out of beds, you'll be the first to go....

She knew Booker hadn't been completely serious when he made that statement, but there were no promises between them. He'd loosely given her six months, but he could ask her to leave at any point and probably would the moment he met a woman he wanted to date. Then where would she go? How would she take care of her baby?

For the first time since she'd gotten pregnant, Katie considered the unthinkable. Was she really the best person to raise this child?

CHAPTER ELEVEN

BOOKER HAD SET UP Katie's computer system on Monday. She'd installed all the software then, too, but it had taken several more days to receive Internet service. Now, on Friday, she was finally up and running and wanted to build a sample Web site and experiment with her new tools. But she couldn't seem to concentrate. Ever since her doctor's appointment, she found herself staring off into space for long stretches of time, wondering what would be best for her child.

Certainly a complete family would provide a better foundation. She didn't need a psychologist to tell her that. A married couple with a home, at least one job between them, and some savings. A couple just like Josh and Rebecca.

But Katie didn't know how she could ever let her baby go. Even to Josh and Rebecca.

The telephone rang. She picked it up, knowing it was Booker. She'd called him earlier, just because she needed to hear his voice. But he'd been dealing with a customer and Delbert had taken a message.

"Hello?"

"You called?"

He sounded busy, which made her feel guilty for bothering him.

"I wanted to tell you I got my Internet service this morning."

"The satellite company came through, huh?"

"Yeah."

"Great. So what are you working on?"

She frowned at the blank screen. "A sample Web site. I—I need to get some stuff out there to show prospective clients."

"Sounds like a good idea."

There was a long silence. She knew Booker was waiting for her to either finish the call or tell him whatever she'd phoned to tell him. But she wasn't sure what that was. She just needed…*something.*

"I'll let you go," she said.

He hesitated. "Katie?"

"What?"

"You feelin' okay?"

She closed her eyes. "Yeah, sure," she said and hung up.

JON SMALL, HIS WIFE and two kids lived in a nice rambler on a piece of land not far from his parents' place, his brother's, and his cousin's. Booker knew the whole Small clan and didn't like any of them. They were part of a Good Ol' Boy network that valued loyalty over honesty, an attitude that reminded him too much of some of the supremacist groups he'd encountered in prison. They put a different face on it, of course, but that hypocrisy bothered Booker more than anything else.

Getting out of his truck, he shoved his keys in his pocket and strode up to Jon's front door. He was worried about Katie and the way she'd sounded on the phone earlier. He should go back to the shop, pick up Delbert and Bruiser, and get home. But he had a few things to say to Jon first.

Jon's wife, Leah, answered his knock. As soon as she saw who it was, she hid behind the door and peered out at him like a frightened child. "Booker? What are you doing here?"

Booker didn't bother disliking the women in the Small family. Mostly he felt sorry for them. They had money and maybe even a little prestige, thanks to Daddy Dave. But Jon and his brother drank a lot and Booker suspected, judging by how quiet and withdrawn their wives were, that the men tended to be controlling and possibly even abusive.

"I'm looking for your husband," he said. "Is he home?"

"What do you want with him?" she asked. "We don't need any trouble. We've got kids here."

"I'm not out to cause trouble. I just want to talk."

"He…he's not here."

"That isn't his truck sitting in the driveway?" Booker motioned to the brand-new Chevy he'd seen Jon driving around town.

With a sigh, Leah closed the door. Booker heard the bolt slide home, but he was willing to wait patiently. He knew Jon would eventually appear. The man felt too safe not to agree to see him. And not losing face mattered a great deal to the Smalls.

Sure enough, Jon appeared a few minutes later—with a split lip and a black eye to show for their fight a week ago. "What are you doing here?" he asked.

Booker jerked his head toward the yard. "You got a minute?"

Jon didn't seem nearly as brave now that he was

sober and on his own. He cast a glance at his wife, who stood behind him, then stepped outside and closed the door.

"We've never had any problems between us in the past, Booker," he said, his voice low. "I don't see why that has to change now."

"It doesn't have to change, Jon, so long as you remember one thing."

"What's that?"

"Stay the hell away from Delbert Dibbs. Otherwise, the situation will end a lot worse than it did last time."

"Why are you getting involved?" he asked. "Delbert's not family to you. Granted, we were a little drunk and stupid, but we were just having fun."

"I'm telling you to have your fun a different way from now on."

A truck pulled up in the driveway. Jon's brother, whom everyone called Smalley because of his name and the fact that he weighed nearly three hundred pounds, got out. "What's going on here, Jon?" he said.

Booker knew Smalley hadn't shown up by chance. Jon, or maybe Leah, had called him.

Jon didn't answer, but he stood a little taller and swelled his chest. "You're a crazy son of a bitch to come out here and threaten me, you know that, Booker?" he said, his voice strident for the first time since Booker had arrived. "If you're not careful, you're really going to piss me off."

"Do I look like I care?" Booker turned his gaze to Smalley, so they'd know his message was meant for both of them. "Just leave Delbert alone. Or you boys'll be asking for more trouble than you can handle." With a wave at Leah, who was watching them through the living room window, he walked away.

WHEN BOOKER GOT HOME, Delbert and Bruiser in tow, Katie was upstairs at her computer. He knew she'd heard him come in when she hollered to say there was some coleslaw in the fridge to go with the rolls, and ribs and barbecue beans waiting in the oven. But she didn't leave her room. Booker didn't see her all through dinner, or even afterward while he was watching TV.

It was understandable that she'd be preoccupied. She finally had everything she needed to get her Web site business going. But he'd become accustomed to her attention and—he twisted on the couch to look up the stairs—she hadn't even bothered to stick her head into the hall.

"You want Katie to come down?" Delbert asked. "You want her to play chess with you?"

"I was just wondering what she's doing," Booker muttered. He was definitely more transparent than he'd realized if Delbert could pick up on his thoughts. With a scowl, he went back to watching *A Few Good Men* while Delbert played with Bruiser.

After another thirty minutes, Delbert went to his room, presumably to play the X-Box Booker had bought him for Christmas, which he loved. Booker watched the news, but he could hardly remember how he'd occupied his nights before Katie had shown up again.

Glancing at the clock, he decided that maybe he should go to the Honky Tonk. It was Friday night after all, and he hadn't been out in weeks. Ashleigh Evans had brought him a chocolate shake at the garage earlier, wanting to know if he'd be in town tonight.

He cast another glance up the stairs toward Katie's room. He didn't really want to go anywhere, but he wasn't about to let himself get too comfortable with his new roommate. Certainly he wasn't going to allow himself to depend on her in any way....

Using the remote to turn off the television, he went to take a shower.

HOLDING A COLD BEER, Booker leaned an elbow on the bar as he studied the crowd. The music pouring from the jukebox was loud, patriotic and definitely country, but it had a good beat. He found himself enjoying it, even though he'd always been more of a classic rock fan. He supposed, given a few more years in Dundee, he'd be wearing a hat and a pair of cowboy boots, too.

Billy Joe and Bobby Westin were playing a game of darts with a couple of girls who looked too young to be drinking, let alone hanging out with men in their thirties. Mike Hill sat in the corner with a couple of business types. Folks came from all over to check out the Hill brothers' breeding enterprise. And since the Running Y Resort, Conner Armstrong's golf course and dude ranch, had opened up last spring, there were more strangers in town than ever before, even during the winter, thanks to the discounted rates through the cold months.

The constant influx of fresh faces created some interesting possibilities and was certainly good for Dundee's economy. For the first time in twenty years, the Honky Tonk had built on and they'd added a mechanical bull. A few preppy types were trying to ride the bull now. Booker usually enjoyed seeing them get thrown, but nothing seemed to hold his interest tonight. He couldn't forget Katie. He wondered what she was doing, if she was finished yet, if she might be ready for a game of chess. Bored and angry with himself that he'd prefer a quiet night with her to drinking and dancing and mingling, he forced himself to stay longer.

But he regretted that decision the moment he heard someone yell, "Hey, Andy, how was San Francisco?"

Andy? Booker's blood ran cold as he turned and saw Andy Bray standing with his cousins at the end of the bar. How he'd missed spotting him earlier, Booker wasn't sure. Except that Andy had changed quite a bit. He'd pierced his nose and wore large silver hoops in his ears. His dark hair, which was very short in the back, had a blond streak in front that fell almost to his chin, effectively covering most of his face. Dressed in a wrinkled white shirt, black pants and black platform dress shoes, he looked like something out of *The Matrix Reloaded.*

So the great pretender was back. Booker should have expected it.

Torn between the prospect of breaking Andy's jaw and simply walking out, he pushed his beer away. Then he pulled his drink toward him again, downed the rest and ordered another. He wasn't going to get involved. He didn't care if Andy was in town. Why should he? He'd been trying to help Katie, as a friend. That was all. He had no emotional stake in her situation beyond that. Which meant he had nothing to lose, right?

Right. Booker was just finishing his second beer when he felt a hand on his shoulder.

"There you are," Ashleigh said. "I guess a girl's got to beg to get you to come to the Honky Tonk these days, huh?" She smiled coyly, batting her eyelashes at him, and he decided he'd been crazy to closet himself away at the farmhouse for the past few weeks. What had he been thinking—that his life had somehow changed?

"Did you want me to come out tonight for a reason?" he asked.

She blinked at his sudden frankness, probably because he'd been so careful not to let her corner him in the past. But she recovered quickly. Striking a sexy pose, she slid her tongue along her top lip as she looked him up and down. "I think you know what I want," she said.

Booker finished off his beer and tossed some money on the bar to pay for it. "Why don't you spell it out for me?" He wasn't in the mood for games. Seeing Andy again had created a sense of déjà vu that made him inexplicably angry. He kept hearing Katie say, "Andy tells me I'll feel differently in a few months," kept seeing her door close in his face, kept feeling as if a horse had just kicked him in the gut.

Ashleigh leaned closer, giving him an ample view of cleavage. "I want to know if you're really as good as your reputation."

That spelled things out, all right. "And tomorrow?" he said, wondering what kind of price tag came with the offer.

"No strings attached. But if we have a good time, I suppose anything can happen…."

Booker could hear Andy boasting about the splash he'd made in the big city. "You're sure?" he said to Ashleigh, wanting to give her one last chance to change the rules.

"I'm positive."

"Then I say we dance." Taking her by the arm, he shut out the father of Katie's baby, forced Katie herself out of his mind and led Ashleigh onto the dance floor.

BOOKER WOKE UP in Ashleigh's bed early the next morning and groaned as memories of the night before assailed him. For the first time since Hatty died, he'd gotten terribly drunk and gone back to his old behavior. But it hadn't felt any more meaningful, despite his long sabbatical. And in the end, he hadn't been able to go through with it, anyway.

God, now he knew just how far gone he really was....

Sitting up, he winced against a raging headache and squinted at Ashleigh, who rolled over and flung her arm toward him. When she didn't encounter anything but empty space, she turned onto her stomach and propped herself up on one elbow. "Hi," she said with a sleepy grin.

Booker pictured Katie at the farmhouse with her round, pregnant belly, and tried to convince himself that Ashleigh was more appealing. But Ashleigh couldn't replace Katie now any more than she could last night.

Inhaling a deep breath, he scrubbed a hand over his face. "Hi."

She raked her fingers through her long tousled hair. "What are you doing up so early?"

"I have to work."

"What?" She sat up without bothering to pull the sheet with her, but even the sight of her bare breasts did little to kick-start Booker's flagging libido. "You can't leave yet," she said with a whine. "You were too drunk to do anything last night. You passed out the second I got your clothes off."

Actually, he hadn't passed out quite that quickly. He'd closed his eyes while trying to talk his body into cooperating—and had slipped away only after meeting with complete and utter failure.

"Come here." She slid closer and tried to wrap her arms around his waist, but Booker had no intention of letting her pull him back into bed. He hadn't been with a woman in almost two years, but that didn't seem to make any difference. He *still* wanted only Katie.

Standing, he said, "Sorry, I've got to go."

When Ashleigh saw that he was serious, she gave him a grin designed to tempt him and let her gaze wander over his body. "You're gorgeous, you know that?"

Surprised, Booker glanced up at her while pulling on his pants. "I've been called a lot of things," he said. "But that's generally not one of them."

"Then you haven't been listening to the right people."

He chuckled, wishing he felt something for Ashleigh. But he didn't.

Stacking the pillows behind her, Ashleigh started to pout when her words didn't have the desired effect of enticing him back into her bed.

Booker finished dressing, then hesitated, wondering how to end their botched one-night stand. Did she expect him to kiss her goodbye? He just wanted to leave, but he was afraid that would be unkind. So he compromised by giving her a light peck on the forehead. "Sorry it didn't work out."

"Booker?"

She caught him as he was walking out of her bedroom. "Yeah?"

"Do I just not…do it for you?" she asked.

He let his breath go in a long sigh as he looked back at her. "It's not you, Ashleigh." It was Katie, but he'd be damned if he'd admit that to anyone else. "It's me," he said. Then he left, cursing his own stubborn heart.

KATIE SAT AT the kitchen table in a pair of Booker's sweats, because she could no longer fit into her own, drinking a cup of herbal tea. Through the large side window, she could see Delbert playing with Bruiser outside, just as she could see the end of the drive—and the empty spot where Booker normally parked.

He hadn't come home last night. She was sure of that. She'd called the Honky Tonk at closing time and been told he'd left with Ashleigh Evans, so she was equally sure she knew where he'd gone. What she couldn't figure out was why the thought of Booker with another woman made her feel so bad.

Her hand shook as she brought the cup to her lips. She didn't have any emotional reserves. She'd been agonizing over whether or not to give up the baby. She'd been trying to learn a lot in a very short time. She'd virtually severed whatever ties remained with her parents. The last thing she needed was the added distraction and anxiety of dealing with a man. Any man. Especially an old boyfriend she obviously still had feelings for.

Trying to swallow the lump in her throat that made it difficult to speak, she picked up the phone and called Mike Hill. It was early, but she knew he'd be awake. The Hills rose before dawn and worked until well after dark. She'd heard Rebecca complain about Josh's long hours before.

"High Hill Ranch."

Katie cleared her throat. "Mike?"

"Yes?"

"It's Katie Rogers."

"Hi, Katie. How are you?"

"Fine. Listen, I was wondering…if you were to lease one of those cabins on the ranch—the ones you mentioned earlier—how much would the rent be?"

"They're tiny, Katie, just a place to sleep really, so not much," he said.

"Can you give me a figure?"

"Four hundred a month would be fair, I guess, since we have a cook who handles meals."

Even better. "Fine. I was—I was hoping maybe I could make a trade with you."

"What kind of trade?"

"If you let me stay in one of those cabins for six months, I'll make sure you receive twenty-four hundred dollars in Internet services."

"Internet services?"

"I design Web sites now. I was just on the Internet last night and realized that you and Josh don't have a Web presence."

He sounded surprised by her businesslike tone. "That's true. We've been meaning to hire someone. We just haven't got around to it yet."

"Then you understand how a Web site can be used for promotional purposes."

"Yes. We have Internet service here and use it occasionally, but I know we're not making the most of it."

"Great. I'd like to handle your Web site for you. I'm new in the business, so I don't have a sample of my work to show you, at least not yet. But I've really learned a lot. And I'm a dedicated worker. I think I can create a Web site that will show High Hill Ranch off to perfection. I promise that, at a minimum, you'll get your money's worth."

She bit her lip, terrified by what his answer might reveal. Would he see the value behind her offer? Or would he let her have the cabin out of charity, the way he'd tried to give it to her before?

She needed it to be the former and was inordinately pleased when she heard grudging respect, even a little excitement, in his response. "Sure," he said. "I'd be willing to do that. I've been telling Josh that we need to get a Web site. And a trade won't cost us much of anything."

"Wonderful." Covering her eyes with one hand, Katie breathed a sigh of relief. But her relief was short-lived. Outside, she heard a vehicle pull up and knew that Booker had finally come home.

"When can I move in?" she asked.

"Whenever you're ready."

Now all she had to do was figure out how to get back and forth to the doctor in Boise. Rebecca? Mona? "I'll let you know," she said and hung up just as Booker came through the door.

She turned, expecting him to say something, possibly even ask her who she was talking to so early in the morning, but he didn't. Opening the cupboard, he pulled out the Tylenol and swallowed at least three tablets with one gulp of water.

Katie made fists inside the overlong sleeves of Booker's sweatshirt. "Have a good time last night?"

Booker's glance was brief, and he didn't answer.

She took a deep breath. "That good, huh?"

Again, no answer. He started toward the stairs just as Delbert poked his head inside. "Booker?"

Booker winced as if Delbert's overloud voice had cleaved his head in two. "Yes?"

"Aren't we going to work today?"

"I just told you outside, we're leaving as soon as I shower."

"Oh, that's right. Are you mad at me, Booker?" Delbert asked, looking worried. "Huh?"

A muscle jumped in Booker's cheek, but his voice was low and calm. "No."

"I'll be waiting for you out here, then," he said. "I'm ready whenever you are, Booker, okay? I'm all ready."

With a slow and careful nod, Booker continued up the stairs.

When Booker got out of the shower, he found the sweats Katie had appropriated for her use folded neatly on his bed, which surprised him. She didn't have any sweats of her own. Her old ones didn't fit anymore, and her clothing budget hadn't stretched to include such extras. If she was giving his back, what was she planning to replace them with?

He wasn't sure, but he was eager enough to get out of the house that he wasn't going to worry about it. His head still hurt, despite the painkillers, and he was afraid that if he stopped for a few seconds, he'd wind up thinking about last night, which he definitely didn't want to do.

Pulling on some faded jeans, he shoved the money wadded up on his dresser into his pocket, yanked on a shirt and a pair of work boots, and immediately started downstairs. That was when he realized that something else was a little odd. He could hear Katie in her bedroom, crossing the floor, opening and closing drawers, then crossing back again.

What was she doing?

Changing directions, he knocked at her door.

She opened it, wearing some of her new maternity clothes. "Yes?"

His eyes cut to the bed behind her, where he could see the corner of an open suitcase. "What's going on?"

"I'm moving out," she said, her face a little flushed.

Booker felt as though she'd just knocked the wind out of him. That he'd expected something like this, that he'd *invited* it by going home with Ashleigh last night, didn't make the reality any easier to accept. "Why?"

She let go of the door, and he pushed it wider as she hurried to gather her belongings.

When she didn't answer, he said, "Katie?"

"I don't want to get in your way anymore, that's all."

"You're not in my way."

She kept her head down while she packed.

"Does this have anything to do with Andy?"

"Andy?" She looked at him as though he was crazy. "No."

"He's back, you know. I saw him last night."

That got her attention. Dropping the shoes she'd been trying to stuff into her suitcase, she sagged onto the bed. "You're kidding, I hope."

"No."

"Do you know why he's here?" Her voice was completely deadpan.

"My guess is he's come to take you home. What do you think?"

She stared off through the window for a long moment. Then with a slight shake of her head, she got up and resumed packing, more slowly this time. "It doesn't matter," she said. "I don't want anything to do with him."

"Then what's all this about?" Booker motioned to the clothes strewn across her bed. "Is it because I didn't come home last night?"

"No," she said, but he knew it was. Somehow he'd known even at the Honky Tonk that going home with Ashleigh would destroy whatever relationship was developing between him and Katie. Wasn't that the real reason he'd finally done it? He'd pushed Katie out the door before she could walk out on her own.

“Where are you going?” he asked, the dull ache throbbing in his chest matching the pain in his head. “To your parents’ house?”

“Absolutely not.” She struggled to latch her suitcase. “I’ve rented a cabin from Mike Hill.”

“How?”

“I’m going to create a Web site for him in exchange for room and board.”

Booker tried to search for some logical reason she should stay, even though he knew her leaving was probably best. He couldn’t offer her anything more than he’d offered two years ago. “You just got your Internet service,” he said.

“Mike has service at the ranch. I’ll use his.”

“What do you want me to tell Andy if he calls?”

“Whatever you do, don’t tell him where I am.”

“Katie—”

She finally got her suitcase latched and tried to lift it. He moved to intercept her before she could hurt herself or the baby. For a moment, they were only inches apart. Booker could see tears caught in her eyelashes, which made the tightness in his chest that much worse. He watched one slip down her cheek and raised a finger to wipe it away. “What do you want from me, Katie?” he said softly.

She closed her eyes and shook her head. “Nothing. I don’t want anything from you, except a ride to High Hill Ranch.”

CHAPTER TWELVE

It took Katie only a couple of hours to get settled into her new house. When Mike had said the cabins were small, he wasn't exaggerating. Strung in a chain, like an old-time cabin-style motel, they were only twenty feet square. Each cabin had one room with a small kitchenette in the corner, a sofa sleeper along one wall, an inexpensive oak entertainment center with a small TV sitting across from the sofa, a desk and a chair to the side and a bathroom barely big enough for a tiny shower. There would scarcely be room for the baby's bassinette, provided she ever got one. Katie supposed she could make the baby a bed out of blankets on the floor, but that seemed too primitive, even to her.

She glanced at the book she was just slipping into her desk. *The Adoption Option.* After she'd finished unpacking, she'd taken some time to read real-life experiences of mothers who'd given up their babies. In a candid, nonjudgmental way, the book had discussed why they'd done what they'd done and how they were coping with the results. But reading wasn't making Katie's decision any easier. She was still torn, and she had so many other things to think about.

A vision of Booker's stony expression as he dropped her off this morning flashed through her mind. Her new place seemed strangely quiet and lonely without him,

Delbert and Bruiser. She felt as if she was missing her family. But she knew she'd made the right decision. She couldn't go from living with Andy to living with Booker, because she didn't know how to be friends with Booker. Their relationship didn't fit any one category, and that had never been more apparent than last night when he'd spent the night with Ashleigh. Katie had felt all sorts of things she shouldn't have felt as a friend: pain, betrayal, even envy. She knew what it was like to lie beneath Booker. Knew the way he tasted and smelled and moved—

A knock at the door made her stomach muscles tense. Booker had said Andy was in town. Which meant it was probably only a matter of time before he found her.

"Who is it?" she asked, creeping closer. Her door was pretty bare and functional. It had a lock but nothing as elaborate as a peephole.

"Mike."

Breathing a sigh of relief, Katie swung open the door.

Mike looked up from arranging a white plastic chair and a geranium on the small concrete slab that served as her front porch. "I brought you a couple of things," he said.

Katie was surprised by the gesture. Mike always seemed so preoccupied with work, she hadn't expected him to take special notice of her.

"Are the other cabins occupied yet?" She glanced down the row of bare concrete slabs, none of which had a chair or flowers.

"Most of them. We have one empty." He nodded to his left. "It's down there at the end, but we haven't furnished it yet and probably won't this year because we've hired all the ranch hands we're going to hire."

"Where is everyone?" she asked.

"Still working. I'm sure you'll meet them as they come straggling in." He checked his watch. "They've got an hour or so yet."

She eyed her new chair and plant. "Thanks for the porch accessories."

"No problem. They're not exactly something you'd see on *Lifestyles of the Rich and Famous,* but I hope they'll make you a little more comfortable." She could barely see his grin beneath the shade of his hat, but she knew he wore a pleasant smile. Everything about Mike was pleasant. "Dinner is served at six every night over at the main house," he said.

Mike and Josh used to live together, but since Josh got married, he and Rebecca had built their own place on a more wooded part of the property, near a small pond. Mike now lived alone in one section of the main house. The rest served as the High Hill Ranch offices and, evidently, the mess hall.

"Sounds good," she said.

"Breakfast is at six. Boxed lunches are prepared at the same time, if you want to grab one for lunch. Otherwise, you're on your own until dinner." He started digging in his pocket. "And I've got a set of keys I want to give you."

"Keys for what?" she asked. Not to the office. They'd decided to run a cable from the house to her cabin so she could work whatever hours suited her best and so she could use her own computer.

"I want you to have access to one of the ranch trucks—" his eyes dropped to her belly "—just in case. Of course, if you need me to take you somewhere, you can always knock. But if for some reason I'm not around—" He shrugged. "I just think it would be best."

"But I can't impose on you by borrowing one of your vehicles."

"Sure you can," he said. "These keys are for the little red Nissan parked over by the barn. There's no sense letting it sit there if you need it. Hardly anyone drives it, so it certainly won't hurt to let you use it for the next few months."

She accepted the keys he handed her. "Thank you. I'll be very careful with it."

"Drive it whenever you want. I'm not worried about it." He adjusted his hat, allowing her a clearer glimpse of his hazel eyes. "Any chance you could give me a haircut in the next few days?"

"Of course. We could do it tonight."

He checked his watch again. "I've got to finish a few things before supper. Could I come back around eight?"

Katie had nothing but time. Her computer was set up, but she wouldn't have Internet service for another few days. "That works for me."

"Great." He tipped his hat. "See you then."

KATIE HAD BROUGHT HER scissors from San Francisco. She didn't have the fancy chair with the adjustable seat or the cape she used at the salon, but she wasn't doing a color treatment or giving a perm. This was a simple haircut. She could cover Mike with a towel, shake off the hair when she was done and sweep it up. No problem.

He arrived a little early, and Katie was glad. After the sleepless hours of the night before, she was exhausted.

And the stress of the move, as well as agonizing over what to do about the baby, wasn't helping.

"I appreciate this," he said as she let him in. "I could go to the salon, I suppose, but I'm always so busy I keep putting it off." He removed his hat and set it on the small kitchen table before folding his tall frame into the chair Katie had pulled into the center of the floor.

"Until we run that cable for Internet service, I don't have much to do anyway," she said.

"That should happen by Tuesday or Wednesday."

"I can wait until then." She put one of the four towels from her bathroom around his broad shoulders and used a clip to fasten it at the neck. Then she wet his hair with her spray bottle. She wasn't going to give him a shampoo in her kitchen sink. That was one of the luxuries he'd have to sacrifice in order to get a free and convenient haircut. "How are things with Mary?" she asked.

"Fine, I guess."

She combed through his wet hair to find that it was much longer than she'd expected. "When did you two start dating?"

"We're not dating."

Katie arched an eyebrow at him. "What would you call it?"

"We're just friends. We get together occasionally."

She could hear the dismissal in his voice and wondered why he seemed to be having so much trouble falling in love—with anyone. "Whatever happened to that woman from McCall you were dating? Everyone was so sure you'd marry her."

He gave her a sheepish grin. "She said our relationship wasn't progressing and broke it off to date someone else. She married him almost six months ago."

She started cutting the front of his hair. "Do you regret not making a move when you had the chance?"

"Not really."

"Do I sense that you have a problem with commitment, Mr. Hill?" she teased.

"I'm not afraid of commitment. I just… I don't know. Haven't met the right woman, I guess."

"Well, I, for one, have decided that being single isn't so bad." She moved toward the back of his head.

"What happened between you and Andy?"

Several clumps of hair fell to the floor before she answered. "That's a long, sad story. Bottom line—"

"He's not in your league."

Katie held her scissors aloft, smiling down at him. "That's a nice thing to say."

"It's true."

She sprayed his hair some more because it wasn't wet enough.

"He's in town, you know," he said after a few seconds.

"That's what I've been told." She let his hair slide through two of her fingers as she checked to make sure it was even.

"You haven't heard from him?"

"Not yet." She clipped his hair a little shorter on the left side, where it seemed slightly longer than it should be.

"Would you ever go back to him?"

"Would 'absolutely not' be too strong a response?"

He chuckled. "What about the baby?"

She shook her head but kept cutting. "I'm doing the baby a favor, believe me."

"It was that bad, huh?"

"I should've come home a long time ago. Then I wouldn't be in this situation."

"Aren't you excited about having a child?"

Katie plugged in her electric razor and started trimming his neckline and sideburns. "In some ways," she said. If she wasn't excited, it was only because she felt such a tremendous desperation, felt such responsibility to make the right choice for her child. If things were different, if she and Andy could've made a life together, she'd be thrilled to have a baby. It wasn't as though she was sixteen—she was twenty-five.

She turned off the razor and set it aside. "Do you know if…if Josh and Rebecca have had any luck…you know, getting pregnant?"

He seemed taken aback by her change of topic. "Not yet. I think they're planning to try some alternatives."

She removed the cape from around his neck and shook the hair onto the floor, where she could sweep it up. If Josh and Rebecca were looking into alternatives, adoption was definitely one of those…. "Do you think they might be interested in adopting *my* baby, Mike?" she asked softly.

Mike held her gaze for several seconds. "Are you serious, Kate?"

"I haven't made any firm decisions, but I'm definitely considering it." She swallowed against the lump that suddenly threatened to choke her and resisted the impulse to put a protective hand over her belly. "I just have so little to give this baby. And they…" Her voice failed her. She covered her face so he wouldn't see the tears filling her eyes.

Standing, he pulled her hands away and tilted her

chin up so she had to look at him. "Katie, it won't always be this bad."

"I believe that, Mike. I'm really going to do well at my new business. If only I can get through the here and now…."

"You'll get through it. Give yourself time and keep plodding along. Things will improve."

"I only have a few more months before the baby arrives."

"Then accept some help. You can always repay folks later. I admire your independence, but I don't want to see you make a decision you may regret for the rest of your life."

Frustrated by her emotion, she wiped away her tears. "I knew there was a reason I had a crush on you," she said with a short laugh to lighten the mood.

He didn't look the least bit surprised by her confession and, no doubt, he wasn't. He couldn't have missed the way she'd followed him around like a lovesick puppy for so many years.

With a grin, he retrieved his wallet to pay her, but she shook her head.

"No, I won't accept your money."

"Katie—"

"I need to feel I still have something to contribute to the world around me. I know that sounds crazy, but there it is."

She could tell he didn't want to take no for an answer, but he finally put his money away. "Can I buy you dinner Friday night, then?" he asked.

"You let me move in here on a trade. You're lending me a car—"

"And you're going to design me the best damn Web

site on the Internet, remember? Don't undervalue your services. Besides, it's only dinner."

She smiled. She knew Mike well enough to realize he wasn't offering her anything more than friendship—but a friend happened to be exactly what she needed at the moment. "Sounds like fun," she said.

AS SOON AS Mike left, Katie decided to go to bed. There wasn't anything on television, she didn't want to look at her baby books because she felt like crying every time she did, and she couldn't help wondering what Booker was doing. Was he with Ashleigh? Was he at the Honky Tonk? It was Saturday night. He could be either place....

Rolling over in bed, she glanced at the keys Mike had given her, fighting the temptation to get up and drive through town, just to see if she could spot Booker's truck. She'd told herself when she accepted Mike's pickup that she'd only use it in case of emergency, but the longer she lay awake staring at the ceiling, the more of an emergency finding Booker seemed to be.

She wasn't going to town, she decided. For her, Booker was trouble.

But when she closed her eyes, she remembered there were other sides of Booker that were far from trouble—for anyone. He'd given Delbert a home, a job, friendship. He'd gone to jail trying to protect him. He'd taken her in, even though she'd walked out on him two years ago....

She stared at the simple white phone next to her bed. She could call the farmhouse under the guise of looking for something she thought she'd left behind, just to see where he was or, better yet, hear his voice.

No! She fought with the covers twisted around her legs until she straightened them out, then ordered herself to sleep. But a minute later she sat up, grabbed the phone and called Booker.

“Hi, Katie.”

Delbert had answered. Katie smiled, feeling even more melancholy. “Hi, Delbert. How are you?”

“Not good, Katie.”

Katie blinked in surprise. Delbert was almost always happy—at least he acted as if he was. “What’s wrong?”

“Booker burned dinner. He threw it in the garbage, Katie. In the garbage. The whole dinner. And the pan. It’s all gone.”

“It must have been ruined, Delbert. Did you get something else to eat?”

“We went to the diner.”

“That’s good.”

“Booker’s angry, Katie. I know he’s angry.”

“Why?”

“Because you left us. He doesn’t like it. I know.”

“I don’t think it has anything to do with me,” she said.

There was a long pause. “So he’s angry at me?”

Judging by the sound of Delbert’s voice, this was an even worse thought.

“No, of course not! Booker never gets angry at you.”

“Yeah. Booker’s my friend. But he…he won’t talk, Katie. And he keeps stomping around and stomping around. And he won’t talk. And he keeps stomping around.”

“Let me speak to him,” she said.

She heard a sorrowful sigh. “I can’t. He’s gone.”

Katie immediately pictured Booker with Ashleigh

and felt nauseous. "Where?" she asked, afraid she already knew the answer.

"I don't know. He left. He was driving real fast."

Katie closed her eyes, aching for Booker and wanting somehow to soothe his pain, if she could—despite what he'd done with Ashleigh. Her relationship with Booker was filled with such contradictions. Sometimes he seemed to enjoy having her at the farmhouse; sometimes he seemed to want her gone. Sometimes he treated her as though he still cared; sometimes she was sure he felt bitter and resentful. Her feelings swung in a pretty wide arc, too. But she had to remember that what she'd suffered last night was just a sampling of what she'd endure if she ever allowed herself to get seriously involved with him again. Reputations followed people around for a reason.

"He's just blowing off steam," she said. "I'm sure he'll be fine by tomorrow."

"I hope so, Katie."

"I hope so, too," she said, because no matter how many times she tried to convince herself not to care about Booker more deeply than was wise or safe, it was too late. She was in over her head.

THE NEXT FEW DAYS passed quickly. Mike got her Internet service up and running on Wednesday, and she threw herself into creating a Web site for High Hill Ranch immediately afterward. Some days she was satisfied with what she could do. Other days she was frustrated by how much she had yet to learn. But overall, Mike seemed pleased with her progress, and when she looked at the High Hill site, done in green and blue with gold lettering, she felt a growing sense of pride. She'd created rollover buttons on the menu that changed colors and slid to the right, she'd made moving graphics that highlighted the more famous of the Hill brothers' stallions, and she'd scanned and enhanced photographs of the ranch and its horses.

Maybe she hadn't made any decisions about her personal life, but she was earning her keep. She even enjoyed living at the ranch. Mike stopped by each evening around dinnertime. They checked over the most recent changes to the Web site, came up with ideas for improvements, scanned additional photos or compared what she was doing to other sites already up on the Web. Sometimes they ate with the cowboys, or he took her out to dinner. Quite often they walked over to the ranch house and watched a movie.

On Sunday, two weeks after she moved in, Mike showed up unexpectedly just after ten o'clock in the morning.

"What do you have planned for today?" he asked as soon as she answered the door and invited him in.

"I was just starting a new Web site." She gestured toward her computer as she closed the door. "I'm beginning to get some business from my on-line marketing efforts."

He took off his hat, turning it in his hands as he held it by the brim. "What kind of efforts?"

"Posting on loops and bulletin boards, visiting chat rooms, things like that."

"That's good. But you know what they say about all work and no play. You need to get out."

She pushed a hand through her hair, conscious of the fact that she hadn't showered before sitting down in front of her computer this morning. "I've been getting out," she said. "You took me to McCall for dinner a few days ago, and it was great."

"Well, I'm taking you to breakfast today."

"Where?"

"The diner."

The diner? Jerry's was right across the street from Booker's auto repair shop and, while he wasn't technically open for business on Sundays, he often worked seven days a week. Katie hadn't seen him since she'd moved out of his place. But she wasn't sure she was ready to face him even now. "Looks like we got a little snow last night," she said, nodding toward the window. "Why bother going anywhere? We might've missed breakfast at the ranch house, but I can make us some omelettes or pancakes right here."

Mike put his hat back on. "Are you still thinking about giving up the baby, Katie?"

She nodded. "I want my child to have a complete family. It's what I grew up with. It's the way I was taught life should be."

"Then I was wondering if we could invite Josh and Rebecca to go out with us this morning."

Alarm raised the hair on the back of Katie's neck. "Do they know I'm considering adoption?"

"No, I haven't told them. That's up to you." Before relief could set in, he added, "I just thought it might make the decision easier for you if you were to talk to them as prospective parents. Josh, Rebecca and I are heading to Houston tonight to take a look at a stallion that's for sale, which would give them a chance to think about the situation."

"When I first mentioned that I might put the baby

up for adoption, you told me you were afraid I'd regret it, Mike."

"I am," he admitted. "But Josh is worried about Rebecca. She wants a baby and so far nothing seems to be working out." He straightened his hat. "I don't want to see you make a mistake, but now that Delaney's pregnant again—"

"I hadn't heard."

"She's not saying much about it because Rebecca's having such a difficult time. Anyway, I thought it might not hurt to talk to both Josh and Rebecca about other options."

"I'm not sure talking about it is such a good idea at this point," Katie said. "I don't want to get Rebecca's hopes up before I've made a decision."

The snow he hadn't managed to stomp off his boots melted onto the mat near her door. "She's trying fertility drugs right now so she's not set on adoption. I just want to introduce the subject, in case the fertility treatment doesn't work." He rested a hand on the door knob. "Whether she ends up adopting your baby or someone else's, it might help her to see that there are mothers out there exactly like you who need a good home for their baby."

So he wanted her to show his sister-in-law that all was not lost if she couldn't conceive, that there were other options....

Mike had been so good to her that Katie hated to tell him no. She gazed up into his handsome face, the face she'd admired for so long, and decided to take a chance on this being the right thing. "Okay," she said. "Give me thirty minutes to get ready."

CHAPTER THIRTEEN

KATIE TOYED NERVOUSLY with the Sweet'n Low packets in the middle of the table as she and Mike waited for Josh and Rebecca to join them at Jerry's. They could've all ridden together. They were coming from the same place. But Katie was grateful that Mike had told his brother and sister-in-law they'd meet at the diner instead. The trip into town had given her some time to mentally prepare herself to approach Rebecca with the adoption issue.

"You okay?" Mike said, watching her with a concerned expression.

She cast a surreptitious glance out the window toward Booker's shop. The garage doors were rolled up and the lights were on in his office. She'd taken note of that the moment they drove up. But she hadn't spotted him on the way in, and now she was sitting at too much of an angle to see more than a small section of his property. "I'm fine."

"I guess you've heard about Booker," he said, following her gaze when it returned, almost involuntarily, to the window.

Katie's eyes went immediately to Mike's face. "What do you mean?"

"He had his hearing on Friday for that fight with the Smalls."

"I didn't know." Except for her association with Mike, she'd been completely out of circulation. "How'd it go?"

Mike stirred some more cream into his coffee. "He was fined 500 and, 'in light of his turbulent past,' the court mandated he attend anger management classes once a week in Boise."

"How do you know all this?" Katie asked.

"Rebecca told me when I called to invite her and Josh to breakfast this morning."

"Did anything happen to the Smalls?"

"No. They weren't even cited."

"That's so unfair." She shoved the sweetener packets away. "Booker didn't start that fight. He was only trying to protect Delbert."

"I believe that."

Katie hadn't expected Mike's support. "You do?"

"I don't really know Booker. Most people don't. He's not particularly trusting. But Rebecca would do anything for him. And I can tell you care about him, too. He must be a decent guy."

"He is."

Mike slid the menu the hostess had given him off to the side. "I remember seeing you and Booker around town quite often a few years ago. I thought you two were an item."

"I guess we were," she said.

"What happened?"

Katie wasn't sure how to explain. She'd gone over the past again and again, wondering how she'd fallen so far from where she'd always wanted to be. But even now it wasn't easy to separate the "should haves" from the "shouldn't haves." Her love life at that time had been complicated. "When I met Booker, my parents and just about everyone in town warned me to stay away from him, but I still had such a crush on you. I wasn't worried about falling in love."

He tipped back his hat and grinned at his part in the story, and she chuckled briefly before continuing. "Anyway, I dated Booker sort of halfheartedly at first. But then things started to get serious. When I realized how much I was beginning to care for him, I thought I had to do something about it. I was losing my heart to an ex-con who'd never made me a single promise about anything." Katie paused as Taylor Simpson, one of the waitresses at the diner, set glasses of water in front of them before bustling off again. "Then Andy moved in with his cousins for the summer."

"But Andy's the exact opposite of Booker," Mike said.

"I think that's what attracted me. I was also trying to start a singles club for the elderly over at the Elks Club, and Andy jumped right in and helped me. He was far more gregarious and demonstrative than Booker. He had a degree in communications and he was a fantastic salesman. Once he pitched in, we had no trouble raising the money we needed to refurbish the dance floor."

Mike took a sip of water. "So did you quit seeing Booker?"

"Yes. I spent more and more time with Andy. He seemed so safe, you know? So close to the family man I'd been looking for—much more like you," she said with a wry smile.

"Only he didn't treat you like a little sister."

"Definitely not. Before long, Andy was telling me he loved me and wanted to marry me. And he painted such an idyllic picture of heading to the big city for a few years before starting a family that I bought in to the whole thing."

"You'd think your parents would've been relieved you got away from Booker. But from what I've heard, they didn't like Andy much better."

"No. They'd heard his aunt and uncle grumbling about how lazy he was and that always bothered them. They wanted to know why, if he had a degree, he was living off his family and wasting time in Dundee instead of beginning a career. But Andy was free-spirited and fun-loving, and I didn't find it so hard to believe he'd take a break after graduating from college."

"How did Booker react when you broke off with him?"

The baby kicked her, and Katie gazed down at her belly, marveling at how much bigger she'd gotten in the past two weeks. "He didn't say much." He'd just stared at her with those dark, inscrutable eyes, and a muscle had twitched in his cheek. Katie knew she'd never forget how he'd looked in that moment.

"I guess it hurt that he seemed to let me go so easily. After that, I poured all my time and energy into Andy," she said. "Then to my surprise, Booker showed up just after Hatty died and asked me to marry him."

Mike sat back. "No kidding? I never pegged Booker as the marrying kind."

"Most people would agree with you."

"What did you say?"

"I told him I'd already made my decision to leave with Andy." She frowned and opened the menu, even though she already knew everything Jerry's served. "Ironic how it all worked out, don't you think? I was probably the only virgin to graduate in my senior class, yet I come home unmarried and pregnant. Andy, Mr. Smooth, turns into a crackhead. And Booker, who doesn't even have a high school diploma, becomes a successful businessman."

"I should've swept you off your feet and saved you from both of them," Mike said.

"Except you didn't love me," she murmured, laughing.

A smile quirked his lips. "I've always cared about you."

"That's different."

The bell sounded over the door, and Mike waved to get Josh and Rebecca's attention as they came in. Josh guided his wife to their booth, but Rebecca barely looked up. She was too busy saying something to Josh about a robbery.

"What was that?" Mike asked when they were close enough.

"Mrs. Willoughby was robbed last night," Rebecca said.

The ice in Mike's water clinked as he set his glass down. "*Old* Mrs. Willoughby? The lady who lives just a couple miles from us?"

"Someone broke into her house wearing a nylon stocking over his head," Josh explained.

"And he flashed her and nearly scared her half to death," Rebecca added.

Rebecca slid into the booth next to Katie while Josh sat by his brother. "He also waved a hunting rifle in her face and cleaned out her jewelry box," he told them. "Hi, Katie."

"Hi, Josh," Katie said. "Do they know who's responsible for the robbery?"

"Slinkerhoff's nephew has been accused of the other robberies in town," he said.

Katie remembered Mary saying something about that the day they saw each other at Jerry's.

"He's been out on bail for several weeks, so I'm sure they're checking his whereabouts. But at this point, Chief Clanahan is saying they don't know much."

"How would you like to identify someone's pecker in a lineup?" Rebecca said, her lip curling in disgust.

"Did it have any identifying characteristics?" Mike asked, obviously joking.

"If he'd flashed me, there'd be a few scars," Rebecca muttered.

Always high-spirited, Rebecca was more dramatic than most women. But Katie had always liked her. She had a big heart to go with her temperamental nature. Katie knew she'd be as good a mother as she was a friend.

"Mrs. Willoughby only lives a couple of miles from the ranch?" Katie said. She hadn't had any qualms about living alone before. But the knowledge that there was an exhibitionist thief on the loose in their small community made her nervous.

"You know my grandfather's house next door?" Mike asked.

"Next door" to the ranch was actually several acres away, but Katie knew the place Mike was talking about. To the Hill family's extreme embarrassment, thirteen years ago his grandfather, Morris Caldwell, had divorced Mike's grandmother and married Red, a known prostitute who was half his age and had three small children. It had created quite a scandal. He'd adopted her kids and finished raising them, but Red got tired of waiting for Morris to die so she could inherit his money and property and tried to poison him. He'd survived and divorced her just before he died of natural causes. In the end, she didn't get a cent, but he kept her kids in his will. Casey and Reed, the two boys, had eventually sold their property to Josh and Mike and moved out of state. Lucky, the only girl, inherited the house but, even though Red had died shortly after, Lucky wouldn't sell. She lived out of state, too; Katie wasn't sure where. But the house had sat vacant for so long and was falling into such disrepair, it had developed a spooky reputation among the children and teenagers of Dundee.

"It's the big Victorian, right?"

"That's the one. Mrs. Willoughby lives in a mobile home on a corner of the property," Mike told her.

"That *is* close," Katie said. "You don't think the thief could be one of your cowboys, do you?"

"No," Josh said. "I've worked with most of those boys before, and I can't see any of them scaring an old lady, let alone robbing her."

Taylor came by to take their orders. Rebecca and Josh decided on a stack of pancakes each and a skillet of potatoes, eggs, onions and bacon. Mike ordered eggs Benedict and Katie chose the cheapest thing on the menu—two eggs any style with two strips of bacon and a piece of toast.

Rebecca's eyes dropped to Katie's belly the moment the waitress left. "How's the pregnancy coming along?"

Katie rubbed the spot where the baby liked to kick. Recently she'd been having a lot of backaches that felt disturbingly like the premature labor pains she'd experienced in San Francisco. They hadn't developed into anything, so she figured they came from spending so much time sitting at her computer. "Fine."

Rebecca's face reflected envy—Rebecca's face always revealed whatever she was thinking or feeling.

Katie said "Fine," as Mike and Josh both started talking at once, in an obvious attempt to distract Rebecca.

She scowled at them. "I'm okay."

Katie opened her mouth to bring up the possible adoption. She thought now might be a good time. But she couldn't do it. Instead she said, "Rebecca, I was hoping you'd be able to meet us here today because… because I wanted to ask if you'd be my coach during the delivery."

Rebecca's jaw dropped, and Josh and Mike looked alarmed—until a smile crept over her face. "You mean you want me to go to classes with you and help you breathe right and all that?"

Katie nodded. "Classes start next Wednesday. But they're in Boise. Is that okay?"

"That's fine."

"Great." Katie shot Mike a glance that said she wasn't willing to go any further today, and he gave her a subtle nod to let her know he understood.

"I would've been your coach," he said, acting hurt.

"You were next on my list," she told him, then realized Rebecca was watching her intensely. "What?"

"Booker's in love with you. You know that, don't you?"

Katie was too shocked to speak. This was the last thing she'd expected to hear.

Josh shifted uncomfortably in his seat and ducked

his head to catch his wife's eye. "Do you think that's information Booker would want you to share, Beck?"

"I want him to be happy," Rebecca stated as bluntly as she stated everything else. "I want them *both* to be happy. Anyway, I'm not betraying a confidence. Booker's never told me he loves her. I just know in my heart that he does."

"You must be mistaken," Katie said. "He's seeing Ashleigh Evans."

Rebecca grimaced and shook her head. "I can't figure out how he got involved with Ashleigh. She was coming on to him long before you showed up, and he might've been friendly, but he didn't show the slightest inclination to take her up on anything more."

"Well, I'm pretty sure that in the last few weeks he's taken her up on plenty."

Rebecca propped her chin in her palm and stared at Katie. "Unless you stake some sort of claim on Booker, he has no reason *not* to see other women."

Katie knew she had no right to be angry with Booker over Ashleigh. But that didn't change the fact that she hurt whenever she imagined them together. "Andy cheated on me so many times. I just… I can't—"

"Booker is nothing like Andy," Rebecca said, her voice soft yet fierce.

Katie looked at the door, suddenly eager to escape. But their food hadn't even arrived. And she'd ridden with Mike.

"Beck, take it easy," Josh murmured as if sensing Katie's panic.

Mike slung his arm over the back of the booth. "Katie's got a lot to deal with right now. What's wrong with letting her hang out with me?"

"Nothing's wrong with it, if that's what she really

wants," Rebecca replied, resisting Mike's attempt to lighten the mood. "I'm just telling her what I think because I'm her friend as much as Booker's."

"Well, thanks for the input." Mike squeezed Katie's shoulder. "You gonna be okay?"

Katie forced a smile despite the unsettling ache in the pit of her stomach. "Sure, I'm fine."

"Katie?" Rebecca pressed.

Katie reluctantly raised her eyes to Rebecca's.

"Ever since you moved out, Booker has barely spoken to Ashleigh. He's barely spoken to anyone, even to me. He works eighteen hours a day. If you care about him, think about the fact that he's hurting right now."

Booker's angry, Katie...because you left us...he doesn't like it... I know... Delbert's words, though delivered in a simpler form, mirrored what Rebecca had just said. Could Rebecca and Delbert be right?

"I'm pregnant with another man's baby," Katie said, stating the obvious. "This isn't the time to worry about what I feel or don't feel for Booker."

"There isn't a better time. This is when you need him, Katie." Rebecca leaned back and crossed her arms. "I think you're seriously underestimating him, just like everyone else."

BOOKER SHOVED HIS HANDS in the pockets of his faded jeans as he stood at his office window. He'd done the right thing, forcing the issue with Katie by going home with Ashleigh. It was over. For good. No more "what ifs." And he was satisfied. Better to put a decisive end to whatever was developing between them than to walk into the same brick wall, right?

But all the logic in the world did little to stifle the

regret or the longing that tore through him at the sight of her.

The inside door banged open as Delbert entered the office, but Booker didn't flinch. He was too mesmerized watching Josh, Rebecca, Mike and Katie leave Jerry's Diner. Katie had been staying out at High Hill Ranch for more than two weeks, and this was the fourth time Booker had seen her come into town with Mike. Even more telling was that Mike hadn't been seen with Mary Thornton lately.

Once again, Booker had the privilege of standing by, at close range, while Katie fell for another man....

"Katie's at the diner, Booker," Delbert announced. "I just saw her."

Booker didn't respond.

"There she is." Delbert pointed as though Booker wasn't already staring at her. "She's leaving right now. Can we go say hello? Can we, Booker?"

"Go ahead," Booker said. "I'm staying here."

In the next second, Katie glanced up and met his eyes. The yearning he felt threatened to expose him. So he gave her a look that said he didn't give a damn about her and turned away.

"MIKE TOLD ME Katie's been living out at the ranch," Barbara Hill said.

Tami Rogers frowned at her best friend. They'd been poring through quilting books in the craft room of Barb's basement, searching for a pattern they wanted to use for their next project. They both liked to quilt, especially through the long summer evenings, and often worked on a quilt together or shared bits of fabric or patterns. They usually sold their quilts at the church's harvest festival each fall, and it was a matter of pride that they garnered the highest bids—second only to Roy White's hand-tooled saddles.

"At the ranch? Since when?" she asked, even though she knew better than to let Barb bait her into having this conversation. Barb didn't agree with how she and Don had handled Katie and had been looking for a chance to say so.

"It's been almost a month."

"Well, that's a better place for her than out at Booker Robinson's, I guess," Tami said, fingering a calico fabric that might be nice for a traditional wedding ring pattern.

"I don't think there's anything wrong with Booker Robinson," Barb said.

Tami raised a questioning eyebrow. "You sure thought something was wrong with him two years ago when Katie was dating him."

"I didn't know him then. He's been around long enough now that I can tell he's a decent fellow."

"Since when have you gotten to know Booker Robinson?"

"Since we started taking our cars over there to have them serviced. He's honest and quick and always respectful."

"I don't want to talk about Booker," Tami said. "I don't have anything against him as long as he stays away from my daughter."

Barb began folding the fabric they'd spread out on the utility table and stacking the books. "You haven't wanted to talk about Katie, either. Meanwhile, my son's telling me how destitute she is and asking why my best friend, who happens to be her mother, isn't helping her."

"Did you tell him it's because she needs to deal with the mess she's created?" Tami said, her tone challenging.

"I told him that, yes." Barb put the fabric away in the plastic containers where she stored her supplies.

"What did he say?"

"That everyone needs a little help once in a while."

Tami shook her head. Even though she was beginning to have her own doubts about the way they were handling Katie, she knew Don still felt certain they'd made the right decision. Admitting that she no longer fully agreed with her husband felt too disloyal. "She'll be better off if we don't rush to her rescue," she said, repeating what Don always told her.

"Did you say she'll be better? Or *bitter?*" Barb replied, sliding her glasses down her nose so she could look over them at Tami.

"Barb—"

"Tami, I know you and Don have strong feelings about this. But it's tough for me not to offer Katie the help you won't give her. If we weren't best friends—if I didn't owe you my first allegiance—I would've gone to her long ago."

"You *should* support me. I'm taking a stand for what's right. How is that so terrible?"

"You're trying to tell her how to live."

"She's my daughter!"

"She's twenty-five."

"And she wouldn't be in the situation she's in now if she'd listened to me!"

Barb's lips pursed in disapproval. Obviously she had more to say but was trying to hold back.

Tami considered leaving before they ended up in an

argument. But the second thoughts she'd been experiencing had poked too many holes in her resolve. Shoving the quilting books aside, she leaned forward. "Go ahead and say what's on your mind, Barb."

Barb hesitated for several seconds, but finally nodded. "Okay, I'm wondering where you think this is going to lead."

"What do you mean?"

"What good can come out of the stand you've taken?"

"Maybe Katie will listen to us next time."

"Next time? Hard as this may be to hear, Tami, your role in her life has changed. You need to support her in a different way now that she's older."

"That's easy for you to say! You're not coping with a daughter who's made a mess of her life and you're not fighting to get a fourteen-year-old turned around. Your boys are all grown up and doing great."

Barb stopped straightening up for a moment. "We've had our rough spots, you know that better than anyone. Both my boys were a handful growing up. And I thought I'd die when Josh decided to marry Rebecca. But I wanted a relationship with my future grandchildren, so I had to trust that he knew what he was doing. And I'm glad I did. Rebecca's a good woman. I wouldn't trade her as a daughter-in-law."

"So you think I should forget about the fact that Katie's having a baby out of wedlock and welcome her back with open arms?"

Barb sighed. "I'm saying we all make mistakes. Sometimes we have to give the people we love a hand—and a little extra room to figure out life's lessons on their own."

Tami pictured Katie standing on her doorstep in the

rain. At the time, Tami had been so disappointed, so angry. She'd told herself she was doing the right thing when she turned Katie away. But was she really?

THE NIGHT STRETCHED before Booker, quiet and lonely. He was too exhausted to head back to the shop, but he couldn't sleep, either. He did some chores around the house, missing Hatty in a way he hadn't missed her in months. He'd changed his life, knew his grandmother would be proud of him. But he was still restless. Maybe he always would be. Maybe it was just his nature.

Unable to think of anything else to do, he watched TV for a half hour before climbing the stairs for bed. Delbert had turned in several hours earlier, but Bruiser nosed Delbert's door open when Booker reached the hall and followed him to the entrance of Katie's room.

Squatting to pat the dog's head, Booker gazed at the empty bed and empty dresser. *Empty* seemed to describe the whole house these days.

"See that? We're finally rid of her. Life can get back to normal now, huh, boy?" he muttered.

Bruiser cocked his head and gave him a pitying look that made Booker laugh. "God, even you." He stood to leave, but something peeking out from under the bed caught his eye.

Moving closer, he realized it was the spine of a book. Evidently Katie had forgotten something. He expected it to be one of the computer manuals she'd studied so religiously, but when he pulled it out, he saw that it was a library book about babies.

"What do you think?" he asked Bruiser, showing the dog the picture of the newborn on the cover.

Bruiser yawned, obviously not impressed. Booker,

on the other hand, was curious. He sat on the bed and thumbed through page after page of pictures, some of pregnant mothers, some of the birth process. But the photographs and diagrams that fascinated him most were of the developing baby. Katie was seven months along. According to the book, a seven-month-old fetus weighed about three pounds and could open and close his eyes. His brain was developing quickly, he was aware and led an active emotional life. It said he could even learn things and recognize his mother's voice.

Booker had never dreamed a seven-month fetus was so developed. He'd never even thought about it. Becoming a parent hadn't been high on his agenda. But that seemed to be changing. He remembered putting his hands on Katie's belly and enjoying the contact, feeling almost as if he was part of a circle that included her and her baby. Which was crazy, of course. He wasn't part of anything.

"To hell with it." Scowling, he snapped the book shut. He was just getting up to go to his own room when the telephone rang. A glance at his watch told him it was nearly two o'clock. Who would be calling at this time of night?

He reached the phone on the third ring. "Hello?"

"I saw Delbert in town earlier."

The caller had a raspy, muffled voice, so muffled it was hardly discernible.

"What?" Booker said.

"You might not want to let your little retard ramble around on his own anymore, Booker. Poor thing might get hurt again."

"Who the hell is this?"

A raucous laugh. "Wouldn't you love to know."

"Jon, if this is you, you're an even bigger son of a bitch than I thought."

"Careful, Booker. You might be in for a surprise."

"Meet me now, at the park in town," Booker said. "We'll see who's going to get a surprise."

Another laugh. "You aimin' to land yourself back in jail?"

"I'm aiming to take your head off if you so much as look at Delbert the wrong way."

"Tsk, tsk. Such temper. Those anger management classes might do you some good. They've done wonders for me. Can't you tell?" More laughter echoed in Booker's ears, then the line went dead.

Booker stared at the phone, breathing hard. It was Jon Small. It had to be. Dragging out the phone book, he looked up Jon's number and dialed. A sleepy female voice answered.

"Is Jon there?"

"Who is this?"

"Booker Robinson."

"What are you doing calling here so late, Booker? If you don't leave my husband alone, we're going to get a restraining order."

"Just let me talk to Jon."

A long pause. "He's not home."

"Where is he?"

"How should I know? He doesn't exactly check in."

Booker cursed under his breath. "When you talk to him, tell him I'm looking for him," he said and hung up.

CHAPTER FOURTEEN

KATIE GAZED AT the new Web site she'd created. "Booker T's Auto Repair" was emblazoned across the top in large black letters. Below that she'd positioned a picture of Booker's shop next to a map showing its location. A menu with bold red letters, including buttons for "Services," "About Booker," and "Testimonials" lined the left side and leaped into a different font when her mouse rolled over them. To finish off the page, she'd added some graphics that included an animation with checkered flags.

The site looked good, but Katie wasn't convinced Booker would like it. She wasn't planning to show it to him, anyway. She wasn't even sure why she'd created it. Booker didn't have much need for a Web presence. His business came from locals and his shop was clearly visible, right on Main Street. This site was just something she worked on during long, lonely nights like this one, when she couldn't sleep. Besides, if Booker ever changed the name of his business, she didn't know if he'd use his middle initial. But she liked the sound of "Booker T's" and thought it was about time he made the shop "officially" his own.

Pressing a hand to her aching back, Katie stood and stretched. She needed to call her doctor in the morning. The pains she was experiencing seemed to be getting more acute. She'd been doing so well the past couple of months she doubted they were anything serious, but there were moments when she worried....

Sleep would help. If only she could relax. If only she could quit thinking about the look on Booker's face when she'd seen him earlier. She could've sworn he hated her. Which meant Rebecca had to be wrong. Booker didn't love any woman. He guarded his heart too fiercely.

But he'd let his defenses down once....

Lying on the bed to ease the tension in her back, Katie stared up at the ceiling and remembered the night they'd first made love. They'd been at the two-bedroom rental house she shared with her best friend Wanda, making chocolate-covered pretzels to fill Christmas tins. Wanda was at work and, just prior to sunset, a snowstorm darkened the sky. Booker built a fire while she melted chocolate—which never made it to the pretzels. When she called him to begin dipping, Booker started playing around, lifting her shirt and dropping warm chocolate on her stomach, then licking it off. What had begun as a game quickly flared into something more when he snapped open her bra, dropped chocolate on her nipple and took the chocolate and her nipple in his mouth.

Katie felt her breasts tingle just thinking about it. Never had she experienced a more erotic evening. Booker had aroused her so completely she'd practically begged him to take it further. And he had. But he was so gentle and careful, despite the urgency they were both feeling, that she knew right then—when he covered her body with his—that she was falling in love with him. The man who went to prison for grand theft auto. The man who made the police chief grimace and the mayor complain. The town's black sheep…

And that was when she'd panicked.

As the wind picked up outside, whistling eerily beneath the eaves, Katie's mind shifted to the night Booker had appeared at her house just before she left with Andy. He'd stood outside in the dim glow of the porch light looking darkly handsome, even dangerous, with his stubbled chin and enigmatic eyes. And he'd asked her to marry him. She'd turned him down, but she hadn't been able to stop shaking for hours afterward.

Now, putting herself in his shoes, she winced. It had been difficult enough for her; she could only imagine what *he'd* gone through, standing there on her porch, laying his heart bare. She'd hurt him, and he hated her for it, and she could understand why.

Close your eyes. Go to sleep. Forget him.

The wind was getting stronger, making noises that sounded like someone outside the cabin. Katie knew it was probably nothing, but she couldn't help feeling vulnerable when she remembered what had happened to poor Mrs. Willoughby in her trailer.

She glanced at the phone, wishing Mike was home tonight. The ranch house was only an acre or so away. She would've felt better knowing he was close—especially when she heard very distinct footsteps on her porch.

She tensed, sending another pain shooting through her abdomen, and grabbed the phone. But before she could call anyone, there was a solid knock at the door.

"Katie? It's me, Andy."

Andy! He'd been in town for a month, and she hadn't heard a word from him. But she'd known he'd show up eventually.

Hanging up, she went to the window and peeked out to see him hunched against the cold, wearing a pair of black pants and a white shirt with no jacket. "What are you doing here, Andy?" she called, moving to the door.

"I need to talk to you, Katie!"

"About what?"

"Come on. You're carrying my baby. Surely that means something to you. I'm freezing my ass off out here."

With a sigh, she opened the door. She didn't want him to wake the cowboys on either side of her, although she doubted anyone could hear him above the wind, which was getting louder by the minute.

"It's about to storm, Andy, and it's very late. Why are you here?"

"I want the money you owe me." He slid past her, rubbing his arms and looking as though he was long overdue for a haircut. Even though she'd asked him not to, he'd had his nose pierced while she was living with him in San Francisco. The garish streak of blond in his hair was new.

"What money?" she said.

"Did you think you could sell off our stuff and run out on me without giving me *anything?*"

Dumbfounded, Katie blinked at him. How could he feel entitled to a dime of that money after everything she'd done to support him? "I bought all that stuff in the first place," she said.

"I worked—" he staggered a bit "—occasionally."

He hadn't even glanced at her belly. He didn't care about the baby. He didn't care about her. He hadn't seen her for two months, yet all he could talk about was money.

Large drops of rain began to pelt the ground. Andy was already inside the cabin, so she closed the door. "*When* did you work? You partied. And you spent almost everything I earned on dope and alcohol!"

Scowling, he gazed around the room. "Come on, Katie. I need a fix. You know how it is. Just give me fifty bucks and we'll call it even."

"I don't have fifty bucks," she said. "And even if I did, I couldn't give it to you. How do you think I'm going to support this baby?"

"Looks like you're doing fine to me. From what I hear, you've got Sugar Daddy Mike taking care of you. That son of a bitch is richer than Midas."

"Who told you Mike's taking care of me?" she cried.

"Some woman named Mary pulled me aside at the Honky Tonk tonight. She's not very happy with you, by the way. She doesn't like that you've set your sights on her man."

"I haven't—" Katie caught herself before the denial could even pass her lips, and raised her hands in a helpless gesture. "You know what, Andy? I've got enough problems without you and Mary. I want you to leave."

"Then give me fifty bucks. Or a couple of twenties, at least. *Something* to get me by."

Katie covered her face and tried to take deep breaths. Her backache seemed to be getting worse. It was difficult to remain standing, but she didn't want Andy to know she wasn't feeling well, didn't want him to have any more advantage over her. "I'm broke, Andy. I don't have the money to give you. Now get out of here."

"That's a lie!" he shouted. "Look at you. Look at all this computer stuff. Computers aren't cheap."

Panic chilled Katie's blood as Andy singled out her

computer. Her future rested on that machine. Quickly inserting herself between him and the desk, she pointed at the door. "Go, before I call the cops."

He shoved her aside. "I'm going, but that's going with me."

"No!" A pain stabbed through Katie's abdomen as she moved, but she wasn't about to let him take the one thing she depended on. She was just starting to recover from the past two years, just starting to glimpse the life she could build with her new job....

"Get out of my way!" he snapped, yanking the cord from the wall.

She grabbed him by the shirt. "I won't let you do this!"

He easily shook her off. "This ought to be worth fifty bucks."

When he headed out with her CPU, she hurried after him. But he kicked her desk chair aside, knocking it over and tripping her at the same time.

Katie twisted to protect the baby as she fell, but she went down hard. She felt her water break, soaking her pants and puddling on the floor as yet another pain gripped her stomach. This one was so strong she didn't realize Andy was gone—until the pain eased and she became conscious of a cold rain blowing in from the open doorway.

Curling up, she fought sudden terror, along with a new stab of pain.

She waited for the pain to subside, but it didn't, and she knew she had to move. If she didn't do *something,* she was going to lose the baby. She was only thirty-two weeks, and two hours away from a neonatal unit.

Thunder cracked in the distance as she dragged herself over to the bed and tugged the phone to the floor. A moment later, a dial tone hummed in her ear, but she was panting for breath and wasn't sure who to call. There wasn't any ambulance service in Dundee. Mike, Rebecca and Josh were gone. She didn't know the phone numbers for any of the cowboys staying in the other cabins. She didn't even know them by more than first names. And her family was absolutely last on her list.

She'd call the police, she decided. They'd send a squad car. But she felt too vulnerable to have Orton arrive at her door. And deep down, there was only one person she wanted: Booker.

THE PHONE RANG, startling Booker. He jumped out of bed, thinking it might be Jon. He was eager to talk to him whether it was the middle of the night or not. But when he picked up, no one spoke.

"Who is it?" he said, his voice an impatient bark.

There was no reply. He almost hung up. But then he heard a weak, reedy voice call his name and apprehension rolled down his spine. It was Katie. Something was wrong.

"Booker?"

"What is it?" he said, his heart thumping.

"I need…help."

He was pretty sure she was crying. "Where are you?"

"My cabin."

"Where's Mike? He's much closer."

"Gone."

"Are you hurt? Is it the baby?"

"Will you come?" she gasped.

He was pulling on his jeans as they spoke. "I'm on my way."

BOOKER'S HEART JACKHAMMERED against his chest as he tore through Dundee going over seventy. Without another soul around, there wasn't much chance of causing an accident. And he didn't give a damn if all three members of Dundee's police force tried to pull him over en masse. They could chase him if they wanted to. He wasn't stopping until he reached Katie.

The weather forced him to slow down when he started into the mountains on the other side of town. But he didn't curse the wind or the rain; he knew he probably had the storm to thank for the fact that he heard no sirens behind him and would therefore have less trouble doing whatever needed to be done.

He arrived at High Hill Ranch in record time and came to a sudden halt in front of Katie's cabin. The driveway had ended five hundred yards earlier, but he didn't care about that, either.

Her door stood open. The sight of it made his throat constrict. What'd happened? Was she hurt? How badly?

Hopping out, he left his truck idling and ran inside. He didn't see her at first, but there was an overturned chair on the floor. When he called her, she moaned, and he found her lying on the other side of the bed, rolled up in some blankets she'd managed to pull down. Her eyes were closed, and she was shivering violently.

"Katie?" Kneeling beside her, he smoothed the hair off her forehead. "It's Booker."

Her eyelashes lifted, and he read pain in her eyes. "The baby," she said. "The baby's coming."

Booker took a deep breath and jammed a hand through his hair. He'd been afraid of this. He had to get her to a doctor.

"Let's go." Wrapping her in the blanket, he gathered her in his arms as gently as possible and carried her out to his truck.

The rain ran down his neck and beneath his jacket as he deposited her in the passenger seat. Chilled by the blustering wind and his fear of what was to come, he hurried to the other side and climbed in. "You'll be fine," he told her, trying to turn the truck around without jolting her too badly.

"Are we going to Boise?" she asked.

"No. Hatcher's only fifteen minutes from here." He couldn't risk taking her any farther. What if the baby came right away?

"We have to go—" she grabbed her middle but struggled to speak "—to Boise. It's too soon for the baby. Getting to the hospital is probably—" she paused, gasped "—the baby's…only chance."

Booker scowled and shook his head. "No way. It's too far. Anything could happen in two hours. You need a doctor now."

"You don't…*gasp*…even trust Hatcher."

"He's better equipped to handle this than I am. Somehow that goes quite far toward inspiring my trust."

"But I've finally—" she clenched her jaw and groaned, her face so pale it seemed to shine in the semi-darkness, which scared the hell out of him "—made a decision."

"What decision?" He tried to distract her from her pain while he focused on driving so they didn't wind up in a ditch.

"I'm keeping my baby…if she lives…."

This gained his full attention. "I didn't know keeping the baby was ever in question."

"It's not…anymore," she said. "Will you…take me to Boise?"

"Katie, with the mountains and the storm, I won't be able to use my radio if we get into trouble. And there's no cell coverage out here. I don't even own a cell phone."

"Please, Booker." Tears slipped down her cheeks. "If you've ever—" she drew a ragged breath "—felt anything for me at all…do me this one favor."

Too many things could go wrong. What if the baby's lungs weren't developed enough and it couldn't breathe on its own? He suspected Katie was bleeding already. What if she lost too much blood? "You're asking me to risk your life for the baby. I can't do that."

"It should be my— *Oh God!*" she cried. "My decision, right?"

Watching her suffer made him angry—angry at the pain, angry at Andy for getting her pregnant in the first place, and angry at himself for being so helpless. "Damn it, Katie! Do you really want to take a chance like that?"

She didn't react to the edge in his voice. She closed her eyes and leaned her head against the door. When the pain seemed to subside, she looked at him again. "This baby's part of me, Booker," she said fiercely. "It's mine…to protect."

"You have to be alive for that," he spat.

"I'll be fine. I can't let my baby down. She's all I have."

What was he going to do? This was crazy, foolish. And yet he couldn't ignore the determination in her voice and the desperation in her eyes.

The pictures from that baby book flashed through his mind.

Katie's baby was helpless—a true innocent, like Delbert. Booker understood. The same feeling had come over him when he'd jumped into that fight with the Smalls.

But risking himself was one thing. Risking Katie was another…

"Please?" she whispered.

Cursing, he turned left at the highway. Fifteen minutes later, he passed Hatcher's dark office and hoped to God he was making the right decision.

KATIE TRIED TO REST between contractions, but they were coming too hard and fast.

Work with me, baby. Come on, she pleaded and glanced over to see that Booker was as focused as he'd been from the moment he'd picked her up off the floor. Jaw set, he grasped the wheel with two hands—distinctly different from his usual careless pose—and he seemed to mark each of her contractions by tightening his grip.

Katie silently drew comfort from the fact that she was on her way to the hospital and that, barring an experienced doctor, Booker was the one person among her friends and acquaintances she wanted with her right now. He had good instincts, loads of common sense and he could drive really fast. If anyone could get her to Boise in time, he could.

The weather, especially with the twisting, turning highway, was no help at all. Katie braced herself against the door as the truck swerved around one corner and then the next, listening to the wipers swish across the windshield. Sixty swishes between contractions… Fifty-eight swishes…

Thoughts of Andy and her missing computer threatened to creep in, but she willed away the desolation that loss inspired. She'd deal with the rest of her life later. One hour at a time....

"Did something happen tonight?" Booker asked, reaching out to support her so she wouldn't slide off the seat as they took a particularly tight curve. "Why was your door standing open when I got there and that chair overturned?"

Katie couldn't answer right away. She felt another contraction coming on. Gritting her teeth, she focused on breathing through it as best she could. Her baby would face enough difficulties even with a normal delivery. She had to pray she didn't deliver in Booker's truck.

The pain finally released her, and she sagged against the door.

"Katie?" Booker prompted.

She forced her eyelids open but didn't have the energy to lift her head.

"What happened before I arrived?"

"Andy stopped by," she said.

"Did he want you to come back to him?"

She chuckled bitterly. "No, he wanted me to give him money."

"Did you do it?"

"I didn't have any to give him." She seemed to make an effort to calm down. "I've landed a couple of Web site jobs, but I haven't got far enough to warrant a progress payment."

"So...what happened?"

She shook her head, staring at the glowing instrument panel as thunder cracked overhead and the rain fell harder. She couldn't talk about Andy, couldn't let dark thoughts steal her resolve. "Nothing."

"He didn't hit you, did he?"

"No." The pain swelled suddenly with another contraction—only this time it was much worse because she wanted to push. Panicking, she fought the urge, knowing it would be at least an hour before they reached Boise.

Stall. Refuse to let go of the baby. Hang on...

But it was no use. Her body no longer seemed to be taking orders from her brain. Another contraction ripped through her, and another, just seconds apart. Soon she was sweating and shaking so badly, she knew that in a few minutes she'd run out of strength.

To her alarm, she felt the baby move lower, into the birth canal. Then Katie experienced a new kind of pain—the pain of delivery?—and knew they weren't going to make it.

CHAPTER FIFTEEN

BOOKER GLOWERED AT the wet, shiny road. They'd only been driving for fifty-three minutes, but he'd spent every one of those minutes cursing the rain. And the road. And the pain. And the panic. And Andy. And Mike Hill—he didn't know why he was angry at Mike, he just was. And everything and everyone else he could think of, including himself and his inability to drive any faster without risking their lives. He'd been crazy to let Katie convince him to take this chance. Except he couldn't help siding with her in wanting to reach Boise and *real* help, if at all possible.

"Booker?" Katie said breathlessly.

He grunted, following the dotted white lines in the center of the road like a safety rope.

"Booker?" she repeated, the pitch of her voice significantly higher.

"What is it?" He finally looked over, but he didn't like what he saw. She was crying and sliding closer to him so she could lie down.

"You have to...*pant, pant*...stop."

"We can't. There's nothing here, no one to help us. We'll make Boise in another forty-five minutes. Just hang on, okay? The road will straighten out in a few more miles and then I can shave off—"

"Booker, please!" The words, torn from her, filled him with dread.

"The baby's coming right *now?*"

Tears pooled in her eyes. "I can't stop it."

At that moment, he would rather have faced a whole gang of Hell's Angels bent on taking him apart piece by piece than help Katie deliver her premature baby out in the middle of nowhere. But what choice did he have? The worst seemed inevitable. There was no way out.

Swallowing a fresh string of curses, he slowed and looked for a safe place to pull over. After a short distance, a narrow road materialized on the right, heading into a forest. It was remote and muddy, but Booker had a four-wheel drive, and they had to take what they could find.

Tree branches scraped the sides of the truck as they bounced through potholes and puddles. When they'd traveled a hundred yards or so from the highway, he parked but left the engine running so he could keep the heater on. Warmth was the one thing he *could* provide.

Katie was turned the wrong way for him to assist her, but he knew it would be a lot harder for her to change positions than for him. Reluctant to get out in the rain and blast her with cold air, he flipped on the cabin light so he could see and carefully maneuvered his large body around hers in the cramped space. A moment later he was on the passenger side, crouching with one knee on the seat and one foot planted on the floor.

"Close your eyes," she said. "I—I have to take off my pants."

"Close my eyes?" he repeated, astonished. Somehow this wasn't what he'd expected. "You're worried about modesty *right now?*"

"I know it seems silly, but I'm hurting and bleeding and—" her chest heaved as she worked to catch her breath "—I've never felt so vulnerable or unattractive in my whole life. And now my…my pants have to come off and—" She suffered through another contraction.

"And?" he prompted.

She caught her breath. "And I'll be…completely exposed, at my absolute worst."

Booker shook his head in bewilderment. "So? I'm going to see it anyway."

She couldn't answer immediately. Her eyes closed as she endured yet another pain, then she muttered, "I'll do it myself. This…this is my problem, not yours."

"You're not making sense."

"What will Ashleigh think about you being here with me?"

"Forget about Ashleigh," he snapped. "She doesn't have anything to do with…anything. And I might not be the best person for this, but I'm all you've got."

Their eyes met and Katie's filled with tears again. "Do you love her?"

He couldn't believe they were having this conversation. Katie was about to have a baby!

"No," he said. "I never did. Now let's get these pants off." Nudging her hands away when she moved to help him, he stripped off her jeans and her underwear, and tossed them on the floor. Then he turned up the heat, to make sure the baby would be warm enough, and supported Katie's legs. At first she resisted his attempts to gently open them so he could see what was happening with the baby, but another pain convinced her she had no choice about that, either.

"Men should have to suffer—" she swallowed "—such indignities."

Booker would've smiled, except he was too scared. With each contraction, blood and fluid leaked out. But he saw no baby. He thought they might have given up on the trip too soon, that they might have made it a little farther down the road if only they'd kept going. But then she cried out and bore down in earnest—and a tiny bald head slowly emerged.

At his first sight of the baby, Booker felt as though someone had landed a right hook to his chin. His pulse raced and he saw stars. For a moment, he thought he might pass out—drop right there on the floorboards of his truck.

"Booker?" Katie cried, obviously realizing something was wrong.

Steadying himself with a hand on the dash, he closed his eyes and found the anger he'd felt earlier, let it bolster and sustain him. He'd handle this the best way he knew how. He would *not* wimp out on her. "I'm here," he said. "I'm here. I'm fine."

"Okay. I believe you. But I'm so scared...."

"You're going to be okay. Everything's going to be okay." He was trying to reassure himself as much as her because he had no idea if it was normal for the baby's head to appear without the rest of it.

Breathing heavily, Katie tried to see the baby while Booker sorted through the snippets of childbirth scenes he could remember from various television shows or movies. Linens and boiling water. They always asked for linens and boiling water. But he didn't have either and wouldn't have a damn clue what to do with them, anyway.

Using the inside of his T-shirt, because it was cleaner than anything else available to him, he wiped the blood and fluid from the baby's face. Its eyes were closed. Its mouth, too…

Several seconds passed. When nothing else happened, Booker felt his panic rise. Surely this wasn't normal. Surely the baby couldn't survive very long half in and half out. It looked dead already….

God, what now?

"Push," he said because he couldn't think of anything else.

"Okay." She nodded. He could tell she didn't have any strength left, but she gritted her teeth and bore down until the veins stood out in her neck, and he'd never been so proud of anyone in his life.

"That's it, honey. There you go," he said and, miraculously, the newborn slipped out, right into Booker's hands.

It was a boy, he realized vaguely. A very tiny, bluish boy.

Bluish… Was he alive? Booker pulled the baby to his chest, holding him like a football and drying him off with the bottom of the blanket. After their mad dash toward Boise, and all the pain and the panic, it didn't seem possible that the baby could be here, in his arms.

It also didn't seem possible that anything so tiny could live. Katie's son couldn't weigh more than a few pounds. And he still wasn't moving….

"Booker?" Katie tried to rise up on her elbows, but she was wedged between the steering wheel and the seat, and let herself fall back almost immediately, panting with exhaustion. "Is my baby…okay?"

"It's a boy." He didn't know what else to tell her. He

had no idea if things were going to get better or worse from this point forward. But he was betting on worse. A lot worse.

"Why isn't he crying?" she asked. "Can he…*gasp*… can he breathe?"

Booker passed one finger through the baby's mouth to check his air passage for mucous or a blockage of some sort, found it clear, then gently turned the slippery infant upside down and spanked its tiny bottom. Whether that was the correct thing to do or some old wives' tale, he had no idea. But he had to try something.

The baby just hung there, limp and unresponsive.

"Booker?" Alarm rang through Katie's voice when she saw what he was doing.

Sweating from the stress and the heat in the truck, he spanked the baby's butt a little harder, just enough to get a response—he hoped—then held his breath and prayed. He hadn't appealed to God since he was a young boy. It'd been that long since he'd felt particularly deserving of divine intervention. But he pleaded with Him now. *Let this baby live, God. Please. Not for me. For Katie.*

A split second later, the baby let out an angry squall.

BOOKER USED A calling card to phone home, then leaned against the wall, still wearing his bloodstained T-shirt and jeans, because he had nothing to change into. He'd spent the past hour staring blankly at a television screen in the hospital waiting room, trying to calm down. But he could barely stand. He'd never experienced such a rush of adrenaline in his life—and he'd taken more than his share of risks, including the dare that had landed him in prison.

On the other hand, he'd also never experienced such incredible relief as when he'd pulled up to the Emergency entrance at Saint Alphonsus Regional Medical Center in Boise, and watched Katie and the baby being whisked away to receive medical care. The doctors had assured Booker he'd done the right thing in drying off the baby and keeping him warm—they'd driven the last forty-eight minutes with the infant tucked against Katie's breasts, skin to skin, and covered with Booker's leather jacket. Fortunately, the baby's lungs were well enough developed for him to breathe properly, or so the doctors said. And although Katie was bleeding a lot, the doctors didn't seem to think it was excessive.

Delbert finally answered the phone. "Hello?"

"Hi, Delbert."

"Who is it?" he said, sounding a bit apprehensive.

"It's me—Booker." Remembering the strange phone call he'd received earlier, he added, "Why? Has someone else bothered you since I left?"

"Bothered me? No. But…why aren't you in your room?"

"I'm at the hospital."

"What hospital?"

"Saint Alphonsus in Boise," Booker said, even though he knew Delbert wouldn't recognize the name. Delbert had only been to Boise once. After his father died, Booker had taken him to have a look at the special home where he could have lived. They'd both decided it wasn't the right place for him, and that was settled.

"What are you doing at the hospital, Booker? Are you hurt?"

"No, I'm fine. Katie had her baby last night." Booker had washed his hands and face in the restroom shortly after they arrived at the hospital, but there wasn't anything he could do about the blood smeared on his T-shirt. He gazed down at it now, shaking his head in disbelief. "It's a boy," he told Delbert.

"A boy?" he shouted excitedly.

Booker winced and held the phone away from his ear. "Yes. A very tiny one."

"What's his name? Pete? Or Henry? Or Chase, like Chase at work? Huh, Booker? Or—"

Booker broke in, knowing Delbert could go on all day. "I don't know yet."

"Oh." He paused. "Can I talk to Katie?"

"Not right now. The doctors are checking her. I just wanted to let you know where I am. I won't be back in time to open the shop today, so I'll call Chase and have him do it. You just stay put until I get back."

"Stay put? Does that mean I can't go to work?"

"I won't be there to give you a ride."

"I can hitchhike. I always hitchhike. Don't I, Booker? Don't I always hitchhike?"

Booker considered the raspy voice of his mystery caller: *You might not want to let your little retard ramble around on his own anymore, Booker. Poor thing might get hurt again.* "You normally do," he said, "but I don't want you hitchhiking for a while, okay, buddy? You can get rides from me or Chase or someone else you know well, like Rebecca or Delaney. But don't walk alone."

Delbert paused for a long moment, and Booker imagined a confused expression on his face. "Why?" he said at last.

"Because I think Jon Small might be holding a grudge."

"Oh."

Booker started to end the call, but Delbert interrupted.

"What's a grudge, Booker?"

"Nothing you have to worry about," he said with a chuckle. "Just do as I say for a while, and everything will be fine."

"Okay."

When Booker hung up, he called Jon Small. This time Jon's daughter answered.

"Is your daddy there?"

"He's asleep."

"Tell him Booker's on the phone."

She hesitated, but finally agreed. "Hang on."

He heard her set the phone down. A few minutes later, Jon picked it up, sounding groggy and not pleased to be disturbed. "What do you want?"

"I want to know if it was you who called my house in the middle of the night."

"What?"

Booker pulled a handful of change out of his pocket to see how much money he had for breakfast. "Do we have a continuing problem, Jon?"

"I don't know what you're talking about."

"Someone threatened Delbert last night."

"It wasn't me."

"You're sure?"

"Call Earl Wallace. I was playing poker with him and some other friends until two o'clock."

"What about your brother?"

"He was playing poker, too. If you don't stop harassing me, I'm going to call the cops," he said and hung up.

Booker slowly returned the phone to its cradle. He didn't want to believe Jon, but Jon had seemed genuinely surprised by the whole conversation. Which meant last night's call was a crank.

Or someone else was out to hurt Delbert…

MESMERIZED, KATIE STARED DOWN at the tiny infant in her arms. Four pounds, two ounces. That was all her baby weighed. But, thank God, the doctors were very hopeful that her son would thrive. He needed to be kept in an incubator for a while, they said, to maintain his body temperature until he could put on some weight. But he could breathe and suck and swallow, which meant he wouldn't have to be on a respirator or be fed through a tube.

How she'd pay for everything was an entirely different question, but she refused to let reality steal the peace of these few moments with her son. She'd just finished nursing for the first time. Because the baby's temperature seemed stable, they were letting her hold him a little longer.

Adjusting the blue knit cap that was supposed to keep him from losing heat through his head, she tried to think of a name for him.

Matthew, after her favorite actor, Matthew McConaughey? Brandon, a popular boy's name she happened to like? Eric, after her mother's brother who lived in San Diego?

A shadow fell across the floor and she glanced up to see Booker standing in the doorway. Her breath caught at the sight of him, looking rugged and unkempt but as darkly handsome as ever.

"There you are," she said. "I thought maybe you'd gone home."

"Not yet." He sauntered into the room as if he owned

it, and she couldn't help smiling at the way he'd stood by her last night. He'd tried to act as though he was taking the birth in stride—that he wasn't disturbed by such a natural process. But the appearance of the afterbirth had definitely rattled him. He'd turned white as a ghost, very unusual for Booker whose skin was always swarthy, and had to put his head between his knees to keep from passing out.

"What's so funny?" he asked, his eyes narrowing.

"You."

"Me? I generally don't elicit that kind of response."

She knew what kind of response he generally elicited, at least from women.

His eyes seemed to search her face for…something, Katie didn't know what. Then his gaze dropped to the baby.

"Want to hold him?" she asked.

He shook his head. "I don't think so. He's pretty… small."

"You were the first person to touch him, Booker. After last night, I think you can handle it. Sit down."

He didn't look convinced, but he pulled the recliner that was next to her bed a little closer and took the baby.

Katie smiled at the contrast between Booker and her tiny, fragile son. Her baby's skin was pale, almost translucent; Booker's was scarred and dark. Her baby's hands were delicate, perfect; Booker's were nicked and calloused. Her baby was just starting out; Booker had traveled the road of hard experience. And yet, despite Booker's obvious discomfort, they seemed to fit together perfectly.

"I'm trying to figure out a name for him," she said. "Any ideas?"

He was studying her son. "You don't have a couple of names in mind?"

"No."

"Because you were going to put him up for adoption?"

"I was thinking about it."

"Why?"

Katie pulled her blankets higher, the euphoria she'd felt since her baby's birth giving way to exhaustion. "Considering my situation, you have to ask? I don't have anything to give him, Booker. A couple like Josh and Rebecca could provide so much more. And yet—" she sighed "—now I realize I could never let him go. So I guess the two of us are stuck with each other."

She thought of her computer and wondered how she was going to get by in the future. Maybe she'd have to go back to work at Hair and Now until she could save up for another computer. Maybe she'd have to build her Web business on the side.

But if she returned to cutting hair, who would babysit while she worked?

"What's wrong?" Booker asked.

Katie smoothed the worry lines from her forehead and attempted a careless shrug. "Nothing I want to talk about right now."

The baby squirmed, and Booker looked alarmed.

"He's okay," she said, laughing.

With a scowl, Booker changed the subject, probably because he didn't like being so transparent. He typically held his cards closer to his chest. "Tell me what happened with Andy last night," he said.

"I already did."

"You said he wanted money and you wouldn't give

him any. You didn't tell me how that chair got overturned or why your door was open while you were lying on the floor clear across the room."

"When I wouldn't give him fifty bucks, he took my computer. I tried to stop him and fell over the chair. That's all."

"And then what?"

"He left."

"With your computer?"

"Yes."

His face hardened, reminding Katie of how he'd looked the night the Smalls had picked on Delbert. Somehow she fell under his protection now, and he wasn't going to allow Andy to hurt her. "Did he know you were in labor?"

"He didn't stop to find out. He needed a fix, and that was all he could think about."

Booker cursed under his breath. "Someday he and I are going to have a serious discussion."

"I just hope he leaves town soon. There's a lot of drinking and foot-stomping that goes on in Dundee, but we don't have a huge social scene. Most people work hard, go to bed early and get up early. Surely he'll get bored and head back to San Francisco."

In one smooth movement, Booker stood and settled the baby in her lap. "Maybe I'll suggest he do that."

"Booker, no," Katie said. "You already have court-mandated anger management classes. Don't ask for more trouble."

His hand rasped over the stubble on his chin. "Get some sleep. I'm going home so I can shower."

"You don't have any suggestions for the baby's name?"

"I think you should call him Troy."

"Why?"

"Troy's cool."

The half smile on his face made Katie suspicious. "Troy wouldn't be the 'T' in Booker T., would it?" she asked.

He grinned. "Maybe it is. But I *did* deliver him. And you asked me what I thought."

"Troy Rogers," she said, trying it on for size. "I like it. What about a middle name?"

"Troy's my best shot."

He started to leave but she called him back. "Thanks for last night," she said.

With a nod, he was gone.

CHAPTER SIXTEEN

BOOKER SLEPT MOST of the day. When he woke at dinnertime, he took Delbert and Bruiser to the shop, because Delbert was going stir-crazy being cooped up in the house all day and Booker wanted to help Chase close up. Nothing out of the ordinary had happened in his absence—except that the mayor had dropped off his Lincoln Continental so Booker could fix the knocking in the engine. Rebecca's father typically took his vehicles to the next town for service. That he'd brought his car to Lionel & Sons gave Booker the town's official seal of approval—at last. But Booker had never vied for Rebecca's father's good opinion and certainly hadn't been holding his breath.

"Good job today," Booker told Chase, clapping the nineteen-year-old on the back as Chase prepared to leave. "What time did you tell Mayor Wells we'd have an estimate on his—"

A feminine *hem hem* interrupted.

Booker looked up to see Mary Thornton standing just outside the open door to his office. Dressed in a red suit and spiky heels that matched her flashy little sports car, which was parked at the edge of the lot, she smiled sweetly. "Sorry to interrupt. I was hoping you might have a minute to speak to me, Booker."

"Is something wrong with your BMW?" he asked.

Mary also typically took her car to the next town for service. She hadn't cared for Booker since the day they met. When he was fifteen, he used to sit in the bleachers during cheerleading practice and make fun of her and the other cheerleaders. She'd told him way back then that he'd never amount to anything, and liked to treat him as though she hadn't changed her mind, although he was beginning to notice that, as his business prospects improved, so did her opinion of him. She'd begun to wave or smile whenever she saw him.

He hoped the fact that he never responded with much enthusiasm would keep the waving and smiling to a minimum. He didn't find himself as eager to be friends with Mary Thornton as she seemed to think he should be.

"No, nothing's wrong with the Beemer," she said, dimpling. "Although it could probably use a good oil change if you—"

"We're pretty busy around here this time of year," Booker said. "You might want to see whoever's been doing it in the past."

Chase coughed into his hand at Booker's response, and Mary blinked as if she found it surprising he'd turn away a whole 29.95. "Well…can we talk at least?" She glanced at Chase. "Privately?"

"I was just leaving," Chase said. "See you tomorrow, Booker."

As soon as Chase scooted past Mary, he turned and waggled his eyebrows at Booker.

Booker waved him away. "What can I do for you, Mary?"

Her bottom lip came out in a calculated pout. "I don't

know how you feel, but I think we're long overdue to resolve some of the issues between us."

"What issues?"

She cleared her throat. "Well…the resentment, for one. I mean, we're close to the same age, live in the same town, know the same people, go to the same places. And yet I've never felt comfortable around you. Surely after fifteen years, we can put our differences behind us."

Delbert came out of the garage carrying the CV joint he'd removed from Bill Wytrop's minivan. "Booker, can you—" His words fell off the moment he spotted Mary. "Hi, Mary. You look beautiful today." He hurried closer, always eager for company. "Are you going out? Are you going somewhere special? Huh, Mary?"

She slid to her right, as if she thought Delbert might infect her with a contagious disease. But she didn't seem any happier to encounter Bruiser, who'd followed Delbert out of the garage and circled around to sniff her on the other side. "I'm just on my way home from work," she said.

As usual, Delbert didn't pick up on her negative response, which made Booker willing to overlook it. Mary certainly wasn't the first person to snub Delbert. As long as whoever was doing the snubbing didn't take it too far—like the Smalls—Booker let it go.

"You look nice," Delbert repeated.

"Thank you." She attempted a smile, but it was almost pained. "Anyway," she went on, immediately turning her attention back to Booker, "I was wondering if you could meet me for a drink at the Honky Tonk later on."

"I was up late last night. I don't think I'll be coming in to town tonight. But if I do, I'll look for you." He hoped a noncommittal approach would get him off the hook without damaging her pride. It wasn't as if he disliked Mary with any real intensity. He'd never been impressed by her shallowness or, more specifically, her need to pretend she was more than she was. But he realized she was lonely and embarrassed that her life hadn't turned out to be the success story she'd expected. Caring so much about other people's opinions had to be a terrible burden.

"Okay, sure." Her smile faltered for a moment, but then a more purposeful gleam entered her eyes. "I'll hang out there and hope you stop by. Now that Mike and Katie are seeing each other, the two of us should stick together, don't you think?"

"Mike and Katie?"

"Yes. They've been seen together all over town. And now that she lives on the ranch, who really knows *what's* going on."

Suddenly Booker thought he understood the intent of Mary's visit. She was afraid she was losing Mike to another woman the way she'd lost Josh to Rebecca. She wanted to rile Booker, make him jealous so he'd get in the way, cause a problem, maybe even win Katie back. But Booker had already played all his cards—two years ago. Now he was stepping out of the way, not getting further involved. "I don't like being manipulated," he said. "So don't bother trying."

"What?" Her eyes widened in feigned surprise.

"Quit playing games," he said. "I'm the last person who'd do anything to stop Mike and Katie from getting together. She's loved him since she was a girl. Everyone knows that."

"You don't care?" she asked, sounding crestfallen.

Booker could no longer deny, at least to himself, that the exact opposite was true. Last night he would've walked through fire to reach Katie. He was still in love with her, and no amount of denial or logic could change that. But he also knew he cared enough about her to let her have the one man she'd always wanted. A man he knew would be good to her and the baby.

He'd recognized the truth the night he spent at Ashleigh's. But he hadn't completely released Katie, or he wouldn't be planning to head back to the hospital tonight.

He had no business going back, he decided. He needed to stay away. And he needed to get a message to Mike Hill so Katie wouldn't be alone in that hospital for long.

"No," he said and added a manufactured shrug to make it convincing.

MIKE SAT IN O'RILEY'S, a trendy pub in downtown Austin, watching a basketball game on the TV in the corner and having some buffalo wings and beer with Josh and Rebecca. Patty's Charm, the stallion they'd come to see, had turned out to be as beautiful an animal as they'd been told, and they'd decided to purchase him. For the past twenty minutes, they'd been tossing figures around, trying to come up with an offer. But for once, Mike's mind wasn't really on business. He'd tried calling Katie earlier in the day, right before dinner and again just a few minutes ago, and hadn't been able to reach her.

He was beginning to find it strange that she was gone

so long. Especially because she spent most of her time on her computer and didn't generally leave the cabin.

"Hello? Are you going to answer me?" Josh nudged him with an elbow.

Mike quit staring blankly at the TV and focused on his brother. "What was the question?"

Josh scowled. "What's wrong with you, man? You haven't said more than two words all night."

"What are you talking about?" Mike responded. "We've been putting together an offer."

"*Rebecca and I* have been putting together an offer. Your contribution is an occasional grunt. And, for a while there, we lost you completely. What's going on?"

"Nothing. I just—" He glanced at Rebecca, knowing instinctively that she wouldn't like what he had to say. She could sense that his interest in Katie was changing and, because she was so protective of Booker, she didn't like it. But Mike couldn't hold her preferences against her. Rebecca was fiercely loyal to everyone she loved, and Booker had been her friend long before Mike had become her brother-in-law. "I'm just wondering why I haven't managed to reach Katie," he admitted.

"Why have you been trying?" Rebecca immediately pounced on the statement, as he'd known she would.

"I just want to check up on her," he responded, keeping his voice neutral.

"We've only been gone a day and a half."

"So?"

He could see her eyes narrow even in the dim interior of the bar. "Are you two an item?"

"I wouldn't say that, no."

"But you're interested?"

"Maybe."

"I thought you regarded Katie as a little sister." She raised her eyebrow. "You've said so time and time again."

"That was before."

"Before what?" Rebecca asked.

"Before she came back."

Josh's expression bore a noticeable amount of skepticism. "What's changed?"

Mike couldn't really say. "She's matured," he replied with a shrug.

"She's pregnant," Rebecca pointed out.

"That's pretty tough to miss."

"It doesn't bother you?" Josh asked. "In case you're confused, a pregnant woman isn't a casual date. Pregnant women nest. They want to marry and settle down."

Rebecca pushed her small plate away. "Usually the words 'settle down' are enough to send you running for cover. And with Katie, you're talking about someone who's had a crush on you for decades, so you know she's going to want a ring."

Mike took a sip of his beer. "I'm not sure she has a crush on me anymore. Like I said, she seems different. And I'm not afraid of commitment. How many times do I have to tell you that? I just haven't met the right woman."

"But you think Katie might be the right woman?" Rebecca asked.

Mike let his breath go in a long sigh. "I don't know. She needs someone right now. That's all. I'm trying to be her friend. If our relationship develops from there, then—" he wiped the condensation from his beer "—then we'll make adjustments."

Josh gave Rebecca a significant look. "What do you think? Is my big brother finally falling for someone?"

"I'm afraid he might be." Rebecca propped her chin on her fist. "Poor Booker. Why does it have to be Katie?"

Mike stood and tossed some cash onto the bar. "I wouldn't make any wedding plans yet," he said. "I'm going to my room to check my messages."

"Mike?" Rebecca called as he was walking away.

He turned to look at her.

"Katie can't go wrong with either one of you," she said.

Tipping his hat, he grinned. When Josh had first said he was marrying Rebecca, Mike had thought he was making a terrible mistake. But he'd since come to appreciate Rebecca's passion, determination, loyalty and, more than anything, the depth of her love for his brother.

He supposed he and Rebecca were becoming family.

AS KATIE'S BABY SUCKLED at her breast, she stared down at him, overcome by the powerful emotions she felt whenever she held him, thought of him or nursed him. The slight weight of Troy Matthew in her arms, bundled tight in delivery blankets, along with the sweet scent that clung to him, satisfied some deep inner craving. She was a mother. At this point in her life, she had few close friends, no computer and only a small cabin in which to live, but suddenly she didn't care. She'd find a way to provide. This child was hers, and she was going to stand by him and protect him at all costs.

A dark-haired nurse breezed into the room, wearing a purple flowered smock, white slacks and white squishy shoes. "Hi there," she said. "You just about done?"

Katie frowned at the sight of her. Not because she didn't like this particular nurse but because the appearance of any nurse while she had the baby generally resulted in his being taken away and returned to the incubator in the Neonatal Intensive Care Unit.

"Can't we take his temperature and see if he's stable enough to stay with me a little longer?" Katie asked.

"We did that fifteen minutes ago," she replied.

"Can we do it again? I'm waiting for someone." Katie cast a hopeful glance toward the door, listening, as she had during the past few hours, for the approach of booted feet. She wanted Booker to see Troy now that he was a day old. She felt certain Booker would come. He'd been so good to her during the delivery, so strong and determined when she needed him most. His tenderness toward her throughout the whole affair indicated he cared about her, at least a little. Enough for a visit to the hospital, surely.

"I'd like to let your baby stay longer, Ms. Rogers," the nurse said. "But I'm afraid he's been out long enough."

Stifling any further complaint, Katie relinquished her son. It was nearly ten o'clock, which was pretty late for Booker to arrive in Boise, anyway. Especially when he was facing a two-hour ride back. She'd probably been wrong to think he'd bother with such a long trip now that he knew she was in good hands.

Suddenly far more tired than she'd been only moments before, she decided to get some sleep. But once the nurse and the baby were gone, the hospital noises seemed amplified. How was she supposed to rest with so much activity going on right outside her door? Instruments beeping, rattling carts, low voices, nurses coming in every couple of hours to take her blood pressure, check her heart rate and monitor her bleeding....

Massaging her stomach the way the nurse had shown her earlier, to make sure her uterus was contracting as it should, she rolled over and stared at the wall, thinking of her family. Should she call them with the news of Troy's birth? She hadn't wanted to include her parents in her pregnancy. She'd wanted to stay completely away from them. But now that the baby was here, it seemed petty to withhold him from them, to withhold them from each other.

She looked at the phone, wondering how her parents might receive her call. She wasn't sure she could endure much emotional upset tonight. But if her parents were even *slightly* positive, she thought it might be best to make peace. All the books she'd read said that grandparents and aunts and uncles were very important to a child.

Lifting the phone, she started to dial. But she didn't have a credit card that would let her make a long distance call, and she couldn't bring herself to call collect. Not after the way things had ended at the restaurant.

After replacing the handset, she got up and went to the bathroom. Seeing her messy hair and gaunt-looking face in the mirror, she tried to convince herself she was glad Booker hadn't come. It didn't quite work, but when she climbed back into bed she fell asleep at last.

KATIE FELT AS THOUGH she'd been sleeping for only about ten minutes when she heard a man's voice calling her name. She struggled into wakefulness, thinking Booker had finally come. He was here. He hadn't forgotten her. He was just later than she'd expected....

But when she opened her heavy lids and blinked, the blurry figure standing over her bed came into focus and she realized it wasn't Booker at all. It was Mike Hill, holding a vase of tiger lilies. He was dressed in the same kind of clothes he wore most of the time—a blue button-down shirt, a parka and a pair of Wranglers—but he looked rumpled and unshaven.

She'd never seen him looking rumpled and unshaven….

"Mike," she murmured, her brow furrowing. "What are you doing here?"

"Booker left a message on my voice mail telling me you had the baby, so I—"

"*Booker* called you?"

"Yeah. He thought I'd want to know, and he was right." He set the flowers on her bedside table.

"Thanks," she said, "but he shouldn't have bothered you. You were away on business—"

"I've already seen the horse and agreed we should buy it. Rebecca and Josh said they'd handle the rest."

"Oh." She fumbled for the remote that controlled her bed, found it buried under the covers and pushed the button that would raise her into a sitting position. The light of day gleamed around the closed blinds, but she knew it was still early. "What time is it? You must've come the moment you heard."

"It's nearly eight-thirty. I was lucky enough to catch a red-eye out of Austin. And I had my car at the airport, so I was able to drive right over."

"That's good." Obviously he'd gone to a lot of trouble….

"How's the baby?" he asked.

A smile curved Katie's lips. "Great. Want me to call a nurse so you can see him?"

"You bet."

She pressed the button that signaled the nurse. "So, Rebecca and Josh are staying in Austin a few more days?"

"They want to continue meeting with the stallion's owner, see what they can negotiate. This horse is special. We'd love to buy him, but at this point, the owner's asking more than we're willing to pay."

Katie knew Mike and Josh owned a couple of million-dollar studs, so she couldn't imagine how much that might be. "I see."

Mike scowled as he sat in the recliner next to her bed. "When I returned Booker's call last night, he mentioned something about Andy stealing your computer."

"Can you believe that?" She wrinkled her nose in disgust.

"Don't worry about it. I'll get it back for you."

"I'm sure he's sold it by now. I don't think there's any chance of getting it back. I'm just hoping he stays away. If he leaves me and the baby alone for a year, it's considered abandonment and I can petition the court to revoke his parental rights."

"Sounds like you've been checking into legalities."

"I've pulled up a few things on the Internet. I need to talk to a lawyer to double-check that what I've read applies to the state of Idaho, but I'm pretty sure it does."

"Do you think Andy will come back into your life at some point and give you trouble?"

"He wanted me to have an abortion when I got pregnant, so I know he's not interested in being a father right now. But he could change his mind later on."

"Would that be so bad—if he straightened up, I mean?"

"I don't know. He used to be a decent enough guy, before the drugs and the parties and all that. Maybe he'll find that person again. But maybe he won't. Either way, I don't want to deal indefinitely with the possibility that he could show up here and interfere in my child's life."

"What about his folks?"

"I plan on calling them in a few weeks and giving them a choice as to whether or not they want to be involved in their grandson's life. From what I know of them, they're basically good people. I feel I owe them that much."

"Sounds pretty generous to me."

"It's fair." She gazed at the vibrant lilies, wondering if she should tell him that Mary had been the instigator of Andy's appearance at her cabin. Finally she decided to broach the subject. "Are you still dating Mary?"

His scowl darkened as he stripped off his parka. "I told you, we were never really seeing each other—certainly not on a regular basis."

"I don't think she understands that."

"She should. I've never indicated that I'm interested in anything other than being friends."

"Well, you might want to give her a call and… I don't know, straighten out a few things."

"Why?"

"She seems to believe I'm getting in the way of your relationship. She told Andy that you're providing more than a place for me to live, which is why he felt justified in taking the computer. She also said some other stuff—unwarranted stuff."

"Like what?"

She chuckled as though it was too incredulous to

believe. “She intimated that I’m offering something more personal than Web services in exchange for rent.”

“She thinks we’ve been having sex?”

“I guess so.” Katie grinned. “She doesn’t realize that you look at me as a little sister.”

His gaze lingered on her face, his eyes assessing. “I *don’t* look at you that way…anymore.”

Katie caught her breath. When she was only a teenager, she’d made a list of the perfect man’s attributes. Mike fit every category. Handsome. Loyal. Brave. Sexy. He had a college education, a great reputation and he came from a good family. He was even rich.

But some traits seemed more important to her now than others, and Booker seemed to possess all the ones that really mattered. Maybe he wasn’t nearly as “perfect” as Mike—at least not according to the obvious criteria. He had a dysfunctional family and a dark past. He cursed a lot and sometimes drank too much. But he was every bit as handsome and, to her, even sexier because of his rough edges. Now when Katie imagined the ideal man, she pictured Booker carrying her into the bathroom to make her take a bath when she couldn’t get out of bed on her own; Booker’s cut and swollen hands the night he came to Delbert’s rescue; the wonder that had dawned on his face when he’d touched her pregnant belly; Booker supporting her shaky legs and telling her not to be scared when she was delivering Troy in the middle of nowhere.

“Mike, I—”

The nurse walked into the room. “Do you need me, Ms. Rogers?”

Katie decided to let her conversation with Mike go, for the moment. He was afraid of commitment, anyway. She didn't have to worry about him pressing for more than she was willing to give. "How's my baby?" she asked the nurse.

"He's doing great."

"Any chance we can see him?"

"Sure. It's time to nurse again. I was just trying to give you a few more minutes because I thought you were still sleeping."

The nurse bestowed a friendly smile on Mike, to acknowledge his presence, and said she'd be right back.

"I'm glad Booker was around to get you to the hospital," Mike said as she disappeared through the door.

"He wasn't too happy when we had to pull over."

Leaning forward, he rested his elbows on his knees and let his hands dangle between his legs. "Something go wrong with the car?"

"What?"

"Why'd you have to pull over?"

She looked at him more closely. "To have the baby."

"You didn't make it to the hospital?"

"No. I delivered in Booker's truck."

Pushing his hat back, Mike scratched his head. "Really? And how did Booker handle *that?*"

"He was…incredible. He took charge of the whole situation."

Mike's eyebrows rose. "I'll be damned. Booker said you went into labor out at the ranch and couldn't reach me, so you called him and he drove you to the hospital. That's it. He didn't say anything about delivering the baby on the way."

"He wouldn't," Katie said, still thinking of possible motives for Booker to have called Mike in the first place. "You'd have to know Booker to understand how he downplays everything."

At the naked admiration that rang through her voice, a curious expression claimed Mike's face, and she knew she'd given herself away. "Things have changed since you used to wait for me to ride by on my bicycle, haven't they?" he said.

"I'm afraid so," she admitted. Things *had* changed a lot since she was that young, but they hadn't changed much over the past two years. She'd been in love with Booker when she left Dundee. She was in love with him now. But after what she'd been through with Andy, and what Booker had done with Ashleigh, she wasn't sure she could trust him enough to ever tell him that. And—even if she could—considering how badly she'd hurt him, he might laugh in her face.

Anyway, she had a son to think about and a life to rebuild. She was better off alone for the time being. Maybe Mike was coming around, but it was more than two years too late. And Booker probably felt the same way about her.

The nurse showed up with the baby.

"Meet Troy," Katie told him, taking her son in her arms and turning him so Mike could see his face.

"Troy? How'd you pick that name?" Mike asked.

"Booker suggested it. It's his middle name."

Mike's eyebrows shot up. "You named your baby after Booker?"

"He delivered him," she said.

"Is that the only reason?"

Katie couldn't meet his eyes.

"Katie?"

"What?"

“Does Booker know how you feel?”

“I don’t think so,” she said.

“Well, you should tell him. He’s tough to read, but Rebecca knows him better than anyone, and she already gave you her opinion.”

“I heard her say that Booker’s never told her *how* he feels. He probably cares about me the way he does about the other poor unfortunates he helps. That’s all. Anyway—” she pulled her baby’s cap down over his tiny ears “—I have enough to deal with right now, don’t you think?”

He studied her and Troy for a minute. “Maybe you’re right.”

CHAPTER SEVENTEEN

REBECCA SAT ON the closed lid of the toilet while Josh hovered over her shoulder, trying to get a glimpse of the pregnancy indicator and praying that this time it would show pink. They were in the bathroom of their Austin hotel room, doing this yet again. It seemed they'd done countless pregnancy tests over the past year—too many, in his opinion. He wanted to put the whole baby thing on hold for a while, have his wife step back and come to grips with the fact that she might never get pregnant. It tore him up inside to see the devastation on her face at each new disappointment. Somehow she'd gotten it into her head that she'd be less of a woman, less of a wife to him, if she failed to give him children. He had to convince her that he loved her for better or worse, regardless.

But he knew, for her, it wasn't that simple. Her insecurities stemmed from her youth and the fact that she'd never felt good enough to please her father.

"Honey, we could always adopt, you know that, don't you?" he said, the tension in the room increasing as they waited. "And there's no rush."

She looked from the second hand on her watch to the indicator, and didn't respond.

"Honey?"

"I'm pregnant this time. I know it," she murmured. "I feel different."

She always said that. They'd immediately rush out to buy an in-home pregnancy test and learn that it had all been wishful thinking. Afterward, she'd be depressed for days. She'd eventually rebound and be herself for a week or two. Then the whole hope-disappointment-despair cycle would start all over again.

"Besides—" her eyes continued to dart back and forth between the watch and the indicator "—I missed the birth of Katie's baby. Surely fate wouldn't be so cruel."

"Rebecca, I can't keep watching you do this to yourself," he said. "I care more about you than I do about having a baby. And this isn't good for you. You hate needles, so the daily fertility shots are bad enough. But the pressure of this—" he sighed "—this constant trying and hoping and testing is miserable."

"It's going to be worth it," she said. "Delaney and I are going to be pregnant at the same time. You'll see."

Delaney… Ever since Delaney had gotten pregnant, Rebecca had been that much worse. "I want to rethink our plan," he said. "I want to check into adoption."

The indicator turned blue, and his wife's shoulders slumped, just as he'd known they would.

Shit! He hated this.

"Beck, come here." Taking her in his arms, he held her close. "Can't we forget about trying for a baby, just for a while?"

"Your family didn't want you to marry me in the first place," she said.

"That's got nothing to do with this. Anyway, they didn't really know you."

"We grew up across the street from each other."

"They're growing to love you more every day. Look at how well you and Mike are getting along."

"I just want a baby. Is that too much to ask?"

"I've been trying to tell you that we can adopt. Adoption is perfectly fine as far as I'm concerned."

"But I want *your* baby," she said. "That's all I've ever wanted."

He lifted her chin and kissed her. "I love you. But I'll only allow you to go through this one more month. Then I'm going to insist we put everything on hold for at least a year."

No response. Just the tears that wet his shirt as he held her.

"Okay?" he prompted.

He knew she'd finally had enough, too, when he felt her nod.

"KATIE HAD HER BABY last night. Everyone's talking about it," Tami told her husband as he came in the back door of the bakery after taking out the garbage.

The closing door cut off the bright ray of afternoon sunlight that had momentarily blinded her. "Who told you?" he asked.

"Louise over at Finley's Grocery told Mona at Hair and Now, who told Mrs. Bertleson while she was getting her nails done."

"That was Mrs. Bertleson in here a minute ago?"

"Yes."

"I thought she was on a diet."

Tami curled her fingernails into her palms. "She was buying doughnuts to take to her grandkids. Aren't you listening to me?"

He sighed and shoved a hand through his hair. “I heard you. Mrs. Bertleson said Katie had her baby. What is it, a boy or a girl?”

“I don’t know. She congratulated me on becoming a grandmother. I didn’t want to let on I didn’t know about the birth of my own grandchild by asking the sex!”

“So, what *did* you say?”

“I mumbled thanks, but my heart was beating so fast I could hardly speak. It’s only April, which means Katie had the baby two months early. Two months! A baby that premature can face so many problems—”

“If the baby wasn’t okay, Mrs. Bertleson would have said something about that, too. Word spreads fast in a town this size.” He turned his back on her and started sweeping.

Tami struggled to ignore the way he discounted her worry, but she felt her irritation grow with every swish of his broom. “So what are we going to do?” she pressed.

“What do you mean?”

“We need to go to the hospital and check on Katie. We need to see about the baby, too. Barbara told me just the other day that Katie’s been staying at High Hill Ranch, creating Web sites for a living. But I’m sure she hasn’t had time to save much money.”

“If she wants money from me, she’s going to have to give me the apology I deserve,” he said.

Tami closed her eyes. “Don, haven’t the last few weeks taught you anything?”

“What do you mean?”

“We owe her as much of an apology as she owes us.”

He stopped sweeping to glare at her. “What do we need to apologize to her for?”

"I've been thinking about it for a long time, and it took Barb to make me see. More than anything, we were angry at her for embarrassing us in front of our friends and neighbors, and we were trying to punish her for it. Only she's a big girl now, living her own life. She's got a right to choose for herself, without emotional blackmail."

"We're not blackmailing her! We're just trying to teach her what's right." He went back to work, but Tami grabbed the broom handle, determined to stop the annoying noise and get him to listen.

"I'm not saying she's made good choices. But what's right, Don? What's right for *us* to do?"

"The way I see it, the ball's in her court."

"You're wrong this time," Tami said. "You're wrong, and you have too much pride to admit it. But I don't. Not anymore. Some things are just too precious to lose." She stripped off her apron.

"Where are you going?" he asked.

"To see our daughter."

TAMI STOOD IN THE HALL, the new infant car seat she'd purchased slung over one arm. She'd been trying, for the past several minutes, to get her heart to stop pounding so she could step into Katie's hospital room with an unfaltering smile. But it was no use. She was afraid Katie would tell her to leave, refuse to let her see the baby. In a way, she felt Katie would be justified in doing just that. As Katie's parents, she and Don had couched the complexity of their reaction—all the anger, hurt pride, disappointment and desire to control—in righteous indignation. They were right, and she was wrong. Period.

Or so she'd thought until she'd had that talk with Barbara…

Tami wanted to believe that if she hadn't been so preoccupied and worried about Travis, she would've come to this point sooner. But at least she was here now. Somehow she had to find some middle ground between taking a stand for the right and being there for her children, even when they did the exact opposite of what she told them.

She just wished it was easier to find that middle ground.

Nodding politely at a nurse who bustled past, she drew a deep breath and stepped into the room.

A game show was playing on the television. Katie was asleep, but she must have heard the rustle of Tami's movements or sensed her presence, because she opened her eyes almost immediately.

"Mom?" she said, sounding confused.

Tami put the car seat on the floor and stepped close enough to grip the bar on the side of Katie's bed. Katie looked wan and tired. Tami remembered what it was like when Katie was born, how precious she'd been and still was, and wanted to hug her daughter. But she doubted a hug would be welcomed.

"Hi, Katie. How do you feel?" she said, then held her breath as she waited for her daughter's response.

"Fine."

"How's the baby?"

"He's perfect, beautiful," she said softly. "Have you seen him?"

"Not yet. I wanted to check on you first."

A tear trickled out of the corner of Katie's eye and rolled into her hair.

"I'm sorry, honey," Tami said. Then she nearly cried herself when Katie offered her a tremulous smile and held the back of one hand against her cheek.

BOOKER DROPPED THE packet of information he'd received at his first anger management class on the kitchen table and went in search of a pen. His instructor, Mr. Boyle, had given each student homework—or *improvement exercises,* as he called them. Booker had to do all the homework in order to get Boyle's signature at the end of the seven-week course. And he had to get Boyle's signature in order to avoid going back to jail. But Boyle treated the entire class as though they were walking time bombs and spoke in a soft, singsong voice purposely manufactured to show how well he'd mastered his own temper. Booker was afraid that if he had to sit through many more lectures like the first one, he *would* have an anger problem.

"Booker, what are you doing?" Delbert asked, coming in from the living room.

Booker scowled as he dug through the utility drawer next to the sink. "Homework."

"I hate homework." Delbert opened the fridge and helped himself to a soda.

"Me, too," Booker grumbled, but he found a pen, so he returned to the table and slumped into the closest chair.

The phone rang. Delbert answered. "It's Rebecca," he said. "She wants to talk to you."

Booker accepted the handset and propped it against his shoulder so he could still write. Ever since Rebecca had returned from her trip to Austin three weeks ago, she hadn't really been herself, and Booker was worried about her. "'Lo?"

"What's up?" she said.

"I just got back from my first anger management class."

"I know. I talked to Delbert an hour ago."

"He didn't say anything to me."

"I told him I'd call back. What'd you learn tonight?"

"That I'd like to choke the teacher."

He heard her laugh for the first time in more than twenty days. "Oh, that's a good start," she said sarcastically.

"My thoughts exactly. I can already tell I'm going to be one of his top students." He grinned because she was still chuckling. "I'm doing my homework right now."

"What does anger management homework entail? Yoga?"

"Looks like I'm starting out with some kind of questionnaire— 'Are you too angry? Find out by answering the following questions as honestly as possible.'"

"What are some of the questions?"

"When I am angry, I tend to:

a. Hold my feelings inside until I can't hold them in any longer.
b. Immediately strike out verbally or physically.
c. Identify the cause, then take steps to direct or manage my anger by using it in a constructive way."

"That's it?" she said. "That's all the choices? What

if you want to say 'all of the above, depending on the situation'?"

Delbert got a box of a doggy snacks and ambled out of the room. A few seconds later, Booker heard him trying to get Bruiser to roll over and play dead. "There is no 'all of the above.' So what do you think? 'B' might give my instructor some validation."

"'B' might get you held back."

"Some teachers are looking for growth."

"You want him to think you're homicidal?"

"He already does. The class is court-mandated, remember?"

She hesitated. "Okay. 'B.'"

He marked it before reading the next question.

"How do you feel when you're angry?

a. Powerless

b. Worthless

c. Unappreciated

d. Justified."

"Powerless," Rebecca said decisively.

"Powerless?" he repeated.

"Yes! I hate that I can't control my own situation."

She was talking about babies, of course. Unless her body finally cooperated, there wasn't a damn thing she could do about getting what she wanted. And she'd already mentioned, two weeks ago, that Josh was only willing to keep trying for one more month.

"I don't feel powerless," he said.

"How do *you* feel?"

"When I'm angry, I'm angry. It's not complicated."

"Then put 'powerless' for me."

"Okay."

They answered eight more questions and Booker turned to the next section, "Ways to Alleviate Anger."

"What suggestions does it give?" Rebecca asked when he'd read the title aloud.

> "When you're feeling angry, try sitting down and answering the following questions:
> How am I feeling?
> Why am I angry?
> Who am I angry with?
> How can I better approach the problem than to—"

Rebecca made a noise of impatience. "You're supposed to do this *before* you explode?"

"That's what it says."

"But if you had enough control to sit down and analyze your feelings…"

"No kidding."

"I hope this course gets better."

And she hadn't even *met* Mr. Boyle. "So do I." He paused, eager to get to the part of the conversation he'd been waiting for. "So?"

"So what?" she said.

"Are you going to give me an update?"

"I don't know what you're talking about."

Booker slid low and rested his head on the top slat of his chair. "Yes, you do."

"You want to hear about Katie?"

"Who else?"

"It's the first time you've ever come right out and asked me."

He stared at the ceiling, remembering as he did so

often those tense minutes when he was delivering Katie's baby. That experience was the most frightening of his life—except coming face-to-face, five years ago, with what he'd be if he didn't change.

He sighed. The baby's birth might have scared the hell out of him, but it was also the closest thing to a miracle Booker had ever experienced, and he knew he'd never forget it. "How is she?"

"Good. Once she got out of the hospital, she stayed in a motel in Boise so she could continue to nurse the baby, since he couldn't come home yet. But they've released Troy now, and they're both at the ranch."

Troy. Booker smiled at the name. "That's good."

"I stopped by with a few baby things."

"Does Katie need anything else?"

"I don't think so. Delaney and I took her a bassinet and some cute little clothes. Delaney even made her a baby quilt. And her mother bought her a baby tub and a rocker, as well as a car seat."

"So her mother's still helping her?"

"Yeah. I saw them in town yesterday. Tami was holding Troy."

Sitting up, he doodled in the margins of his questionnaire. "Did Mike ever get Katie's computer back?"

"No. He's going to lend Katie a computer until she can afford one of her own."

"I've been over to Andy's cousins' house half a dozen times, but they always tell me the same thing—Andy's gone."

"He must've headed back to San Francisco. I know if you were looking for me the way you've been beating the bushes for him, I'd hightail it out of here."

He chuckled. "No one could scare *you* off."

"Well, no one's seen Andy. Did I tell you Katie's going to start working at Hair and Now tomorrow? She doesn't know it yet, but we're giving her a baby shower in a couple of weeks."

"Who's going to watch the baby while she works?"

"I told her she could bring him with her, but I think her mother's planning to take care of him for the first few weeks."

"Sounds like she's patched things up with her parents."

"From what Katie told me, relations are still strained between her and her father, so Tami's agreed to watch Troy out at the cabin."

Booker pictured Katie holding her newborn in the hospital. He could recall the scent of the baby so vividly…. "That's convenient."

"Yeah."

"Is she still seeing Mike?"

"They're just friends."

"You said he was interested in more."

"He is, but she's not responding."

Booker dropped his pen and shoved the questionnaire away. "She grew up wanting to marry him."

"Maybe things have changed."

"Or she's waiting until the baby's older."

A knock sounded on the front door. "Hang on. Someone's here."

"I've got to go," Rebecca said. "Josh is getting impatient. Just call me tomorrow."

"Okay." He hung up and walked into the living room, but Delbert answered the door before he could reach it. "Booker," he called, "it's Officer Orton!"

Judging by his stance, Orton had come on police

business, but Booker couldn't imagine why. He'd paid his fine and was attending the anger management classes. The misdemeanor assault charge was almost behind him.

"I've got it, Delbert." Booker stepped outside instead of inviting Orton in. Closing the door behind him, he shoved his hands in his pockets and refused to act surprised or worried while he waited for Orton to speak.

Orton let the silence stretch. "There's been another robbery," he finally said.

"Tonight?"

His watery eyes gleamed in the darkness. "That's right."

"Where?"

"You don't know?"

The hair on the back of Booker's neck stood on end at the accusation in Orton's voice. "How would I?"

"Because it happened at 1028 Robin Road."

Booker didn't recognize the number. But he didn't need to. He knew only one person who lived on Robin Road: Jon Small.

KATIE FELT FAIRLY confident that she could smile and be polite when she saw Ashleigh at the gas station or passed her in the grocery store. But she didn't want to work with her. Just the thought of standing across from her at the salon while everyone was swapping stories about the men in their lives, as they often did, made Katie cringe. She didn't want to hear the intimate details of Ashleigh's experience with Booker, didn't want to remember that it had even happened.

But she had to go back to work. Thanks to Mike's willingness to lend her a computer, she could continue to build her Web business on the side. But she needed immediate cash to take care of Troy, to make payments to the hospital for his birth, and to repay her mother the money she'd borrowed over the past few weeks. Katie and her father still weren't speaking, which put her mother in a difficult position, and Katie was especially sensitive to that.

Gathering the bag that held her scissors and beauty supplies, she got out of the red Nissan Mike insisted she use and went into the salon. She wasn't going to sit in the parking lot, dreading Ashleigh. It was better to hold her head high and get their initial meeting over with.

Ashleigh was standing behind the cashier's desk when Katie walked in. At the bell, she glanced up, then smiled brightly, and hurried over to give Katie a big hug. "Katie, I'm so glad you're back!"

Katie pasted a smile on her face and tolerated the embrace. She and Ashleigh had gone to the same school, but Ashleigh was two years younger, she ran with a faster crowd and they'd only worked together for a few months before Katie quit.

"Thanks, it's good to be here." Katie immediately looked to Mona who, at the moment, was the only other person in the salon.

"Good to see you again, Katie," Mona said while she organized her station. "How's the baby?"

Katie felt her smile grow genuine. "He's so wonderful, Mona. I love him more every day. When he gets a little older, I'll bring him in so you can see him."

"I bet he's a doll."

"I can't wait!" Ashleigh chimed in.

Ashleigh's enthusiasm over her return caused Katie a flicker of guilt. Ashleigh found Booker attractive, and had been aggressive in her pursuit, just like the woman named Chevy from the mall. Katie couldn't complain about either one of them. As Rebecca had already pointed out, she had no claim on Booker. But somehow that didn't make what had happened any easier to accept.

"I scheduled Heather Frye with you for an 'up do' in fifteen minutes," Ashleigh said. "Prom's tonight so a lot of the high school girls are coming in to have their hair curled and styled."

Katie liked styling hair for special occasions. She nodded and went into the back to stow her purse. On her way to the front, she waved to Winnie McGiver, who'd just come in to have her nails done, and called her mother to check on Troy. She'd left home only twenty minutes earlier, but this was the first time she'd trusted someone besides the hospital to take care of her son. She needed to assure herself that he wasn't crying uncontrollably.

"He's fine," her mother said. "I've raised two kids of my own, remember? I can handle him."

"Call me if you think he wants to nurse."

"I've got that bottle you expressed. I'll let you know if we need more."

"He likes to lie on my chest and sleep. If he's fussy, you might try that."

"He's not fussy," Tami said. "He's sleeping soundly."

"And the rocking chair helps if—"

"Katie!"

"Okay, I know. I'm worrying about nothing. Everything's fine."

"Don't you have work to do?"

"Yes, my first client's here. I'd better go."

Hanging up, Katie smiled at Heather, who was just coming through the door. “So you’re going to prom tonight, huh?” she said. “What did you have in mind for your hair?”

As they walked to Katie’s station, Heather told her she wanted the front of her hair up and the back falling in ringlets. Katie was draping a cloak around Heather when she heard Winnie say something that caught her attention.

“I don’t know why the police haven’t figured out who’s doing these darn robberies. It’s a shame when a person isn’t safe in her own home.”

Katie glanced over to see Mona painting Winnie’s nails with what looked like a shimmering opal lacquer. “Are you talking about what happened to poor Mrs. Willoughby, Winnie?” she asked.

The bell over the door tinkled just then, and Mary Thornton stepped in. Her sunglasses made it difficult to read her expression, but she was wearing a purple suit and her face turned a similar shade the moment she saw Katie.

Katie couldn’t believe she had to face Ashleigh and Mary on the same day. “Hi, Mary,” she said, deciding to make the effort to be friendly.

Winnie and Mona said hello to Mary, too. Ashleigh was on the phone, and Rebecca wasn’t around. Katie thought it was probably no coincidence that Mary had scheduled her nail appointment for Rebecca’s day off. Rebecca had never liked Mary, and Mary certainly felt no love for Rebecca. Especially now that Rebecca was wearing Josh’s ring.

Mary gave her a chilly nod, but smiled at the others, then removed her sunglasses and sat down to wait for Mona.

"Winnie was just talking about the robbery last night," Mona told Mary.

"Everyone's talking about it," she murmured, thumbing through a magazine.

"You're defending Slinkerhoff's nephew, right?" Winnie said. "Do the police think he did this, too?"

When Mary raised her eyes, she looked at Katie, even though it was Winnie who'd spoken. "Haven't you heard?"

"Heard what?" Katie said, feeling oddly singled out.

"It was Jon Small's place that was broken into, and nothing much was stolen. It's more like an act of revenge."

Katie's heart leaped into her throat, but she refused to show her fear. "So?"

"They think Booker did it."

CHAPTER EIGHTEEN

After her first day of work, Katie was in a hurry to get back to Troy. But she couldn't pass Lionel & Sons without stopping in. Considering what Mary had said, Katie was worried about Booker. Somehow, that took precedence over the decision she'd made in the hospital to keep a safe distance from him.

She couldn't see Chase or Delbert. They seemed to be gone for the day. But she could hear Booker talking on the phone as she approached his office. She knew he hadn't noticed her pull up when she knocked softly on his open door and he glanced over his shoulder—and blinked in obvious surprise.

"I'm telling you I think there might be a problem with those tires," he said into the phone. "I don't care about that… I sell more snow tires than anything else… Listen, I've got someone here. Call me tomorrow, okay?"

He twisted away to hang up, then turned back to face her, and the tension in the air seemed to crackle like static electricity. Stretching his legs out in front of him, he crossed them at the ankle and his gaze dropped to Katie's high heels and slowly worked its way up her legs, over her short denim skirt and stretchy T-shirt before meeting her eyes again. "What's up?"

No wonder women fell at his feet. Just the way he *looked* at her made Katie breathless. She had a sudden impulse to cross the room, slip into his arms and let him kiss her with that wicked mouth of his while her hands roamed over the muscles and contours she remembered so well. But she supposed her hormones were still a little screwed up, because Booker wasn't part of her immediate plans. She wasn't even sure he was part of her long-term plans. She was a mother now and was going to move much more cautiously in the future than she had in the past. She'd only come to *talk*...and support him, if there was any way she could.

"I heard Jon Small's place was broken into last night," she said.

He turned a pen over and over in his hands. "Who told you?"

"Mary Thornton. She just came into the salon."

"Watch yourself around that woman."

"Why would I need to watch myself?"

He tossed the pen onto the desk. "Because you've got the man she wants, and she's out to get him back."

"I don't 'have' Mike. We're just friends."

He cocked an eyebrow at her. "I thought you were going to marry him someday."

"Is that why you sent him to the hospital?"

"I didn't *send* him to the hospital. I just let him know you'd had the baby."

"You didn't tell him you delivered Troy."

"I didn't figure he'd be interested in that part."

She folded her arms and tapped one foot. "So now you're playing Cupid?"

"No, I'm just getting out of the way."

"I have to work with Ashleigh now," she said, and wasn't sure why she'd said it, especially so sullenly.

With a sigh, he closed his eyes and ran one finger

over his left eyebrow before looking up at her again. "If you don't care about me, Ashleigh shouldn't make any difference, right?"

"Tell me what happened between you and Jon Small," she said, trying to get back to the reason she'd stopped by in the first place—before the conversation could drift any further into topics she'd rather not discuss.

"Nothing."

"Then why do the police think it was you who broke into his house?"

"Because folks around town aren't particularly happy there's a robber on the loose, so the police need a suspect. Problem is they don't know how to actually *solve* a crime. They can only pick someone they don't like and go with that."

"Then tell me you have an alibi—preferably one that doesn't depend on Delbert. Or Ashleigh," she added before she could catch herself.

She hoped he was going to ignore this latest jab but knew better when he stood up and shut the door. "I'm sensing some hostility here," he said. "Maybe we should talk about it."

"No, never mind. I didn't mean anything by what I said." She took a step back for every step he took toward her, but it didn't do any good. A moment later, he had her backed up against the wall and closed the remaining distance between them in two long strides.

"First of all, you left me for Andy," he said, propping an arm against the wall over her left shoulder.

"I—I know that." The scent of leather, mingled with Booker's aftershave, distracted her as he moved closer.

"Second of all, you never looked back."

That wasn't entirely true. She'd spent many nights in

San Francisco, lying awake, missing Booker. She just hadn't had any confidence that her life would've turned out better if she'd stayed with him. She'd always told herself her only mistake in getting away from Booker was jumping from the fire into the frying pan. "And third?" she said, her heart beating so hard she could feel it knocking against her ribs.

"Third, we weren't committed in any way when I went home with Ashleigh."

She stared up at him because she couldn't argue. She might have looked back once she'd left him, but she certainly didn't do anything to let him know it. And he was right about the other two.

"So why are you holding Ashleigh against me?" he asked.

She could smell wintergreen on his breath and knew he'd probably been snacking out of the vending machine Delbert loved so much. "I—I'm not."

"Sounds like it to me."

She couldn't think when he was standing so close. "Maybe that's because you forgot about number four."

"What's number four?"

"That night you broke my heart." His eyes lowered to her lips, and she knew he was going to kiss her. She also knew she should push him out of the way so she could leave. But her legs felt cemented to the spot. Closing her eyes, she tilted her face up—and was surprised to realize that her arms went around him before his ever came around her. He *hadn't* been about to kiss her. But it didn't matter. Her body had a will of its own. She found his mouth, and kissed him as though she was half-starved for the taste of him.

His kiss was familiar and satisfying, everything

she'd missed. She groaned as he offered her his tongue, remembering and reacquainting herself. He responded by kissing her more deeply while pressing into her.

Feeling the hard planes of his body as well as his erection caused warmth to pool low in her belly.

"Booker, I don't think they remembered your pickles." Delbert flung open the door as he charged inside with Bruiser, carrying a take-out bag from the diner.

Booker quickly pushed Katie away from him, but it wasn't quite fast enough to go unnoticed. Delbert glanced between them, looking confused. "Hi, Katie."

Katie took a deep breath, trying to even out her pulse, and moved away from Booker to give Delbert a hug. "Hi."

"I heard you had your baby." Bruiser nudged her with his wet nose as Delbert touched her stomach. "Look! You're skinny again."

She smiled, but her lips seemed to tremble with the effort. "I'm getting more back to normal each day."

"Booker said he'd bring me over to your place. I really want to see the baby. I keep asking him and asking him but—" a sulky expression appeared on his face "—he's always too busy."

"Of course he's busy, but you're welcome anytime." She sidled toward the door.

"Can we visit tonight?"

"Sure, okay," she said, fully conscious that Booker hadn't spoken a word in the last sixty seconds. She'd wanted to rip off his clothes a moment ago, could hardly speak now for the pounding of her heart, yet she couldn't tell whether their kiss had had any lasting effect on him.

"Is it okay if we go over there tonight, Booker?" Delbert pressed.

Booker didn't answer, so Katie chanced another look his way. "Are you coming over tonight?" she asked, then held her breath as she waited for his answer.

"Maybe," he said. "We'll see."

"BOOKER, IT'S GETTING LATE. If we don't leave right away, the baby will go to sleep," Delbert complained, nagging him, once again, about going to Katie's.

Booker muted the television and glanced at his watch. Eight o'clock. The minutes had been dragging by, and Delbert's impatience wasn't making things any easier. Booker had hoped that if he stalled long enough, Delbert would forget about the baby, at least for tonight. After what had happened in his office, Booker wasn't sure he wanted to see Katie. He'd been down the same road with her once before, and it hadn't led anywhere.

"I think Troy sleeps most of the time, anyway," he said.

"I don't care. I want to see him. Please, Booker?"

Booker considered allowing Delbert to hitchhike to Katie's. Ever since that threatening call, he'd stopped letting him ramble around on his own. But nothing worrisome—at least as far as Delbert was concerned—had happened in the past few weeks. Booker was almost convinced that strange call had been some kind of joke.

But he remembered finding Delbert the night the Smalls got hold of him and decided there was always the possibility that it wasn't....

Tossing the remote aside, he stood. "Okay, I'll drive you out there. But Bruiser has to stay home."

"Okay. Thanks, Booker. Thanks a lot!"

Booker shrugged into his jacket and headed to the door. Delbert ran to his room and brought back a gift, crudely wrapped in newspaper with an excess of tape.

"What's that?" Booker asked.

Delbert's smile stretched across his face. "It's for the baby."

"What's inside?"

"A surprise."

KATIE NORMALLY SPENT her evenings nursing and bathing Troy, and rocking him in the chair her mother had given her. Or she slept, if she could. Troy was getting up at least twice every night, and she hadn't yet adapted to the new schedule.

Tonight her son required little attention, but she didn't go to bed. She curled her hair and touched up her makeup, just in case she had visitors. She was trying on clothes and checking the mirror to decide which outfit looked best, when the phone rang.

She eyed it nervously, wondering if it was Booker. "Hello?" she said, sinking onto her bed wearing jeans and a cream sweater that made the most of her returning figure.

"How's the baby?" her mother asked.

Katie looked over at Troy, who was lying in his bassinet. "Fine."

"He's such a doll. He was so good for me today while you were at work. I gave him a car ride over to see Travis."

Katie wondered if she'd also shown him to Don, but didn't ask. "I really appreciate you taking care of him. What with prom tonight, I made some good money."

"I'm so glad. Are we on for tomorrow, then?"

"Isn't Dad going to get angry that you're coming here and helping me instead of staying at the bakery?"

"My day's mostly over before yours begins. He just sells what we have left after the morning rush while he cleans up the place."

"I don't want this to come between you, though," Katie said.

"Don't worry. I think it's a stand I need to take."

There was a knock at the door, and excitement filled Katie at the prospect of seeing Booker. She knew she was crazy to be feeling the way she was, but she couldn't help it. She wanted another kiss…tonight.

"I have to go, Mom," she said.

"What time do you need me tomorrow?"

"Ten o'clock. But I'll come home and nurse after the first couple of hours."

"Okay."

Katie ended the call. Now that she and Tami were getting along, she didn't want her mother to hear Booker's voice in the background and resume her old complaints.

As soon as she opened the door, Delbert nearly bowled her over. "Hi, Katie! We're here. Booker brought me. We're here to see the baby."

Booker stood off the concrete porch, a toothpick dangling from his mouth, hands in his pockets. When Katie looked out at him, he gave her a slight nod. In deference to the baby, they'd obviously left Bruiser at home.

"Come in," she said.

Delbert handed her a rectangular shape wrapped in thick bunches of newspaper and masking tape. "I brought you something. It's for the baby."

Katie smiled as she accepted his gift. "Thank you, Delbert."

"It's from Booker, too."

"It is?" She raised an eyebrow at Booker and saw a flash of white teeth as he grinned and shrugged.

Spotting the bassinet, Delbert headed right over to it. "Is this the baby, Katie? Can I hold him, huh? Can I hold him now while we're here?"

"Sure." She set his gift aside so she could lift Troy. "Sit on the couch there, and I'll hand him to you."

Delbert obeyed immediately, his eyes wide as she settled Troy in his arms. "Whoa," he breathed. "He's *little.*"

"He is little. So be sure you hold him very carefully, okay? Keep him in the crook of your arm like this."

"Oh, I'll be careful. I wouldn't ever let anything happen to him." Delbert sat very, very still. "He's wonderful. He's wonderful, isn't he, Katie?"

Katie smiled. "He's sweet like you."

A blush tinged Delbert's cheeks, but he continued to stare at the baby. After several minutes, he remembered his gift. "Are you going to open my present now? I think the baby will like it."

"You bet."

Booker stood at the edge of the room, near the door. Katie was conscious of him watching her and had a difficult time focusing, but she wanted to give Delbert the attention he deserved.

Sitting on the couch so she could help him with Troy if necessary, she tore the wrapping off the package to find the model car he'd shown her, with such pride, that first night at Booker's house.

"Oh, Delbert!" she said. "Are you sure you want to give this to Troy? It's your most prized possession!"

"Booker helped me build it," he said.

He'd already told her that. Several times. She realized now that was why the model held such worth. That Booker had cared enough about him to help him build it. And he was giving this treasured item to her....

Fighting tears, Katie looked over at Booker. He took helping Delbert in stride, treated him like a brother instead of a burden. She didn't know anyone else who would have done so much, so ungrudgingly.

"You and Booker are pretty special," she said. "I'll put this car up on my shelf where I can see it all the time, and it can remind me of the two of you, okay?"

She made a big production of letting Delbert find just the right place to put the car, which turned out to be a prominent spot on her entertainment center, then gave him a hug.

"Aren't you going to hug Booker?" Delbert asked when she stepped away.

"Uh...yeah, of course. Thanks, Booker," she said and gave him a very brief, formal hug.

"Booker, you want to hold the baby?" Delbert asked.

Katie thought Booker would mumble something about how late it was and slip out the door before Delbert really cornered him. But he didn't. He walked over and lifted Troy gently out of Delbert's arms, then sat in the rocking chair. "Got any movies?" he asked.

THEY WATCHED THE NEWS and an old sitcom because Katie didn't have a VCR or a DVD player. Delbert fell asleep on his end of the couch almost immediately, and Katie felt her eyelids grow heavy soon after. Somehow, sleep was even more inviting when there was someone around to help watch over her son. Then she didn't feel as though she needed to jump up every few minutes just to be sure Troy was breathing.

"Do you want me to take him?" she murmured softly as the sitcom went to a commercial, wondering if Booker was getting tired, too, and wanting to go home.

"I'm fine." He still sat in the rocking chair. "Go ahead and get some rest."

She dozed off after that. She thought she heard the baby fuss a couple of times, but Troy didn't cry in earnest. When her son finally demanded her attention, she was surprised to see by the glowing numerals on her alarm clock that nearly three hours had passed.

"He's hungry," she said, trying to wake up enough to find her feet and get him. But she didn't need to go anywhere; Booker brought him to her.

At some point, Booker had turned off the lights and lowered the volume on the TV. Even with Delbert sleeping on the couch, the room felt close and quiet. Katie put her back to Delbert and settled the baby so he could nurse, and Booker started to move away. But she didn't want him to leave. Catching his hand, she rubbed his knuckles against her cheek.

Booker met her eyes for a long moment, then lowered them to watch Troy nurse. Feeling his interest, his curiosity about the whole baby process, she pulled her shirt slightly higher.

Kneeling beside her, he trailed one finger lightly over the swell of her breast to Troy's mouth. "Beautiful," he murmured.

The reverence in his voice surprised her. She let him watch a couple of minutes longer. "Booker?"

"Hmm?"

He bent his head. She thought he was going to kiss the place he'd touched on her breast. Her stomach tensed with anticipation and she caught her breath, but he kissed Troy's head.

"You're a soft touch," she said.

He chuckled. "Yeah, well, just don't tell anyone, okay?"

She admired his dark eyes, and the thick lashes that framed them. "I'm scared."

"Of what?"

"Are they going to arrest you?"

He sighed. "No. There were a few things taken from Jon's house. If Orton's warrants come through right away, he'll search the farmhouse and the garage in the morning. But when he doesn't find anything, I'm hoping he'll let it drop."

"What if he doesn't?"

"There's no evidence linking me to that crime. I was in Boise or driving most of the night."

"Then how can they even believe it was you?"

"They're saying I could've done it on my way home, but I think they'll eventually realize that I wouldn't have had time. Anyway, a good lawyer should make a big difference."

"I hope so."

Delbert stretched and yawned, and Booker stood. "Come on, Delbert," he said. "We're leaving now."

"Thanks for holding Troy so long and letting me sleep," Katie said.

While Delbert was rubbing his eyes, Booker lifted her shirt for another quick peek at Troy nursing. "It was worth it," he said with a devilish grin. Then he and Delbert left.

KATIE COULDN'T BELIEVE IT. Booker liked the baby. A lot. He certainly didn't strike her as the cuddly baby sort. But she remembered him holding Troy last night, remembered his hands on her belly when she was pregnant and how involved he'd been in getting her the maternity clothes and the doctor she needed, and realized that he'd been fascinated by her pregnancy from the beginning. When she considered why that might be, she supposed she could understand. Booker was drawn to people who needed him, and no one was more dependent than a newborn.

Smiling as she pictured the sweet kiss he'd given Troy last night, she leaned closer to the mirror to finish applying her mascara. At this speed, she'd be late for work, and Rebecca had already called to let her know she had a ten-o'clock appointment.

Troy cried, interrupting her rush to get ready, but her mother showed up only a few minutes later. Holding her son close, Katie pressed her cheek to his bald head for a moment, then passed him to Tami. "I expressed some extra milk. It's in the fridge," she said, grabbing her purse and keys. "And—"

"I know." Her mother chuckled. "Call you if he needs anything."

Katie smiled and threw her arms around Tami. "Thanks, Mom. I don't know what I'd do without you. After Andy took my computer…well—" she glanced nervously at her watch "—you're a godsend, let me just say that."

"I'm enjoying the time with my grandson."

"Dad didn't have a problem with you coming today?"

"He'd have less of a problem if you'd go over and talk to him."

Katie grimaced. She wanted peace with her father, but she wasn't sure she wanted it on his terms. "I'll think about it," she said and hurried off.

When Katie arrived at the salon, Rebecca was in the back opening product shipments. Delaney was sitting next to her, drinking a small bottle of orange juice while they talked. Emily, Delaney's little girl, was probably with her daddy, because she wasn't around.

"Where is everyone?" Katie asked after leaving her purse in a locker.

"Mona phoned to say she's running late," Rebecca said. "She's already rescheduled her first appointment, though. And Ashleigh doesn't come in until one."

Katie breathed a sigh of relief. She had a few things she wanted to ask Rebecca, and she didn't want to do it in front of Ashleigh.

"Have you heard anything yet?" she asked, interrupting Rebecca as she was writing prices on the small green stickers they used to mark the hair products they sold.

"About what?" Rebecca asked.

"About Booker."

Delaney put the lid on her orange juice.

"What about him?" Rebecca said.

"You know there was a break-in at Jon Small's house, right?"

Rebecca's forehead wrinkled in confusion, and her "no" was quickly echoed by Delaney's.

"Two nights ago someone broke into Jon's house. They messed up the place, stole a few things, and—"

"Don't tell me the police think it was Booker," Rebecca said.

Katie nodded.

"Because of that fight a few weeks ago?"

"And his reputation, I'm sure."

"That's crazy!" Delaney said. "Booker would never do that."

"Booker's grown up, changed," Rebecca concurred. "He'd never steal from anyone. That car he took before was because of a dare. He didn't really even want it."

"I guess Officer Orton was hoping to search the farmhouse and the garage this morning to see if he could find the stuff that was stolen," Katie told them. "I don't know what time he was planning to do that, but I thought it might've happened early."

Worry knitted Rebecca's eyebrows. "Booker called me yesterday, but Josh and I were so busy I never got back to him. I just figured I'd call him today."

"He doesn't seem too concerned," Katie said.

"Weren't you with Booker two nights ago?" Delaney asked Rebecca.

"No, but..." Rebecca tapped her lip with one finger. "That's the night I talked to him on the phone. He'd just gotten back from Boise. He had anger management class."

"They think he did it on his way home," Katie said.

"You're kidding!" Delaney cried.

"No."

"That's it," Rebecca said. "I'm calling my dad."

Katie and Delaney, who was barely starting to show, followed Rebecca to the phone and waited nervously while she dialed her parents' house, then City Hall before managing to track down her father. When she finally had Mayor Wells on the phone, Katie curled her fingernails into her palms and prayed for good news.

"But I know he'd never do anything like that, Dad," Rebecca said. "I don't care what he's done in the past.

It's not right that the police should automatically assume it's him just because he spent some time in prison several years ago… So? Whoever broke into Jon's place is probably the same person who robbed Mrs. Willoughby, and I know for a fact that Booker would never expose himself…. He doesn't need to get cheap thrills like that… He can have almost any woman he wants… What?"

Katie watched Delaney lean closer, so she could hear Mayor Wells' response, and did the same.

"Leah Small says Booker's been harassing Jon. Jon's daughter confirmed it," he said. "Booker went out to their house one day to threaten Jon. And he's been calling him at all times of the day and—"

"Booker's not the aggressor in that relationship, Dad," Rebecca broke in. "I told you he was defending Delbert against the Smalls. That's what started the whole thing."

"And I believed you. But now I'm wondering if he's decided to get revenge for the arrest and whatever else happened that night."

"Booker's not after revenge! He just wants the Smalls to stay away from Delbert."

"Then it shouldn't matter if they search his place. What's wrong, Rebecca? Are you worried they might find something?"

"I'm not worried at all! I—"

"I know Booker's your friend, Beck," her father said. "But I can't step in just because you two are close. Believe it or not, I'm actually starting to like him. However, I still have to let the police do their job."

Rebecca glanced from Katie to Delaney and shook her head. "Fine," she said into the phone. "Just call me when they're done, okay? I want to hear you say the police were wrong."

Katie's ten o'clock came in just as Rebecca hung up. A recently divorced Sheila Holley wanted a completely new style. Katie felt it was about time Sheila cut off her long straggly hair, but Katie didn't enjoy the transformation as much as she would have if her thoughts hadn't been on Booker and the police who were searching the farmhouse while she worked.

Delaney promised to check in later and left. The hours dragged as Katie went from Sheila's cut and style to a perm and then home to nurse Troy and back to do a color. Ashleigh arrived at one o'clock, but Katie barely noticed her. She was too focused on the telephone, jumping every time it rang.

Rebecca's father didn't call until well after lunch. Katie was doing Mrs. Reese's weekly set, but she paused, comb in hand, as Rebecca took the call.

Katie could tell instantly that it wasn't good news. Leaving Mrs. Reese in the chair, she crowded beside Rebecca at the front desk, feeling as though her stomach had just turned into lead. "What did they find?"

Rebecca shoved a hand through her hair as she hung up. "I can't believe it. I just can't believe it."

"What?" Katie touched Rebecca's elbow. "Tell me."

Rebecca forced her eyes away from some indefinable point in the distance. "They found a car."

"A *car?*" Katie echoed.

"It was in a gully on Booker's property, and covered with brush. My father was just out there. He said it's quite obvious that someone went to great lengths to hide it. So, of course, now they think the worst."

CHAPTER NINETEEN

WHEN KATIE PASSED Booker's shop on the way home from work, it was closed—just like it had been when she'd gone home for lunch. She wondered if the police had arrested him. If so, they were wasting their time. Booker couldn't have stolen that car. There had to be some other explanation. She knew he'd made some stupid mistakes when he was younger, but that chapter of his life was over.

Too upset to continue home, she stopped at the diner and used the payphone inside to call the farmhouse.

No one picked up, not even Delbert. Tempted to drive out there to see if she could learn what had happened since the mayor's call, she glanced at her watch. Troy needed to nurse again. And she had to let her mother leave. Tami had been babysitting for nearly seven hours.

With a sigh, Katie gave up trying to reach Booker and drove to the ranch.

"What's wrong?" her mother asked the moment she walked through the door.

"Nothing. Why?"

"You look upset."

Katie *was* upset. She wanted to talk to Booker, make sure he was okay. But at least Troy seemed to be doing well. He was sleeping peacefully in his bassinet, despite the fact that it was feeding time. “I’m just tired,” she said. “And it’s hard to leave the baby.”

Tami used the remote to turn off the television. “Oh. I thought you might’ve heard about Booker.”

Katie’s stomach muscles tensed. Surely word hadn’t spread already.... “What do you mean?”

“Don called me from the doughnut shop. I guess Officer Orton stopped in for a cup of coffee and mentioned that Booker’s stolen another car.”

The news *had* spread. Only in Dundee... “Orton doesn’t know that.”

Her mother’s thinly penciled eyebrows notched up. “So you *have* heard about Booker?”

“Rebecca said something about it at the salon earlier. But I haven’t been able to get hold of Booker to find out what’s really going on.”

“I’ll tell you what’s going on,” her mother said. “He’s been stealing cars and harassing the Smalls.”

“Mom—”

“Trudy Johnson, my new next-door neighbor, is a good friend of Leah’s. They play Bonco together once a week. And Trudy said Leah told her that Booker’s out to get even with Jon. He blames Jon for getting him thrown in jail a few weeks back.”

“He *should* blame Jon,” Katie said. “Booker found Jon, his brothers and his cousin beating up on Delbert. Booker stood up for Delbert.”

“Maybe that’s what Booker told you, but—”

“I know what happened. I was living with Booker at the time. I saw him and Delbert when they got home.” Troy began to stir and she went over to pick him up. “Delbert’s the one who told me what happened.”

“He’d say anything to protect Booker. He idolizes him.”

"He wouldn't lie. I don't even think he knows *how* to lie."

"When someone's not right in the head, you can't take anything for granted," her mother said, gathering up her purse and her coat.

Katie had been about to feed Troy, but the Model-T that Delbert had given her sat on the top shelf of her entertainment center, reminding her how sweet Delbert was—and how good Booker was. After listening to her mother's derogatory tone, Katie had too much adrenaline pumping through her to sit down. "I care about Booker," she said abruptly.

Her mother hesitated at the door. "I know you've always liked him, but—"

"No." Katie broke in. Troy's squirming had progressed to fussing, but Katie couldn't feed him just yet. She'd finally reached the point where she could no longer deny or avoid the truth. "I don't only like Booker, Mom. I'm in love with him."

Her mother's hand dropped from the doorknob. "What?"

"It's true. I haven't wanted to admit it, even to myself. That's why I left here to begin with. I was in love with Booker and afraid I was making a terrible mistake. Only leaving with Andy was the real mistake."

"Katie, Booker's a car thief!"

"I don't believe it."

"Then, where did that car in the gully come from? Cars don't materialize out of thin air."

"The police are checking. I'm sure they'll realize it was an old car of Hatty's or…or something," she said, although she doubted Hatty was the type to leave an old car on her land. Scrupulously clean and frugal, Hatty had waged war on dirt and waste the whole time Katie had known her.

Her mother tapped her own chest, as though she was finding it difficult to breathe. “But…but what about Mike? I’ve been hoping the two of you would get together. You’re perfect for each other. His mother told me before you had the baby that he’s interested in you. Can you imagine? The man you’ve always wanted is interested in you after everything that’s happened? How many men would be that open-minded?”

Mike *was* wonderful. Katie didn’t know how she would’ve gotten through the last few weeks without his friendship and support. He was definitely her childhood ideal. But her heart belonged to Booker.

“I’m sorry, Mom,” she said. “I know you and Dad don’t like Booker, so—”

“Think of the life you’d lead if you married Mike. Think of the home you’d have, the father he’d be.”

Troy was now crying so loudly that Katie could barely talk over him. She pulled up her shirt and settled him to nurse without sitting down. “I can’t change the way I feel, Mom. I’ve already tried—for more than two years. And I’m right back where I started.”

Tami’s shoulders slumped, making her look older than Katie had ever seen her—old and exhausted. “What am I going to tell your father?”

“Tell him—” she took a deep breath “—why not tell him to have some faith?”

“Faith?”

“In me.”

Her mother stared at her for several long seconds. “Are you sure Booker’s who you want?”

“He’s who I want. That doesn’t mean I’m going to

get him. He asked me to marry him once, and I turned him down. I'm not sure I'll have another chance."

"I guess there's hope in that," Tami said. But she smiled grudgingly when she said it, and Katie couldn't help laughing.

KATIE WAITED BY THE PHONE that night, hoping Booker would call. She'd left several messages on his answering machine, but now that it was nearly eleven o'clock, she was afraid she wouldn't hear from him.

Briefly, she considered calling Rebecca. Surely Rebecca would've talked to Booker at some point today. Even if she hadn't, she'd know more about what was going on, from her father or the police. But Katie didn't have call-waiting and she'd been afraid to use the phone in case Booker tried to reach her. And now it was too late to call Rebecca.

After a long evening that had passed with painful slowness, she placed Troy in his bassinet and took a shower. She let the hot water run over her body, hoping she could relax enough to sleep. But she kept picturing Booker in a jail cell, with Orton telling everyone around town that he'd stolen another car.

Where had that car come from? And why was it hidden on Booker's property?

She couldn't answer those questions, but she knew there *was* an answer. And it wasn't that Booker had stolen it.

Turning off the water, she stepped out to towel off and realized she'd never be able to sleep without talking to Booker first. She hated to take her son outside while he was still so young. But if she bundled him up, she didn't see how a little car ride would hurt him.

Once she'd made the decision to go, Katie felt better almost immediately. She'd find Booker, wherever he was, and reassure herself that he was okay. She'd figure out what really happened—and convince others to believe in him as much as she did. And if he *was* in jail, she'd do what she could to get him out. Lionel & Sons Auto Repair seemed successful, but she didn't know whether Booker had any money. If he couldn't make bail, she'd ask Mike to lend her the money.

BOOKER WAS FEELING the tension of being held at the police station the entire day when the fax they'd been expecting finally arrived. Officer Bennett collected it as soon as the fax machine stopped humming, and carried what looked like two sheets of paper into Chief Clanahan's office.

The white-haired Clanahan retrieved a pair of reading glasses from his desk. He glanced at Booker, who was sitting across from him, and at Orton, who was standing in the doorway, then perched his glasses on his nose and studied the document.

"Looks as though he's telling the truth," he said at last.

The lines in Orton's forehead deepened into grooves. "So that *was* Katie's car we found?"

"She's not on the title yet, or the registration, either," Clanahan mused. "Evidently she didn't take care of any DMV paperwork before she left San Francisco. But the Martins say they sold it to her, and this here looks like a valid Bill of Sale to me. Even her signature is legible."

If only the Martins had been home to answer the phone earlier, Booker thought. Maybe he'd be on his way by now. But he couldn't blame them. He should've handled his own DMV paperwork and sent in the Certificate of Nonoperation he'd been planning to file.

"Whether the Bill of Sale looks valid or not, I think we should contact Katie and see what she has to say about all this," Orton said.

Irritation showed on Clanahan's face. "It's after eleven o'clock, Orton. I'm not going to call Katie Rogers right now. It would wake her for nothing, and it'd be a waste of our time. If she'd had her car stolen, don't you think she would've reported it?"

Orton moved closer to his boss's desk. "Probably. But something's off."

"What?" Booker demanded, growing impatient after so many hours. "Like I said before, her car broke down before she ever reached town. After I fixed it, she couldn't pay me. So she gave me the car in trade. I tried to sell it, but it wasn't generating any interest, so I finally decided it was a waste of space and moved it out of the way. What's so hard to understand about that?"

Booker knew better than to tell the story as it had really happened. Number one, he'd paid Katie in cash, so he couldn't prove, without involving her, that money had changed hands. And number two, he knew Orton and the others wouldn't understand why he'd buy a car only to hide it in a gully.

Bennett was standing at Clanahan's elbow, his lips pursed as he gazed down at the Bill of Sale. "I saw the car for sale at Booker's shop," he said, obviously more convinced by Booker's story than Orton was. "It sat there for a good coupla weeks, at least."

"I saw it, too," Orton said. "But that doesn't mean he came by it honestly."

"Katie would've said something," Clanahan insisted.

"So why is he hiding it?" Orton asked. "Tell me that."

Booker kept his eyes hooded. He knew his insolent expression angered Orton, and couldn't resist for that reason. "What I do with my own property is my business. I can shoot it full of holes if I want, right? Just so long as I own it."

Orton's jaw tightened and his eyes glittered coldly. "Listen to him, Chief. Are we really gonna let him wriggle out of this?"

"Wriggle out of what?" Clanahan said. "Unless you boys found something else at his place today, something you didn't tell me about that ties him to the Small robbery or some other crime, we don't have anything to hold him on. The mayor's already called here twice. I'm not pushing this any further." He shoved the Bill of Sale off to the corner of his desk. "Now, you two take Booker home."

Orton shook his head and cursed under his breath, but when Clanahan fixed him with a pointed glare, he looked at Booker and muttered, "Come on."

Releasing a long, silent sigh, Booker followed Orton across the reception area.

Bennett moved ahead of them and held the door.

"Where'd you put the stuff you took from Jon Small?" Orton asked as soon as Booker stepped outside.

"You tell me," Booker said with a taunting grin. "You boys are the ones who searched my house and my shop."

"This isn't over," Orton promised.

"I agree with you there," Booker said and headed to the patrol unit.

WHEN ORTON PULLED OVER a mile outside of town, Booker stiffened in surprise. "What now?" he asked from the back seat of the same police cruiser they'd used to bring him into the police station earlier.

"Let him out," Orton said to Bennett, who was riding in the passenger seat.

Bennett shot a surprised glance at Orton, then seemed to take in the raw land on both sides of the dark highway. "What? Here? He's probably a good twelve miles from home."

"And I'm not driving him a mile closer. If this asshole wants to get home, he can friggin' walk."

"Clanahan said—"

"Clanahan's not here."

"But—"

"But nothing. Let him out."

"Clanahan won't like it," Bennett said.

Orton arched a challenging brow. "And who's gonna tell him?"

Worry creased Bennett's forehead as he looked back at Booker. "What if *he* does?"

Orton shrugged, and a menacing smile curled his lips. "I'll just tell Chief he was cursing and calling me names and generally making my life miserable, so I refused to take him any farther. We don't *have* to give him a ride home. It's a courtesy. Anyway, it'll be his word against ours. Who do you think Clanahan's going to believe?"

Bennett hesitated, but Booker knew he'd cave in eventually. Bennett wasn't strong enough to fight Orton on anything. "Whatever, man," he said.

Orton jerked his head toward the door. "Get going."

A moment later, Booker slid out of the car while Bennett held the door. In a previous time, Booker would have evened the score between him and Orton. But he was determined not to let Orton get under his skin. Allowing his temper and his outrage to get the better of him would only complicate matters. He'd learned that the hard way. Now he had a home and a successful business to take care of, and he had Delbert to think about. Delbert would be shipped off to that special home in Boise almost immediately if Booker ever went to jail for any length of time.

"Maybe you boys should start looking for whoever's robbing the good citizens of Dundee instead of wasting your time harassing me," he said.

Bennett slammed the door and climbed back in front.

"Except that I'm pretty sure we don't have to look any farther than right here," Orton said, chuckling.

Booker bent down to see Orton's mocking face through Bennett's open window. "Which doesn't say much for the intelligence of our police force."

Orton's smile faded, and he stepped on the gas, spewing dirt and gravel as he wheeled around and headed back to town.

His jaw and hands clenched, Booker stood watching until the cruiser's taillights disappeared. What he wouldn't give for five minutes alone with Orton, he thought, and started walking.

THE POLICE STATION WAS locked up tight. Katie knew that either Orton or Bennett patrolled Dundee each night until the Honky Tonk closed, catching drunk drivers and breaking up fights. But she hadn't seen a cruiser as she passed through town, and had no idea where Orton or Bennett might be. So she decided to drive out to the farmhouse to see if maybe Booker had come home since she'd tried calling there.

When she arrived, she found Booker's truck sitting in the drive and his motorcycle parked just inside the garage. She could also see Delbert through the kitchen window, pacing worriedly, his lips moving constantly as though he was muttering to himself.

Taking Troy with her, she knocked on the door. Delbert glanced up and seemed to recognize her, but he wouldn't respond. He just kept pacing and muttering.

Katie tried the door and, fortunately, found it unlocked. "Delbert?" she said, carrying Troy inside.

Delbert blinked faster and increased the speed of his pacing, but that was it.

"Are you okay?" she asked.

No answer.

"Where's Booker?"

Again, no response. But when she paused long enough, she could hear what he was muttering.

"He'll be back soon. He said he'll be back. They won't put him in jail. He lives here. He hasn't done anything wrong. He'll be back soon. He said so. They won't put him in jail...."

She'd never seen Delbert so agitated. "Well, now I know why you're not answering the phone," she said. "This whole thing has you in quite a state."

Setting Troy's infant seat on the floor, she went over to stop Delbert's rapid movements and capture his full attention. "Delbert, listen to me," she said, touching his arm while using the most soothing voice she could muster.

He kept muttering, but he didn't fight her.

"I'm going to find Booker, okay?"

His frantic eyes latched on to her face.

"You don't have to worry about him. Everything will be okay. Do you understand?"

The volume of what Delbert was saying increased, but that was the only sign he'd even heard her.

"I'm going back to town to see if I can find him," she reiterated. "Do you want to come with me? I've got Mike Hill's little Nissan, which doesn't have much room with Troy's car seat in there, too. But I think you might feel better if you came with me."

"He'll be back soon. He said he'll be back—"

"Delbert! I know you're upset. But if you want to come with me, please answer."

He shook his head, which meant her words had registered, after all. They just didn't have much impact. Pulling away, he resumed his pacing.

"Okay. You wait for him here," she said. "I'll be back as soon as I know something."

"Katie says to wait here," he responded, adding that statement to his litany. "Booker will be back soon. He told me he'd be back. He said, 'Sit tight, I'll be home in a few hours…'"

With a sigh, Katie lifted Troy and headed out to the truck. Booker must've gone to the Honky Tonk, she decided. Where else could he be? It was nearly midnight. But with both his vehicles, as well as Hatty's Buick, right here, how was he planning to get home?

An image of Ashleigh flashed across her mind, but Katie refused to believe Booker was with Ashleigh or any other woman. He wouldn't leave Delbert at home, frantic. He'd have come back…if he could.

CHAPTER TWENTY

BOOKER COULD HAVE sworn the little Nissan that passed him a few minutes earlier was the truck he'd seen Katie driving around town. But it had to be someone else, he told himself, most likely someone staying in the cabins farther up the mountain. Katie was probably at home with her new baby. She had no reason to be out in the middle of the night, no reason to be anywhere near the farmhouse....

Pulling up the collar of his leather jacket against the chill wind that whistled through the trees around him, he shoved his hands in his pockets and kept moving. He'd been walking for nearly an hour, but the passing miles had done little to soothe the old aches, the ones inside that he thought he'd outdistanced. He felt dark, sullen and, for the first time in a long while, he was craving a cigarette.

Headlights appeared as a vehicle came around the bend in the road up ahead. Booker hunched deeper into his coat and waited for it to pass. If it had been going the other way, he would have stepped off the road into the trees, as he'd been doing all night. He had no intention of drawing anyone's attention. He was too angry to ask anyone for a ride, too angry to need anyone. He just wanted to be left alone.

The truck passed before he realized it was the red

Nissan he'd seen earlier. Standing in the road, he turned to glance behind him. The person he'd briefly glimpsed behind the wheel had certainly *looked* like Katie….

Whoever was driving threw on the brakes. The truck came to a sudden stop, then the gears shifted and the engine whined as the driver backed up.

A moment later, Katie rolled down her window and stared out at him.

"What are you doing here?" he asked, not at all sure he was happy to see her.

"What do you think?"

He didn't know what to think. Katie hadn't come to the farmhouse since she'd moved out. "Where's Mike?"

"At his house, I guess."

"And the baby?"

"In here with me."

"Isn't it a little late to be taking him out?"

"*Someone* had to find you."

He zipped up his jacket. Now that he'd stopped moving, the air felt even colder. "I can take care of myself."

She let her breath go in a dramatic sigh. "To be honest, I'm beginning to wonder about that, Booker. The 'T' in your middle name must stand for trouble."

When she smiled, he felt a responding grin twitch at the corners of his mouth—but resisted the lightening of his mood. "You're not the first person to draw the connection."

She peered in her rearview mirror. "Are you going to climb in before I get rear-ended?"

The wind whipped his hair across his forehead. "I'm not good company tonight, Katie."

"I'm not asking you to entertain me. I just want to

know you're home safe so I can sleep. And *maybe* I want to hear why the police think you've stolen another car."

He raised his eyebrows. "Maybe?"

"If it's not going to upset me."

Booker's momentary levity disappeared. "Are you afraid I did it?"

She seemed to sober, too. "I know you didn't, or I wouldn't be out here."

She meant it—he could tell—and the fact that she trusted him seemed to press back the darkness and the cold.

"Why are you walking?" she asked.

"Let's just say Orton wasn't as excited about giving me a ride home as he was about hauling me down to the police station."

"I don't like that man."

"That makes two of us."

Headlights bore down on them as an approaching car rounded a bend farther up the mountain. "Someone's coming up behind you," he said. "You'd better get going."

Katie gave the truck some gas, but only enough to pull over, out of the way. "Come on." Her voice carried across the road. "Delbert's about to have a nervous breakdown."

Booker raised his voice above the engine of the advancing car. "He's not asleep?"

"He's pacing a hole in your kitchen floor, muttering over and over that you'll be home soon."

"Oh, boy." Finally overcoming the stubbornness that had driven him all day—the last hour especially—he waited for the car to pass, then jogged over and climbed in next to Troy. Immediately the comforting smell of fabric softener and baby powder enveloped him and made him feel more like the man he'd been for the past few years than the angry child of the first twenty-five.

Maybe everything was going to be okay. Maybe he *was* what he thought he was and not what he used to be....

"Baby's asleep, huh?" he said, staring down at the tightly wrapped bundle that was Troy.

"He likes the movement of the truck." Katie turned the Nissan around and headed toward the farmhouse. After a few minutes, she looked over at him. "So where did the car come from?"

"What car?" he asked, stalling.

"The car the police found in the gully."

He shrugged.

"You don't have any idea?"

He turned to stare out at the dark trees moving past his window. "I guess it was abandoned—more or less."

"And the police now realize this?"

"That's why they let me go."

"What about the robbery at Jon Small's?"

"Orton still seems to think I had something to do with it, but they didn't find any evidence linking me to the robbery when they searched the farmhouse or my shop. They don't have any witnesses, no one who so much as saw my truck in the neighborhood that night." He propped his elbow on the window ledge, shifting so he could see her better in the darkness. "They can't arrest me on suspicion alone."

"Good."

Booker checked her ashtray, halfheartedly hoping for a toothpick, and was surprised to actually find one.

Her eyes flicked his way when he opened the wrapper and stuck it in his mouth, and she smiled again, but she didn't say anything.

"What's Mike doing tonight?" he asked a few seconds later.

"I haven't seen him."

She fell silent, but the expression on her face indicated she was deep in thought.

"What are you thinking about?"

She pulled into the drive and cut the engine. "Mike."

"You've been together a lot lately."

"Yes." She bit her lip, as if she had more to say, and Booker braced himself for what was probably coming next. *You know I've been in love with him my whole life, Booker. Now things are changing between us, and I wanted you to know I'm hoping to marry him in a few months. I feel I should tell you, just in case last night meant something to you. I didn't want you to get the wrong idea about what happened....*

Briefly Booker closed his eyes at the memory of watching Katie nurse. The incredible purity of a mother's love for her child, and the intimacy of being a witness to it, had touched him deeply. He'd almost told her right then that he was still in love with her, that Troy might not be his baby but he knew he could be a good father to him.

Obviously, he'd been delusional to think she might welcome such a confession. Rebecca had said Katie wasn't responsive to Mike, but he couldn't imagine why she wouldn't be. Mike was everything she'd always wanted. She must have figured *that* out.

Clenching his jaw, Booker forced himself to look at her. "What about Mike? You got some kind of special announcement to make?"

Her chest rose as though she'd just taken a deep breath. "Yes, I guess I do."

He'd been expecting it, and *still* the impact of that admission hit him hard. He wished he could let her ease her conscience and then reassure her that he had no false hopes. But he wasn't capable of it. Not tonight. He felt too open, too…vulnerable. And he was afraid he might embarrass himself again by trying to convince her that *he* could make her happy—like he'd tried to do once before.

"I'd rather skip this next part, if it's all the same to you. But I hope the two of you will be happy," he said. Then he got out and headed for the house, hoping she'd give him a break and leave it at that.

KATIE SAT IN HER TRUCK long after Booker disappeared into the house. She'd been on the verge of telling him that she'd finally realized the difference between the crush she'd had on Mike Hill and falling in love—that Booker had been the one to show her what falling in love was all about. Only she had to explain her feelings over the past two years and she didn't know exactly where to start. He hadn't given her enough time to get her thoughts sorted out.

Inside the house, she saw Booker, then Delbert, walk past the window as they talked. Booker was obviously reassuring Delbert, calming him down. Katie knew Delbert was going to be okay when he appeared again. He was smiling and moving toward the stairs, probably on his way to bed.

The kitchen light went off. Booker didn't even glance out to see if she was gone. Then the porch light went dark, too. He was turning his back on her, sending her the signal to go home. But she wasn't ready to leave. She kept remembering the night Booker came to her door to ask her to marry him—and wondered if she had the courage to take the same risk.

Her heart began to pound as she unbuckled Troy and got out. She *thought* Booker might snub her on principle. Simply for revenge. She deserved it after what she'd done to him. But deep down, she didn't believe he was that petty. And she owed him the truth, even if he no longer returned her feelings.

"Here we go," she murmured to Troy as she carried him up to the door. Her stomach muscles tensed as she knocked. After having lived in Booker's house, she felt she should be able to walk right in, as if she belonged here, and hated feeling as though she was now being shut out.

She heard someone approach.

"Please let it be Booker," she whispered to herself. If Delbert answered the door, chances were he'd hang around to see her and the baby, and then she didn't know what she'd state as her purpose for knocking in the middle of the night. She certainly didn't want an audience when she told Booker how she felt about him.

Fortunately, when the door swung open, the full moon behind her lit the face of the man she wanted to see. Barefoot and bare-chested, Booker looked so good he made her mouth go dry.

He didn't turn on a light, and she was glad. The darkness seemed to lend her some security. "You left before I could finish," she said.

"In case you didn't notice, that was intentional."

She hoisted Troy higher. "You're not going to make this easy for me, are you?"

He took the baby from her and set him inside the house, out of the wind, but he didn't invite her in. "Why would I want to stick around to hear you tell me you're in love with another man, Katie? You've wanted Mike since you were little. I've heard it all before."

"That's just it," she said. "Mike and I are only friends. I'm *not* in love with him."

Distrust lingered on Booker's face, but he was watching her closely. "Since *when?*"

"Since I fell in love with…since I fell in love with—"

"Who?" he prompted.

Cursing herself for being such a coward, she swallowed hard and forced the word out. "You."

Gently pulling her inside, he closed the door. Katie could hear the clock ticking over the stove and smell the familiar scent of Booker's kitchen, and felt as though she'd just come home. The next few seconds would tell whether or not that was really the case….

"Katie, nothing's changed," he said softly. "I have a record. Your parents hate me. I'm still the same man you walked away from two years ago."

"I know that."

"And?"

"Leaving you was a mistake, Booker."

He ran a finger down her cheek, moving lower to brush lightly over her bottom lip, and she wished he'd kiss her or…or *something.*

"Well?" she said, her arms aching to hold him.

His dark eyes lifted to hers.

"This is the part where you respond," she told him. "Preferably with something similar to what you said two years ago."

He leaned close, pressing his lips to her neck. Katie

felt an answering flutter in her belly and knew she *had* come home—to Booker.

"Refresh my memory," he murmured, his breath warm on her skin as his mouth moved up to her ear.

She let her hands skim over his bare chest and muscular arms and finally settle securely around his neck so she could pull him fully against her. "You said, 'Marry me, Katie. I know I can make you happy.'"

"I did?" He kissed the corners of her mouth before kissing her more deeply.

"I think you were right. You can make me happy. I'm starting to get happy already," she said. "Let's go upstairs."

He chuckled, then sobered when he looked down at Troy. "Isn't it too soon?"

"Doctor said to wait a month."

"How long's it been?"

"A month."

"Are you sure?"

"It's been twenty-eight days since Troy was born, but I've never been very good at math."

He gave her a sexy grin. "Me, neither."

Lifting Troy by the handle of his infant seat, he slung an arm around her shoulders and led her to the stairs. "Let's see if we can make you downright ecstatic."

"I CAN'T BELIEVE you wouldn't make love to me," Katie complained almost as soon as she opened her eyes the following morning.

Booker yawned and drew her closer. "I guess I'm better at math than I thought."

"You're overprotective, you know that?"

He scowled and rubbed the stubble on his chin lightly

against her shoulder. "Come on, you'll ruin my reputation."

Katie rolled her eyes and rose up on her elbows. "You're such a big softie. I can't believe you have *anybody* fooled with that big, bad biker stuff."

"And I can't believe you're complaining about last night," he said. "We did almost everything I could think of. I should get extra points for creativity."

Katie couldn't wipe the smile off her face. "It was good," she admitted. "*Very* good."

"It must've been. You were screaming so loud I thought you'd wake Delbert."

She gave him a playful kick. "I wasn't screaming."

"That was me?" He looked boyishly handsome with his mussed hair and sleepy smile.

She laughed. "Just tell me you were saving the best for last."

When she snuggled closer, she could tell his body was ready to take her up on her offer, but she knew he wouldn't act on it until he was sure he wouldn't hurt her.

"Ask me that in a week or so."

"A week sounds like forever."

"Is it long enough to plan a wedding?"

Katie propped her chin on his chest. "I don't see why not. We don't have to invite very many people. My parents won't even come."

"Does that bother you?"

She drew light circles on his shoulder. "I wish there could be peace between us, but I'm not going to let that stop me from being with you."

"Do you want me to talk to them, try to work things out?"

"I'll do that." She found his hand and entwined their

fingers. "Are you sure you can forgive me for the past, Booker?"

"I say we start with a clean slate."

"I like the sound of that."

"Which means—"

Troy wailed then, and Booker rolled away to look over the edge of the bed. "I think our baby's hungry," he said, scooping him out of his infant seat and settling him between them.

Our baby… Katie kissed Troy's soft cheek and laughed when he immediately began to root for her breast. "Which means what?" she said, returning to their earlier conversation.

"Which means you forget about Ashleigh. And you believe me when I say I didn't sleep with her."

Katie stared at the man she loved. "You went home with her."

"But we didn't do anything."

Could that be true?

Even if it wasn't, they'd both made mistakes. If he could forgive and forget, she could, too.

"I wouldn't have gone home with her if we'd been together. You know that, don't you?" Booker said. "I would never cheat on you, Katie."

She admired the clean lines of his face, the wide brow, the high cheekbones. "I know that," she said, happier than she could ever remember being.

Troy's squirming grew frantic, and he began to cry in earnest.

"I think someone's growing impatient." Booker shifted to allow her more room to maneuver.

"He needs to be changed."

"Did you bring diapers?"

"I brought a diaper bag, but it's in the truck."

"I'll get it while you feed him."

"Booker?" Delbert called. Judging by the closeness of his voice, he was standing directly outside their door.

Booker had just gotten out of bed and was pulling on his pants. "What?"

"Is *Katie* in there with you?" He sounded confused.

Booker raised his brows at Katie, as though requesting her permission to tell Delbert what he must already know. She nodded.

"Yes," he said. "Why?"

"I want to hold the baby again."

"The baby's eating right now," Booker told him. "You can hold him when we come down for breakfast, okay?"

Delbert agreed, but Katie didn't hear him move away.

"I think he's still out there," she whispered.

"Is there something else?" Booker asked.

"Yes…"

"What?"

A long pause, then, "Someone called for you last night."

Yawning, Booker yanked a T-shirt over his head. "Who?"

"Um…can you come here?"

"Why?"

"I want to whisper it."

Katie felt her eyebrows gather and glanced at Booker questioningly. "That means it was a woman."

"Just say it out loud," Booker said, sitting on the edge of the bed while pulling on his boots.

"Her name was Chevy," Delbert said. "Chevy, like

the car. She has a car name. Isn't that funny, Booker? She wants to come over. She wants to see you."

Katie struggled to sit up while keeping Troy at her breast, but Booker pressed her gently back against the pillows. "Relax," he murmured, and leaned across Troy to kiss the top of her head.

"Go ahead and call her back," he told Delbert.

"Me?" Delbert said.

"Yeah. Why not?" Booker got up without bothering to lace his boots, and put on a ball cap.

"What do you want me to say, huh, Booker?" Delbert asked. "What should I say?"

Booker's eyes rested on Katie, and she watched him slowly grin. "Tell her I'm getting married."

CHAPTER TWENTY-ONE

REBECCA STOOD IN the feminine hygiene aisle at Finley's Grocery, staring at the pregnancy tests. She bought one almost every month—had tried every brand—but it was getting harder and harder to go through the check-out line and face the sympathy in Marge Finley's eyes.

She took a test off the shelf, a brand she hadn't tried in a long time, wondering if she'd have better luck try-ing it again. Then with a sigh, she put the box back. She'd wasted enough time and money—and hope—on pregnancy tests. Josh was tired of the whole thing. He'd given her one more month to realize her dream, and now that month was over. She'd taken her fertility shots until the very end, but she knew she didn't need to buy a pregnancy test. She couldn't be pregnant; she'd just started her period.

Slowly she meandered around to the next aisle, in-exorably drawn to the baby supplies: bottles, rattles, diapers, rubber-tipped spoons, powder and diaper ointment. She'd pored over every item in this aisle so many times she could have quoted the prices. She'd even bought a few things—and hidden them in the attic so Josh wouldn't see them and become forlorn that he couldn't give her what she wanted so badly.

Running a finger over the picture of a baby on a box of Oragel, she felt the familiar yearning and closed her eyes. She needed to accept that she and Josh would never have children of their own—accept it and forgive herself. Almost everyone she met suggested she adopt. But she was too angry and bitter to consider that an option yet. She'd imagined holding Josh's child in her arms too many times, could already picture what his child would look like….

Suddenly she heard Mary Thornton's voice. Hoping to escape before Mary saw her in the baby aisle, Rebecca immediately headed in the opposite direction. If Josh had ended up with Mary, she would've been able to give him children, and Mary wasn't about to let Rebecca forget that. Whenever they bumped into each other, Mary made a point of asking if Rebecca and Josh were planning to start a family soon, even though she must have heard about the fertility problems they were facing. Rebecca always pretended the question didn't bother her and responded with "Maybe someday." But it *did* bother her. And now she knew "someday" would most likely never come.

As she hurried away, she heard Mary say something that made her pause.

"If Booker's going to steal a car after all the time he's been out of jail, he hasn't learned his lesson."

"Stealing a car isn't necessarily the same as robbing someone's house," another voice said. Rebecca couldn't figure out who the second voice belonged to, but it sounded familiar.

"Why not?" Mary went on. "Booker has no scruples. You should've seen how he treated me when I went to his garage a few weeks ago."

"What were you doing at Booker's garage?"

There was a slight hesitation. “I needed my oil changed.”

“I thought you took your Beemer elsewhere for service.”

“Uh... I usually do but I didn’t have time to make the drive.”

“Right.”

“Why’d you use that tone?”

“Just tell me what your visit to the garage has to do with the robbery.”

“Booker’s the type to get revenge. And he’s the only one in town with a history of violence and stealing.”

Rebecca finally placed the second voice. It was Candace, a friend of Mary’s since high school. The two were so engrossed in their conversation that they passed the aisle where Rebecca was now standing and continued down another aisle without even glancing her way. But Rebecca no longer cared about going unnoticed. She had a thing or two to say to Mary and Candace.

“Mary, the police didn’t find any evidence at his house or his shop that tied him to the robbery,” Candace said as Rebecca began to follow them.

“So? That doesn’t mean anything. I know it wasn’t Slinkerhoff’s nephew.”

“How?”

Rebecca rounded the end of the aisle and was about to call Mary’s name when she heard her say, “Because he was with me that night,” and froze in her tracks.

“What was Joe Slinkerhoff doing at your place?” Candace asked.

Rebecca was wondering the same thing.

“Having dinner and watching a movie.”

What? Rebecca covered her mouth. Mary had pursued Josh, and then Mike, for years, hoping for a wedding proposal. She'd let everyone in town know that she'd settle for nothing but the very best. So why was she spending time with Joe Slinkerhoff? He was nearly ten years her junior, worked at a fast-food burger joint—the only one in town—and still lived at home, for crying out loud.

"Was Nick around?"

"No, he spent spring break with his father."

"Still," Candace said, "isn't Joe a little young for you?"

"He's only nine years younger. And a girl's got a right to have a little fun," Mary responded, giggling. "He treats me like he's lucky to tie my shoes, and he's not bad in bed."

"So you're giving up on Mike?"

"Of course not. Mike's not married yet. He might be seeing Katie, but it won't last. She's just the latest novelty."

"You don't think he'll mind that you've been sleeping with Joe?"

"He's not going to know. Anyway, who's to say he's not sleeping with Katie?"

Rebecca stepped into view. "I am," she said. "Mike and Katie are only friends."

Mary looked up at her and the color fled her face. For a moment she seemed to have trouble finding her voice. "Rebecca, I didn't see you."

"I know," Rebecca said. "But just to set the record straight, Booker did *not* steal that car they found at his house."

"That's not what Orton's wife is saying," Candace said.

"Orton's wife doesn't know anything. I talked to my

father early this morning. The car they found is the car Katie drove here from San Francisco. She gave it to Booker when she couldn't pay him for repairs."

Candace looked almost as uncomfortable as Mary. "Oh. I guess Janelle was wrong."

"You're damn right she was."

"We were just going by what we've heard," Mary said.

"Right." Rebecca turned to go, but Mary caught her arm.

"You're—" she cleared her throat "—you're not going to tell Mike about Joe, are you?"

Rebecca hesitated. She'd been about to say, "Of course I am." But suddenly there seemed so little point. Mary was obviously miserable and grasping at whatever she could find to fulfill her. She deserved sympathy, not derision.

"No," Rebecca said and even managed to smile before she walked away. Maybe she wouldn't be able to have a baby. But life wasn't *all* bad. Now that she realized how pathetic Mary truly was, Rebecca knew Mike would never fall for her.

KATIE HAD ALMOST DECIDED not to go to work today. Booker had made her a big breakfast and helped Delbert hold the baby while she showered. She'd wanted to spend the rest of the day with him. But she'd promised to work for a few hours in the afternoon and didn't want to leave Rebecca in the lurch.

After yesterday's fiasco with the police, Booker said he needed to take care of a few things at the garage, anyway. So they'd come into town together. Only now that Booker was at the garage and Katie was sitting in her own chair at a mostly deserted Hair and Now, she couldn't help thinking about her parents. How was she going to tell her father that she planned to marry Booker?

With a frown, she glanced over at Troy, who was sleeping in his infant seat. She'd canceled the baby-sitting she'd lined up with her mother for today because Ashleigh and Rebecca had been asking to see the baby—and she felt bad about accepting her mother's help when she knew how upset Tami would be to learn that Katie had acted on her feelings for Booker, and that he'd responded. She planned to marry him with or without her parents' approval. She knew now that she was so in love nothing could stop her. But it would certainly be nice to have their support for a change....

Rebecca swept into the salon, her face flushed from hurrying. "Sorry I'm late," she said. "I had to drop off some film to be developed at Finley's and ran into...a distraction."

The way she said *distraction* made Katie curious. "What kind of distraction?"

"Mary Thornton."

"Oh, *that* kind of distraction." Katie went back to looking through the magazine on her lap. "Well, being late is no problem. As you can see, it's slow around here."

"Where is everyone?"

"Ashleigh's in back, straightening the storeroom while I watch the front. Mona's taking the day off."

"What about our appointments?" Rebecca stopped at the desk to check the scheduling book. "Rita Price was supposed to come in for a perm at one." She glanced at her watch. "That was nearly forty minutes ago. Didn't she make it?"

Katie put her magazine aside. "I haven't heard from her. I tried to call her a couple of times, but there was no answer."

Rebecca tucked her dark blond hair, which was getting quite long and conservative for Rebecca, behind one ear. "She's usually more reliable than that. She has a standing appointment every two months for a cut, every four months for a perm."

"What are you two talking about?" Ashleigh asked, emerging from the back. "Didn't Rita show?"

Rebecca tapped a pencil against the desk. "No, which is strange. And Katie said she's not answering her phone."

Troy started to fuss, but before Katie could take two steps in his direction, Ashleigh rushed over to get him. "Oh good, he's waking up. Can I hold him?"

Katie smiled and nodded. She wasn't sure *what* had happened the night Booker had gone home with Ashleigh. But from the beginning, Ashleigh had been open and friendly, and Katie was finding it surprisingly easy to like her.

"You brought the baby?" Rebecca crossed the salon to huddle over Troy as well.

Katie shrugged. "Since I'm only going to be here for a few hours, I thought it might be okay."

"It's fine. I told you, you can bring him anytime." Rebecca pulled back the blanket so she could peek at his face. "Look at him…."

Katie wasn't sure bringing Troy into the salon was such a good idea when she saw the expression on Rebecca's face. She wondered how Rebecca's fertility treatments were going, but was afraid to ask for fear the answer wasn't the one she wanted to hear.

"He's beautiful," Ashleigh gushed. "I can't wait to have kids of my—" Her words fell away as she glanced at Rebecca. Clearing her throat, she immediately turned the conversation in a different direction. "I mean, I met the cutest guy at the Honky Tonk last night. You two should've seen him. Tall and blond and—"

"I thought you had a thing for Booker?" Rebecca interrupted, her gaze still on Troy.

Katie stiffened as she awaited Ashleigh's response.

"Booker's gorgeous and all that," she said. "He's nice, too. But it isn't going to work out between us."

"Why not?" Rebecca asked.

Ashleigh rubbed the top of Troy's head with her thumb. "I can tell he's not really interested in me." She shot Katie an envious smile. "If you want to know the truth, I think he's still in love with Katie. *She* might have moved on, but he's never gotten over her."

Rebecca arched a brow at Katie. "I told you," she said. "Everyone can see it but you."

"Actually…" Katie was about to admit that she and Booker were seeing each other again. The excitement she'd felt before she started thinking about her family had returned, making her miss Booker already, even though she'd only been away from him for an hour. But the bell rang over the door and, when she looked up, she saw her mother walk in. Travis was with Tami and, to Katie's complete amazement, so was her father.

"Katie, we'd like a word with you, if you don't mind." Her mother settled her purse more firmly at her elbow and folded her arms. "We tried to reach you at your cabin early this morning, but you weren't home."

Tami's formal tone didn't bode well. She'd said, "You weren't home," as if there was something innately wrong with her being gone.

Katie felt her pulse kick up as she looked from Rebecca to Ashleigh. "Can you…can you watch Troy for me?"

As far as Katie knew, her father had never seen Troy before. She noticed the way his eyes kept moving to the baby, but he seemed intent on whatever purpose had brought him and didn't come any closer.

"Should we go in back?" Katie asked.

Tami nodded. "If you think that's best."

Katie had no idea *what* was best. She had no idea what had precipitated this little family gathering, especially after her father had gone so long without even speaking to her. "This way," she said, and led them to the stock room.

"Is something wrong?" she asked as soon as they were alone.

"Your mother told me what you said about Booker yesterday, Katie," her father began.

Katie noticed that Travis was wearing a dark scowl. When their eyes met, he raised his hands and shook his head. "I'm not really part of this. I'm only here because they made me come."

Katie returned her attention to her father. "What did you say?"

"That your mother told me you think you're in love with Booker."

"I *am* in love with Booker."

A muscle jumped in her father's cheek. "Katie, after everything you've been through, I'd expect you to use some caution. Surely you don't want—"

"Katie?" Rebecca called from the front.

Katie stuck her head out of the stockroom. "Yes?"

"Booker's here. He's brought you something to eat."

Leaning farther into the hallway, Katie could see Booker standing at the desk, holding a take-out bag. Oh God, they were all here together....

She hesitated, wondering what to do. She wanted to tell Booker to take the food to the garage, that she'd meet him there later. But if her family was ever going to accept him, she'd better start including him. "Booker? Could you come back here?"

"Katie, this is a family meeting," her mother said, clearly not pleased.

"Booker's part of *my* family," Katie insisted.

A moment later, Booker strode into the stockroom wearing the faded jeans and Lionel & Sons T-shirt that served as his warm-weather apparel. He must have set the food he'd brought her someplace else because his hands were now free. He spread his legs and crossed his arms as he eyed Don and Tami, his expression shuttered. But he nodded a hello to Travis.

"I'm not part of this," Travis reiterated.

"Maybe it's better that Booker's here," Don said to Tami. "I think it's time we got this out in the open."

"*What* out in the open?" Booker asked.

Katie stepped closer to him and felt the reassuring weight of his arm as he slid it around her shoulders.

"We've heard about your recent troubles with the law," Don said. "First the fighting, then the robbery. And now we hear you've stolen another car."

"He hasn't stolen anything." Katie's voice had risen enough that she knew everyone in the salon could probably hear, but she didn't care.

"You don't have to defend me," Booker muttered.

"I don't see how anyone *can* defend you." Tami had picked up on his words, even though they were only intended for Katie. "Katie has a baby to think about now. And we're that baby's grandparents. We have a responsibility to look out for Troy, too. She doesn't need to be getting involved with the likes of you—*again.*"

Katie could tell by the hard line of Booker's jaw that he was angry, but she knew she could rely on him to hold his temper. She'd grown to trust him a great deal since she'd come back.

"I'll take responsibility for the fight," he said, "But—"

Katie whirled to face him. "You will not take responsibility for that fight!"

He ignored her. "—but I didn't rob the Smalls or anyone else, and I didn't steal another car."

"Then how do you explain the car they found hidden in that gully at your place?" her father asked. "We just saw Orton at church. It's like he said. No one hides a working car beneath a bunch of brush and lets it sit there for months without having some reason. We knew Hatty well enough to know that she took care of her land and property. She never would've left a car in a gully to rust. Which means it must've gotten there after she died."

"Maybe it did," Booker said. "But I didn't steal it."

"You expect us to take your word for it?"

"Check with Chief Clanahan, if you want."

Katie could hear Troy crying out front. She didn't want to leave Booker on his own with her family, but she needed to comfort her baby. She was just about to get him when his cries grew louder and Rebecca appeared. "Troy wants you," she said, passing her the baby.

"Thanks." Katie kissed and held Troy close, and he quieted almost instantly.

But Rebecca didn't leave. "I know this is none of my business," she said. "But I can't stand what's happening." She glared at Katie's parents. "Why don't you two come out here and let me call my father? He'll tell you what he told me this morning. The car they found in that gully on Booker's property belonged to Katie."

"To me?" Katie echoed. "What are you talking about, Rebecca?"

Rebecca's confidence seemed to falter. "You don't know about it?" She looked to Booker. "Booker?"

He shook his head. "None of that matters. That car is nobody's business but mine."

Her car? Since she'd sold the Cadillac, she didn't have a— Suddenly the memory of Booker handing her three thousand dollars flashed through Katie's mind. "Oh, my gosh! It's the Cadillac, isn't it? They found the Cadillac in that gully!"

He didn't answer.

No wonder he'd given her cash! He couldn't write her a check without revealing that he was the one who was buying her car—a car he didn't need. He'd basically *given* her that money. When her own parents had turned their backs on her, he'd taken her in, fed and clothed her, and bought her that computer and all her software.

"Booker, is it true?" she asked.

His scowl darkened. "It's no big deal. I can always sell it."

"But you haven't been trying to sell it. You've been hiding it so I wouldn't know you gave me three thousand dollars for nothing. Just because I needed it. Why?"

His gaze shifted to meet hers and his expression softened. "Why do you think?"

Warmth filled Katie as she thought about all the good things Booker had done for her. She didn't care about his reputation or the mistakes he'd made in the past. She didn't care about anyone else's opinion of him. She *knew* him. He'd been there for her when she had no one else. It was his love that had nourished her.

Bringing Troy to her shocked mother, she threw her arms around Booker's neck. "I've never known anyone with a more beautiful heart than yours," she said and kissed him.

Booker looked a little uncomfortable having an audience to such praise. Certainly he wasn't accustomed to it. But Katie could tell he was fighting a smile. And she knew Rebecca understood how she felt because of her silly grin. Even Katie's parents seemed awestruck.

"So what now?" Don asked.

"We're getting married," Booker said.

Tami held Troy against her shoulder and patted his back. "When?"

"As soon as possible."

"At least wait a while to make sure—" Don started, but Tami placed a hand on his arm.

"It's too late for that, Don." She turned her gaze on Booker. "Just tell me you'll take good care of my grandson. You don't mind that he's not your baby, do you?"

Booker reached out and took Troy from her. "He *is* my baby now."

"What about Delbert?" Don asked.

"He'll stay right where he is," Katie said.

"You're going to let him live with you?"

Katie knew Booker felt responsible for Delbert, as

a big brother of sorts, and could never send him away. She didn't want him to. She loved Delbert, too, loved knowing that Booker's heart was big enough to include him. "Yes."

"Hey, can I live with you, too?" Travis asked, and chuckled weakly when his parents glared at him. "Just kidding."

Katie looked at her father. "Will you come to the wedding, Dad?"

"I don't know, Katie. I—I don't know what to think."

"Will you at least consider it?"

He nodded as Ashleigh came rushing into the storeroom. "Rita Price just called," she announced. "You're never going to believe why she missed her appointment today."

Katie and Rebecca both said, "I hope she's okay."

"She's fine. But someone broke into her house this morning while she was at church—and he was still there when she got home."

"The poor thing's got to be sixty!" Rebecca cried.

"And she lives alone," Tami added.

Ashleigh rubbed her hands together. "She might be a widow, but guess what? She caught him! He flashed her but couldn't get his pants up fast enough to make his getaway. He tried to run out the back, tripped and fell, and she hit him over the head with a skillet. Knocked him out cold."

"Who was it?" Booker asked.

Ashleigh grinned. "Are you ready for this?"

Rebecca nudged her. "Just tell us."

"Officer Orton's son."

CHAPTER TWENTY-TWO

"Do you think my father will come to the wedding?" Katie asked as she and Booker packed up her belongings later that day.

"I don't know," Booker replied. "Why don't you call him?"

Katie didn't want to call her father tonight, just in case the answer was no. She planned to make dessert for her new family—Troy, Delbert, Bruiser and Booker—and afterward relax in Booker's arms while watching a good movie. She hated to let anything spoil the simple peace of it. "I'll call him tomorrow."

"We could stop by their place on the way home if you want," he said.

She definitely didn't want to take *that* much of a risk. "No, it's okay. They rushed off because they had company coming. I'll handle it later."

A knock on the open door caused Katie to turn. Mike was leaning against the lintel, his hands in his pockets. "You two need any help?"

"I think we got it," Booker said.

Mike tipped his hat back. "You know you stole my girl, don't you?" he said to Booker.

Booker glanced at Katie as he finished latching her suitcase. "It was nip and tuck there until the very end."

Mike chuckled and shook his head. "No, you had me beat a long time ago."

Booker set Katie's suitcase on the floor. "So, are you going to start seeing Mary again?"

Mike rolled his eyes. "I was never *seeing* Mary! I was bored and wanted an occasional dinner companion, and she was available. But I'm beginning to believe I'll never live it down."

Laughing at Mike's exasperation, Katie put Troy in his infant seat and arranged a blanket around him. "I don't think she's the woman for you."

"No."

"But there'll be someone."

"Let's hope I find her before I turn forty."

"First you have to overcome your fear of commitment," she said.

"I'm *not* afraid of commitment!"

Katie heard Booker laugh softly at her baiting and liked having him with her. He was part of her. They belonged together, for better or worse. "Thanks for everything, Mike," she said, giving him a hug as Booker carried out her suitcases.

"Actually, I came out here today to tell you I found Andy."

Katie froze. "Where?"

"In San Francisco. He's living with someone named Margot."

The women who'd worked with her, the one he'd had the affair with. "How did you find him?"

"His cousins put me in touch with his parents who put me in touch with him. I guess he's been calling them for money, so they had the information."

"Did he say what he did with my computer?"

"No. I'm afraid I couldn't get that back."

"It's okay, Mike," she said. "Thanks for—"

He held up a hand. "But I got something better. It's my wedding present to both of you." Pulling an official-looking document out of his pocket, he passed it to her.

"Waiver of Parental Rights," she read aloud. Then her eyes skimmed rapidly through several paragraphs of fine print. *I, Andy Bray, hereby relinquish all parental rights to my son, Troy Matthew Rogers....* At the bottom she found Andy's signature.

Katie pressed a hand to her chest. "I can't believe it! How did you get this?"

Mike straightened. "I wish I could say it was hard, but it wasn't. I called him to see if I could reclaim your computer, but he didn't have it anymore. So I told him I'd forget about the computer and pay him a small fee if he'd sign this and mail it back to me. He agreed, and I received it yesterday."

"How much did you have to pay him?"

"A hundred bucks."

Giving up Troy for a mere hundred bucks was a sad commentary on Andy's state of mind, but Katie wasn't about to complain. Mike had solved the one thing she'd been worried about—that her past might someday come back to haunt her, and possibly hurt Booker and Troy. "Thanks, Mike. You're a wonderful friend," she said and felt it to the tips of her toes.

Booker returned from the truck and peered over her shoulder. "What's going on?"

"Mike just gave us our wedding present. Early." Katie let a smile of hope and relief blossom on her face as she handed the waiver to Booker.

He read it, then looked from her to Mike, blinking several times. "This means I can adopt Troy."

"That's exactly what it means," Mike said, his pleasure in the gift evident on his face.

"When I talked to Mike after Troy was born, I mentioned that I wanted to be sure Andy couldn't come back and cause problems later," Katie explained. "And he took care of it."

Mike shoved his hands in his pockets. "Well, I do expect a little compensation."

"What's that?" Katie asked.

"You've got to finish my Web site as soon as you get another computer."

She grinned when he winked at her. "Of course. I love building Web sites."

Booker gave her back the document and took Troy. "I'm already getting her a computer."

"So is that what you're going to do from now on?" Mike asked.

"Not exclusively," Katie said. "I've decided I'd like to do hair one or two days a week, just to get out. The rest of the time, when I'm not taking care of Troy, I'll build Web sites or help Booker with whatever paperwork I can do for him at the garage."

"That's the beauty of owning your own business," Mike told Booker. "You can bring your wife and son to work with you."

"Just wait until I have her changing oil and greasing hubs," Booker said, giving Mike the keys to the red Nissan. "Thanks for looking out for her while she was here."

Mike accepted the keys and shook Booker's hand. "I'm just glad you're off the market," he said. "Maybe now I can get myself a girl."

BOOKER COULDN'T BELIEVE he was bringing Katie home for good. She was going to marry him in a week, and they'd have more children someday. They already had a family. He'd never really been able to picture himself settling down, but he'd done a lot of settling in the past few years. This was just the final step.

Surprisingly, he wasn't afraid of the commitment. The timing was right.

Reaching over Troy, who was sleeping in his infant seat, he squeezed Katie's shoulder. She glanced at him and smiled.

"Happy?" he asked.

She nodded. "I should've married you two years ago."

"Maybe we wouldn't have appreciated what we have the way we do now."

He turned into the farmhouse and was surprised to see a Toyota Camry sitting in the driveway.

"Who's here?" Katie asked.

Booker hoped it wasn't Chevy. She'd called him twice, even after he'd had Delbert tell her he was getting married. He hadn't been there to accept the call either time. Had his lack of response precipitated a visit?

As he drew closer, however, he could tell his visitor wasn't Chevy. "It's Leah Small," he said and looked around, wondering if Jon or Smalley or any of the rest of the Small clan had accompanied her. But he couldn't see anyone else.

"What do you think she wants?"

"I have no idea."

While they parked and got out, Leah waited at the front door, her hands clasped tightly in front of her.

"Hello, Leah," Booker said as they approached.

Her eyes darted quickly to Katie. “Could I speak to you alone please, Booker?”

Booker handed Troy to Katie. “I’ll get the suitcases in a minute.”

She nodded and went inside, and he offered Leah a seat on the porch swing.

“No, thanks,” she said. “This won’t take long.”

He leaned against the porch railing. “What’s up?”

“I—” Her voice faltered, so she started again. “I’m afraid I owe you an apology.”

Booker felt his eyebrows draw together. “For what?”

“For all that business about the police thinking it was you who broke into my house.”

“You knew it wasn’t?”

She pulled her limp brown hair over one shoulder. “No. I thought it was you, or I wouldn’t have said so. But—” she took a deep breath “—I wouldn’t have thought it was you if I hadn’t been stirring up trouble between you and Jon.”

Booker had to work to keep his jaw from dropping. Mousey Leah Small had been stirring up trouble? For her own husband? She didn’t seem the type. “What kind of trouble?”

“It was me and Tripp Bell who called you that night and threatened Delbert. You know Tripp, don’t you?”

“Yeah, he brings his car in to have it serviced.”

“He’s my neighbor.”

“And he wanted to stir up trouble, too?”

“Let’s just say he’s sympathetic to me because of the way my husband treats me….”

“So it was the two of you who called here and threatened Delbert. Why?”

"After what happened in the park, I knew you'd think it was Jon. And I wanted you to teach him a lesson."

"You mind explaining your motives?"

Her eyes had remained fastened on her feet, but now they met Booker's. "I did it because he's a mean son of a bitch, and I hate him."

"Wow." Booker jammed a hand through his hair. He would never have guessed Leah could feel so passionate about anything. "Why didn't you simply leave him?"

"It's not as easy as it sounds. I didn't think he'd let me go. I'm still not sure he will. We've got the kids and… and there's his pride. He's not going to like being embarrassed in front of his family, in front of the whole town. But I'm going to marry Tripp and make a better life for myself. I refuse to put up with Jon's abuse any more. Twenty years is long enough."

The soul behind the eyes that looked up at him seemed to hold a world of painful memories. Booker immediately sympathized with Leah despite what she'd done. "Why are you telling me this?"

"Because I'm not like Jon. Once I found out it was Orton's son and not you who broke into my house, I knew I'd been wrong to do what I did. I'd caused people to turn on you because of your past, and you haven't done anything bad in a long time. I'm sorry for that."

Booker shrugged. "It worked out okay."

"I'm sorry about Delbert, too. I don't wish him any harm."

"I know, Leah."

"That's it, then," she said shakily. "I just wanted to tell you the truth."

"I appreciate it," he said. "I know it couldn't have been easy coming here."

She nodded and headed to her car, and Booker watched her go.

"Leah?" he said as she was about to get in.

"Yes?"

"Good luck leaving Jon. I think it'll be worth the fight."

A brief smile touched her lips. "You're twice the man he is, Booker," she said, then drove away.

Katie stepped onto the porch as soon as Leah was gone. "What was that all about?"

He sighed. "Desperation."

KATIE WAITED NERVOUSLY inside the entrance of the small whitewashed church to see if her family would show. Three days ago she'd called their house with the date and time of her wedding, but Travis had said their parents were in Boise picking up some new equipment for the bakery, and Katie hadn't heard from them since.

Booker was standing next to her, wearing a shirt and tie for the occasion. He looked spit polished, but Katie liked him best in the more casual leather and jeans he typically wore. Leather suited his personality and highlighted his rugged magnetism. He wasn't the indoor type.

"Will you be okay if they don't come?" he murmured, kissing the back of her hand.

Katie brushed a wrinkle out of her new cream-colored sheath dress, which fell just past her knees, and nodded. She knew she could accept whatever happened. She was so in love with Booker that she wasn't going to allow anyone to spoil this day. Besides, they'd filled several pews already. Mona, Erma and Ashleigh were there from the shop. Rebecca, Josh and Mike from the ranch. Several of Katie's hair clients. Her old piano teacher. Chase and Delbert. Delaney and Conner Armstrong. Millie and Ralph, the old couple who had raised Delaney. Mike and Josh's parents. For a small, hastily planned wedding, the chapel was quite crowded.

But the day would be even more wonderful if only her family would make an appearance and at least try to help her close the gap that had sprung up between them.

Troy began to cry, and Katie turned to see Rebecca stand up and jiggle him gently on her shoulder. Rebecca had reached for him the moment she arrived and hadn't relinquished him to anyone else yet, despite numerous requests for a chance to hold him.

"Look," she told Booker. "Rebecca loves babies so much. I wish she could have one."

Booker didn't say anything, but he squeezed her hand, and she knew he felt the same way.

"Katie, it's about time to start." Pastor Richards had come up quietly behind them. "Do you and Booker want to take a seat now?"

"Can't we wait just another few minutes?" she asked.

He smiled. "Of course."

The door opened, and Katie caught her breath as afternoon sunlight burst into the cooler, darker church. But it wasn't her family. It was Rebecca's parents.

Mayor Wells smiled and shook Booker's hand. "You did a great job on the Lincoln, Booker. It's running like a charm," he said, then he and his wife congratulated Katie.

Katie heard the door close as they moved away and decided her parents weren't coming. Don and Tami knew Booker hadn't robbed anyone or stolen any cars recently, but they'd held a grudge against him for a long time. Evidently, they weren't able to let it go. Or perhaps they were embarrassed for judging him so harshly.

Taking a deep breath, she forced a smile onto her face for Booker's benefit. "Let's go ahead and start."

"Are you sure?" he said. "We could wait a little longer."

"No, they're not coming."

"I'm sorry," he whispered as he kissed her temple.

"It's fine." She pumped up the wattage of her smile. "Really."

Pastor Richards stood when he saw them, and waved for them to take their seats on either side of the aisle. "Good afternoon," he said. "I'd like to welcome you all to help celebrate the union of Booker Robinson and Katie Rogers this beautiful spring day. We have reason to be joyful, for—"

The door opened again. This time Katie didn't even look around. She didn't want the lump that clogged her throat to turn into tears if she was disappointed again. But Booker caught her eye and jerked his head toward the back. When she followed his gaze, she saw her mother, father and Travis filing in.

Her mother looked at her and smiled. Then her father smiled, too, and Katie felt a tremendous weight lift from her shoulders.

Rebecca immediately jumped up and led the Rogers family to the pew where she and Josh were sitting, and relinquished the baby for the first time—to Katie's father.

EPILOGUE

Six months later...

TROY KICKED HIS LEGS and chewed his fist as Booker held him in one arm and stood back to see the effect of his new sign. Booker T & Son's Automotive Repair. He liked the look of it, liked the sound of it, too. He'd paid Lionel off, and now he and Katie were expanding their business to the lot next door. They needed the space right away, because Katie had built a thriving Internet business selling tire rims through Booker T's Automotive Web site.

"What do you think?" he asked Katie, glancing over at his wife.

It had snowed heavily last night. Katie was wearing a parka, jeans and boots, and her breath misted on the early morning air. "It's great," she said, smiling widely. "But we're going to have to change it as soon as we have another child. You know that, don't you?"

"We should have a couple of years yet. Troy isn't even walking." He kissed his baby's cheek, and Troy immediately started babbling, "Da, da, da."

Booker raised his eyebrows. "Hear that?"

Katie was still staring at the sign. "What?"

"Troy's saying his first words."

She turned her attention to their son, but Troy jammed a finger in his mouth and stopped talking. "He's not saying anything."

"He just said Dada. Listen." Booker put his forehead to Troy's, pulled the baby's finger out of his mouth and met his eyes. "Say it again, Troy. Say 'Dada.'"

Troy blinked, his round blue eyes staring innocently up at him, and Katie started to laugh. "You're dreaming."

"Wait. He said it a minute ago. Come on, Troy."

"No!" Katie told their son, scowling playfully. "Say Mama… *Ma-ma.*"

Troy looked from Katie to Booker and broke into a drooly grin. "He'll say it in a sec," Booker told her, but a car pulled into the lot, distracting all three of them, and he turned to see Rebecca driving a new Jaguar. Delaney, who'd just had a baby boy three weeks earlier, was in the passenger seat.

"Whoa, early Christmas present?" Booker asked as Rebecca lowered her window.

Rebecca exchanged a look with Delaney. "It *was* going to be my Christmas present," she said. "But I'm taking it back."

He and Katie moved closer. "Why?"

Tears welled up in Rebecca's eyes, yet she was smiling. "Because I just got a better one."

"What's that?" Katie asked, sounding as confused as Booker felt.

"The lab called yesterday."

"The *lab?*" Booker repeated.

"I went there because I was afraid to trust the test I did at home." A tear escaped and ran down Rebecca's cheek. She wiped it away, sniffed and gave them a watery smile. "I'm pregnant!"

* * * * *

Books by Brenda Jackson

Harlequin Desire

The Westmoreland Legacy

The Rancher Returns
His Secret Son
An Honorable Seduction
His to Claim
Duty or Desire

Forged of Steele

Seduced by a Steele
Claimed by a Steele

Visit her Author Profile page at Harlequin.com, or brendajackson.net, for more titles.

TEMPERATURES RISING

Brenda Jackson

To the love of my life, Gerald Jackson Sr.

To the Mother Nature Matchmakers' author team—Carmen Green and Celeste O. Norfleet. I enjoyed working with you ladies on this one.

To everyone who joined me on the 2009 cruise to Canada. This one is for you!

He that troubleth his own house
shall inherit the wind: and the fool
shall be servant to the wise of heart.
—*Proverbs* 11:29

CHAPTER ONE

"SHERRI, I WOULD be honored if you joined me for dinner at my club tonight."

Sherri Griffin never, ever got headaches, not in all her twenty-seven years. At least not until recently, when she'd taken the job of producer and program director of WLCK, a Key West radio station. That was when she had encountered Terrence Jefferies, a former NFL player for the Miami Dolphins and one of the station's sports commentators.

He was also the owner of Club Hurricane, a popular nightclub in the Keys frequented by celebrities. From what she'd heard, when Terrence began playing pro football he had been nicknamed the Holy Terror by sportscasters because of his oftentimes surly attitude on the field. Besides Mean Joe Greene, there had not been another defensive tackle that had been so respected and feared. But when it came to pursuing women, he used an entirely different strategy. He was all smooth and debonair and never came across as intimidating or bad. Just relentlessly determined.

The man was also handsome as sin.

Drawing in a deep breath, she pulled herself together before looking up from the document she was reading to acknowledge Terrence's entry into her office. Her answer today would be the same one she'd given him yesterday, the day before and for the past few weeks. Little did he know, it would take more than a gorgeous face, broad shoulders and tight buns to make her change her mind. She had to admit, though, there was definitely something about muscle shirts and jeans that clearly defined a well-built male body.

"Thanks for the invitation, but I'll be busy," she responded.

He simply smiled, and that softening around his lips actually sharpened her senses…as if they weren't keen enough already where he was concerned. "One of these days I'm going to follow you home to find out just how you're spending your evenings," he said in a deep and throaty voice.

Definitely without you in them, she thought, wondering if perhaps she was making a mistake by avoiding him, as her best friend, Kimani Cannon, claimed. According to Kim, whenever the Holy Terror made a pass, any normal woman would run with it and rush for the goal line, not turn away like she constantly did. Kim thought the man was as gorgeous as any man had a right to be, and wildly sexy. Grudgingly, Sherri could only admit Kim was right.

But Terrence also had a reputation a mile long, one she would never be able to tolerate. She hadn't been at the station a week when his breakup with some wealthy socialite had been plastered all over the front page of the *Key West Citizen.*

"Sherri?"

She returned her attention to him, wishing he wouldn't say her name like that. Doing so always caused her to remember him in her dreams. And yes, she would admit she'd dreamed about the infuriating man a few times, but as far as she was concerned that meant nothing…other than the fact that she was a woman who could appreciate a stunning male with definite sex appeal.

She placed the documents in her hand down on her desk as she met his gaze. "How I spend my evenings shouldn't concern you, Terrence."

He smiled again and she tried like heck to ignore the little shivers that ran down her spine. The man had a dimple in his right cheek, for heaven's sake! She let out a sigh. He was getting to her, and dimple or no dimple, she was determined not to let him. She knew getting her into his bed was all a game to him—a game of conquest that she had no intention of playing.

"And what if I said I wanted to make it my concern?" he asked, sitting on the edge of her desk and leaning in close.

She tried to ignore the clean and manly aroma of his aftershave. "In that case I would say you have more time and energy than you really need. You might want to channel them elsewhere."

She watched as his mouth—more specifically, his sinfully sculpted lips bordered by a neatly trimmed mustache and beard—eased into a grin. The grin showed his dimple again. She let out a slow breath. If she thought his smile was sexy, then his grin was guaranteed to take a woman's breath away.

"I've been trying to channel them elsewhere for about a month now," he said in a way that told her he still wasn't getting her message. "From the moment I first laid eyes on you I decided to channel all my thoughts, my time and my energy solely on you."

Sherri could only stare at him and wonder if he ever

ran out of pick-up lines. Reluctantly, she would even admit he was good at delivering them. It was a good thing that, thanks to Ben Greenfield, she was immune. “Don’t waste your time, Terrence.”

He shook his head and chuckled, and just like the smile and grin before them the chuckle was explosive. She could feel goose bumps forming on her arm. “It will be time worth wasting,” he said, leaning in closer.

She wished she could tell him that she was technically the boss of the radio station and that he was an employee. But she knew that wouldn’t work. Terrence and the station’s owner, Warrick Fields, were good friends and Terrence’s contract stipulated he reported only to Warrick. Everyone’s job was to keep the Holy Terror happy, especially since his show received high ratings each week and pulled in huge sponsorships. There was even talk of the show going into syndication next year.

It didn’t help matters that Warrick Fields was her mother’s twin brother. He had taken her complaints about Terrence with a grain of salt, which proved in this case blood wasn’t thicker than water. Uncle Warrick actually thought Terrence’s “innocent” flirtation was amusing.

“I can see your mind is busy at work,” Terrence said, interrupting her thoughts. “I appreciate a woman who enjoys mulling over things, but now it’s you who’s wasting time. You can’t deny this chemistry between us.”

No, she couldn’t deny it. Nor would she act on it. “I hate to rush you off, Terrence, but as you can see I have plenty to do.”

He glanced at her desk. “I’m going to have to talk to Warrick about that. He shouldn’t work you so hard. You should have playtime.”

She rolled her eyes and imagined just what kind of playtime he was talking about. “I don’t need you to run interference for me. I can hold my own. Thank you.”

“If you’re sure,” he said, smiling and getting to his feet.

“I’m positive.”

“Then I’ll let you get back to work.”

Sherri let out a relieved breath when he turned and headed toward the door. Just her luck, he stopped before walking over the threshold and turned back around. When he caught her gaze, she felt the thud deep in her chest at the same time a heated sensation traveled down her spine. He stood there in her doorway, all six foot three of him, and she could only stare at the well-built body. And his dark eyes were focused right on her.

“I won’t give up, Sherri. I think you know that,” he said in a determined tone. Not intimidating, not threatening. Just promising and unwavering.

Yes, she did know that, and the thought that one day he just might succeed made her pulse pound. But she would continue to resist him since getting involved in a relationship was the last thing on her mind. Building a career at the station was her top priority.

She made no response to what he’d said. He really didn’t give her a chance since he then turned and walked out the door, closing it behind him. Only then did she lean back in her chair and breathe. His masculine scent lingered in her office and she reached out and touched the spot on her desk where he’d sat. It was hot. The man was so hot-blooded he was capable of leaving heat behind.

He was determined to make trouble and she was just as determined not to let him. She had a job to do.

Uncle Warrick was thinking about retiring in another year and he wanted her to be ready to take over as station manager when he did so. She would prove to her uncle that his faith in her was not a mistake, and that she would be more than capable of managing the day-to-day operations of WLCK. Although it seemed the Holy Terror was not going to make her job easy, there was no way she would let him get in the way of her achieving her goal.

She stood and walked to the window and looked out. Key West was a beautiful seaport city and WLCK served the people by being one of the most popular stations in the area. She loved working here.

She had arrived almost a month ago and discovered the radio station that her uncle owned was a nice size compared to others she'd seen. Although the pay scale wasn't any higher, not too many other stations could boast of having an ocean within walking distance.

The first change she had implemented upon taking the job was reinstating the dress code. According to Uncle Warrick, there had always been a dress code, but somewhere down the line the employees had ignored it, reasoning that it didn't matter how they looked since the audience couldn't see them.

Sherri believed in dressing professionally, and in the end she and the staff had compromised. The too-laid-back attire of shorts and flip-flops had gotten ruled out and replaced by business casual, with the majority of the employees wearing jeans and tops. Personally, she'd never been a jeans-wearing woman. While working around a more aristocratic crowd at her uncle's station in D.C., she had gotten used to business suits. Going from professional to casual wasn't as easy as she'd thought, but she was working on it.

She glanced at her watch and walked back over to her desk. Terrence's sports talk show would be airing in a few minutes and she wanted to tune in. Each office was equipped with an intercom that broadcasted all the shows so you could listen at will. Not that she was all into sports, but she made a habit of tuning in to his show, which filled an hour time slot twice a week.

Flipping on the dial of the radio unit beside her desk, she leaned back in her chair and slipped off her shoes with a long sigh. She'd spend the next hour with Terrence Jefferies. The man who was trying to get next to her—and the man she was determined to ignore.

TERRENCE COULDN'T HELP but smile after hanging up the phone from talking to his sister. Olivia was happy and he was happy for her. It seemed the ugly hands of disaster hadn't caught her in their clutches the way they had his father.

His mother had walked out on his old man, leaving him with the task of becoming a single father with three kids to raise. Terrence had been ten at the time, Duan twelve and Olivia only three. Things might not have been so bad if the man his mother had run off with hadn't had a wife and kid of his own.

He was glad Olivia hadn't listened to their father a few months back when he found out she'd gotten serious about a guy—a guy who just happened to be running against their father for a senate seat in the Georgia General Assembly. She had married Reggie Westmoreland and now she had a man who loved her and a huge family who had embraced her with a warm and sincere welcome.

Terrence glanced at his watch. He had already touched base with Cullen Carlisle, better known as CC, whom he'd hired to manage Club Hurricane a few years ago. According to CC, things were pretty busy for a Tuesday night, which wasn't surprising considering this was the first week in June. Every year at this time college students headed south before making the trip home, wherever home was for them.

So far there had been only one situation where CC, who stood two inches taller than Terrence and weighed close to two-fifty, had had to intervene to bring order. A lamp on one of the tables had gotten broken and the man responsible quickly paid for the damages. Terrence chuckled. Knowing CC, it was either pay up then or have pieces of the broken lamp shoved down your throat. To say CC took his job seriously was an understatement.

Terrence decided to do something he rarely did—be in bed before ten. Might as well since he hadn't managed to talk Sherri into joining him at the club.

Sherri Griffin.

It took a lot for him to admit that he was virtually obsessed with the woman and had been since walking into Warrick's office a month ago and finding her standing there.... Bending over was more like it. She had leaned down to pick a paper clip off the floor. He had appreciated the look of her shapely backside before getting a chance to see her face, and when he had, he had been pleased with the total package.

As he removed the last piece of his clothes to step into the shower, he couldn't help but recall the exact moment she had straightened her body, turned around and looked into his face. He had stood there, literally transfixed while drinking in the lusciousness of her curves before taking an admiring visual path up to her face.

If there was such a thing as instant, mind-blowing physical attraction, he had experienced it right then and there. A woman being pretty was one thing, but being punch-in-the-gut beautiful was another. First there was the most mesmerizing pair of sable-brown eyes he'd ever seen. Then there was a rounded chin on a medium-brown oval face, the two somehow totally in sync with each other. In addition to the softness of her high cheekbones and her shoulder-length styled hair, she had a pair of lips he would have given anything, possibly even his Heisman Trophy, to get a taste of.

Sizzling heat had instantly invaded his body, and it had taken Warrick saying his name twice before he had dragged his gaze away from her. But not before that same gaze had studied her hands and found her fingers ringless. And not before he'd decided that his six months of sexual draught were about to come to an end.

While Warrick had gone about making introductions, Terrence could tell by the set of Sherri's jaw that she hadn't liked the interest he was showing in her and she wouldn't make things easy for him. No problem there since he was a man who appreciated a challenge every once in a while. Trouble was, he hadn't counted on her still being a difficult case almost an entire month later. He refused to believe he was losing his touch or that the physical attraction hadn't been mutual. He had seen the flame that had come alive in her eyes, although she had immediately tried to douse it.

For him, Sherri Griffin projected a number of things

and sexual pleasure headed the list. There was something totally feminine and sensually captivating about her. While she tried coming across as all business, he refused to go there with her. The only level he was willing to meet her on was a sexual one. The effect she had on him would make it impossible for things to be otherwise.

So since she wanted to play hard to get, he would start turning up the heat. What the hell. At thirty-four, he still enjoyed having fun and there hadn't been any excitement in his life since finding out about Olivia's involvement with their father's political enemy. And as the warm rush of water trickled over his skin, he quickly came up with a plan to deal with Ms. Griffin.

By the time he got in bed less than an hour later, his body was relaxed and his mind was clear. He didn't intend to overwhelm her or pressure her. Instead, he would use the oldest trick known to a desperate man, one that included seduction that was impossible to resist. He wasn't called the Holy Terror for nothing.

CHAPTER TWO

"I CAN'T BELIEVE you turned him down again."

From the top of the stairs, Sherri looked at Kim, who was still standing below with an astounded expression on her face. Three days a week she and Kim met to jog along the beach where their condos were located. After leaning over and inhaling slow and deep, Sherri straightened her body and placed her hands on her hips.

The disappointment in Kim's voice was evident, and Sherri couldn't help wondering why. "Really, Kim, it's not that bad. He'll get over it, but now I'm worried as to whether or not you will. What's with you wanting me to go out with him, knowing his reputation?"

Instead of answering, Kim jogged up the stairs to join her. After taking a huge gulp of water from the water bottle, she said, "Because I know you can handle him."

If only Kim knew just how wrong she was, Sherri thought. She was still reeling from the side effects of that visit he had made to her office two days ago.

"Besides, you need to indulge yourself in a fling," Kim added.

Now it was Sherri whose face was filled with astonishment. She couldn't believe her friend had made such an outlandish statement. "Let me get this right. You think my way to handle him is to have an affair with him?" She saw the smile that lit Kim's features and wasn't all that pleased it was at her expense.

"Hey, get the daggers out of your eyes," Kim said, laughing. "I'm just reminding you of the promise you made to me last year."

Sherri lifted a brow. "And what promise was that?"

"The promise that once you got out of here and were settled, you would let go of that situation with Ben Greenfield and concentrate on meeting someone else."

Sherri dragged her eyes away from Kim. "I've been busy," she said, which in a way was true.

Kim wiggled her brows. "Now that reminds me of another promise you've broken, the one where you swore you would never let work interfere with pursuing a worthwhile relationship with a man. Especially because Ben claimed the reason he was breaking off your engagement was that you could never make time in your busy schedule for him, so he—"

"Found someone else," Sherri finished for her softly. At the time she'd felt it had been a lousy excuse for his infidelity. His betrayal had hurt.

"You said you wouldn't give another man the chance to make that claim," Kim reminded her.

"Which is the reason I refuse to get involved with anyone," Sherri said. "I don't have the time right now. I need to learn all I can and—"

"You know all you need to know about running a radio station, Sherri. Come on, this isn't the first one you've managed. All you had to do is become familiar with the setup of WLCK. You're good at what you do," Kim said as they began walking slowly toward Sherri's bungalow.

"Thanks."

"You're welcome. Now back to the reason why you won't go out with the Holy Terror," Kim said while looping her arms around her friend's shoulders.

Sherri couldn't help but smile. Kim refused to let up, and it served Sherri right for convincing her friend to move to the Keys with her when she had gotten the job offer from her uncle Warrick. Since Kim was a nurse, it hadn't been hard for her to get a job at one of the hospitals here.

Sherri had just opened her mouth to say something when she saw the floral arrangement in front of her door. "Wow! I wonder where these came from."

She picked up the vase filled with a beautiful arrangement of mixed flowers. "They're gorgeous, aren't they?"

"Yes, so who sent them?" Kim asked.

Sherri pulled off the card and opened it up. Moments later she massaged the bridge of her nose and closed her eyes, not wanting to believe the message written on the card.

"Well, Sherri, who sent them?"

She opened her eyes and frowned at Kim. "They're from Terrence, like you really wouldn't know," she said.

Kim placed a hand over her mouth in surprise. "The Holy Terror sent you those?"

Sherri lifted her heard and quirked a brow. "Don't tell me you're really surprised about this," she said.

Kim shrugged. "Well, I am. I did my research on the guy and everything I've read about Terrence Jefferies indicates that when it comes to pursuing women he doesn't put out a lot of effort or give it much thought. He doesn't have to since women usually flock to him."

She glanced at the floral arrangement. “I would think a lot of thought went into ordering those.”

Sherri would think so, too, but then, she hadn’t gone to the trouble of doing an investigation of Terrence like Kim had done. “I can’t get weakened by this,” she decided to say. “I’ll thank him for the flowers but make absolutely sure he understands that nothing has changed. I still won’t go out with him.”

She looked at the flowers and couldn’t help but smile.

Her smile faded when she noticed the sympathetic look on Kim’s face. Kim knew her better than anyone. “I’m headed for troubled waters, aren’t I?” she asked her friend softly.

Kim chuckled. “Yes, and I hope you can swim.”

LATER THAT NIGHT after taking her shower, Sherri put on her silk bathrobe and then curled up on the sofa with the card she’d received with the flowers. Again she read the message Terrence had written.

Please have dinner with me tomorrow night at my club.
Terrence

The man just wouldn’t give up. She wondered what would happen if she refused him again. Would he continue to be persistent? She felt her body tremble at the thought.

During her first week on the job, Terrence had been out of town attending his sister’s wedding. But from the moment her uncle Warrick had introduced them, she had felt this pull, this sexual chemistry. Unlike him, she had been willing to ignore it, to move on and place her focus on more important issues like becoming acquainted with the day-to-day operations of the station. But that didn't mean he hadn't crossed her mind a few times or that he wouldn't give her system one hell of a jolt whenever she would run into him in the corridors.

She recalled seeing him at the water fountain one day, and the sight of him bending over and drinking water—how his mouth adjusted to take in the liquid—had made her senses whirl and her blood rush through her veins. And when he'd finished, he had licked his lips. She had been totally embarrassed when he had glanced up and seen her staring at him like a ninny.

She reread his card. The least she could do was call and thank him for the flowers, she thought, glancing across the room at them. She had found the perfect spot, right in front of the window. She had the window open and a soft breeze was flowing through, wafting the fragrance toward her.

Before she changed her mind, she called him.

"Hello."

Even with the noise she could hear in the background, Terrence's deep masculine voice came through the phone loud and distinctively clear. It moved over her skin like a soft caress. "Terrence, this is Sherri."

"I know. Your name popped up," he said, and she could just imagine the potency of the smile he had on his lips.

"Thanks for the flowers. They're beautiful," she rushed on to say, deciding to stick with the reason she'd phoned and end the call.

"You're welcome. I'm glad you like them." There was a pause. Then he asked, "What about dinner? Will you join me tomorrow night here at the club?"

Sherri closed her eyes. In the recesses of her mind, she could actually pick up the scent of his aftershave and could see that enticing smile on his lips, the one that made her feel as if something akin to liquid fire flowed through her veins. She then thought of his body heat, the heat she felt whenever she was around him. The same heat he had left in her office. She opened her eyes when she actually felt the phone tremble in her hands.

She could think of all the reasons she should not have dinner with him. She had gone over them a number of times before, most recently just an hour ago while she was in the shower. In essence, nothing had changed. Yet for some reason she wanted to have dinner with him.

"Yes, I'll join you for dinner," she said quickly, accepting that although nothing had changed, she needed to get beyond this thing with him. Maybe having dinner with him this one time would help her do so.

"All right. Do you want me to pick you up or would you rather we meet here?"

She did not want him to pick her up. Him coming into her home for any reason was something she'd rather avoid. "I can meet you there," she said. "Will six o'clock be okay?"

"Fine. Do you know how to get to Club Hurricane?" he asked.

"Yes. Although I've never been there, I've passed by it a few times. It looks like a real nice place."

"It is. And I look forward to showing you around."

There was something about the way he'd made that last statement that warned her to keep her senses in check while around him. Not doing so would be reckless. "I'll look forward to it. Good night."

"Good night, Sherri."

Sherri clicked off the phone, feeling warm and tingly all through her body. Terrence had a way of making her feel that way, even when he was miles away.

IT TOOK A few seconds after disconnecting the call from Sherri for Terrence to remember he had visitors. He glanced across the table at the two men who'd dropped by the club to see him, his best friends, Lucas McCoy and Stephen Morales. The three had met while attending the University of Miami and had instantly bonded. Lucas was engaged; his fiancée lived in New York but had agreed to move to Key West after the wedding. He was building a beautiful house for them on his family property.

Stephen, whose birth name was Esteban, was a deputy sheriff. A few years ago he had given up a rather plush job with his father's successful construction company to work with his paternal grandfather, the local sheriff.

"Are we keeping you from your date, Terrence?" Stephen asked, plastering a huge smile on his face.

"Yeah, man, we can check you out later if we're in the way," Lucas followed up by saying.

Terrence returned their gazes, not giving any sign that he was taking either of them seriously. "You're fine. My date isn't until tomorrow night."

"Anyone we know?" Stephen was curious enough to ask.

"No, but eventually you will." After he'd said the words, he wondered why he was so certain. It wasn't as if he intended to make Sherri a permanent fixture in his life. In fact, he intended for anything between them—once it got started—to be short-term. At the moment, she was an itch that needed scratching. Bad.

And when had he ever wanted his two closest friends to meet any woman he was involved with? Things with Vicki Waller had been different because she had somehow gotten it into her head that she would one day become Mrs. Terrence Jefferies, although he had told her time and time again that she wouldn't. Their breakup had made the papers, but only because she had erroneously informed a number of people they were planning to get married.

"So we're still on for this coming weekend?" Lucas was asking, reclaiming his attention. They had made plans to get some boating time in. Forecasters had predicted nice weather.

"Only if you're sure Emma isn't coming to town," Terrence said, referring to Lucas's fiancée. Terrence saw the tightening of Lucas's jaw, and even before his friend spoke he knew what he was about to say. Lucas and Emma had been doing the long-distance-dating thing for almost a year now, but lately it seemed Lucas was traveling more to New York than Emma was coming to Florida.

"I'm sure she won't be coming," was Lucas's terse response.

"Okay, then," Terrence said, reaching out and squeezing Lucas's shoulder. "Our weekend on the water is all set."

"Okay, pal, don't think we're letting you off the hook that easy," Stephen said, grinning. "Who is this woman that just brought a sparkle to your eyes?"

"You're imagining things," Terrence said, rolling those same eyes.

"I don't think so," Stephen countered. "We want a name."

Knowing they wouldn't let up, he said, "Her name is Sherri Griffin. She's Warrick's niece and works at the station as a programmer and producer. However, Warrick's grooming her to be manager when he retires."

"Is she pretty?" Lucas wanted to know.

Terrence didn't say anything for a minute while sipping his drink, and then he said, "She is stunning. I mean jaw-dropping gorgeous, even in her business suits."

Lucas chuckled. "The woman actually wears business suits? Here in the Keys?"

Terrence smiled. "Yes, but I'm sure sooner or later she'll be coming out of them." *And I'm going to make sure she does.*

LATER THAT NIGHT Terrence strode through the door of his condo, satisfied that he'd finally gotten Sherri to have dinner with him. Now he had to continue to move forward. Remain calm. Stay in control. Yet he couldn't overlook the same key questions that persistently reared their inquisitive heads. Why did it matter? Why was getting under Sherri Griffin's skin so important to him? Why when he thought of such a thing happening did his heart thump furiously in his chest?

He moved to the window and looked out of it with serious eyes. Intense eyes. And to top it off, warning signals were going off in his head. He was not a man who thrived on escalating relationships. For reasons instilled deep within him, he much preferred affairs that led nowhere, and he certainly never considered the thought or possibility that he would diligently pursue a woman who refused to reciprocate the interest.

Yet he was.

He exhaled deeply as he moved toward his bedroom, fully aware that he still had his work cut out for him. For the moment, he wouldn't spend time questioning why reaching his goal of bedding Sherri Griffin was of vital importance to him.

CHAPTER THREE

SHERRI INHALED DEEPLY as she walked through the doors of Club Hurricane. After deciding a change of clothes was in order, she had rushed home from the station to quickly strip off her business suit and shower before slipping into a short pleated skirt and a silk top.

She glanced around and was impressed with the decor of the establishment and its ability to blend both casual and tailored, thanks to a solid wall of glass that provided a panoramic view of the ocean. Immediately she knew she had entered Terrence Jefferies's domain. It was as high-class as the man himself.

She was greeted by a hostess. "Ms. Griffin?"

Sherri was surprised the woman knew her name. "Yes?"

The hostess smiled. "Mr. Jefferies has asked that I escort you to him."

Sherri returned the smile. "All right."

They passed the bar and stage on the way to the part of the club where food was served. Terrence stood there waiting. Sherri's breath caught the moment she saw him, dressed casually in a pair of white linen slacks and matching long-sleeve shirt that hung outside his pants and made him look muscular and toned. Appearances were important, personally and professionally, and he'd cornered the market for both.

"Thank you, Debbie. I'll take over from here," he said, taking Sherri's hand.

Debbie nodded before walking off, leaving Sherri alone with Terrence. He looked at her and smiled. "Thanks for joining me tonight."

She felt the nervous tension in her stomach from just the feel of her hand in his. "Thanks for inviting me," she said.

He then looked down at her from head to toe before returning an appreciative gaze to her face. "You look nice."

"You look nice, as well." And she meant it. He was definitely one fine-looking man.

He tightened his hand around hers. "I promised you a tour, so let me show you around."

"All right."

"The club is really divided into three sections. When you first enter you have the bar with the big screen for sports enthusiasts. There we not only serve drinks but sandwiches, salads and appetizers. The area across from the bar is where the music is set up so it can be heard in all parts of the club."

They stopped walking and he gestured to where the band was still setting up. "We have live music on Tuesdays, Thursdays and the weekends. A huge dance floor separates these two areas from the restaurant, which overlooks the ocean."

She glanced at the huge glass wall that covered the length of the back of the club. "Nice setup."

"Thanks. It was designed to take into consideration all age groups, from the twentysomething up to the fifty-and-over crowd." They walked slowly back to the dining area. "This part of the club is my favorite. I tried capturing the Key West flavor while maintaining a classy opulence," he said proudly.

She glanced over the restaurant. "And I think you succeeded." On each of the mahogany tables sat a hurricane lantern on top of an ocean-blue tablecloth. The chairs, padded with contoured backs, were shaped like seashells. The design of the chairs and the ocean on the other side of the glass window combined to create a seashore atmosphere while maintaining a high level of classiness.

He then gave her a tour of the kitchen and the rest of the club. "What made you decide on the name?" she asked when they returned to the restaurant area.

He smiled. "Two reasons. First, I played football for the University of Miami Hurricanes, and second, this area is susceptible to more hurricanes than any other part of Florida. I was in my first year of college when Hurricane Andrew blew up. Let's just say hurricanes have given me a whole new respect for Mother Nature."

"Hurricanes and all, you do like it here." It was more of a statement than a question.

He chuckled. "Yes, I like it here. I enjoy going back home to visit, but as far as putting down roots, I can't imagine living anywhere else."

He glanced at his watch. "I hope you're hungry," he said, keeping a firm grip on her hand while leading her toward an elevator.

Sherri nervously glanced around. "Yes, but aren't we eating here?"

Another smile touched Terrence's lips. "No. For space and privacy, my suite upstairs will be better. Do you mind?"

She glanced up at him, searched his face for any indication that she should mind. There was still chemistry between them, she couldn't deny that, but she didn't feel threatened at the thought of being alone with him. She forced herself to relax. "No, I don't mind."

They stepped into the elevator, and after Terrence pressed a button, the door closed. She'd never noticed just how intimate the inside of an elevator was until now. Nor had she known how hard it was to resist temptation until now. Terrence stood looking at her but saying nothing. He didn't have to. His eyes said it all.

What she hadn't read in them before stepping into the elevator was clearly in his gaze now. That longstanding desire she had tried to ignore was obvious. Whether it was because he saw her as a challenge or just the new woman on the block that he had to have a piece of, she wasn't sure. But there was no doubt in her mind that he wanted her, and, if given the opportunity, he wouldn't waste any time getting her.

That's where temptation came in. She was tempted to give in to Kim's way of thinking: that her constant rejection of his advances was absurd and that women with their heads screwed on right didn't hesitate to date someone like Terrence. As far as Sherri was concerned, even being here tonight spoke volumes, but she wasn't ready to throw all caution to the wind. She had a tendency to take things slow, wade in the water before actually taking a dive. But still, all she would have to do now was to reach out and touch him. Feel his muscles. Taste that smile right off his lips.

Before desire could play havoc with her common sense, the elevator door swooshed open. His hand touched the center of her back as he led her out of the elevator, and it took everything within her not to moan from his touch. Her breasts suddenly felt tender. Her nipples felt hard against the fabric of her blouse. And the body heat emanating from him was stirring sensations deep inside her.

They stepped off the elevator into a brightly lit hall, and with his hand still firmly placed on her back, he led her to a room that had a balcony facing the ocean and a table for two had been set. Candlelight and soft music told her they would be sharing a romantic evening.

She glanced around and saw a king-size bed against the wall. When her gaze met his, he read the question in her eyes.

"It's needed," he said softly. "On weekends the club stays open until two and it's easier for me to crash here instead of going home. You're free to take a look around and enjoy the view of the ocean from the balcony while I phone the kitchen so they can deliver our food."

She nodded and gave an appreciative glance around the room, making sure her main focus was no longer on the huge bed. As she walked toward the balcony she couldn't help but be impressed. Just like downstairs, the suite was immaculate. The only difference was that the furnishings in here were modern.

"Would you like something to drink while we wait?"

She stopped walking and glanced over her shoulder. He stood there, braced against a table, his eyes unerringly on her. Her body responded. Just that simple. Just that easy. She wondered if he could gauge her response to him. "Yes."

"White wine okay?"

She saw his gaze lower to her legs, and instinctively she smoothed the hem of her short skirt along her thighs. "That would be fine. Thanks." She turned around and continued walking, knowing his eyes watched every step she took. A part of her wished he wouldn't pay so much attention to her body. Then another part, the one that appreciated the fact she was a woman, didn't mind at all; in fact, that part was glad he noticed. He was a man, after all. It would be up to her to stay in control and keep things in perspective.

Before stepping out on the balcony she glanced over at his bed once more, wondering how many women he'd had between those sheets and deciding right then and there that no matter how much sexual magnetism he transmitted, she wouldn't be one of them.

WITH TWO WINEGLASSES in his hands, Terrence moved toward the balcony then suddenly stopped when he glanced ahead and saw Sherri. She leaned against the balcony's rail while the wind gently blew in her hair. He sucked in a deep breath, felt his body get hard and quickly decided it would be best to stay just where he was for the time being. No problem. She hadn't noted his presence, which gave him the opportunity to notice hers.

She looked sensational, sexy and hot all rolled into one. She was tall, around five-eight, curvy, with a small waist and dark hair that billowed around her shoulders in soft, bouncy waves. Even now her outfit made sweat bead out on his forehead. She had the perfect legs for her short skirt and the perfect breasts for her low-cut blouse and he would love the chance to taste both legs and breasts. If ever there was a reason to call a woman delectable, then this would be it. He could just envision starting at the soles of her feet and working his mouth upward toward her lips, taking time to fully savor the feminine part of her in between. He knew that degree of lovemaking would come later. Right now he needed to work his way up to a simple kiss.

He smiled then, thinking that when they kissed there wouldn't be anything simple about it. It definitely wouldn't be anything close to a brush across the lips or a light smooch. He intended to make up for lost time. Work his tongue in her mouth in a way that she would know, would always remember, that he had been there.

SHERRI TURNED WHEN she heard the sound of Terrence returning. She took a deep breath and tried to calm herself. He was just a man. A man who, if given the opportunity, could change her life forever…but not for the better. She refused to let that happen. She had given one man total access to her heart and she would never do so again.

"Here you are," he said, handing the glass of wine to her.

"Thanks." She glanced back at the ocean. "This is such a beautiful view from here. So peaceful."

He followed her gaze. "You should be here to see it one morning at sunrise."

She looked at him over the rim of her glass. Was he issuing her an invitation? If so, it was definitely wasted. Instead of responding to what he'd said, she decided to change the subject. "Tell me about Terrence Jefferies."

He lifted a brow. "What do you want to know?"

"Anything you want to tell me."

He took a sip of his wine, and it was a few moments before he spoke. "My family lives in Atlanta. There's my father, my older brother, Duan, who is thirty-six, and my sister, Olivia, who got married last month. Olivia is twenty-seven."

"What about your mom?"

She saw the way his jaw tensed when he said, "I don't have a mother."

She felt bad for asking. Thinking his mother had evidently passed away, she said, "I'm sorry."

He lifted a brow. "Why? You didn't do anything."

"I shouldn't have asked about your mother," she said softly.

He stared back at the ocean before meeting her gaze. "My mother isn't dead, if that's what you're thinking. She and my father split when I was ten, Duan was twelve and Olivia was only three. She gave my father full custody of us, kept walking and never looked back."

"Oh." Sherri didn't know what to say. Her parents were still happily married after thirty years, and she couldn't imagine a woman not keeping in touch with her children. Deciding she needed to change the subject yet again, she said, "How long have you owned the club?"

"About four years. I purchased it right after an injury caused me to stop playing for the Dolphins and I decided to settle here instead of moving back to Atlanta."

"What made you decide to remain in South Florida?"

"Close friends from college, Stephen Morales and Lucas McCoy. We attended the University of Miami together. Stephen is a deputy sheriff and Lucas renovates houses. Another reason I decided to stay is that I like the area, especially the beaches."

As he spoke, she noticed his gaze had shifted from her eyes to her lips. A second of silence passed before he said in a deep, husky tone, "There's something I've wanted to do ever since the first day I saw you."

She fought to quell the sensations flowing through her. "What?"

"This." And then he lowered his head, skimming her lips lightly a few times before capturing them fully with his.

She felt the room tilt when he masterfully deepened the kiss, deliciously tempting her to submission. She moaned when his tongue roamed freely everywhere in her mouth before grasping hold on hers, toying with it, mating with it, feasting greedily on it. Her control crumbled in the intense and sensual assault of his mouth.

She felt the hardness of him pressing against her middle, and at that very moment her senses, the ones still operating, were thrown into overdrive, and her body felt like it was actually overheating. As shards of pleasure cascaded through her, her stomach tensed. Her nipples pressing against his chest ached. Heat flared between her legs and her pulse beat relentlessly.

When he finally pulled his mouth away, she dropped her face to his chest and stifled another moan. Her defenses were all but shattered as the result of one kiss. She hadn't expected it. Hadn't been fully prepared for it. Her mouth had yielded for him in a way it had never yielded for another man.

She lifted her head and met his eyes. The look he gave her was intense. Deep. Sensual. The air surrounding them actually seemed to thicken. She didn't know what sort of tactics he'd used when he played on the football field, but here, right now, he was using his own sensual weapon to advance and he clearly was determined to reach the goal line with her before the night was over. She opened her mouth to tell him that it was not going to happen when she heard a doorbell.

"Our dinner has arrived."

His words filtered through her chaotic mind, and before she could say anything, he had taken her hand and was leading her back inside.

HE INTENDED TO invade her territory.

Although Terrence figured she wouldn't like it, it would be done. He had gotten a taste of her, a taste that even a full-course meal later, he couldn't let go of.

Their conversation over dinner he'd dismissed as chitchat. She'd told him about being an only child with a lot of cousins and the only one of them interested in following in her uncle's footsteps by working in radio. She'd told him about her best friend, Kim, who had decided to move to the Keys with her. She'd told him how she intended to go shopping for a new car by the end of the year. One thing she hadn't mentioned was her love life, specifically the guy her uncle had mentioned, the one who supposedly had broken her heart last year.

He glanced across the table. After a long, drawn-out silence while they'd enjoyed another glass of wine, he decided to stir up conversation again by coming out and asking point-blank, "Do you engage in affairs?"

From the way her head snapped up and the surprised look on her face, he knew his question had caught her off guard. He watched as she regained her wits and released a long, slow breath. He even felt when the shiver passed through her.

Then he saw a slow smile touch her lips when she said, "I understand that you do."

She hadn't answered his question but had made a comment instead, one he fully intended to answer. "Yes,

I do," he murmured truthfully. "Short-term affairs. I don't do long term."

"Commitment phobia?"

"Not necessarily. I just decided very early in life that I would die single. Matters of the heart are not for me."

There was no need to tell her he felt that way because of the pain he'd seen his father endure after his mother had walked out on them for another man, nearly destroying their family in the process. Nor would he mention how as a child he had watched a once happily married man learn to cope as a divorced husband and a single father. A man whose life was filled with pain and sadness and for whom the only thing that mattered in his life was his children. Terrence was convinced to this day that his father had never gotten over the betrayal of his wife.

Just like he had never gotten over the betrayal of his mother.

"Then what about that article I read in the newspaper the first week I arrived? The one about your broken engagement."

He glanced over at her and decided to set the matter straight. "There was never an engagement. I don't ever plan to marry, and she knew it. I can only assume that she was hoping I would change my mind."

Deciding he needed to make sure Sherri fully understood so there would never be any misunderstanding, he held her gaze and then added, "That is one thing I don't intend to ever change my mind about. I will never marry."

SHERRI COULD ONLY NOD. Terrence was making his position absolutely clear to her, and she appreciated it because she now knew how to handle him in the future. Virtually the same way she'd been doing in the past. She didn't regret having dinner with him. It had been both enjoyable and enlightening.

It would be easy if she were the type of woman who had no qualms in engaging in the same type of affairs that he did, but she wasn't. Her parents were enjoying a relatively happy marriage, and although at this point in her career, marriage was the furthest thing from her mind, she still wanted the same for herself one day. A man who would love her and cherish her, give her his babies, his life, his world. Terrence had just told her in no uncertain terms that he was not the man for her. He lived for the moment, and the women he dated would never, ever get close to his heart. She wondered if the way his mother had walked out of his life was the reason. In a way, his take on things was no different from Kim's. As a child, she had watched her father physically abuse her mother, and because of it, although Kim did on occasion indulge in what she considered a healthy relationship, she never intended to marry.

Thinking the silence between them had extended long enough, she said, "Thanks again for dinner, Terrence. The steak was delicious. I commend your staff. It was the most incredible meal I've ever eaten."

He smiled at her compliment. "Thanks. We aim to please. I suggest you visit on a Wednesday night. It's ladies' night and our specialty dessert is a key lime pie that is to die for."

A smile touched her lips. "I think I will." She glanced at her watch. "It's getting late. I'm due in at the station rather early in the morning, and I need a good night's sleep."

"You can always stay here for the night."

She took his kindness for what it was. An invite to roll between the sheets with him. "Thanks, but I prefer my own bed," she said, getting to her feet.

"You're sure I can't entice you to enjoy dessert before you leave?" he asked, getting to his feet, as well. His voice was low and husky, making her wonder just what kind of dessert he was talking about. She had a feeling it wasn't anything his cooks could whip up in their kitchen. Rather, the two of them would be stirring up all the ingredients.

"Yes, I'm positive. I do need to leave." *Either that or be tempted to take you up on your offer.* Although she knew where he stood, he was still temptation, the type she was finding it hard to resist. Even now she could feel sexual tension flowing in the air between them, heightening her full awareness of him as a man.

The kiss they had shared hadn't helped matters. A part of her wished she could toss caution to the wind and engage in the type of affair he was used to, but she was too quick to give her heart. An involvement with Terrence would be heartbreak just waiting to happen.

But boy, was she tempted…

"If you're sure that you're ready to leave, I'll walk you down."

His words filtered through her mind and interrupted her thoughts. He was giving her a chance to change her mind, to reconsider his invitation. But she wouldn't. "Thanks, and yes, I am sure."

"All right."

She watched as he rounded the table to walk toward her, and her heart pounded deep in her chest with every step he took. He would escort her down but he intended to kiss her again before he did. She felt it in her bones. She felt his intentions in the very air she was breathing. It was there on his face, in his expression, especially in the eyes that held her in their direct gaze.

She suddenly felt hot, light-headed. When he came to a stop in front of her, saying nothing but concentrating on her mouth, she felt weak in the knees. Although she wanted to deny it, desire was flooding her body. Blood rushed fast and furious through her veins. A hard thump pounded in her chest and a pool of heat gathered between her legs. The last thing she needed at that moment was all these sexual feelings, but they were there, complicating things.

He shifted his gaze lower, and, following the path of his gaze, she saw what now held his attention. Her nipples had hardened and were pressed against her blouse, making her arousal obvious.

His eyes returned to her mouth and he stood there for several moments before finally reaching out and placing his hands at her waist. The smile he gave her made her breath catch, and then he lowered his head and in one absolute imprisonment confined her lips to his.

She wound her arms around his neck. It was either that or slither to the floor from the impact of his kiss. The moment he captured her tongue, she was a goner. Then he released it, taking free rein of her mouth, unrestricted. She felt every touch, every flicker, every bold movement of his tongue—direct, unguarded, unrestrained.

A moan escaped from deep in her throat. She felt her resolve weakening when a scene of her in that bed across the room flashed through her mind. And he was there in that bed with her, hovering over her, making any resistance melt away.

A loud bang below had her jumping back out of his arms, drawing in a deep breath. She suppressed an inner shiver when she met his heated gaze, and she knew if given the chance he would pull her back in his arms and kiss her again, even take it to another level. Lord help her, but she needed to get out of there.

"I need to leave. Now," she said in a strained voice.

As if he understood, he nodded. "All right."

Taking her hand in his, he led her out of the room and toward the elevator. Lucky for her the doors opened the moment he pressed the button, and she quickly stepped inside.

When she saw he was about to join her, she said quickly, "You don't have to ride down with me."

The smile he gave her made her breath catch. "I know, but I wouldn't have it any other way. Regardless of what you might think, I can be a gentleman," he said, pushing a button for the lower floor.

Instead of speaking, she just nodded. She would be sure to add *gentleman* beneath *good kisser* on her list of his many attributes. Though she tried to ignore him once the elevator closed, he stood against the wall staring at her like he wanted to cross the space separating them and devour her.

She released a deep breath when the elevator stopped and the door swooshed open. She quickly stepped out and headed for the exit door. It was then that she heard the music. The band had started playing and the slow tune they were performing was one of her favorites. She unconsciously slowed her pace.

"Let's have at least one dance before you leave," Terrence whispered close to her ear as he took her hand in his.

She nodded, and within seconds he led her toward the dance floor. Heat surged through her the moment he pulled her into his arms. A frisson of sensual awareness invaded her entire being and the air surrounding them seemed supercharged. As if they had a mind of their own, her arms wrapped around him the same way his embraced her. She closed her eyes and placed her head on his chest despite thinking that she really needed to leave, go back to the safety of her home, and that dancing with him this way was too risky. But then, being held in his arms felt good, and like always when they were this close, she could feel her body responding to the pure masculinity of him. His muscles felt hard and firm beneath her fingers and she felt herself pressed even more tightly against him. Then her mind began wondering again. She wondered how it would feel to have his skin beneath her fingertips, how the texture of it would taste on her tongue.

"Sherri."

It took her a full minute to realize he had called her name. She looked up into the darkness of his eyes, desire lining his pupils. "Yes?"

"I was dead serious when I invited you to spend the night," he leaned down and whispered huskily.

She considered his invitation, really considered it. Although it had been a long time since she'd been involved in a physical relationship with a man, she still wasn't ready to give herself to him so fully and completely. Because of Ben, she was going out of her way to safeguard her heart from further hurt and pain, and she believed an affair with Terrence would lead to just that.

The song had ended, but they were still standing in the middle of the dance floor. "Come, let's sit over here," he said, leading her to one of the tables near the windows.

"We want the same thing, Sherri," he said when they were seated. "I think you know that."

She glanced over at him. "I want more from a relationship than just the physical. I'll never settle for just that again, Terrence."

He nodded. "And a physical relationship is all I can ever offer a woman."

Sherri stared at him for a few moments before slowly standing. Her words held finality when she spoke. "Then it would never work between us, because we want different things." She sighed deeply. "I'm leaving, since we fully understand each other."

And then she headed for the exit door without looking back.

CHAPTER FOUR

"This is the Holy Terror, and you're tuned to WLCK, the Keys' most important stroke on your radio. Although some of you die-hard football fans want to get a head start discussing the coming season, today on *Sports Talk* we're talking about Wimbledon, the oldest tennis tournament in the world, which starts shortly. There're many tennis fans out there in the audience, and I want to hear from you."

Sherri stood in the glass-enclosed booth next to where Terrence sat with a computer monitor flashing in front of him. Mark, the person who was usually available to screen incoming calls for *Sports Talk,* had called in sick and with a limited staff working during the summer months, she'd pitched in to help, which would have been fine if it hadn't put her in close contact with Terrence.

It had been almost two weeks since that night he had invited her to dinner. Two solid weeks during which time they'd passed each other in the halls and sat across from each other in meetings while trying to ignore the sexual tension radiating between them. Sexual tension that her parting words to him hadn't been able to eradicate.

Sighing deeply, she checked the clock in the hall. Terrence's show lasted an hour, and it had just started.

Even separated from him in the booth, she felt the effect of him just by listening to his voice. He had what most in the industry would refer to as a stroking voice, one that could pull a listener in.

He had gone into advertisements, giving five minutes before he was ready to take the first call.

As if he knew she was in the booth, he turned off his mike, took off his headset and looked her way. Their gazes locked. She felt the sensations she'd been trying to ignore, sensations she'd convinced herself had actually been a figment of her imagination. At this very moment he was proving her wrong. He was also making her remember that night the two of them had shared dinner alone. The kisses. Their dance. For her the Holy Terror experience was coming back in full force.

Her lips tightened when he leaned back in his chair and continued to study her. He should be keeping an eye on that computer monitor instead of on her. Likewise, she should be screening his incoming calls. She tried to ignore him but felt his gaze still glued to her, like that of a hungry predator with its next meal in focus.

Her only saving grace was that the jingle was about to end. She watched as he sat up straight in his chair, put his headset back on and turned the mike back on. Only then did he shift his attention from her.

She released a deep sigh. It was destined to be a long hour.

"HI, HOLY TERROR, this is Monica."

Terrence couldn't help but smile. Monica Kendricks was a frequent caller no matter what sport they were discussing. And she was a notorious flirt. "Monica, what can I do for you today?"

"Several things," she said in that feminine chuckle that actually had the tendency to grate on his nerves. "But the one I'm safe in requesting of you is for you to end a disagreement between me and several of my girlfriends. They say the nineteen courts at Wimbledon are composed of just rye grass but I remember reading somewhere it was Bermuda grass."

The first thing that came into Terrence's mind was who gave a crap. Were there really women somewhere who'd been arguing about the type of grass on the courts at Wimbledon? He shook his head. "I hate to tell you this, Monica, but you lose. All the courts at Wimbledon are composed of rye grass." And before she could comment, he moved to the next call.

"This is the Holy Terror."

"Holy, this is Thomas."

"Yes, Thomas. What's your question?"

"It's about Serena and Venus."

"What about them?"

"Rumor has it you use to date one of them," Thomas said.

"And if I did?"

"Will you be joining one or both in London later this month?"

"No, sorry to disappoint you," Terrence said, smiling.

"Hey, you could never disappoint me, man. I was there that night when the Dolphins clobbered the Cowboys to go to the Super Bowl thanks to your winning touchdown. You're the greatest."

He chuckled. "No, Muhammad Ali is."

"Oh, then you're the second greatest, and if you did

date one of the Williams girls, then you're also my hero."

Terrence shook his head again. It was one of those days.

AN HOUR LATER Terrence turned off his mike and removed his headset again before standing to work the kinks out of his body. He had gotten a record number of calls today. It seemed everyone had to say something about the Grand Slam season.

He glanced over at the glass booth. He could see the top of Sherri's head, which meant she was still there, probably telling disappointed callers the show was over. His lips curved into a smile when she stood and caught his eye. They hadn't said a word to each other for a couple of weeks while effectively waging one hell of a mental battle. As far as he was concerned such a battle could be fought anywhere but could only end in the bedroom.

Okay, so they were at opposing crossroads. She had happily ever after in her sights and he had no plans of indulging in anything remotely close. But what did that have to do with overactive testosterone and raging hormones? They were adults. They had needs. Who said they couldn't enjoy each other without any promises of tomorrow? No expectations. No obligations.

He imagined she assumed that she'd had the last word, and for the past couple of weeks he'd let her. That had given him time to think, make a few decisions and formulate a revised plan. The bottom line was that, for a reason he still hadn't yet figured out, he wanted her. He'd wanted other women in the past, but none with this degree of wanting. It kept him up at night with thoughts of how it would feel to slide between those luscious-looking thighs.

The two kisses they'd shared that night had done more damage than good. He thought if the kisses alone were that explosive, how would it feel to get naked with her, share her bed, get inside her body and take the word *stroking* to a whole other level and then some? He got hard just thinking about it. With him, being hard equated to one thing: getting laid.

Playing Mr. Nice with her hadn't gotten him anywhere, so it was time he lived up to his name. Determined, he moved toward the booth at the same time she came out of it. He stopped dead in his tracks wondering how a woman could look both professional and sexy at the same time. She liked wearing those business suits, and one of these days he intended to peel one right off her body, along with whatever she was wearing underneath.

He began walking again and came to a stop in front of her. He felt the sexual tension, a lot stronger today. "Hello, Sherri."

"Terrence. It was a nice show."

He smiled. "Thanks. And you look nice."

He hated making small talk when what he really wanted to do was scoop her up into his arms and take her somewhere—her office was one consideration—and make love to her until she begged for more and then start the hot and delicious process all over again until they were out of each other's systems.

"Thank you."

"So what are you doing for lunch?" he asked, looking at his watch.

"Haven't made any plans yet," she responded softly. "More than likely I'll work through lunch."

He looked back at her and smiled. "And miss the opportunity of going off somewhere with me to make out?"

Any doubts he'd had that she wanted him as much as he wanted her dissolved then and there. Desire was there in the eyes looking back at him. It was there in her expression, although she was trying like hell to hide it. Why was she so opposed to a short, no-strings-attached affair? Why couldn't she forget about that jerk who evidently hadn't appreciated her? And couldn't she temporarily suspend the idea of a little house and white picket fence? That could come later with some nice, willing guy who shared her views on the whole forever-after thing. What she and he needed to concentrate on was the needless torture they were going through now.

"How many times do I have to tell you that an affair between us won't work, Terrence?" she said with impatience in her voice.

"As many times as I'm going to tell you that it will not only work but it's a necessity."

She rolled her eyes. "A necessity? That's a good one." Her lips twitched in a smirk.

Now he was the impatient one. "Don't let me wipe that smirk off your face in a way that will have you moaning my name, Sherri."

Her smirk immediately turned to a frown. "I think you've said enough. My uncle may have given you free rein to say or do what you please around here, but I'm not included on your agenda."

He moved a step closer. "Baby, starting today you are my agenda," he said, his voice a low rumble. "Don't confuse the Mr. Nice and Persistent guy from before. Now all is fair in love and war."

She lifted her chin and glared at him. "Oh, now are you saying you're capable of falling in love?"

Now it was his turn to frown. "No, what I'm saying is not even close. But actions will speak louder than words. You'll see what I mean."

"I'm opposed to whatever you're thinking of doing."

A mischievous smile touched his lips. "Okay, I'll keep that in mind."

She inhaled deeply. "You really don't get it, do you?"

He chuckled. "Yeah, it's kind of hard for me to get it when you're emitting such hot vibes whether you want to send them or not. Now I'm giving you fair warning that I plan to act on them. And trust me when I say that you'll be the one *getting* it. Now if you will excuse me I need to go check on things at the club. You're welcome to join me for dinner if you like."

"No, thank you," she said firmly.

He smiled. "If you change your mind, just show up. I like surprises."

"HE LIKES SURPRISES. The nerve of the man!" Sherri muttered under her breath as she made her way back to her office. She had a good mind to turn around and tell him just where he could stick those surprises he liked so much.

Her footsteps halted when she saw her uncle walking quickly toward her office. "Uncle Warrick, you need to see me?"

"Yes, I just got a call from Jeremy Wilkins. He's decided to sell WSOV after all and wants to give me first dibs."

Sherri couldn't help but smile. "Uncle Warrick, that's wonderful. I know how long you've wanted to operate a station in Memphis."

"Yes, well, keep your fingers crossed that the negotiations are successful. Wilkins can be hard as nails at times, and he knows how much I want that station. The worst thing you can ever do is to let your opponent know how anxious you are to get something."

Evidently nobody ever told that to Terrence, she thought. "How soon will you be leaving?"

"Just as soon as I can get to the airport," he said as they walked toward her office. "Wilkins has sent his private jet for me. I put my feelers out, and from what I hear he's in a little financial bind. He might know I want to buy the station, but it helps me to know just how much he needs to sell it."

Sherri admired her uncle. His goal had been to own at least five radio stations before he turned forty, which he'd done. Now, at fifty-five, he owned fifteen across the country.

"That means I'm leaving you completely in charge while I'm gone," he said as they entered her office. "It might take me a full week to work out all the details and return as owner of station number sixteen."

Her uncle's excitement was contagious. "Don't worry about a thing while you're away. I'll handle everything and everyone."

His brow raised. "What about the Holy Terror? Have the two of you been getting along any better than the last time we talked?"

With her hand, she waved aside any of her uncle's concerns. "Everything's fine," she lied. "Terrence and I understand each other," she added, wishing that were true. She and Terrence did not understand each other. After two weeks of good behavior he was back to being difficult.

Her uncle studied her. “Are you sure? Because if not, I can talk with him.” He smiled. “I think he makes a pest of himself with you because he likes you.”

Sherri had to refrain from telling her uncle that Terrence didn’t like her, he *wanted* her. There was a difference. “I doubt that’s true, but like I said, Terrence and I understand each other. Don’t worry about anything back here. Just go on to Memphis and work out a good deal with Wilkins. I’ll take care of everything while you’re gone.”

CHAPTER FIVE

JUST WHEN SHE'D thought her and Terrence's paths wouldn't be crossing any more that week, she ran into him, of all places, on the elevator. And to make matters worse, he was the lone occupant.

"Going down, Sherri?" he asked, his voice lowering to too husky a pitch for her peace of mind. And it didn't help the situation to know that for some reason he had invaded her dreams last night in ways he hadn't invaded them before. They had been sexy. Naughty. And in her dreams he had been the one going down. The memory of it had the insides of her thighs feeling damp. Now there he stood, leaning against the wall and looking sexy as all outdoors.

"Yes." She hesitated a moment before stepping in and moving to one side, a safe distance away from him. The man was way too much temptation.

"Don't think you can control yourself in here alone with me?" he asked in a teasing voice.

"I'm the one who should be asking you that," she said, snapping out the words. Too late, she wished she hadn't when she saw the darkening of his eyes. The look he was giving her had the pulse beating erratically at the base of her throat.

"Since you brought it up," he said, his gaze roaming

her figure from head to toe, "I was going to be a gentleman and control myself, but now I don't think I will."

She backed up and lifted her chin. "You will force me to do something against my will?" she asked.

He smiled that sexy smile of his and she knew she'd lost the battle already. That darn dimple did her in. "No, but I may force you to admit something you're being rather stubborn about. Although our relationship goals in life are different right now, this very moment in time, we want each other and there is no way you can deny it."

"I do deny it."

"Let's see for how long."

He moved away from the wall and reached out and pushed the button to stop the elevator. Then he took the few steps separating them. She refused to back up, determined to hold her ground with him.

"I need this kiss, Sherri, so if nothing else, please humor me," he murmured in a low voice.

The words he'd spoken had come as a surprise, and despite her reason for not wanting it to happen, she inwardly admitted that she needed the kiss, as well. So she did what he asked and humored him, although when his mouth settled on hers it was obvious neither of them was amused. Instead they were filled with one gigantic need.

Judging by the depth of their kiss, it was a need they were determined to fill. Just like the two other times their mouths had been joined, what they were experiencing was ultimate pleasure. The kind that slaughtered your senses, sent shudders through your body. As if they had a will of their own, their bodies pressed closer together in a way that bordered on indecent.

Sherri's purse fell to the floor when she wrapped her

arms around Terrence's neck and sank even deeper into the kiss. She felt heated sensations all the way to her toes. This was the reason she'd tried to resist him. He had a way of making her not think straight. The last thing she should be doing with him was locking lips, getting some tongue play.

Yet that was exactly what she wanted to do—and she was enjoying every minute of it.

When he pulled his mouth away, she nearly moaned in protest. But he didn't move his mouth far. His tongue played around the corners of her lips. His actions ripped into what little control she had left. She felt overwhelmed by desire.

"Tell me I can come over tonight, Sherri. Let's finish up what we started here," he whispered against her moist lips.

She was tempted to concede. He was stirring up emotions within her that she'd never had to deal with before. The only excuse she could come up with was that her hormones were obviously out of whack. How long had it been since she'd been intimate with a man? Two years? Probably longer than that given the fact that she and Ben had never made love on a frequent basis. Whenever they could fit it into their schedules had worked well for them…or so she had thought. She'd found out later he'd been making love to someone else, a woman who worked for him. Someone who had no qualms about banging her way to the top. Sherri drew in a deep breath, not wanting to think about Ben's betrayal.

"We've held this elevator up long enough. Time to get out of here," Terrence said, breaking into her thoughts and taking her by the hand.

As soon as the elevator door opened, he stepped out

and tugged her with him. Luckily they were in the parking garage, because he then pulled her into his arms and kissed her again. Sherri felt weak in the knees and felt blood rush to her head with every precise stroke of his tongue.

When he pulled back, she held on to him because it seemed the world around her was spinning. “Do I get to follow you home and spend some time with you?” he asked.

She looked at him, making a quick decision. She had tried to avoid him for two weeks and look what happened. Now she was behaving like a woman in heat. She needed to do whatever it took to get him out of her system, and if spending one night with him was the answer, then she would go through with it. Terrence had an allure she could not resist. At least not tonight.

“I need to think about it,” she said softly.

He nodded. “Promise me you’ll give it a lot of thought.”

She stared up at him, becoming hypnotized by the eyes staring back at her. Deep. Dark. Hungry. He wanted her. There was no doubt in her mind. And she wanted him, but she had never been a person to engage in casual affairs. After her fiasco with Ben, maybe it was time to grab what she could and not believe in the forever after.

There was something about Terrence, the way he looked at her, the arrogant way he acted around her. In a way, she liked his arrogance. He was a self-assured man. Confident. A man who was persistent in going after what he wanted.

“I promise,” she said softly, not sure what was happening to her to even consider such a thing.

A struggle was taking place within her, and she

wasn't sure of the outcome. The only thing she did know was that since day one she had fought her feelings, tried to ignore her desires for Terrence, and it wasn't working. She hated to admit it, but he had been a part of her every thought even when she hadn't wanted him to be. Evidently he felt being smooth and debonair didn't work with her and was now behaving like a bad boy. She'd never messed with bad boys before. All the guys she'd dated in the past, even Ben, had gotten a stamp of approval from her parents.

"If you make a decision in my favor, I'll be at home tonight. I won't be at Club Hurricane," he said, breaking into her thoughts.

She doubted she would make a decision about anything tonight. She knew that any affair with Terrence, even a one-night stand, was destined to change her life forever. He was determined to set fire to a passion within her that had been left dormant for the past two years. Her nerve endings tingled at the thought of that happening.

"I've got to go," she said, moving away toward her parked car.

"All right. And I hope to see you later. You do have my address, right?"

She nodded. Although she'd never been to his home, she knew his address. It was within a mile of where she was currently living. "Yes."

And then she walked away and forced herself not to look back.

FEELING A SENSE of impending doom, Terrence stood with his hands deep in his pockets and watched Sherri walk away. Never had any woman's decision meant so much to him that it had his stomach tied in knots. From the beginning he'd thought that he was the one calling the shots.

Now he wasn't so damn sure of that.

When he'd first seen her he had quickly decided she was someone worth looking at, and there was no harm in looking. Once he'd discovered she was Warrick's niece, any thoughts of hitting on her vanished, although he'd seen no harm in a little innocent flirtation. But then he discovered looking and flirting weren't good enough. He wanted to touch and taste her, to join their bodies together. The more he'd seen her, the more he had wanted her. Now he was driven with an impulse to strip her naked each and every time he saw her.

She affected him like no other woman had. For two weeks they had tried avoiding each other and he'd been fine with it, deciding a woman with marriage on her mind was the last type of woman he needed to get involved with. Yet the moment he had glanced at the glass booth and seen her in it, it was as if a part of her had called out to him, had made his desire for her keener, his obsession with sharing a bed with her even more defined.

He stood there and continued to watch as the car she'd gotten into drove off and disappeared. Now the waiting would begin. Taking his hands out of his pockets, he walked toward his car, thinking he needed to make love to her like he needed to breathe.

For him to want any woman that much wasn't good. But for the time being, he was trapped by his desires and only she held the key for his release.

SHERRI WALKED INTO the house, thinking that during the drive home her head should have cleared and her senses should have been back in check. But if that was the case, then why was she contemplating taking a shower, changing into something sexy and paying Terrence a visit?

And why on the drive home had she felt the need to constantly remind herself that she was a forever-after kind of girl, and just because Ben hadn't appreciated her that didn't necessarily mean the next guy wouldn't? On top of all that, she also reminded herself she didn't have the time to put into an affair, long or short. Her concentration was on her work at the station. She felt good knowing her uncle believed in her capabilities enough to leave her in charge of everything and everyone.

Including Terrence.

But only technically, since being in charge of the station included responsibility for anyone associated with it.

She moved through her living room and headed straight for the kitchen, needing a cup of tea. She always thought better while sipping tea.

A short while later she was sitting at the kitchen table sipping tea and trying to decide what she should do. Why would a logical person like herself even contemplate doing something so illogical as having an affair, and with of all people, the Keys' bad boy? A man with a reputation as a ladies' man. A man who never, ever intended to marry. What was the sense in that? She took a sip of her tea and summed up the answer in five words.

She needed a memorable experience.

She was twenty-seven and had yet to experience the big O. At least not a real one. She hadn't ever told anyone, including Kim, that her time in bed with Ben had always left her so unsatisfied that she had begun wondering what all the hoopla was about regarding sex. Though Ben had never complained and had in fact several times complimented her on the degree of passion she could generate in their bed, she'd always inwardly felt shortchanged. She smiled, thinking that she would love to see Ben now and confess that all those times she'd actually been faking it.

Her smile quickly vanished when another thought crossed her mind. What if Ben had been faking it, as well? What if the reason he had left her for another woman had nothing to do with her spending more time on the job than with him? What if that had only been his excuse for her replacement?

She took another sip of tea and thought about all those possibilities. A short while later she knew she had to know the truth. Could she satisfy a man in bed? Could a man satisfy her? She nervously placed her cup back down in the saucer. Maybe she was thinking too hard. She'd never underestimated herself as a woman. She was healthy, in good shape, dressed nicely. Men looked at her, Terrence wanted her. But all they saw was the book's cover. What was really on the pages? What if she wasn't capable of delivering when a man needed it the most?

She had to know the truth.

Convincing herself that she was doing this more for herself than for Terrence, she made her decision. One night with Terrence ought to give her the answer she wanted. One night and not any more and she would make certain he understood that. To make absolutely sure she wouldn't be another notch on his bedpost, she went to get her cell phone from out of her purse.

She called Terrence. He answered on the first ring. "Hello, Sherri."

She frowned. At times she detested caller ID. "Hello, Terrence. I've decided not to come over to your place. But you're more than welcome if you'd like to come over to mine."

He didn't say anything for a second, and then, "I'd love to."

"And, Terrence, just to make sure things are absolutely clear, tonight is the only night you'll get invited to my home. There will only be tonight for us. There will not be any repeats."

Again he didn't say anything for a second, and then, "I'll be there shortly."

Sherri hung up the phone. She refused to be just another notch on his bedpost, but he could definitely be a notch on hers.

CHAPTER SIX

BY THE TIME Sherri had showered and changed into something more comfortable, Terrence was ringing the doorbell. Although her outfit, a printed skirt and blouse lounging set, was supposed to be relaxing, she found that she was a nervous wreck.

Twice she was tempted to call Terrence and tell him that she had changed her mind, but each time she decided to go through with it. She deserved to know the truth about herself.

Taking a deep breath, she opened the door. He stood there, not surprisingly looking positively jaw-droppingly sexy. The man was as macho as they came. He had changed out of the outfit he'd had on at the station and was dressed in a pair of jeans and a pullover. His hair appeared damp, which meant he'd showered and shaved.

"Terrence, welcome to my home," she said, attempting to add a degree of warmth and hospitality to her smile. "Won't you come in?"

"Yes, I definitely want to come in," he assured her, stepping over the threshold when she moved aside.

When she closed the door and turned, he was standing in the middle of her apartment and glancing around. "Nice place, Sherri. It suits you."

She chuckled, not sure what he meant by that.

"Thanks." She gestured toward the sofa. "Please have a seat. Would you like anything to drink?"

"No thanks, I'm fine," he said, sitting down.

"All right, then I'll get dinner—"

"Dinner?"

She saw the surprised expression in his eyes and understood. Evidently he'd assumed that he would be escorted immediately to the bedroom. "Yes, dinner. After the wonderful meal you had prepared for me at the club, there was no way I could invite you over and not return the hospitality. Although I didn't have time to prepare anything, so I ordered from a nice Chinese restaurant around the corner. I understand you like Chinese food."

"And who told you that?" he asked, looking at her intently.

"Um, I think I overheard one of the technicians mention it one day during lunch. So do you enjoy Chinese food?"

He leaned back in his seat. "Yes, I enjoy a number of things and Chinese food happens to be on the list."

"Good. It will only take me a second to set things up." She turned toward the kitchen.

"Sherri?"

She turned back around. "Yes?"

He met her gaze, and she could tell from the look in his eyes that he definitely had an agenda. He confirmed it when he asked, "Dinner isn't the only thing I'm getting tonight, right?"

Her reaction to his bold question was instantaneous. Her nipples hardened and heat began forming between her thighs. "Why? Is there something else that you want?" she asked, trying to keep her body from quivering.

He smiled, and her gaze shifted from his eyes to his mouth. She immediately recalled the kisses they'd shared, and just thinking about the intensity of them had goose bumps forming on her arms.

"Yes, there's something else I want. Do you want me to tell you what it is?"

She swallowed deeply. Not at any time did she doubt that he would. "I don't think that will be necessary, and as far as what else you'll be getting tonight, we will have to see. Some things are better when they are not planned or expected."

He shook his head. "I happen to disagree. I have nothing against spontaneity, but it's nice to know what's in store. Accidents can happen when things aren't planned or expected."

She nodded, catching his drift. But in this case, as he would find out later, he had nothing to worry about since she was in good health and on the pill. "True, but a smart man and woman are always prepared regardless."

Deciding not to say anything else on the subject, she moved toward the kitchen.

TERRENCE WATCHED SHERRI walk away. He was definitely prepared, since he'd put several condoms in his wallet. And just in case they decided to make it an all-nighter, he'd put a few in his jeans pockets, too. To be quite honest, although he'd hoped that she would, he'd been sort of surprised that she had called him. He wasn't sure of the reason, but he was not about to complain.

He heard her moving around in the kitchen and decided to check out the various paintings on the wall. A friend once said you could tell a lot about a woman by the pictures on her walls. In that case, Sherri must love animals, because he noticed several framed portraits of them. And one could safely say she liked live plants, judging from the many she had. Obviously she did a good job keeping them alive. Too bad he couldn't say the same about himself.

"Dinner is ready."

He glanced over in her direction and every nerve ending in his body vibrated. He'd meant to tell her earlier how much he liked her outfit and how good she looked in it. This was only the second time he'd seen her dressed in anything other than a business suit, and he couldn't wait for later when he got to see her wearing nothing at all. Deciding the sooner they finished dinner the sooner they could move on to other things, he crossed the room to her.

"I hope you're hungry," she said.

He couldn't help but smile at that. He was hungry, and once he got a taste of what he *really* wanted, he planned to gobble it up. "Yes, I'm hungry."

And then, taking her by surprise, he leaned forward and captured her mouth with his, causing heat to immediately flare within him. And her. He felt it when he used his tongue to tangle with hers, stroking pleasure she probably didn't want to respond to. But she was doing so anyway.

He broke the kiss and pulled in a deep breath. Just that first sensuous vibration made his stomach tremble and tempted him to lean over and capture her mouth again. But he didn't.

"What was that for?" she asked in a low, stunned voice, searching his face and at the same time licking her lips.

He grinned. "I'd thought it was time to let you know that although you're providing dinner, I intend to serve the dessert."

He intended to serve dessert.

All Sherri could do was sit across from him at her dinner table and make an attempt to enjoy what was her favorite food—shrimp fried rice—while trying not to imagine what kind of dessert he would be serving. She had ideas, of course. And those ideas had heat settling between her legs.

"You okay?"

She quickly glanced over at Terrence. He was sipping his wine and looking at her. She wondered if he knew what she was thinking, and if so, if he was amused by it all. "I'm fine. Why do you ask?"

He smiled. "No reason, other than you've barely touched your food."

She glanced down at her plate. She had eaten enough. "I had a huge lunch today."

She glanced over at his plate. It was clean. "I take it that you were hungry."

He chuckled. "Yes, evidently. Well, at least since it was takeout, there're no dishes to wash. Saves time."

She met his gaze. Was getting her into bed all he could think about? From the look in his eyes, evidently so. She stood and began clearing off the table, and he automatically stood to assist. "You don't have to help," she said, hoping that he wouldn't.

"Why don't you go on into the living room and get comfortable," she suggested. "You might want to check out my selection of DVDs. There might be something you want to see."

"A movie?" he asked with the same surprise that he'd had when she'd mentioned dinner.

She couldn't help but smile. "Yes. It won't take me long to finish up in here."

He glanced at the table. “Are you sure you don’t need my help?”

“I’m positive.”

“Then I’ll be waiting for you in the living room.”

I just bet you will. As soon as he was gone, she let out a long breath. Anyone could tell she was out of her element with Terrence and serious doubt began to cloud her mind. What if the reason Ben had left her was because she’d been a disappointment to him? That meant chances were she probably wouldn’t be able to satisfy Terrence, either. How would she handle seeing him around the station knowing she’d been a failure in bed?

She leaned against the kitchen counter. Why hadn’t she thought this through before inviting him over? She knew the answer to that one. After that kiss in the elevator, she hadn’t been thinking clearly.

By the time she’d finished wiping off the table, she was a nervous wreck and knew just what she had to do. Terrence was expecting a little hanky-panky tonight, and somehow she was going to get out of it. After placing the chairs back neatly under the table, she pulled in a deep breath before walking out of the kitchen.

IT DIDN’T TAKE a rocket scientist to detect Sherri was nervous about tonight, and that was probably the reason she was stalling, Terrence thought while flipping through her collection of DVDs, none of which he cared to watch. None of them would be able to hold his attention. The only action he was interested in was the one that would take place in Sherri’s bedroom.

If he thought he wanted her with a passion before, now his craving had doubled, possibly even tripled. It had been pure torture sitting across from her at the table while inhaling her scent, watching her eat and how, every so often, their gazes would meet in a heated clash. More than once he'd been tempted to push the food containers aside and have her then and there.

He needed to have tonight with her. Hopefully when it was over she would be out of his system, and his mind and body would go back to a normal state. He and Sherri understood what sharing a bed meant. Neither of them had any expectations beyond tonight.

"Terrence?"

He turned at the sound of her voice and once again he felt a tightening in his gut as he watched her cross the room to him. And when she came to a stop, it took all he had not to reach out and pull her into his arms and kiss her crazy. "Yes?"

"About tonight..." She was nervously twisting her fingers and her voice sounded unsteady.

He had an idea what she was going to say and knew immediately that he couldn't let her. They were too close to turn back now, and he needed to reassure her that things would be all right.

She opened her mouth to speak, but he quickly placed a finger to her lips. "Don't say it, Sherri. I feel your uncertainty about this, about us, but I want you to do something that you might find difficult to do."

He saw her throat tighten when she swallowed. "What?"

"Trust me enough to believe that in this situation, I know what we both need."

He watched as she studied his features and figured she was wondering how he could be so sure of what she needed. Inwardly, he was asking himself that same thing. It was scary, but he actually cared how she was feeling and he wasn't running a game on her just to get her in bed. He was being completely honest. For a reason he couldn't explain, one-night stand or not, he couldn't and wouldn't treat this affair like all his others. Although tonight would be all they had, it still meant a lot to him that she wanted things to happen as much as he did.

And he truly believed that she wanted him as much as he wanted her. He'd discovered that she had the ability to say one thing while meaning another, and as a man who was used to picking up vibes from women, he'd been able to home in on it. That was the reason he had been so persistent, working like hell to break through her resolve, wear down her resistance, so the two of them could have a night together they would both enjoy.

It was a gimme that he desired her more than any other woman, but there was something else between them, something he'd been trying to downplay, practically ignore. And it was something he wasn't capable of walking away from until she was out of his system. He needed tonight.

"Trust has to be earned, Terrence," she said softly, breaking into his thoughts.

"And I agree," he said, holding her gaze. His stomach clenched when she moistened her lips with the tip of her tongue. "Earning trust would be the normal course of action for most people, but we aren't most people, Sherri. I need you to trust me enough to believe this is the best course of action we can take to move on, to work each other out of our systems. This physical attraction has turned into a physical obsession, and there's only one way to end it. But I need you to feel safe with me."

Her lips tightened. "I do feel safe with you, Terrence, otherwise you wouldn't be here."

That's what he needed to hear. "Good." He reached out and took her hand. "Come here. Let's sit down and talk awhile."

Now it was her turn to look surprised. "Talk?"

He chuckled. "Yes, talk. And if we go beyond just talking, it will be left up to you."

She allowed him to lead her to the sofa, and when she moved to sit down beside him he pulled her into his lap. She started to get up, but his firm arms kept her immobile. "Stay still. I won't bite."

She parted her lips to say something, but then immediately closed them. Good thing. He would have been tempted to break his promise and make the first move by kissing her. He had such a weakness for her mouth, it was almost unnerving.

He shifted positions on the sofa, and once he had her tucked in his lap the way he wanted, he glanced down at her to find her staring at him. "Comfortable?"

"Yes."

"So," he said, trying to ignore the furious pounding of his heart, "what do you think of Key West so far?"

That question kicked off a series of others, sparking a lot of conversation between them, some of it serious, most not. His goal was to keep her talking so she could feel relaxed with him. And it was working. She sat up in his lap and shared with him how her cousins—Jackie, Reatha and Alyson—used to get into all kinds of trouble with their parents while growing up, and how Warrick was the one who would always come to their rescue. He could tell she was close to her uncle and sensed a special bond between them.

He couldn't help but study her while she talked. That she had loosened up was obvious in her face. No frowns.

No scrunching up of her forehead. No glaring of the eyes. She had smooth skin, beautiful skin. And her eyes, ears and nose were perfect. Then there was her mouth. He quickly decided not to go there.

In good time the conversation switched to him, placing him in the spotlight. And he did something with her that he typically didn't do with other women. He shared a little about his pro career, his retirement from the game, his siblings, his father. He even went so far as to mention that his father was dating the woman who had been his secretary for over fifteen years. A woman everyone knew had been in love with him for years. He expressed just how happy he and his siblings were about the developing relationship and how they hoped to hear something of a planned wedding soon.

It was only after sharing that bit of news that he noticed just how cozy he and Sherri had gotten together. Sometime during the past hour or so, they had eased into a more comfortable spot on the sofa. He was reclining sideways with his back against the armrest and she was sprawled all over him. Only when there was a lag in conversation did either of them realize it. Sherri quickly made a move to sit up.

The hand he placed on her shoulder halted her. "Please stay."

She held his gaze for a long moment. Somewhere in her house he could actually hear the ticking of a clock, but for them it seemed time was standing still. That realization gaze him pause, and he continued to stare at her with the same intensity as she was staring at him. He became entranced, totally and irrevocably mesmerized, by the look in her eyes. In response, his body started getting hot; his desire was on the rise…

as well as a certain part of his anatomy. The need to kiss her, touch her and play out his fantasies—the ones that invaded his nightly dreams—surged in him. But he fought back the temptation, determined to do what he'd promised and let her be in control. He had placed her in the driver's seat, and he was willing to go wherever she transported them.

"It's your call," he said in a deep, husky voice. "You can play or you can pass. Which do you want to do?"

She continued to hold his gaze, and then she closed her eyes for a brief moment. When she reopened them, he immediately sensed a change in her and was well aware that she had made her decision. And by the look in her eyes, he had a gut feeling just what that decision would be. Yet his heart appeared to have stopped beating until she spoke aloud to confirm his assumption.

"I want to play."

He simply nodded as intense heat fired up his blood. After inhaling deeply, he said, "Your serve."

She slowly raised her body to lean forward, and he could feel the beating of her heart against his chest. Her hardened nipples felt right pressing into him, and her body's heat was combining with his, causing a frisson of electric energy. Never before had he wanted a woman more, and when she tilted her mouth upward toward his, he leaned in to meet her halfway.

Her mouth closed over his, and in that moment the full impact of what they were doing blasted through his loins and he felt his arousal pressed solidly against her thigh. If she minded the hard contact, she didn't show it. She was too busy tangling her tongue with his and stretching up as far as she could to take the kiss deeper and make it last longer.

He grabbed her around her waist and gently pulled her body closer. With a compulsive need, he deepened the kiss like it was the greatest gift he could ever receive. Something he had been waiting his lifetime to have.

What made it even more special was that she had been the one to initiate it. She was surrendering herself to him willingly, and he was taking her mouth greedily. He had been right all along: she was a very passionate woman. He could feel her passion, taste it. And more than anything, he wanted to bury himself in the very heat of that passion, right inside her.

When breathing became necessary, she pulled away from his mouth and leaned against the back of the sofa to breathe in deeply while staring into his face. Their positions had shifted again and somehow she had him on his back beneath her.

Her lips were swollen from their kiss, her eyes aflame with desire, her face flushed with sensual need. At that moment he realized that Sherri Griffin was no ordinary woman. No ordinary woman had the capability to do the things she was doing to him. She had his entire body throbbing, his blood rushing through his veins, his insides on fire.

"It's your turn," she said, severing his thoughts.

His breathing deepened to a feverish pitch. "Are you sure?"

He knew what giving him a turn meant, but he wanted to make sure she knew, as well. Before she could respond to his question, he said, "I think it's only fair to warn you that I've wanted you from that first day in Warrick's office. Since then I've dreamed about you and me together this way countless times. Fantasized about it, as well. Once I take my turn, Sherri, I might not be able to stop. Chances are that I won't."

To indicate that she fully understood, she nodded. And then she swallowed deep in her throat before asking in a breathless tone, "Do you intend to play or pass, Terrence?"

He shifted both their bodies sideways and then leaned in closer and said in a deep, husky voice, "I intend to play."

"Then it's your serve."

That was all he needed to hear.

CHAPTER SEVEN

TERRENCE HAD KISSED HER several times before, but nothing, Sherri thought, could have prepared her for this. He wasn't just kissing her. He was staking a claim to her mouth that one would think went beyond a mere one-night stand. There was an urgent need within him. Demanding. And she felt it all the way through to her bones.

He was kissing her like she was the core to his very existence, and she could do nothing more than respond while her insides quivered and sensations surged through her nerve endings.

Then his hands seemed to roam everywhere, on her breasts, underneath her skirt, touching her as if she belonged to him, not just for tonight but for days to come, weeks, months, years. The absurdity of that thought stuck in her mind, but not for long. The moment he used his legs to nudge her thighs apart and then put his hand between them to touch her intimately through her panties, any and all thoughts dispersed from her mind on a breathless moan. He pulled his hand back then and broke off their kiss, but she had a feeling he was just beginning.

And he proved her right.

Their eyes caught just seconds before he pushed back enough to start removing her clothes. He pulled her blouse easily over her head. Tossing it aside, he undid the front clasp of her bra in one smooth flick of the wrist. Once he had taken that off her, his gaze feasted on the twin globes and the hardened buds of her nipples. He sat back on his haunches, examined them in detail with his eyes, and she felt the heat of his gaze as it trailed all over her chest.

After getting his visual fill, he stood to remove her skirt. Words were not spoken between them. None were needed. It was accepted. Understood. She knew they wanted the same thing, and tonight they would be getting it.

With his fingers in the waistband of her skirt, he gently eased it down her legs, baring all of her to him in the process. She was wearing a pair of bikini panties, but from the way he was looking at her she might as well not have been wearing anything at all.

The skirt went flying over the sofa, and she tilted her head back to look up at him. He smiled, and at that moment she was lost in a sea of desire so deep she felt herself drowning in it. But she knew there was no way he would let her go under. Tonight was far from over, and when he leaned down and picked her up in his arms, she knew it would be a long, hot night.

FOLLOWING SHERRI'S DIRECTION, Terrence headed for her bedroom as a gigantic need roared to life inside him. It had been there all the time, increasing steadily in slow degrees, but now it seemed to have taken on a life of its own.

He placed her on the bed and then followed her, easing back into the soft bedcovers with her, craving the taste of her mouth again. Tangling with her tongue sent erotic sensations rushing down his veins, and when he finally pulled back from the kiss, he knew he would take pleasure in removing the last garment from her body.

Straddling her, he began easing her panties down her legs. As soon as he tossed them aside, his gaze latched on to the area between her thighs. That part of her held his gaze tightly, and he seemed unable to release it. He finally shifted his eyes to roam over her entire body, and the only word that came to his mind was *beautiful*. Every delectable inch of her.

He stood and began removing his own clothes and couldn't get out of them fast enough. Seeing her in that bed naked and waiting for him was almost more than he could handle. He'd had more than his share of sexual encounters before, but none had him quivering from the inside out like this one.

He had taken off his shirt, but before he removed his jeans, he took out his wallet and retrieved the condom packs and tossed them on the bed. He pulled the others out of his back pocket.

She gave a little laugh. "So many?"

He undid his zipper. "Those are just a few. I have more in my car if we need them."

Her smile was replaced by supreme wonder. "You're kidding, right?"

He held her gaze. "No, I wouldn't kid you about something like that. Evidently you don't know how much I want you."

When he pushed his jeans down past his thighs, he saw her take in the size of him through his briefs. She inhaled deeply before saying, "If I didn't before, I do now."

He smiled and when he kicked his jeans aside he knew he had to get inside her body fast. There was pleasure and then there was pleasure, and he had a feeling they would be experiencing it to the highest degree tonight.

He could barely remove his last stitch of clothing knowing her eyes were directly on him. Once he did and looked up, he saw that her eyes were glued to his aroused member, both amazement and uncertainty etched in her features.

After sheathing himself in a condom, he decided not to waste any more time. He strolled over to the bed and, lifting a knee onto it, reached out his hand. "Come here."

Unhesitatingly, she came to him, placing her hand in his and going willingly when he pulled her into his arms. She responded to him when he leaned in and closed his mouth over hers.

He slowly broke off the kiss and pulled back slightly. Meeting her gaze, he asked in a gruff voice, "Ready to play?"

The desire in her eyes deepened when she said, "Yes, I'm ready."

Satisfied with her response, he traced her heated flesh from the pulse point in her neck to her breasts. When he touched the hardened tips, she sucked in a deep breath. He watched the play of emotions on her face and knew her breasts were a hot spot for her, one he would enjoy using to push her over the edge.

Now was as good a time as any.

Lowering his head, his tongue replaced his fingers and he greedily began devouring her nipples. They seemed ready for his mouth. Her moans were sensuous music to his ears. As his mouth had its way with her breasts, his hands joined in and cupped them, tenderly kneading the firm mounds.

And then his mouth moved lower and he felt her shudder, which only heightened his need, flamed his desire. When he got to her stomach, his tongue blazed a wet trail around her belly button before finally moving lower.

His hands closed over her thighs, held them immobile as he lowered his head to the apex where her feminine mound awaited. With a guttural moan, he dived in with a possessiveness that nearly drove him over the edge of sanity. He felt her response when he began tasting her with his tongue and now understood why he had wanted her so much. The primitive part of him was absorbed in her sensual scent, her delectable taste, in every single thing about her.

The lower part of his body began throbbing with the need to be joined with hers, and moments later he gave in to the need. He lifted his head, met her gaze and smiled before slowly easing his body upward over hers, sweeping her into his arms.

He needed to hold her, kiss her, share with her sensations that were affecting him through to his bones. And when he released her mouth he knew he had to love her in the most primitive way known to man.

For him it was no longer an option. It was a necessity.

His eyes held tightly to hers when he eased between her thighs and lifted her hips high in his hands. With the head of his hard and heated erection poised at the entry of her feminine mound, he nearly trembled in greed. His gaze remained focused on her, studying her eyes, scrutinizing her face. He wanted to see her reaction, needed to hear her response, at the exact moment his body entered hers. Why such a thing was so important to him, he wasn't sure. All he knew was that it was.

It was then that he decided to seize the moment, capitalize on the sensuous chemistry and sexual awareness surrounding them. His pulse was beating rapidly at the base of his throat, and his erection was throbbing hard in need. Slowly and with uninhibited deliberation, he pushed deep inside her, all the way to the hilt. Surprise then pleasure lit her features when her body accepted the full length and thickness of him. He heard her gasp, followed by a soft moan. Then he pulled out, just to thrust back into her again, watching her eyes dilate each time.

He held still for a second or else he would have exploded inside her, then and there. He needed to savor the moment, especially since this was the last time for both of them. He had to remember this was a one-night stand, but at that very moment, while on the brink of a sexual abyss, he didn't see how that could be. How in the world, after this, he could not come back for more. And more.

Something within him uncoiled and propelled him to move. Maybe it was those sexy sounds she was making, or the scent of their joining that was floating around them, over them, cloaking them in the potent aroma of a man and woman mating.

"Terrence!"

He held on to her, dragging in a deep breath when her feminine muscles clamped him tightly, squeezing and demanding the hot rush of his release. He gripped her hips and with one final thrust gave her what she wanted, what they both needed, and felt her come apart in his arms at the same moment he was ripped apart in hers. The same sensations that swept through him did likewise to her, rippling from head to toes.

His lips parted as he cried out her name, and when he felt his entire body get swept away, seemingly to the stars and beyond, he wondered if he would ever drift back down to earth again.

SHERRI SUDDENLY UNDERSTOOD what it meant to be totally consumed in the art of making love. Terrence had taken her to a level of pleasure that she'd never traveled to before. The thought that this was what she should have been experiencing all those times she had been faking it hit a deep nerve. How was it possible for one man to so eloquently do what another one could not? How had Terrence given her the experience of a lifetime, her first big O, when Ben hadn't even come close?

She pulled in a deep breath, deciding not to think about it since it didn't matter any longer. Terrence had given her pleasure beyond measure, and from the way she saw things, she had pleased him, as well, which lifted a great burden off her shoulders. Nothing was wrong with her. She could be both the recipient and giver of pleasure.

Something else Terrence had shown her was the fact that she was capable of falling in love again, because as much as she didn't want it to happen, as much as she didn't need it to happen, she was afraid she could be falling in love with him. She inhaled deeply, thinking that he was the last person a sane woman would want to give her heart to.

"Sherri?"

She glanced up and met his gaze. He had slumped

down beside her and was drawing in deep breaths of air. "Yes?"

"We're not through yet tonight. I gave you fair warning."

She nodded, remembering. He had. She felt his touch between her thighs and immediately her body responded. And then he was there, leaning up on his elbows, all in her face, about to get all in her mouth. And the only thing she could think of at that very moment was that she was ready, willing and able to go the next round with him. More than anything, she wanted to make love with him again. She would share her body with him, but she was determined to keep her heart under lock and key.

THE OPENING AND CLOSING of the bathroom door jerked Terrence awake, made him recall just where he was and in whose bed he had spent the night. He glanced out the window. It was morning.

He stretched his body and then leaned up on his elbow to glance at the clock on Sherri's nightstand. It was just a little past seven. When he heard the sound of the shower going, he slumped back down beneath the covers. He was tempted to go join her but doubted he could move his body. To claim he was sensuously exhausted was an understatement.

Just how many times had they made love? How many orgasms had they shared? Hell, he wasn't sure. At some point he had stopped counting. Her need to mate had been just as fierce as his. Before last night he'd never had a reason to care about any woman's past relationships, but in Sherri's case he had a feeling her past lover hadn't been taking care of business properly. Some of the positions they'd tried had been new to her, but she hadn't hesitated to go for it, finding satisfaction and giving him his. He smiled when he remembered he had basically ridden her to sleep right after an orgasm had hit them both. He hadn't been able to stop his body from thrusting into her until he had nothing else to give. It had been only then that he had slumped down beside her and pulled her into his arms, where they both succumbed to blissful slumber.

He threw his hand over his eyes when something occurred to him. He had known making love to her would be powerful, but what he hadn't expected was for her to blow his mind in such a way that the very thought that this would never happen again between them was totally, absolutely unacceptable.

He inwardly groaned. When had the thought of leaving a woman's bed without looking back ever bothered him? Most of the time when the sex act was over, he was the first one gone. But not this time. He wondered how he could convince her that last night should be the beginning for them and not the end. And he knew why. The woman had gotten under his skin, and one night of lovemaking wouldn't be able to get her out.

He actually liked her. He liked her smile, which she was giving him more of these last couple of days, and he liked the way she looked at him when she thought he wasn't looking. He liked the way she made those little sounds right before she came and the way her body responded so quickly whenever he touched her.

Amazingly he was beginning to understand her, something he'd never taken the time to do with other women. He doubted she realized it, but when they had been holding their in-depth conversations, he had listened carefully and had heard everything she'd said and had picked up on a number of things she hadn't said. He couldn't help but admire a woman who knew what she wanted and worked hard to achieve it. She wanted to one day manage WLCK, and he could respect that and had no doubt she would achieve that goal.

But what he needed to show her was that she could have the best of both worlds. A career and a man. From the information he'd been able to weasel out of Warrick, her fiancée had broken their engagement, claiming she had made her desire for a career more important than her desire for him. Meanwhile he'd sought the attention of another woman. Jeez. What kind of ass reason was that to cheat? Even he was smart enough to know it was the quality and not the quantity of time that mattered in a relationship. His father had proven that when he had juggled being a single father and an attorney. Evidently no one had explained it to Sherri's boyfriend.

He glanced at her nightstand and saw all the empty condom packs there. They sure had gone through plenty, but there was more where those came from. The last thing he wanted was to get any woman pregnant. He closed his eyes, and in the outer reaches of his mind he saw Sherri. She was standing at the window in his club, and she smiled at him. When he glanced down the full length of her body, he saw she was pregnant, with his child. His hand went out to touch her stomach, to feel the movement of his—

He forced his eyes back open. How could he possibly imagine something like that? Why would he imagine something like that? He'd sworn never to be a husband or a father, so why had such thoughts entered his mind?

When the answers came, they hit him as one sharp

kick in his gut. For the first time in his life, he had fallen for a woman. That was why he had been pursuing her like an obsessed moron this past month. But for some reason he wasn't thrown into an extreme panic attack as he should have been.

Nor was he in a state of denial.

He turned over in bed and smothered his head in the pillow, immediately picking up her scent. And then his mind became filled with memories of last night, and he couldn't think of a better way to start off the day. With that thought deeply entrenched in his mind, he got out of the bed.

THE WARM WATER flowing down on her made Sherri realize just how sensitive certain areas of her body were. When she glanced down and saw all the marks of passion practically everywhere, she couldn't help but recall the intensity of her and Terrence's lovemaking.

The man had given her what no other man had—her first sampling of sexual fulfillment. And it had been good. Over-the-top. For the past month he had made it blatantly clear that he wanted her. And last night, when he'd finally gotten her, he had delivered big-time. He had been capable of stroking desires she hadn't known she had. She hadn't just managed a single orgasm; on more than one occasion, he had driven her to multiples.

The man was a sexual sensation on legs. Where did he get his energy? His staying power? His ability to make her scream to the point where her throat felt sore? And he was still there in her bed. At least that was where she had left him. She was surprised he was still there when she had awakened. From what she'd heard, he was good at making quick escapes the morning after.

If he had decided to sneak out while she was in the shower, she would hope that he remembered their agreement—not that she thought he would forget. Men like Terrence wouldn't forget. Last night might have held a lot of revelations and satisfaction for her, but it meant nothing to him other than finally scoring. He would move on. It was expected.

In a way she was glad he had that attitude since that made it easier for her to scoff at the idea, the mere possibility, that she was falling in love with him. She didn't want to become involved with a man no matter how good he was in bed. She reminded herself that the only thing she had time to concentrate on was achieving her goals.

She had made love enough times with Terrence last night to last a lifetime. Somewhere out there was a man who would love and cherish her, but she didn't want him to find her any time soon. Working on a relationship took up too much time, time she didn't have to spare. Although she still resented the way and the reason Ben had left, his leaving had in truth been a blessing. He would never have agreed to quit his job with that prestigious law firm in Cleveland to move to the Keys. He would have flatly refused, and she would have given up the chance to pursue the dream of a lifetime.

"Mind if I join you?"

She jerked around so fast she almost slipped and would have done so if a naked Terrence hadn't reached out to steady her. "W-what are you doing here?" she asked.

"I spent the night here, remember?" he said, smiling as he reached out to grab the soap out of the dish behind her.

She stood there, speechless, and watched as he rubbed the soap—*her* soap—over his chest and stomach before moving down his thighs and legs, working up a lathery foam. She tried to downplay the sensations settling between her legs as she stood there staring.

"You do remember that I spent the night," he said, in an attempt to get her attention again.

She dragged her gaze back to his face. "Yes, but I assumed you would be gone when I got out of the shower."

"What would make you think such a thing?" he asked as he continued to scrub soap all over his body. "And do you mind stepping aside for a moment? You're blocking the flow of water."

And getting drenched in the process, she thought, glaring at him as she did as he requested and moved aside. It was a good thing her shower stall was big enough for two. "The reason I thought such a thing," she said, trying to ignore the way the water was washing away the soap foam from his body, "is because it's my understanding—through the rumor mill—that that's how you operate."

Using his hand, he wiped water off his face and smiled over at her. "You've been checking up on my techniques? That's cute. You really didn't have to waste your time doing that. If there was something you needed to know, all you had to do was ask."

She narrowed her gaze at him. "I wasn't interested. It was merely watercooler gossip that I overheard."

He lifted a brow. "That's strange since until last night I hadn't slept with anyone at the station for them to know what I do or don't do."

"Doesn't matter. Apparently they were wrong."

"Technically they were right. I usually don't hang around."

Sherri frowned in confusion. "In that case, why are you here?"

He smiled, and before she could blink he had backed her up against the wall and simultaneously lifted her legs around his waist. "For this."

And then he was kissing her, stoking the same fires within her that he had flaming out of control last night. Her nipples ached and the apex of her thighs throbbed, but she forgot everything the moment his tongue entered her mouth. Then she was helpless to do anything but kiss him back…not that she had any qualms about doing so.

It didn't take long for her entire body to respond. When he spread her legs apart and drove into her, she literally screamed out loud from the pleasure he evoked. Pleasure that overwhelmed her senses and racked her mind. She looked up into his eyes and understood at that moment that he was teetering as close to the edge as she was. And then she remembered one vital thing. He wasn't wearing a condom. What had he said last night? *Accidents can happen when things aren't planned or expected.*

She was on the pill, so she wasn't worried. Still, she would definitely remind him of that statement. Later. Not now. The only thing she wanted to think about now was the way he was making her feel. Like a woman being smothered in bliss and making up for lost time.

Her heels dug into his back with each one of his powerful thrusts into her body. Moments later, when passion overtook them, she felt herself shattering in a million pieces. He broke off the kiss and let out a deep, hard groan the same time she screamed his name. Together they were propelled to a higher plane and reached the pinnacle of sexual gratification.

"YOU FORGOT TO use a condom when we were in the shower."

Terrence swore and stopped short as they walked out her front door. Forgetting something that important had never happened to him before. Never. That just showed how much the woman affected him. He'd envisioned her pregnant in his mind and had done the unthinkable by risking the chance of it becoming a reality. "It wasn't intentional and I apologize," he said. "I'm more responsible than that. I take full responsibility if you—"

"Relax," Sherri said, giving him a wry smile. "I'm on the pill. I just wanted to remind you of what you said last night. Besides, you did bring enough condoms with you. It just slipped your mind. Things like that can happen."

He was grateful for her understanding. "Yes, but if for some reason the pill doesn't work, then I—"

"You'll be the first to know," she said, smiling.

"Would you like to go with me to the club for breakfast?"

She glanced at her watch. "I have to fill in for Uncle Warrick at an off-site meeting this morning."

"Perhaps another time, then."

She didn't say anything for a minute, but when they reached her car, she said, "Thanks for last night, Terrence. It was special. I will remember it for a long time."

He didn't say anything for a minute, and then, "Would you be willing to do it again sometime? Sometime soon, like tonight?"

He could tell his question took her by surprise. "Why would we want to?"

He chuckled. "You can ask me that after last night, Sherri? We're good together. We both enjoyed it. You're not serious about anyone, and neither am I."

She narrowed her eyes at him. "I believe we covered all of that before and it was decided that we don't want the same thing in life. You just want a physical relationship, and I want something more. At least eventually. A smart woman would never let herself fall in love with you, because it would be a love that led nowhere."

He stared at her for a second. The latter part of what she'd said was true, at least that had been the story of his life until he'd realized his feelings for her. She wouldn't believe him if he were to tell her. For women like Sherri, things had to be proven and he had time to do just that.

The Holy Terror *way.* If he had been persistent before, then she hadn't seen anything yet.

Deciding not to argue with her about their future, he said, "Okay, I can see your point. Have a nice day, and I'm sure I'll see you sometime this week at the station."

He then leaned over and placed a kiss on her lips before heading toward his own car.

CHAPTER EIGHT

"HEY, KEY WEST, this is the Holy Terror and you're tuned in to WLCK, 101.5 on your radio dial. *Sports Talk* is about you, the sports-enthusiast, and today we're going to take your questions and facilitate your discussions on whether you think the Yankees have a snowball's chance in hell of winning the World Series this year. Personally, I don't think they do, so if you disagree call in and tell me why."

Sherri smiled as she parked her car in the spot usually reserved for her uncle. Like a number of people around town, she was enjoying Terrence on the air, although she wouldn't call herself a "sports-enthusiast." Point-blank, she enjoyed listening to the sound of his voice. It was husky, masculine, with a low rumble that could conjure erotic thoughts in any woman's head—and probably did, considering the show's high ratings. A number of callers were women, and you couldn't convince her that that many women in the Keys were interested in sports.

Depends on what you're playing, she thought, remembering their fantasy game of two nights ago. Not only had he played exceedingly well, but he had served up something so passionate that she felt her temperature rising just thinking about it.

Had it been two nights ago? No wonder her body

was still in a state of sensual heat. She couldn't even go to bed at night without remembering what they had shared. The man had an intense sexual appetite, and the more he was fed the more he had wanted. And she had obliged, learning a number of things in the process. Like you could have multiple orgasms and that there was such a thing as an erogenous zone, because he had definitely tapped into hers that night.

So what was next? Nothing. She was determined more than ever to move on and tuck away those special memories of their night together. With him out of her system, she would be able to do just that. She understood the yearnings she still experienced at night at bedtime and often during the day. Any woman who had been made love to as thoroughly as she had would suffer periods of loss. She could handle it as long as it didn't get to the point where she was driven to act on it.

That wouldn't be done. Terrence had gotten what he had wanted from her, and she had basically gotten what she wanted from him. They were adults and would act accordingly.

She looked at the clock on her dashboard. The U.S. National Hurricane Service had announced that Tropical Storm Ana had formed over the Dominican Republic and was expected to head west toward Cuba over the weekend. If the storm strengthened it could become the first hurricane of the season. Currently, there was less than a thirty percent chance of that happening, but everyone was still keeping their eyes on Ana just the same. WLCK had an excellent news department, and she wanted to make sure that their station was where listeners would call in to get the most up-to-date and reliable weather reports. To make sure that was in place, she would hold a meeting later that day with Prentice Sherman, the station's meteorologist.

She had gotten a call from Uncle Warrick that morning reporting that the negotiations with Jeremy Wilkins were going slowly. Wilkins, who knew just how much Warrick wanted the Memphis radio station, was trying to be difficult, although it would be in the man's best interest to sell. Uncle Warrick was determined to wait things out, soften the man up a little and make him another offer at the beginning of next week. Meanwhile, she'd keep everything at the station under control.

Getting out of her car, Sherri could immediately feel the change in the air and hoped that the tropical storm would not be coming their way.

TERRENCE GLANCED AT the clock on the wall. He only had time for one more call, and he hoped it was a short one. After the show was over he intended to drop by Sherri's office to see how she was doing. He had deliberately kept his distance for two days, trying to be a nice guy and give her space before he moved in and started gobbling it up. Just thinking about how he intended to do it made him smile. Sherri Griffin wouldn't know what hit her until she was back in his bed again. But he didn't intend to stop there. He had plans for them, plans he would have to orchestrate without her knowing he was doing so. For the first time in his life, he wanted to do more with a woman than sleep with her.

The monitor in front of him started to blink, indicating he had another call. His last one for the day. He rolled his eyes. It was Monica Kendricks. She liked to call in and flirt with him over the air. In the past he hadn't minded as long as no rules were broken. But that was before Sherri.

He plugged into the call. "Thanks for holding, Monica. So tell me, who do you think will win the World Series?"

Her husky, feminine laughter grated on his nerves today. "I'm going to go with the Cowboys."

He couldn't help but chuckle. "Wrong sport. Cowboys are a football team."

"Oh. Is there any way to tell them apart other than the balls they play with?"

He frowned, thinking that was really a dumb question and covered the mike with his hand when Mark, who was manning the booth, let out a gigantic laugh.

He shot Mark a glare although he was fighting to keep from laughing himself. "Yes, there're also the rules of the game, which are totally different, and the uniforms the players wear. Typically there aren't any cheerleaders for baseball and—"

"Why not?"

"Excuse me?"

"Why aren't there cheerleaders for baseball?"

This time Terrence did chuckle. "Now that's a question for another day. Callers, if any of you know the answer to Monica's question, call in on Friday. You will be listening, won't you, Monica?"

"I always listen to you, Holy Terror. And I'm thinking about coming to your club tonight."

He rolled his eyes again. "You do that. We could use the business. Thanks for calling in." Before she could say anything else, he quickly disconnected the line.

"That's it for today. Join me again on Friday so we can see how many of you will be able to answer Monica's question—why don't baseball teams have cheerleaders?" Terrence said to the listening audience as he closed out the show. "Until then, peace and stay safe."

He then switched off the control, turned off his mike and was about to remove his headset when Mark's voice transmitted through one of the speakers. "That woman definitely has the hots for you, Holy Terror. I wonder what she looks like."

He laughed. "Why don't you drop by the club tonight and see?"

"Um, you think she'll show up?"

A lazy grin spread over Terrence's face. "Yes, she'll show up."

"I hate to mess up any plans you might have for her," Mark said. Terrence didn't have to look in the man's direction to know he probably had a smirk on his face. Twenty-five years old and divorced, the young man was working two jobs while trying to go to school and paying child support for one child. Mark had hit the dating scene again running and hadn't slowed down since.

"You won't be messing up any of my plans because I'm not interested. But she might be too old for you," he said to Mark.

"That's okay with me. I've decided to date older women for a while. I heard they're less trouble and lower maintenance."

Terrence shook his head and decided not to intervene. He'd discovered long ago that experience was the best teacher. "Good luck."

He removed his headset and leaned back in his chair. He had to admit that he enjoyed doing the show. It only took a few hours of his time twice a week and it got him out of the club so he wouldn't get in CC's way. But now, with Sherri on his agenda, that meant he had less time to kill. And whether she knew it or not, she was on his agenda. As high up there as any woman could get and ever would get.

He glanced at his watch. He had dropped by her office earlier, and she had posted a note on her door that she had left the station to go to an off-site meeting. He wondered if she had returned and decided there was only one way to find out.

SHERRI TURNED OFF the radio in her office, thinking that the woman who had called in had openly flirted with Terrence and he had flirted back. Okay, he hadn't flirted back, exactly, but when Monica What's-her-name said that she would be showing up at Terrence's club tonight, he had indicated she should do that because he could use the business…a business that didn't have an advertising spot on his show.

She got up from her desk, refusing to admit she was being a little bit unreasonable. Or that she was just a teeny bit angry at the woman. And at Terrence.

And she outright, positively refused to consider that she was jealous.

She began pacing while thinking that she was too much of a professional to do something like that. Her anger had nothing to do with Terrence; what he did on his own time was his business. She just didn't like the fact that he'd given a plug for his club on the air.

"May I come in?"

At the sound of the deep, husky male voice, she whirled around to find the object of her anger standing there in the open doorway. And of all the nerve, he was smiling. Why hadn't she closed her door? If she had, then he could have assumed she'd been busy and would not have disturbed her. And today he was disturbing her. This was the first time she had been in his presence since the night they had rolled around between the sheets and the morning when they had made love in her shower. Just thinking about both suddenly made her feel so hot she wanted to remove her jacket, but she refrained from doing so.

"It seems you're already in," she said after he closed the door and walked across the threshold.

Her smart response only widened his smile, showing that dangerously sexy dimple. It was the same dimple that, in the heat of the moment, she had licked several times.

She inhaled deeply. Now was not the time to think about what the two of them had done two nights ago, about the sensations his lovemaking had evoked, about the numerous orgasms she'd had. And for the first time ever.

"How are you today, Sherri?"

His question interrupted her thoughts, which was a good thing. "I'm doing fine, and you?"

"I'm doing fine, as well, but if you want you can ask me how I can be better."

She tried ignoring the stirring in the pit of her stomach when listening to the deep, husky tone of his voice. "And why would I want to do that?"

"Um, I can think of several reasons."

She frowned at him. He was hinting about the time they had spent together, and she wished he wouldn't go there. Although she didn't regret anything they had done, it was over and there wouldn't be any repeats. They had wanted one night and they had gotten it. However, the lazy grin that appeared on his face reminded her that they had gotten more than one night if you took into consideration the morning after in the shower, which had resulted in them tumbling back into bed between the sheets again afterward.

"Well, I can't think of any reasons," she finally said and decided to quickly change the subject. "I listened to your talk show today."

She figured that there must have been something in her voice that put him on alert. He braced his jean-clad legs apart in that stance she always found sexy and crossed his arms over his chest. "And?" he asked, the single word a husky rumble from his throat.

She lifted her chin. "And I think you got out of line with Monica What's-her-name."

"Kendricks. It's Monica Kendricks, and she's a frequent caller to the show. And how did I get out of line with her?"

She inhaled deeply, knowing in all actuality she shouldn't go there, especially after Warrick had explained on her first day that Terrence's performance and anything related to it was his concern and not hers. But Warrick was out of town and had left her in charge. Surely she had the authority to provide Terrance with whatever feedback she felt was warranted.

"She flirted with you," she heard herself saying.

If the smile he sent her way was any indication, he seemed amused by that observation. "Yes, she flirted with me," he agreed. "She's not the first caller who has and probably won't be the last." He leaned back against a file cabinet. "So what's your point?"

Now she was the one who crossed her arms over her chest. "My point is that you flirted back."

Another amused smile touched his lips. "You think so?"

"Yes, and that was a very unprofessional thing to do."

Terrence studied Sherri's face, and when he saw she was dead serious, he had to refrain from chuckling. "And what do you think was so unprofessional about it?" he asked, needing to know just where she was coming from.

"You encouraged her."

"I encouraged her?"

"Yes."

This, he thought, was getting good. "And just how was she encouraged?" He could feel the vibes coming from her, and she wasn't a happy camper.

"When she said she was coming to your club tonight, you told her to do that and that the club could use the business. Not only was such a statement unprofessional, but since you haven't purchased any advertisement time for your club, it was unethical."

Terrence looked down at his shoes. He could deal with a lot, but for someone to take him to task for something as silly as this was a waste of his time. He had come into her office to kiss her, not to tangle with her, although he would just love tackling her to the floor about now and working that skirt up her waist, getting rid of her panties and—

"Just so you know, I'm going to mention the incident to Warrick when he returns, since you report directly to him. But in the meantime, until he gets back I'd appreciate it if you'd conduct yourself appropriately," she interrupted his thoughts by adding.

He shook his head, deciding she really did need to use her lips and tongue for something other than talking.

"Conduct myself appropriately?" he asked, as if savoring each word, every single syllable.

"That would be appreciated."

With an inward sigh, he straightened his tall frame and crossed the floor to cover the short distance separating them. “And you’re upset because a woman came on to me?”

“That’s not it at all. Women can do what they want to you or with you. That’s not my concern, although I’m curious as to how many of our listeners will show up tonight at your club to see for themselves just how you conduct yourself with her. She’s been calling in for practically every show. Everyone knows the only interest she has in sports is you.”

He reached out and pushed a few strands of hair out of her face. “And this bothers you.” It was more a statement than a question, and he knew she would take it as such.

Sherri rolled her eyes. “Don’t try making this personal, Terrence.”

He smiled. “I don’t have to make it personal since you’re doing a very good job of it for me. Would it make you feel better if I told you that I don’t plan on going to the club tonight?”

“It doesn’t matter to me what you do.”

A devilish gleam appeared in his eyes. “In that case, I’ll see you later tonight.”

Sherri blinked, certain she had missed something along the way. “Excuse me?”

“No need, you didn’t do anything.”

She took a step, got in his face. “And what makes you think you can just come over to my place?”

Terrence couldn’t stop smiling. She looked cute when she was angry. “Because you said you don’t care what I do,” he reminded her. “On that note, I might as well take it a little further, since it seems you're mad at me anyway."

Before a frown could set in her face, Terrence lowered his head and took her mouth, laying claim to whatever biting words she was about to say, effectively wiping them from her lips. Once his tongue slid into her mouth, her response was instantaneous. And when his tongue began moving around her mouth in long, fluid strokes, he heard her moan.

The sound made fire gush through his bloodstream, and he reached out and placed his arms around her waist to draw her closer. He then shifted his hand to cup her backside, liking the feel of that part of her in his hand even through her clothes. His tongue had been playing a cat-and-mouse game with hers, and when it was finally within her grasp, she surprised him and sucked on it in a way that nearly brought him to his knees. But he refused to buckle. He needed to stand upright to torment her mouth the way she was tormenting his.

The palm of his hand glided sensuously back and forth over her cute bottom, kneading it tenderly, while at the same time the hardness of his erection pressed against her stomach. An ache throbbed to life inside him, and it wouldn't take much to push him over the edge and have him take her right there on her desk.

There was no telling how long they would have continued to kiss if there hadn't been a loud knock on the door. Her breath caught the moment Terrence released her mouth. He watched as she breathed in deeply, fighting the urge to kiss her again.

A knock sounded again, and she quickly went to the door, glancing over her shoulder before making a move to open it. Since a hard-on was something he knew couldn't go away quickly, he decided to sit down on the love seat. "Go ahead and open the door, Sherri," he said quietly. "I'm as put together as I can get under the circumstances."

Trying to recoup all her senses, Sherri took a deep breath before opening the door to find Prentice Sherman standing there. It was then that she remembered their meeting. She cleared her throat. "Prentice, sorry about this, but my meeting with Terrence has run over for just a bit. I'll buzz you when we're finished."

Prentice smiled. "Sure thing, Sherri. No problem. I'll be in the break room," he said before turning to leave.

As soon as the door was closed, Sherri whirled around and stared at Terrence with eyes as sharp as daggers. "How dare you."

An innocent look appeared on his face. "How dare I what? Kiss you? In that case, how dare you kiss me back?"

Inhaling a calming breath, or at least trying to do so, she ran her fingers through the mass of hair on her head. There was no way Prentice wasn't suspicious about what they had been doing. First, it had taken two knocks before she had opened the door, and then there was no doubt in her mind that she probably looked like a woman who'd been pretty well kissed.

"This is all a game to you, isn't it, Terrence?"

"Why would you think that?" he asked, getting to his feet.

"Because it was my understanding that after our one night together there would be no more hitting on me. No more trying to get me in your bed. No more of anything. We *did* it."

Terrence couldn't stop the smile that touched his

lips when he crossed the room to stand in front of her. "Yes, we did do it, and it was done in a way that still leaves me breathless whenever I think about it. And for that reason, I need to spend more time with you. I need to do it again."

"No. Once was enough."

He shook his head. "No, once wasn't enough for me, and from your response to our kiss, not for you, either."

She lifted her chin. "You're imagining things."

Amusement darted across his lips. "Trust me, whenever I'm inside your mouth or inside your body, I'm dealing strictly with reality."

He checked his watch. "It's getting late, so I'll leave you to meet with Prentice. I'll call you later to see if—"

"Don't."

He met her gaze, and she met his. "Why are you afraid of me?" he asked softly.

"Leery is a better word, and like I said earlier, I refuse to participate in whatever game you're playing."

He thought about the game they'd willingly played together two nights ago. Their naked bodies tumbling between soft cotton sheets… His mouth tasting the sweetness of her unlimited times with no threat of facing a time-out… Her body while her inner muscles clenched him inside of her, releasing him and then clenching him some more, milking him for everything he had… He no longer had to wonder how it would be to make love to her, because now he knew. That knowledge stirred his insides whenever he thought about it. It was the force behind the hunger, so intense and deep, it racked his senses. It was part of what was channeling his love, something he could admit to freely.

"Do we understand each other, Terrence?"

Her question regained his attention, and he felt it was important that she be the one to understand. He wouldn't tell her that he had fallen in love with her until he had time to work on her heart. Whatever glass case she had surrounding it would be broken into tiny pieces. "Once wasn't enough, Sherri. I want you again. And again. But I'm willing to give you time to adjust to the idea. I'll see you on Friday."

And without giving her a chance to respond, he headed for the door.

CHAPTER NINE

"HAVE YOU BEEN keeping up with the weather report?"

Sherri glanced across the restaurant table at Kim and wiped her mouth before she spoke. "I can't help but keep up with it. We have a meteorologist at the station, and I met with him today. At four o'clock the most recent update from the National Weather Service indicated there was a possibility that Ana could strengthen significantly when she emerges from Cuba's north coast. If that happens, then she has a chance of becoming a hurricane and could pass near here."

"That's scary."

Sherri nodded. Neither she nor Kim had ever lived in a place that was this close to a hurricane's breeding ground.

"Well, there's nothing we can do. It's all in the hands of Mother Nature, but I'm hoping it bypasses here," Kim said.

Sherri couldn't help but agree. Deciding to change the subject, she asked Kim about the doctor she was dating. "He's okay," Kim said, shrugging her shoulders. "He's been divorced twice and that might not be a good sign, but I'm willing to go out with him a few more times. He likes to have fun, and that's good, although I think he's also dating another doctor."

Sherri lifted her brow. “And how do you feel about that?”

Kim shrugged. “Doesn’t bother me, since we’re not exclusive. What about you and the Holy Terror?”

Sherri glanced over at Kim. “What about us?” Kim knew he had spent the night, so Sherri knew that wasn’t what she was inquiring about.

“So you admit there’s an ‘us’?”

Sherri shook her head. “No, it was a slip of the tongue, nothing more, although he evidently thinks there’s an us. We clearly went into that night knowing it was a one-night stand, but now he wants a repeat.”

Kim’s eyes widened. “Really? Everything I’ve read said he doesn’t do repeats.”

“Then what about that socialite he’d become involved with?” If anyone knew the details, Kim would. Her best friend lived and breathed the Internet when she wasn’t working. Sherri sometimes thought it was a wonder she’d never taken a job with the FBI, since Kim had such a keen investigative nature.

“Oh, he only dated her those few times as a favor to her father, this real-estate tycoon on the island. Evidently she put more stock into the affair—if you really want to call it that—than Holy Terror did. After a few dates, when she began to get clingy, he cut her loose, but not before she’d told everyone they were engaged and he was having her ring sized. I’m told her lie pissed him off and he embarrassed her by retracting her claim. End of story.”

Sherri took a sip of her drink and said nothing.

Kim asked after a moment, “So what do you plan to do? You know how persistent he is.”

Sherri nodded. Yes, she knew. "I'll keep telling him no. Eventually he'll get the message."

"Don't be surprised if he doesn't. I think you made quite an impression on him."

Sherri rolled her eyes. "Whatever."

She really didn't care what sort of impression she might have made on Terrence. The bottom line was that a one-night stand was a one-night stand, and she had no intention of modifying their agreement.

When the live band began playing, she decided to try and put any thoughts of Terrence from her mind, but she couldn't help wondering what he was doing now. Had he not gone to the club tonight to meet the infamous Monica Kendricks like he'd said or had he gone?

She wanted to kick herself for caring whether he went. And for caring about the man himself. Though she had admitted to having feelings for him, it was something he would never know. The man was too arrogant already.

TERRENCE PLACED THE book he'd been reading on the nightstand and then shifted positions in bed. He had just finished talking to Stephen, who told him the authorities were gearing up for a mass evacuation because of Ana if one was officially called.

The last time he had talked to Lucas was a few days ago. His friend was waiting for Emma to fly in, hoping she would make it before the flights got canceled. Terrence hadn't wanted to tell Lucas not to hold his breath waiting for the woman since she had promised to fly in numerous other times and hadn't made an appearance yet.

Terrence smiled, thinking how his father, Olivia and

Duan had called to make sure everything was okay. They had heard about the tropical storm on the radio and had been concerned.

He had assured them that he was fine and that chances were the storm would shift and move in another direction. At least he was hoping that would be the case. The Dominican Republic was presently taking a beating, but all they were getting in the Keys was a lot of strong wind. Still, he knew that would be changing if the dark clouds were any indication.

Speaking of dark, he couldn't help but remember the dark frown that had been on Sherri's face when he had walked out of her office earlier. To say he had riled her anger was an understatement.

He shifted in bed again and decided the next time they made love would be over here at his place, in this very bed. No other woman had set foot in his bedroom, but he intended for her to be the first as well as the last. He wondered what she would think about that. In her current mood, she wouldn't think much about it. She'd denounce the very idea that such a thing might ever happen. But whatever it took, he would make sure it happened.

He would love to have her in bed beneath him when she wouldn't be thinking at all, just enjoying the moment. He intended to have that and more. Sherri Griffin might be stubborn, but when it came to implementing plays and rushing them to the goal line, she would discover no one was better than him.

He glanced over at the phone. He was tempted to call her, but he wouldn't. He would give her a couple of days to get adjusted to the idea of what was going on between them. He had broken down her defenses once and intended to do so again.

He wouldn't be satisfied until he not only had Sherri in his bed, but had her as a permanent fixture in his life. He intended to make her his.

Listeners, this is Prentice Sherman, meteorologist at WLCK, and this is another update from the U.S. National Hurricane Center in Miami. All eyes are on Tropical Storm Ana. She has been responsible for at least four deaths in the Dominican Republic. It seems things aren't favorable for us as forecasters have predicted that once Ana passes over Cuba, she will make landfall here in the Keys in two to three days, at which time it is expected she will reach hurricane status. Official evacuation plans are now under way. Residents and tourists are urged to heed evacuation directions.

Sherri stood in her office and looked out the window. The wind had picked up, and the palm trees were swaying back and forth. Coming in to work, she had encountered more traffic on the roadway than ever. Everyone was taking heed of the weather warning. Ana was still a tropical storm but was expected to reach hurricane status by landfall in a couple of days. Since most of South Florida was in Ana's path, the governor had already declared a state of emergency. This morning, tourists had been asked to leave the Keys, and those living in low-lying areas and mobile homes would be evacuating in a timely manner.

She had spoken with Uncle Warrick earlier today and he indicated he would be staying put in Memphis and would depend on her to keep things running in his absence. A lot had been placed on her shoulders, but she was ready to handle things.

The station had received a lot of calls from frantic listeners wanting to know what to do and where to go. According to Prentice, who had lived in the Keys all his life and was used to hurricane evacuations, the most important thing the station could do was to keep providing updates and to maintain business as usual. If they panicked, then the listeners would panic. For that reason, programming would remain the same, other than breaks for periodic updates on the storm. Terrence was due to hit the air in a few minutes.

Terrence.

She tried not to let thoughts of him overtake her mind. Today was the first day she had seen him since that time he had spent in her office. The day he had kissed her with a passion that made her toes curl. Earlier, she had held a meeting with everyone to advise them of her decision not to make any changes in programming.

Like everyone else, he hadn't said much, but she did notice the way he had looked at her and the smile he had given her. It was as if he'd known the importance of what needed to be done under her authority and was sending her his silent support. At least that's what she assumed his smile had meant, but with Terrence one never really knew.

She turned from the window when she heard the knock on her office door. "Come in."

Prentice stuck his head in. "Hey, I just wanted to let you know of our most recent update. Ana is now officially a Category One hurricane."

Sherri nodded. "And her path hasn't shifted?" she asked, hoping that it had.

He shook his head. "No, although she seems to be a

slow-moving gal. She was expected to leave Cuba hours ago, but she has decided to linger. That's good for us but bad for Cuba."

He looked at his watch. "Next radio update isn't for another thirty minutes, during *Sports Talk*."

"Okay, and thanks. I know you've been putting in a lot of hours during the past couple of days, and it is appreciated."

He smiled and said "Thanks" before closing the door behind him.

She did appreciate him. He was one of the first people Warrick had introduced her to. Prentice and his wife, Lucinda, were expecting their first child next month.

Satisfied everything was running smoothly, she went back to her desk and turned on the console to listen to *Sports Talk*.

"THIS IS THE Holy Terror and you've tuned in to another edition of *Sports Talk* at WLCK. Just in case you haven't heard, Ana is now a Category One hurricane and forecasters have predicted the lady is headed our way. During today's show we will give you periodic updates because the last thing we want you to do is get caught unawares."

He leaned back in his chair and said, "Today's show will pick up where we left off when one of our listeners asked the question why there aren't any cheerleaders for baseball. Phone in with your comments. We're going to take our first call after the station identifies itself."

Terrence flipped the switch to break for a commercial and took that time to sip his coffee. He glanced around. At first when Warrick had talked him into taking the job, the small soundproof studio where the DJs broadcasted their shows and from where *Sports Talk* would be aired had bothered him. He was a man used to space. But over the past year he'd gotten used to it and actually looked forward to being inside the booth. It was peaceful, relaxing, and other than Mark, who was holed up in the glass-enclosed booth next to him, he was virtually alone.

Alone with his thoughts.

When he had seen Sherri earlier today, his reaction to her had been instantaneous. Immediately, there had been a stirring in his gut, and his heart had pounded hard and heavy in his chest. She had called a meeting, and in that professional way of hers, she had brought everyone up to date on Ana.

She had surprised everyone by actually dressing down today with her jeans and polo shirt. Still, she had managed to look professional anyway. This was the first time he'd seen her in jeans, and she looked good in them, especially the way the denim emphasized her curvy backside. He was going to have to encourage her to dress down more often.

He sighed as he checked the commercial reel to find he had less than a minute left. He glanced over to see Mark looking through some girly magazine. According to Mark, Monica had shown up that night at Club Hurricane, and she was a looker. A woman in her thirties, she had seemed disappointed that Terrence hadn't been there to greet her. Terrence had chuckled at that, thinking she would get over it.

"Five seconds to airtime, Holy Terror."

Mark's voice interrupted his thoughts, and he turned his attention back to the business at hand.

"Welcome back. This is the Holy Terror, and you're listening to *Sports Talk* on WLCK. Today's topic is why there aren't cheerleaders for baseball." He pressed the button for line one. "Okay, Stan, what's your opinion?" Stan was a regular, and Terrence hadn't been surprised he'd called.

"Hey, Holy Terror, I think there aren't any cheerleaders for baseball because of the danger," Stan said.

Terrence raised a brow. "Danger?"

"Yes. A ball off a bat is more likely to hit a cheerleader and cause serious damage than a basketball, soccer ball or football."

Terrence nodded. "Um, you have a point there, Stan. Thanks for calling to provide your input."

He then clicked on line two. "Okay, next caller, what do you think?"

"I think it's a good question, and a good idea. It will get the fans into the game and give them something a lot prettier to look at than a player chewing tobacco and then spitting on the ground. How disgusting."

Terrence couldn't help but chuckle at that. "Well, every sport has its own idiosyncrasies. Thanks for calling in with your comment."

He disconnected the call, and instead of taking another, he said, "Now it's time for a weather update with Prentice Sherman." He pushed a button to bring Prentice, who was in another sound room, on the air. He then turned off the mike.

He leaned back in his chair while keeping an eye on the computer monitor that would tell him when to reconnect. He wondered what Sherri was doing. He knew that with Warrick away she had her hands full. Any thoughts about getting her to let him into her space would have to be placed on the back burner for a while. Hurricane Ana was the main thing on everyone's mind right now.

CHAPTER TEN

SHERRI STUDIED THE flashing computer screen on her desk while tightening her grip on the phone in her hand. "I understand, Prentice. Your first priority is to Lucinda and to get her to the hospital. Be careful and call me when you find out something."

She hung up the phone and took deep breaths. Prentice had called to say Lucinda had started spotting and the doctor had suggested he take her to the hospital since the baby wasn't due for another month. That meant WLCK wouldn't have a weatherman.

She slumped down in her chair. On top of everything else, two other employees, including Mark, had phoned to say they couldn't come. As far as she knew, the only person at the station, other than herself, was Soul Man, the DJ who was currently spinning the *Old School Hour*. He had been doing a good job of providing weather updates, but he'd been there for twelve hours already, and she couldn't ask him to stay any longer. Besides, her employees needed to go home and take care of personal business. They had lives outside the radio station. That meant she would be doing the solo act for a while. She had no other choice since she refused to go on total autopilot. She'd let music run on autopilot, but she'd stay to give updates on the weather.

She sighed again when she heard the phone ring, wondering if things were about to get worse. "Hello."

"Sherri, it's Kim. I just took a quick break to make sure you're okay."

"I'm as well as can be expected." She told Kim about the call-ins.

"Maybe you ought to follow their lead and go home," Kim said seriously.

Sherri shook her head. "I can't do that. As long as the station stays on the air, I will be here. I packed an overnight bag before I left this morning and brought in extra clothes, so I intend to stay put. Besides, with all the generators in place I'll probably do better here."

"What about your personal belongings?"

"Since I'm on the second floor my apartment should be fine. It's a new complex and, according to my landlord, built to withstand a lot more wind than we're expecting."

She looked at the clock on her wall. "Look, Kim, I need to go. Soul Man is getting off at four today, and I need to take over. I don't want him to think I'll keep him here unnecessarily."

"Okay, you take care."

"You do the same, Kim."

Sherri stood. For the second straight day she had worn jeans in to work, a decision she hadn't been pleased with at the time. But the owner of her local dry cleaner—where most of her business suits were still hanging—had feared Ana's predicted fury and closed the shop and caught the first plane leaving the Keys. Sherri had been surprised since most of the other business owners in the area were adamant about waiting it out and didn't plan to close shop until it became absolutely necessary.

She had searched her closet and had been forced to do some quick shopping at the mall down the street after discovering she didn't own a pair of jeans. Now she had come to the conclusion they weren't so bad and were rather comfortable. Hard habits just weren't easy to break.

She crossed the room, stepped out into the corridor and immediately collided with the hard bulk of someone's body. She knew in an instant, the moment a hand went to her waist to steady her, whose body it was. Terrence.

"You okay?"

The concern she heard in the deep, husky voice almost made her weep, in light of the load she had on her shoulders. Instead, she straightened those shoulders and met his eyes, trying to ignore just how good he looked…as usual.

"Yes, I'm okay. What are you doing here? Didn't you get the message not to come in?" Programming had changed due to the storm and *Sports Talk* was canceled today.

He leaned against the wall. "Yes, I got the message."

She frowned. "Then why are you here?"

He smiled. "I'm here, Sherri, because you're here. I got a call from Prentice and he told me about Lucinda. I knew that would leave you in a tough spot since, according to Prentice, you're not putting the station on total autopilot. So I came in to help."

"In this weather? You came in here?" she asked incredulously.

"Yes."

That didn't make any sense, which pushed her to ask, "What about your club? It's on the ocean. Don't you have to board it up or something? You have an entire back wall that's nothing but glass."

"There was no need," he said easily. "I had hurricane shutters installed a few years ago. Besides, I have people in place to take care of whatever needs to be done."

He looked her up and down and then said, "I like your outfit, by the way. I meant to tell you the other day how good you look in jeans."

She swallowed against the thickness in her throat as well as the fluttering in her stomach. "Thanks."

"So what can I do to help? I've pitched in for Prentice before, so I'm available if you need me to do weather updates."

She sighed deeply. Although she didn't want to admit it, considering her lack of manpower, he was a godsend. "You can do that, but that means you'll also have to be the DJ since Hercules called to say he can't come in and Soul Man has been here for twelve hours already, so there's no way I can ask him to stay any longer."

He nodded. "Where's Mark?"

She shook her head. "Not coming in, either."

"So it was just going to be you here alone handling things?"

At her nod he let out a curse. "Why didn't you just place the station on autopilot and let music play for the next twenty-four to seventy-two hours or longer? With all the modern technology, this station can be programmed to basically run itself, so what are you trying to prove by placing yourself in danger?" he asked in an angry tone.

She glared up at him. "I'm not trying to prove anything. There are people out there, still left in their homes, displaced in hotels, who are tuned in to us and are depending on hearing what we have to tell them about the weather. They need periodic updates that can only come from a live body."

When she saw from his expression that her words hadn't gotten through to him because he knew she was still holding something back, she glanced down at the floor for a moment before looking back up to meet his gaze. "Okay, maybe I do feel I have something to prove, Terrence. I'm running things in Warrick's absence, and I need to come through on this. I have to prove to him and to myself that I can do it."

Why she had shared that with him she wasn't sure. Maybe the stress was getting to her. But she was determined to prevail.

He didn't say anything for a minute. He just stood there and stared at her. Then he smiled and squeezed her shoulder lightly before placing his arm around her. "Okay, then, let's go relieve Soul Man."

SOUL MAN WAS out of there in a flash once they took over. Because Terrence was familiar with the setup, he took over as DJ and Sherri went to work to make sure they were connected to the Hurricane Center for periodic feedback. Once in the glass-enclosed booth, she also checked the equipment to handle incoming calls, making sure it was working properly and at full capacity.

Because they'd moved to work fast, she hadn't given herself time to ponder the fact that she and Terrence were the only two at the station, confined against the approaching storm. So far, there were only high winds and debris flying around, but from the look of the dark clouds, rain was coming. It was imperative that everyone understood the severity of the hurricane and took precautions. She hoped Terrence used his time and influence on the air to stress that to everyone.

He glanced over at her and smiled before putting on his headset. The autopilot was in place to play continuous music with Terrence breaking in every so often to give updates on the weather.

She just wished she wasn't getting that funny feeling in her stomach every time he smiled at her and showed that dimple. The last thing she needed to remember was the night and morning they had made love. She hadn't known just how thorough his mouth had been until she had gotten undressed later that day and found passion marks practically everywhere, especially in the area between her thighs.

Terrence's voice on the airwaves interrupted her thoughts.

"Hey, folks, this is Holy Terror sitting in for the Mighty Hercules. I'll be the voice of calm on your radio and will keep you updated on that voracious hurricane out there, and yes, Ana is acting like a scorned woman, kicking everything in her path, and is presently kicking Cuba's you-know-what."

Sherri placed her hand over her face and cringed. Although he hadn't used profanity, no one had to imagine just what he meant. She glanced over at him, caught his eye and shook her head, letting him know he needed to tone it down. He merely chuckled and continued talking to the audience.

"I'm here with the station's beautiful program director, Sherri Griffin, and she will be assisting me in making sure you get the hurricane facts on a periodic basis. I know many of you thought that you could stay put, but now that's not an option. So get your butts in gear and evacuate. For those who refuse to leave, you need to take every precaution."

Sherri's eyes widened, not believing that Terrence had said "get your butts in gear."

She placed her hand on her forehead. She felt a headache coming on.

TERRENCE GLANCED OVER at Sherri in the glass booth. He didn't intend for her to stay there for long, since there was no need for her to distance herself from him with the station basically operating on its own. For now he would give her the space she evidently wanted, but with just the two of them at the station, he was overflowing with ideas about how they could spend their free time. He no longer had to wonder how it would be to make love to her because he knew and had a burning desire to do so again. His body was getting hard just thinking about it.

Deciding for the time being to switch his thoughts elsewhere, he checked his watch and wondered how Stephen was doing. He had talked to him earlier. An article had appeared in the papers proclaiming Stephen a hero after rescuing some careless tourists from their car that had plunged down a ravine. He'd gotten hurt and sustained a few cuts and bruises, but after a night spent in the hospital, he seemed to be doing fine. And Terrence also needed to give Lucas a call to see if Emma had made it in, although Terrence had a feeling she hadn't, as usual. He and Stephen had had several talks with Lucas regarding why his fiancée never showed up when she was supposed to. As far as he was concerned, Lucas was putting more into this long-distance relationship than his fiancée.

Music was continuously playing, a mixture of everything: old school, hip-hop, rap and R & B. Currently Tamia was blowing out a number entitled "So Into You." He smiled, deciding he was going to make that his theme song in pursuit of Sherri and wondered if she was listening to the lyrics. Probably not, since she was messing around with the transmitter board, not even paying him any attention.

It was time she became his captive audience.

"SHERRI, COULD YOU come here for a minute, please?"

Sherri inhaled deeply upon hearing the deep, husky voice coming through her headset. She refused to shift her gaze away from the computer monitor. She had known the moment Terrence's eyes had lit on her. She had felt it in the way her body had responded and hadn't wanted to give in to temptation and look back. But now she couldn't help herself and tilted her head to look in his direction.

The moment their eyes connected, she'd known it was a mistake.

Need. An overwhelming craving began stirring in her middle and was working its way down her body. Once it reached the area between her legs, she had to tighten her thighs together to find relief. Not that she got any. Terrence had the ability to make her burn…for nobody other than for him.

She slowly released her breath when his voice came in again through her headset. His eyes still locked with hers. "Come here, Sherri."

She swallowed and somehow found her voice. "Why?"

"I need you to do me a favor."

She broke eye contact with him to look back at the computer monitor, trying to resist the pull the sound of his deep, sexy voice had on her. What kind of favor did he need her to do? It had to be about business and not pleasure, right? She didn't want to ask for fear of giving him any ideas.

She figured if she didn't go see what he wanted, he would only ask again, so removing her headset and pushing back her chair, she stood and walked out of the safe haven of the glass booth. His eyes were on her every step she took. She tried looking away but couldn't.

When she came within a few feet of where he was sitting, she couldn't help noticing how his gaze roamed her up and down before zeroing back on her eyes with targetlike precision. And like a bull's-eye getting pierced by an arrow, she felt the direct hit in every part of her body, especially between her thighs.

"What kind of favor?" she asked, watching him continue to study her.

"Stay in here. Keep me company," he said, shifting his gaze to her mouth and pulling out the chair beside his. At that moment she couldn't help but remember the last kiss they had shared, the heat it had generated, the moans she had made.

"I don't think that's a good idea," she said, struggling to put more punch behind her words. "Besides, I have work to do." She knew the latter sounded like the lie it was.

"I think it's a good idea," he interrupted her thoughts by saying. "And as far as you having work to do, how about coming up with another excuse?"

Her lips firmed into a line. "I don't have to make excuses for not wanting to spend time with you, Terrence."

He nodded. "No, you don't. But I would think, considering everything, that you could spare a few moments of your time. You and I are the only two people here."

Sherri wished he hadn't reminded her. She looked around and noticed just how quiet things were. Except for the sound of Ashford and Simpson, all was peaceful. She looked at the monitor as she sat down. "It's time for a weather update, and you have a call coming in."

He followed her gaze and looked at the monitor. "All right." He put on his headset and turned on his mike.

"Hey, folks, this is the Holy Terror with a weather update. Those of you hoping Ana would turn west and spare us a devastating blow may not get your wish. Don't defy the evacuation order that's been put in effect any longer. According to the authorities, anyone refusing to leave—" he looked directly at Sherri "—is on their own."

He looked back at the monitor. "Now for an evacuation tip. Don't forget to get those important papers and special photographs in order and secure them in plastic. Hey, you guys, I wouldn't leave behind those divorce papers if I were you, and please don't forget those hidden pics of old girlfriends. Oh, yeah, you might want to go ahead and destroy that picture of your mother-in-law that you've been using for target practice."

Out of the corner of his eye he saw Sherri get out of her chair and come into his line of vision, furiously waving her hands. "Folks, we're going to have a commercial break and then I'll be back to take some calls. I see the board has lit up," he said into the mike. "Hold on. I definitely want to hear what you have to say."

As soon as he turned off the mike and removed his headset, she lit into him. "You can't say stuff like that!"

He lifted a brow. "And why can't I?"

"Because this is a serious matter," she snapped.

He checked the monitor to see how many minutes he had before pushing his chair back and standing. A hint of a smile touched his lips although he was trying to keep his temper in check. His woman was determined to drive him to drink.

His woman.

He liked the sound of that. He came to a stop in front of her and instead of stepping back she tilted her head back and glared up at him. "I think," he said slowly, "that I know when and how to take a hurricane seriously. I've been through a lot more of them than you have. And furthermore, those people out there are stressed, some are nervous, a lot of them are afraid. They need the humor. They appreciate it. So loosen up. You're wound up too tight."

"If I lose my job you will—"

"Jeez, you won't lose your job. Come here, you need me to help you relax." And before she could protest, he pulled her into his arms and captured the gasp that flowed from her mouth.

The moment their lips touched, she moaned. But so did he. It was like before. Like each and every time they kissed. She pulled something out of him. Something tangible. Deep. Passionate. He wondered at what point she would figure out that her mouth, lips and tongue belonged to him. So did every other part of her. Just like every part of him belonged to her.

He pulled his mouth away because he knew his time was up and he needed to go back to the monitor and take a few calls. "I want more," he murmured against her moist lips.

"You won't be getting it," she countered with a frown.

He lifted his head and smiled. The challenge was on.

RETURNING TO THE seat she had vacated earlier, Sherri watched how, with a smooth transition, Terrence went back on the air.

"Thanks for returning, folks. This is the Holy Terror filling in for the Mighty Hercules at WLCK, and I'm ready to take a call. Caller, what's on your mind?"

"Holy Terror, this is Fred. I agree with what you said about those pictures. I still have every flick I've taken of my old girlfriends."

Terrence chuckled. "Thanks for telling us, Fred. Have you evacuated yet?"

"Me and the old lady, we're moving to higher ground now."

"That's good to hear," Terrence said. "Stay safe."

He then went to the next call. "This is Holy Terror, what's on your mind?"

"Hey, Holy Terror, this is Agnes. Something else people need to grab before they evacuate is deeds to their property. Mine got washed away with the last hurricane, and I had the hardest time with my ex. He tried claiming my house was his."

"I hope you got things straightened out," Terrence said and took a sip out of his water bottle.

"I did. He's dead now."

Terrence choked when the water nearly went down the wrong way. He cleared his throat. "He's dead?"

"But I didn't kill him. He died in bed with his young girlfriend."

Too much information. "Uh, sorry about that. Thanks for calling."

He disconnected the call. "Okay, folks, here's more music for your pleasure. The next weather update will be in about twenty minutes, along with another evacuation tip."

Sherri watched as he turned off the mike, removed his headset and glanced over at her before standing up and moving toward her.

TERRENCE'S CELL PHONE rang before be could pull Sherri into his arms. Muttering a curse, he pulled the phone out of his pocket, checking caller ID. "What's up, Stephen?"

"Just calling to let you know I think you're doing a great job at the station. I like your first tip."

Terrence smiled as his eyes remained on Sherri. "I thought you would. What's it like out there?"

Instead of getting a response, Terrence heard the screeching of brakes and then the sound of Stephen saying a few choice words before he came back on the phone. "You still there?" he asked Terrence.

"Yeah, I'm still here. What happened? Do you need me to send help your way?" Terrence asked, concerned. "I was just about to call in to police dispatch."

"No, I'm fine," Stephen said. After pausing a few minutes, he tacked on in a frustrated voice, "Do me a favor and reiterate that part about staying off the roads. Apparently your audience didn't hear it the first few times you mentioned it."

"What happened?"

"It's what didn't happen. A head-on collision."

"Come again?"

"I just had a near miss with some crazy lady speeding to get to an appointment in town," Stephen said angrily.

"But everything in town is closed," Terrence said.

"Yeah, I tried to tell her that," Stephen said, and Terrence could just see him shaking his head in disgust. "Listen, thanks for spreading the word about staying off the streets. Keep repeating it. I better check in and see about the bridge situation."

"All right, be safe out there. If you need anything else, call me. I'll be on the air for the duration. Do you need anything now?"

When Stephen didn't respond, Terrence got worried again. "Hey, you sure you're okay out there? I can send someone to you," Terrence said.

When Stephen still didn't respond, Terrence frowned and breathed in deeply. "Stephen, you there?" Terrence called out, his voice getting louder.

"Yeah, yeah, I'm here. Just checking something out, that's all," Stephen finally returned to the phone to say. "I thought I saw something. I'm not sure."

"Man, you just got out of the hospital a few days ago. You need to take it easy out there. This isn't the kind of weather you need to play with."

"I hear you. I'm fine for real. So how's your lady doing?"

Sherri had been listening to his half of the conversation and had picked up the panic in his voice. He could tell by her expression that she was concerned, as well. He had yet to introduce her to his two best friends, but he would soon.

"You wouldn't believe me if I told you," Terrence said.

At that moment Sherri's own cell phone rang. She pulled it out of her jeans pocket and then stepped outside the room to answer it.

"Sounds serious."

Stephen's words reclaimed Terrence's attention. "It was serious within two minutes after I met her."

"In that case it sounds like the Holy Terror has finally been tamed. I wish you and your lady the best. Let me know when to get my tux pressed."

Terrence smiled. "Will do. Be safe."

"Back at ya."

CHAPTER ELEVEN

"YES, UNCLE WARRICK, everything is fine. Terrence is at the station with me doing weather updates. How are the negotiations going?"

With her uncle's response, a huge smile covered her face. "Uncle Warrick, that's wonderful. We will celebrate when you get back."

Sherri knew the moment Terrence had stepped outside the room, and swung around to face him. Every single nerve in her body became energized. She wished she could put that kiss they'd shared moments ago to the back of her mind, but couldn't.

Her uncle's words pulled her attention back to their phone conversation. "Terrence? Yes, he's right here. Just a moment."

She handed the phone to Terrence. "Uncle Warrick wants to talk to you." She then went back inside the room to check the monitors.

Terrence watched her walk away before speaking into the phone. "Warrick, this is Terrence."

"Hey, man, I got that station in Memphis. We're going to have to celebrate when I get back."

Terrence chuckled. "Sure thing. I'll spring for the champagne."

"And I want you to watch out for Sherri. Her parents have been calling, freaking out about the hurricane and knowing she's down there in the thick of things. Will you do that for me? Will you make sure she's taken care of?"

A smile touched Terrence's lips. "Don't worry about a thing, Warrick. I can guarantee you that Sherri is in good hands."

"HOW'S YOUR FRIEND?" Sherri asked the moment Terrence walked back into the studio.

"Stephen's fine. The roads are crazy out there, and he wants me to reiterate to everyone to stay inside."

She nodded. "You have less than seven seconds to airtime."

"Thanks." He immediately went to the monitor and sat down. He checked the weather update reel from the Hurricane Center before putting on his headset and turning on the mike. He glanced over at her and smiled before going on the air.

"Hey, folks, this is the Holy Terror. It's time for a weather update. Before I go into the weather, though, I want to again remind everyone to please stay off the roads. Don't go out unless you really have to, and then stick to the evacuation routes. This is not the time to decide you've just got to have a Mr. Goodbar or a Bud Lite. Chances are all the stores in your area are closed anyway."

He leaned back in his chair. "Now for that update on the weather. There has been no change since the last time. It seems Ana doesn't know which way she wants to go and has decided to stall for a while. So, in the meantime, here's another evacuation tip. Think ahead and take video or photos of your property before you leave. This will assist you later with any claims for damages you might need to file. And for heaven's sake, don't forget to take the video or photos with you, and later if you have to turn them in with your claim, make sure you submit the right ones and not the ones taken of you and your old lady skinny-dipping or something else equally intimate."

He glanced over at Sherri, saw her jaw drop and winked at her. "I'm ready to take another call and then you'll be treated to more music after a commercial break."

He clicked a caller on the line. "This is Holy Terror."

Sherri couldn't do anything but shake her head. However, from the callers' comments to Terrence's outlandish take on the evacuation tips, she could see the listeners were actually enjoying it. Go figure.

She stood to stretch her body, knowing his gaze was on her when she went to the window—the portion that wasn't boarded up—and glanced out. Although he had control of the call and was conversing as if the caller's comments had his complete attention, she knew that was not the case.

She had Terrence's complete attention.

She felt it in every part of her body. In every breath she took. When she heard the music start playing again, she knew he would act on all that attention. She wanted to turn around and face him but didn't, not even when she felt the heat of him at her back. He was standing just that close and she almost gasped when he reached out and closed the storm shutters.

She still didn't turn around.

"Sherri."

He spoke her name on a sensual breath that caressed the back of her neck, thrummed warmth through her pores. She didn't want to respond, didn't want her body to react to him, but it was doing so anyway.

"You're an ache inside of me that won't go away unless I'm inside of you. When I'm there, buried deep between your thighs, I'm complete in a way only a woman can make possible for a man. But no other woman will do for me. Only you."

His words were breaking down her control, sweeping her resistance away. They were destroying the last vestige of her sanity. She couldn't fight him any longer because she couldn't stop loving him. Even now, when he could agitate her like nobody's business, she loved him and there was nothing she could do about it.

She slowly turned around. Meeting his dark gaze, she reached out and cupped his face in her hands. He smiled and she lost herself in it. Without any further ado, she leaned up and covered his lips with her own.

Kissing him always did this to her, she thought. Unleashed the feminine desire she'd held closely tethered. When he pulled her closer to the fit of him and she felt his aroused body, that desire broke loose, untamed and undeniable. How could a man make a woman feel this way? So easily, so intensely. From the way his erection was pressed to the apex of her thighs in perfect position, he wanted her, too.

His hand went to her waist, to the snap at her jeans, when the monitor sounded. Muttering a curse, he inhaled deeply and met her gaze. "Don't move," he said before stepping away.

Terrence eased back into his chair and read the blinking monitor. He glanced up at Sherri when she came beside him to read the updated weather alert.

Hurricane Ana was no longer stalling. She was headed straight for the Keys.

CHAPTER TWELVE

"THIS IS HOLY TERROR, and I am providing you with the most current weather update that just came in. Hurricane Ana has made her decision and will be making an unwelcome visit to the Keys. Buckle down, folks. It seems we're about to encounter a very wild ride for the next forty-eight hours or so."

He glanced up at Sherri and a wry smile touched his lips as he continued talking into the mike. "If staying with relatives isn't an option, you might want to consider a hotel. Take my advice and book the room. Who wants to stay with relatives at a time like this anyway? Can you imagine trying to get some private time with your old lady with a bunch of relatives around? Go ahead and get the room so you and that special person can bring the hurricane to town right. With all the bumping sounds going on anyway, who will know that the majority of it won't be coming from the outside but from your room? And be smart. Don't tell your relatives what hotel you're going to. They just might show up."

He chuckled when Sherri poked him on the shoulder. Turning off the mike and removing his headset, he unceremoniously pulled her down in his lap and covered her mouth with his. Her resistance lasted all of two seconds and then she was returning his kiss, tangling her tongue with his and blowing away what little control he had.

Breathing heavily, he broke the kiss and stood and then backed her up against the wall. "I need you now."

He pulled her shirt over her head, tossed it aside. And then his hands were on her, kneading her breasts through her lace bra, undoing the front clasp with a flick of the wrist, freeing her breasts for his hands.

Sherri closed her eyes when a responsive shudder shook her body the moment Terrence took a nipple into his mouth, curled his tongue around it and began sucking.

She pulled in a tight breath, felt the stirrings in the pit of her stomach intensify. Heat flared within her and she felt the moment her panties got wet. She groaned when his mouth went to the other nipple, giving it the same attention and nearly driving her insane in the process.

She was aware of the exact moment his hand reached down to unsnap her jeans. Knew the instant he eased his hand eased inside, finding its way to her hot and ready center.

"I need to taste you first," he murmured while easing down on his knees.

Reaching up, he slid her jeans down past her hips and then down her legs. He helped her out of her shoes and then removed the jeans completely and tossed them aside, and proceeded to do likewise with her panties. When she was totally naked he leaned forward for a moment and buried his face in the juncture of her thighs, as if he needed to consume her scent, feel her heat.

"Terrence."

She breathed his name from her lips when a quiver passed through her.

He slowly raised his head to look at her, and she felt the intensity of his gaze. He seemed to be searching her face, studying every single detail. A seriousness she had never seen before lined his lips.

"Do you have any idea what you do to me?" he asked in a deep, husky voice that was rough and sexy simultaneously. "What you're doing to me now?"

She shook her head. "No. I only know what you did to me. What you're doing to me now."

"And what did I do to you?" he asked, breathing the words hotly against her feminine mound.

She had to tell him. "You gave me pleasure. For the first time in my life, I discovered how things should be with a man and woman in the bedroom. You made me come." There, she figured it couldn't get any clearer than that. He had to understand.

From the smile that suddenly touched his face, the same one that simultaneously touched her heart, she knew that he *had* understood. She'd told him something that he really hadn't needed to know, especially at the risk of escalating his ego, stroking his arrogance. But she had wanted him to know, so he could comprehend what all of this meant to her.

"And I'm going to make you come again. A lot more times. Starting now."

And then he cupped her mound with his hand, opened her up, leaned forward and sank his mouth into her. He licked here, nibbled there, and when she cried out his name he intensified the kiss. She was at a loss to do anything other than let her grip on reality slip, and she groaned in response to the shudders that racked her body.

He didn't let up, nor did he let go. While boneless pleasure ripped through her, his mouth remained latched to her, absorbing everything she had to give, causing her to whimper in pleasure. And when the last shudder shook her body, she opened her eyes and saw he had gotten to his feet and was unzipping his pants.

Time restraints wouldn't allow him to remove them completely, but he was able to push them down past his hips to display his engorged member. He was quick about putting on a condom. Then he gently lifted her off the floor, wrapped her legs around his waist and, meeting her gaze, he rocked his hips against hers, found his target then thrust inside.

She felt him push deep, all the way to the hilt, and she adjusted her body to take him all in. She felt full, and every pore in her body was sensitized to the feelings he had evoked. His body began moving, thrusting in and out of her with whipcord speed, bracing her back against the wall each time he did so.

She fought to hold back the sensations, resist the emotions that took control, but it was no use. Pleasure began overtaking her, shredding her hold on reality and pushing her toward an enormous tide of ecstasy. One more thrust pushed her over, drowning her in sensations.

In response, Terrence screamed her name and held their bodies tight, locked together as quake after quake shook through them, blasting them off the Richter scale. He then leaned forward and kissed her, taking the rest of her trembles in his mouth.

She would no longer deny how she felt, but she couldn't share her feelings with him yet, knowing he didn't feel the same way. For now, this part of their relationship would have to be enough.

"CALLER, YOU'RE ON the line. This is Holy Terror, and this is WLCK. What's going on?"

"Holy Terror, this is Josh. You forgot to take calls after that last weather update and evacuation tip."

Terrence smiled. He hadn't forgotten. He'd gotten into doing something a lot more satisfying. He glanced across the room at Sherri. She met his gaze and a blush tinted her features at the caller's statement. She was pulling back on her jeans. He didn't know why she bothered, since he would be pulling them off her again soon.

"Sorry about that," he said to the caller. "I got sidetracked, but I'm here now. What's on your mind, Josh?"

"Do you think we're going to lose power?"

"I would say count on it, Josh."

"For how long?"

"Hard to say. Could be a couple of days. Remember that no electricity means that the ATMs won't be working, so you need to have some hard cash on hand for any emergencies that might come your way."

"Thanks, I hadn't thought of that. We appreciate the updates out here. You might want to warn your listeners about Domino," Josh said.

Terrence raised a brow. "Domino?"

"Yes, he's a stray dog that roams the streets whenever a bad storm rolls in. You'll be surprised how many female dogs Domino gets pregnant during a storm. So your listeners need to keep any female dogs that aren't fixed behind lock and key or they'll be sorry after Hurricane Ana passes through."

Terrence wondered if the man was serious. "Thanks, Josh, for that advice. Okay, folks, you heard it from Josh, so take heed to his warning. Beware of Domino. And keep in mind that it's unlikely your pet will have a place in a motel or hotel if you decide to check into one. You'll want to find some other place that will keep Fido or Cujo. If you do find a pet-friendly hotel, make sure your cat is blindfolded. If you and your lady decide to get into any action, there's nothing worse than a Peeping Tom." Terrence chuckled, and Sherri rolled her eyes.

"Okay, folks, here's more music. A little bit of Jill Scott will start things off this hour. I'll be back at you in twenty."

After turning off the mike and removing his headset, he looked at Sherri and smiled. "Let's go rob the snack machine. I've gotten hungry."

"So, DOES YOUR brother have a girlfriend?"

Terrence took a sip of his coffee and then smiled. The employees' lounge didn't have a window and he appreciated not having to see the rain and wind he heard pounding the building. "Why? You're already taken."

Sherri chuckled. "I was thinking of Kim. She needs to meet a real nice guy."

He lifted a brow. "Playing matchmaker?"

"Hey, you aren't so bad, so I figure it might run in the family."

"It does, since I have to admit Duan is a nice person."

Terrence's expression then turned serious. "Duan is also a person who has been burned. That's hard for some men to get over."

"Yes, I would imagine," she said, sipping her own coffee.

"And I understand it's the same way for some women," he decided to throw out there.

Sherri wondered what he was hinting at. How much about her had her uncle shared with him? She sighed.

Since she'd already told him that he was the first to give her an orgasm, she figured he deserved the rest of the story, all the boring details.

"Ben was a likable guy. A sweep-you-off-your-feet kind of person. And he definitely swept me off mine. We dated for a year, got engaged and then we moved in together. That's when the problems started. He became needy, wanting all my time, jealous of my work. Then one day over breakfast he told me he didn't want to get married anymore. He accused me of not knowing how to balance my work life and my love life. Unbeknownst to me, he had already packed, and he left, walked out the door a few hours later."

She sighed, remembering that day. "I honestly thought he would be back once he got over it, since he would get pouty at times like a kid. A few days later I discovered he had gotten his own apartment. I got the address and went there and discovered he'd been having an affair. The two of them had already moved in together. I confronted him, and instead of admitting he was the one who had betrayed me, he refused to take accountability and accused me of not giving him the time and attention he deserved."

Terrence reached across the table and lifted her chin up to meet his gaze. "Seems to me that he was the one not giving you the time and attention that *you* deserved."

"I guess we were both wrong for each other. I just didn't see it until too late." She shrugged. "I don't care if I never marry. Sometimes building relationships is too much trouble."

Terrence removed his hand and took another sip of his coffee. "I used to think that very thing, especially seeing how deeply my mother hurt my father when she up and left, committing adultery by running off with another man—a married one at that. You wouldn't believe how many people in our neighborhood knew the story, and their kids had overheard it. I got teased by a good number of them about how no-good my mom was. It made me bitter. I grew up feeling basically like you, not caring if I ever married. Not ever wanting to. But now I believe that not every woman is like my mother. There are women out there who are born to be true mothers, lovers of their man. Trustworthy. Their mate's best friend."

Sherri considered asking when he had figured that out, but didn't. Instead, while he was in a talkative mood, she said, "Tell me about Stephen. I couldn't help but overhear your conversation with him."

A smile touched his lips, and, as always, it affected her, arousing sensations in her stomach. He had mentioned his two close friends before, Stephen Morales and Lucas McCoy, but he'd never actually said much about them other than they'd gone to college together and were still close. "There isn't anything I wouldn't do for Stephen, or Lucas for that matter. Both of my buddies are single, although Lucas is engaged."

He paused for a moment and then added, "And that concerns me."

Sherri raised a brow. "What concerns you? The fact that he's engaged?"

"No, the fact that I believe he's putting more into this engagement than Emma, his fiancée. It's a long-distance romance, and she seldom comes here. He always has to fly to New York to see her, and when she does say she's coming, she never shows up. Like now. He's expecting her in a few days, once this storm lets up. He wants her to see the house he's building for her. Personally, I doubt she'll come. I told Lucas my feelings on the matter."

"You did?"

"Yes, but it's his decision. I just don't want to see him get taken advantage of."

She nodded. "What about Stephen?"

"His real name is Esteban, but he goes by Stephen and he's single and carefree. He had a few family issues in the past with his father, but now he's doing fine. I'd like for you to meet Stephen and Lucas one day."

"And I would like to meet them," she replied. The fact that he wanted her to meet his best friends meant something, didn't it? Did she want it to mean anything? "And I'd like you to meet Kim."

"I would love to."

She checked her watch. "It's time for another update. And about those evacuation tips..."

He leaned back in his chair and met her gaze. "Yes, what about them?"

She smiled. "I'm beginning to like them."

"HOLY TERROR, THIS is Maggie, and what Josh said about Domino is true. The only time I see that mutt is when there's a storm. He got my Mitzy pregnant twice, but they were beautiful puppies. He also got my friend Nancy's dog, Bella, pregnant. He is definitely a rolling stone."

Terrence smiled. "Thanks for sharing that, Maggie. Okay, folks, you heard her. Anyone want to call and describe this famous Casanova on four legs? If you've seen Domino, know how he looks and/or his whereabouts, please call in and let us know."

He clicked on the next call. "This is Holy Terror. What's on your mind?"

"This is Monica. I went to your club, and you didn't show up."

So what does that tell you? he refrained from saying and glanced over at Sherri. She was sitting on the edge of the desk, facing him and listening attentively. "I couldn't make it. I had other things to do. Did you enjoy Club Hurricane?"

"Yes, but it would have been better had you been there."

"But I wasn't. Have you evacuated?"

"I decided to stay put."

"Then stay safe."

He disconnected the call and took another.

Moments later he turned off his mike and removed his headset. It was dark outside, and he glanced at his watch. Nearly eleven o'clock. Time definitely had not stood still.

He stood. "After the music plays, there will be another fifteen minutes of intermittent advertisements, and then that syndicated show from L.A. will kick in until six in the morning. There will be periodic updates directly from the weather station to keep everyone informed. We can chill for a while. Come on," he said, reaching out his hand to her.

She took it. "And just where are we supposed to be going?" There was a hurricane raging out there and she knew he was fully aware of it.

He smiled down at her. "We're going to take a shower and then we're going to bed."

CHAPTER THIRTEEN

"THIS HAS BEEN a well-kept secret, and now I can see why," Sherri said, glancing around Terrence's office. She met his gaze. "How did you get to be so special around here?" His office included a back room that was actually a studio apartment, complete with a bed, flat-screen TV, an equipped kitchenette, love seat and tables. There was even a bath with a shower.

Terrence chuckled as he pulled off his shirt. "I don't know. You tell me."

Sherri smiled. "I've told you why I think you're special, but why this home away from home? You're seldom here."

He lifted a brow. "Are you sure about that? How often do you come down this particular corridor?"

She shrugged. "Not often. It's too close to Uncle Warrick's office. Whenever he calls, it's the same feeling as when you were summoned to the principal's office. He's my uncle, but his expectations of me are the same as everyone else. I get no special treatment, so I don't like going to his office unless I have to," she said, smiling.

He laughed as he sat on the edge of the bed to take off his shoes. "It can't be that bad, unless you've gotten into trouble."

"Who? Me?" she asked incredulously. "I never get into trouble."

"So you say." He glanced over at her. "Is there any reason you still have your clothes on?" he asked, standing to remove his pants. He then proceeded to roll on a condom.

It always amazed Sherri that he had no qualms about putting on protection in front of her, whereas Ben always retreated to the bathroom, saying it was something a man should do in private. She was glad Terrence didn't think that way because she liked watching him prepare himself for their lovemaking and knowing he cared enough to do it. He had slipped that one time, but she trusted he would be more careful in the future.

She smiled. "Yes, there is a reason I haven't gotten undressed," she finally answered. "I checked out your bathroom. It's nice, but your shower isn't as roomy as mine. It will be a tight fit, so I guess you'll go first."

"Don't hold your breath for that to happen. I like taking showers with you," he said.

"Oh, is that what we did that morning? You could have fooled me."

Completely naked, he crossed the room to her and took her hand and brought it to his lips. "I'd rather make love to you instead. So get out of the clothes. The sooner you do, the sooner we'll both be happy and satisfied. Besides, I want to make love to you lying down this time and not on our feet."

Her eyes twinkled. "I didn't have any complaints."

"Neither did I, but now we have time, and I plan to use it wisely. So, are you going to undress or do you want me to do it?"

"You do it," she challenged.

He grinned. "Gladly."

Terrence began removing her clothes, taking his time and enjoying parts of her body along the way, liking the taste and feel of her skin.

"Do you know what one of my fantasies is regarding you?" he asked, moving his mouth close to her breast. "Taking off your business suit."

She smiled. "I'll make sure I wear one next week just to give you the honor."

Terrence grinned. "I'd like that."

Moments later she said in a breathless voice, "I thought you were in a hurry." He had removed her top but had proceeded to take her breasts into his mouth and torture them the same way he had done earlier.

"I am, but I decided to enjoy myself for a while. Some things you just can't pass up. And I've developed an intense craving for certain parts of your body."

"I can tell," she said, throwing her head back when his mouth moved to the other breast.

It took a while before he got to her jeans, but by the time he had removed them from her, she felt shivers consume her all over. His touch alone could send her over the edge.

Holding her gaze, he reached behind her and gently squeezed her bottom. "Do you know this is the first thing I noticed about you?" he said, murmuring hotly in her ear. "The shape of your backside turned me on that day I walked into Warrick's office and saw you bending over."

She couldn't hold back her grin. "Doesn't take much to turn you on, does it?"

He leaned forward and licked the pulse that was beating at the base of her throat and smiled when he heard her sharp intake of breath. "Just for being a smart-ass, I'm going to see just how much it takes to turn you on."

Her body was naked, fully exposed to his view, and Terrence intended to take her over the edge and back, plenty of times. There was a storm raging outside, and he planned to create his own storm inside.

"You know what they say about payback, right?"

He chuckled. "Yes, I think I've heard once or twice."

"Then get ready to experience it for yourself, Terrence Jefferies."

Before he could take his next breath, she surprised him and went for his mouth, wrapping her arms around his neck and easing her body close to his, feeling the hardness of his erection pressed to her stomach.

She kissed him the way he liked kissing her, using her tongue to touch and find every sensitive spot in his mouth before capturing his tongue with hers and mating intensely.

He was the one who pulled back and quickly turned her in his arms, letting her feel his hard erection against her backside. She was fully aware what he wanted to do, and her senses spiraled out of control at the thought that she would let him.

"Bend over toward the sofa. Grab to it and hold on tight," he instructed, and she did just what he said. He pressed closer to her, reached over and let his hands caress her breasts, moved underneath to touch her stomach and then the juncture of her legs. His fingers found her, touched her, stroked her wetness, and she savored the feel of his hands and the pleasure they were giving her.

"I want to get to this from this way," he whispered in her ear just moments before tilting her behind up, pinning her between him and the sofa. Using his knee, he spread her thighs apart at the same time the palms of his hands splayed across her stomach.

Terrence closed his eyes. The feel of warm bottom pressed against him in perfect position made him quiver, and he inhaled the deep, sensuous scent of her, letting it fill his nostrils. Leaning down, he placed a passion mark on her neck, then another on her back, not caring who might know she was his. It didn't matter. The only thing that mattered was the fact that his heart felt full of love for her and he wanted to mate with her for the rest of his life, this way, in all kinds of ways.

He couldn't last much longer, and he gripped her thighs, brought her body back, closer to the intimate fit of him, and tilted her hips for the perfect angle. Then he entered her. In one long, hard thrust he pushed into her heated warmth.

Sherri gasped at the feel of Terrence deeply embedded inside her body. Holding tight to the sofa, she inhaled deeply. She wished there were mirrors in the room so she could see just how her body was fitting perfectly to his and how deeply connected they were.

She could feel him behind her holding still, not moving an inch, as if he was savoring the feel of being inside her this way, pressing hard against the backside that had turned him on. She glanced over her shoulder and saw his eyes closed, his jaw clenched.

Inside, deep in her body, she felt his engorged member throbbing, waiting for him to move, so she clenched her inner muscles and knew he had felt it from his sharp intake of breath.

"Why did you do that?" he asked in a strained voice.

"To remind you that I'm here," she whispered back.

"Sweetheart, there's no way I could forget." He

paused and then said, "I've dreamed about making love to you this way a number of times. If only you knew how many." His grip tightened on the soft cheeks of her backside. "Nice." And then he asked, "Do you feel me?"

The way his staff was throbbing inside her all but had her thighs trembling. She wasn't sure how long she could last. What was he trying to do? Let her anticipation build? If so, it had reached its limit. "Yes, and do you feel me?" she countered, clenching her inner muscles again.

He muttered something, but Sherri wasn't exactly sure what. All she knew was that he had shifted his body again and was beginning to move. She could feel every inch of hard, solid muscle. Heat flared through her with every single stroke, every deep thrust he made, igniting a flame inside her that nearly blazed her brain. The feeling had her calling his name.

The sound made Terrence's nostrils flare, and he inhaled deeply just moments, mere seconds, before he felt her body explode and she jerked, triggering his own body to follow in one earth-shattering release. He gripped her hips tighter, wished at that very moment he was giving her the baby he'd envisioned she would have. Not this time, but he was determined they would share a baby together, after their marriage. Because he would marry her, and it was time she knew it. But first he needed to kiss her.

After the last shudder had touched their bodies, he gathered her into his arms, lifted her up and turned her to him, covering her mouth and thrusting his tongue in deep to mate with hers. He needed the connection. He needed her.

Sweeping her completely into his arms, he broke off

the kiss and carried her into the shower. Hurricane Ana was raising a fury of problems outside, but here on the inside, he was a very happy, satisfied man.

SHERRI'S MOVEMENT WOKE TERRENCE. His thigh was thrown over hers and she'd been trying to ease out of bed.

"Where do you think you're going?" he asked in a sleepy tone of voice, nuzzling her neck.

"To the bathroom, and then to check to see if the weather has changed," she whispered.

"Let it go for now, Sherri. If there's an alert, we'll get a call. Stay in bed with me."

"All right. But only if you at least let me go to the bathroom," she teased.

He loosened his hold on her, and she turned on the lamp and then quickly scooted out of the bed, shivering as she hurried across the room. The air conditioner was on full blast, and she guessed in a way she should appreciate the station's generators. She was certain in some parts of town some residents didn't have any power.

Returning, she decided to borrow one of Terrence's T-shirts. She glanced over at him, glad he had gone back to sleep. She moved quietly across the room to the dresser and opened the top drawer. Instead of clothing, all she saw was papers. She was about to push the drawer closed when something caught her eye. Picking the document up, she held it close to the light.

Shock and disbelief tore through her, and she closed her eyes to fight back tears. Why hadn't anyone told her? Why didn't she know?

Turning back to the bed, she studied Terrence's features as he slept. At that moment, she felt a sense of betrayal. Glancing around, she quickly saw her clothes scattered all about. There was no way she could leave due to the weather, but at least she could go stay in her office until the roads were clear. She continued looking for one of Terrence's T-shirts and found one that suited her. Slipping it over her naked body, she picked up her clothes and bundled them together and left the room. She fought back the tears as she made it to her office and locked the door. For now she needed to be alone.

TERRENCE SHIFTED IN BED and found the spot beside him empty. He opened his eyes, remembering Sherri had left the bed to go to the bathroom, but that had been a while ago. Where was she? Had she gone to the studio when he had told her there was no need?

Getting out of bed, he slipped into his jeans and left his office to head down the long hallway. She wasn't in the studio, and from the look of things, she hadn't been there. He frowned as he made his way back to his office, thinking she might very well have been in the bathroom.

He was about to pass her office when he noticed the light on underneath the door. He tried the door and found it locked. He knocked gently. "Sherri, are you in there?"

"Yes. Go away. I don't have anything to say to you."

Terrence quirked a confused brow. After making love, they had taken a shower, made love in the shower, then gone to bed and made love again. They had fallen asleep in each other's arms, happy and satisfied. What had happened from that time to now? He had never been one to do stupid things in his sleep, at least not that he was aware of. Hell, he needed to be sure.

"What happened, Sherri? What's wrong?"

"Just leave me alone. I don't want to talk to you."

The hell she wouldn't talk to him! He went to his office and got the master key to every door at the station, then returned to open Sherri's door.

From the look on her face, he had caught her by surprise. She'd swung around from where she'd been standing by the window and he couldn't help but notice how good she looked in his Miami Dolphins T-shirt that hit her midthigh.

"I told you I didn't want to talk to you."

Her words grabbed his attention, and he moved his gaze off her legs and to her face. He could tell she'd been crying. "That's tough," he said, crossing the room to her. "We're going to talk, because I want to know what I did to make you leave my bed."

"I don't have anything to say to you, and as soon as the weather clears, I'm leaving."

He crossed his arms over his chest. "No, you're not. Look out that window again, baby. Hurricane Ana hasn't officially arrived yet, and you see how things look. If you think for one minute I'd let you go out in that storm, then you have another thought coming."

Anger flared in her face. "You don't own me. I was just someone you slept with. You lied to me. Uncle Warrick lied to me. All men are nothing but liars," she all but screamed.

Terrence just stared at her. She wasn't making sense. "What the hell are you talking about?"

"I'm talking about the fact that I went into your top drawer to look for a T-shirt and found out the truth, Terrence. Uncle Warrick doesn't own WLCK. You do."

CHAPTER FOURTEEN

TERRENCE BLEW OUT a breath. "Is that what got you upset?" he asked, clearly not understanding what the problem was even if he did own the station.

"Well, is it true? Do you own it?" she asked, glaring at him.

"What does it matter who owns the station?" he asked, throwing up his hands.

She crossed the room to stand in front of him. "Because whoever owns it is my boss, and I don't take kindly to the idea of sleeping my way to the top."

"So are you saying that if I'm the owner and not Warrick, then you would never have gone out with me? Shared a bed with me?"

"Of course I would not have!" she snapped. "Just think of the ethics involved. What would people think?"

He narrowed his gaze. "Frankly, I don't give a royal damn what people think. And as far as my ownership of WLCK, it's merely on paper. For all intents and purposes, Warrick is the owner. As a favor to him, I'm holding the mortgage."

"And why didn't someone tell me?" she spat out.

A deep frown lined Terrence's face. "Frankly, because it wasn't any of your business. It was a business deal between me and Warrick. He needed extra cash flow, and this was the way to do it. It didn't concern you or anyone here at the station."

"No wonder you've been getting special treatment," she said as if his explanation meant nothing to her. "It all makes sense now. You report to no one but Uncle Warrick, you make your own hours, you have this plush office. And on top of everything, you're sleeping with the hired help. Is that how you get your kicks?"

Her words were like a slap to his face. Terrence stared at her for a moment and then asked, "Is that what you think? Do you think I slept with you because you're available and all it meant to me was a fun time in bed?"

When she didn't say anything, he continued. "That says a lot for what you think of me, Sherri. And to think I fell in love with you the first time we made love."

"What?"

"You heard me. But I guess you wouldn't believe something like that, either, since I'm such a horrid person."

"You can't love me. Men like you don't fall in love."

"If you truly believe that, then I guess men like me really don't." Without saying anything else, Terrence turned and walked away.

"THIS IS HOLY TERROR and I am providing you with the most current weather update that just came in. Hurricane Ana is still a Category One, and if you were hoping that overnight she would have changed her mind and shifted positions, I'm sorry to say that didn't happen. Although I'm sure you won't be putting out the welcome mat, you can expect her late tonight. WLCK is committed to bringing you periodic updates. And we want you to stay off the roads as much as possible.

We're getting heavy winds and rain with zero visibility. We'll take a few calls after a couple of announcements from our sponsors."

Terrence clicked off the mike, took off his headset and leaned back in his chair. It was close to noon, and he had yet to see Sherri. She was holed up in her office. Thank God she had more sense than to go out in this weather, no matter how angry she was with him. An anger he considered unjustified.

He felt his cell phone vibrate in his pocket and stood to pull it out. It was Lucas. "Hey, man, how are things going?"

"Fine. I'm just hoping the weather improves and the airport reopens. I'm expecting Emma to arrive when things clear."

Terrence rolled his eyes. "And you're really expecting her this time?"

"I know you and Stephen think she isn't serious about coming and—"

"After a number of no-shows, do you blame us?" Terrence paused, then said, "You're building that house for her, and she hasn't been to see it, not once. I don't want you to get your hopes up and be disappointed."

Lucas gave a dry chuckle. "It won't be the first time with Emma." After a brief moment, he said, "I know you're stuck at the station, so when the weather clears how about dropping by for breakfast?"

"Thanks, I'd like that."

"Good. How are things going with you and Miss WLCK?"

"Don't ask."

Lucas laughed. "You're losing your touch, man."

"Possibly, but she's not like the others. I've fallen in love, and I've fallen hard."

"You?"

"Yes, me. The only thing is that she doesn't believe it."

"Why not? You're certainly not someone who'd claim to love a woman when he doesn't."

"Evidently she doesn't think so," Terrence said, tossing a pencil on the table.

"Well, I guess you're going to have to work on her some more."

"That's not going to happen. If she doesn't take my word for it then that's too bad."

"Sounds like the both of you are stubborn. That's not good," Lucas said. "Well, I guess I'll call and check on Stephen. I'll talk to you again later."

"Okay."

Terrence clicked off the phone and put it back into his pocket. He glanced at the monitor and slid his headset back on and clicked on the mike.

"Welcome back, folks. This is the Holy Terror, and I'm ready to take call number one. You're up, Cheryl. What's on your mind?"

SHERRI LEANED BACK in her chair and listened to Cheryl as she recounted how bad things were in her neighborhood.

Like some others, Cheryl had not evacuated, deciding to ride out the storm and remain in her home. Now she wished she had left. All the streets around her were flooded, and one of her neighbor's trees had fallen on her husband's toolshed. But Cheryl was thankful no one had gotten hurt.

Sherri had to grudgingly admit that Terrence had a way with people. He had a personality that made anyone feel comfortable in talking to him. He had taken several calls this morning, more than he had taken yesterday. Some had been sad and some amusing, and in the midst of a killer storm he was doing his best to keep things upbeat, especially with all those crazy calls regarding the now-famous Domino.

Sherri went to the window and lifted the storm shutter so she could look out. She hadn't realized it had gotten so late. Other than going to the snack machine and grabbing a couple of sodas and snack food, she had remained in her office, hoping she didn't run into Terrence.

She moved her neck around, trying to get the kinks out. She had slept the rest of the night in her chair and awakened with her body feeling abused. It was around four in the afternoon and already it was getting dark. Terrence was still encouraging the listeners to stay inside, and she hoped they did what he asked.

She turned when her cell phone rang and quickly walked back over to her desk to pick it up. "Hello."

"It's Kim, just checking in. The hospital is a zoo. We've been pretty busy all night. This is the first time I've taken a break. How are you and Holy Terror handling things?"

"Professionally, fine. We're keeping everyone informed how the weather is doing."

"And personally?"

Sherri took a deep breath, and she dropped down into her chair. "I think I screwed up."

"How?"

"I found out that Terrence holds the mortgage on the radio station."

"And?"

Sherri rolled her eyes. "And no one told me. If he's the owner, then technically he's my boss. I've slept with him. Ben was sleeping with one of his employees and—"

"Will you forget about Ben? The man betrayed you. Get over it, Sherri. Are you going to mess up something that can possibly lead to something good because your ex-fiancée couldn't be trusted? And I don't care who he chose as his bed partner when he screwed around on you. It doesn't matter. As far as I'm concerned, good riddance. You've said so yourself."

Yes, she had. "I love him, you know."

"Who? Ben?"

"No, not Ben. Not anymore. I'm beginning to wonder if I ever did love him. I love Terrence. I didn't want to fall in love with him. I fought it like hell, but it happened anyway."

She paused a moment and then said, "And last night he told me he loved me, too. And that was after I said some mean things to him."

"Let me get this straight. The Holy Terror, Terrence Jefferies, actually said that he loved you?"

"Yes."

"Dang. Do you believe him?"

"At first, no, but now that I've had time to think about it, yes, I believe him. And he was right. What was between him and Uncle Warrick was a business deal that doesn't concern me. No one else at the station knows about it, and evidently they wanted to keep it that way."

"And how did you find out?" Kim asked.

"Last night, I got cold and went through his drawer looking for a T-shirt, saw the paper and read it."

"He could have said something to you about invading his privacy," Kim pointed out.

"Yes, he could have, but he didn't. I guess he was too upset to think about it at the time."

"Well," Kim said, "my break is over and I need to get back to work. Seems like you have a lot to clean up with Terrence. Good luck. When all this is over, you and I need to sit down and talk."

"All right, and if things work out with me and Terrence, I'll introduce you to his brother one day. I've seen a picture of him. He's a hunk."

Kim laughed. "Trying to play matchmaker?"

"Yeah, but I need to take care of my own business first. Like you said, clean things up. I don't know how Terrence feels about me now."

"There's only one way to find out," Kim said teasingly. "Some people think the way to a man's heart is through his stomach. I personally think the area is a tad lower than that."

"HEY FOLKS, THIS is Holy Terror, and it's time for your weather update. Hurricane Ana is kicking butt, and the Keys are taking a beating. The authorities think the worst is yet to come and are asking everyone to stay inside and do whatever you need to stay safe. I hope you've stocked up on water and propane gas, because you're going to need it. And I understand some of you don't have power and are listening to me on battery-powered radios. Be careful with those candles."

He looked at the monitor. "We're going to take a

commercial break, after which we'll take a few calls. Hang tight."

Terrence turned off the mike, removed his headset and pushed away from the table. He suddenly picked up Sherri's scent regardless of the fact he didn't see her anywhere. He glanced at the door, expecting her. It didn't take too long for her to appear. It was almost six in the evening and the first time he'd seen her all day.

She looked good. Refreshed. Sexy.

She was wearing another pair of jeans, a darker denim than yesterday, and her polo shirt today was black instead of blue. She met his gaze the moment she walked through the door and stood in the middle of the room for a second. He watched as she took a deep breath before strolling over to where he sat.

"Terrence."

"Sherri."

"Can we talk?"

He glanced at the monitor. "Not now. I'm about to take a few calls."

She glanced at the monitor. "I'll wait."

"Suit yourself." Whatever she had to say, he wasn't going to make it easy on her. Trust was important in any relationship, and her actions earlier proved that although they had spent time together, slept together, she still didn't trust him.

Instead of taking the chair, she began pacing, and although he tried not to focus on her, he did so anyway. He noticed how good she looked in her jeans. How curvy her backside was in them. He then remembered that backside that he branded his last night and memories of how he had done so sent trembles through his body, made him hard.

Fighting the feeling, he turned his attention to the monitor. He had three calls holding.

"Hey, folks, this is Holy Terror, and I'm ready to take those calls. First up is Ray. What's on your mind?"

"Hey there, Holy Terror. Enjoying the music. Me and my old lady took your advice and checked into a hotel. Nice. I just wanted to let the listeners know that I saw Domino, and he had a lady friend. If anyone is missing a female Black Lab, then it might be too late."

Terrence couldn't help but smile. "Hey, Ray, thanks for letting us know." He disconnected the line. "Next caller, you're up. What's on your mind?"

Sherri stopped pacing and glanced over at Terrence. He was deliberately not looking at her, and that was okay for now, but she refused to let him ignore her once he had finished taking those calls. She'd admit that she had been wrong to get into his business, and she would apologize and hope he would forgive her. But then she and Terrence needed to do something they hadn't really done. Talk about their feelings for each other. She hadn't known he had fallen in love with her, just like he didn't know she had fallen in love with him.

She wanted to continue to build a relationship if that's what he wanted, and she hoped that it was. But what if it wasn't? What if he wasn't willing to forgive her? With those uncertainties, she began pacing again.

WHEN TERRENCE FINISHED with the last call, he glanced over at Sherri. Their eyes met, and he was consumed with memories of all the pleasure they had shared last night. But then, that pleasure had been tossed aside by her harsh words.

He pushed back in his chair. “You want to talk, go ahead.”

He watched her inhale deeply before she came closer to the table where he sat. “I need to explain why I went off the way I did. It has to do with Ben.”

When he didn’t say anything, but continued to look at her, she continued. “I told you that Ben broke our engagement because of another woman. What I didn’t tell you was that the other woman was someone who worked for him, wanted to bang her way to the top. I detested her for it, and I loathed Ben as an employer for letting her do it. In my mind a person who would do such a thing was unethical, undeserving. And last night, I became that sort of woman when I found out you’re the boss and I was sleeping with you.”

“I am not the boss,” he said in an angry tone. “Let’s get that straight right now, Sherri. And like I said, this is a business deal between me and Warrick and doesn’t concern you or anyone else who works at this station. Now that things have worked out with Warrick and that station in Memphis, he’ll have the financial package he needs to get back control of things.”

She nodded. “I understand, and I want to apologize for everything I said last night. You said you love me. Well, I got one up on you, Terrence, because I love you, too.”

She lifted her chin. “And I didn’t just fall in love with you when we made love. I loved you before then. I just didn’t want to admit it. In all honesty, I tried denying it to the hilt. But I can’t any longer. I’ve realized that loving you is right.”

He didn’t say anything for a long moment, and then, “You said you didn’t believe I loved you because men like me didn’t fall in love. What did you mean by that?”

She glanced down at the floor and then back at him. "Within a week of coming to town, I found out about your reputation as a ladies' man, Terrence. You're one of the most eligible bachelors in the Keys. Women call the station just to flirt with you. They go to your club just to get a glimpse of you. You're an ex-pro-football player. Handsome. Intelligent. Wealthy. You've dated celebrities. Why would a man give that up—the life of a bachelor—to fall in love with anyone? And why me?"

Slowly getting out of his chair, Terrence crossed the room to stand in front of her. He studied her features. "You might want to be asking this question. Why *not* you?"

He gave her a moment for that question to sink in and then he said, "You're beautiful. Intelligent. A career woman who knows what she wants and doesn't mind working hard to achieve it." He paused a second. "You're also a woman who has made me feel things I've never felt before, at least not with the same magnitude. When I'm inside of you, I don't want to come out. You're the only woman that I've envisioned having a baby with. The only woman I allowed access to my heart. So I'm no different from any other man, Sherri. I want love just like the next guy, and I want to think I'm smart enough to recognize it when it comes along and take a chance."

She tried fighting back the tears, but one fell down her cheek anyway. She quickly swiped it away. "So, do you accept my apology?"

"Only if you promise never to doubt my love for you again."

She smiled through the tears in her eyes. "I promise."

"Then I accept your apology."

He leaned in and brushed her lips with his. "I just thought of something that I need to do."

Sherri watched as he walked back to the monitor and took a seat. A commercial break was going on, which would be followed by nonstop music for at least an hour. She lifted a brow when she realized he was about to interrupt and do an unscheduled station alert of some sort right after the commercial.

He turned on the mike and slipped into his headset.

"This is Holy Terror in a very special appeal. This is for all the lovers out there weathering the storm in each other's arms. Tonight is the night not to tell, but to show that special someone how you feel about them. So, brothers, while Hurricane Ana is out there banging on the door, you take care of your business and take your special lady in your arms. Give her love. Show her how much you care. And, ladies, you know what to do. Me, well, let's just say I'm doing just fine right here."

Not realizing he hadn't turned off the mike, he looked over to Sherri and said, "Come here, baby, let's get it on."

Sherri smiled and walked over to him. Her smile widened as she clicked off the mike, removed his headset and slid into his lap just as Marvin Gaye's classic "Let's Get It On" began bathing the airwaves in a melodic and soulful sound.

"I love you," she whispered against his lips.

"And I love you," he whispered against hers.

And then it was on.

He hungrily took her mouth, and her response was immediate. His tongue moved thoroughly and methodically inside of her mouth, showing her the love, making her feel it. She was his and he was hers and that's how things would always be.

Moments later when he raised his head and looked into her eyes, he knew he was seeing his future, the woman who would be his wife, the mother of his children, his soul mate, helpmate, his lover for all eternity.

He stood with her in his arms and headed for the special private haven in his office. Hurricane Ana could do as she pleased, but in the meantime, he intended to take care of business with the woman he loved by putting his own advice into practice.

This was going to be one storm that he'd never forget.

* * * * *